HIS NAME WAS ALOYSIUS JOHN MURTAH.
HE WAS KNOWN THROUGHOUT THE LAND
AS JOHNNY.

Fourteen months previously, he had been arrested by the police in Belfast whilst organizing the establishment of arms and explosives in secret dumps within the city boundaries. Brought to trial for his activities as a member of the Organization, he was given a sentence of seventeen years penal servitude, four months of which he had served before making a daring escape and going into hiding. A large reward had been offered for information which would result in his capture, and an intensive search had been made for him. All without success.

Johnny has become legendary since "Odd Man Out" was originally published; his hopes and agonies have become synonymous with Belfast, Ireland, and the political and religious strife that prevails to this day. Johnny is more than a classic protagonist in literature; he is Everyman in pursuit of freedom. . . .

ODD MAN OUT

by

F. L. GREEN

For Elizabeth Muriel

LEISURE BOOKS
THIS BOOK CONTAINS THE COMPLETE TEXT
OF THE HARDCOVER EDITION

First Leisure Book printing (July) 1971

Copyright 1947 by F. L. Green

ISBN 0-8439-0023-7
COVER PHOTOGRAPH CURTESY

OF THE RANK ORGANIZATION

*James Mason as "Johnny" in the Two Cities Film version
of* **Odd Man Out**

COVER DESIGN BY REX IRVINE

Published by Leisure Books, Inc.
6340 Coldwater Canyon
North Hollywood, California 91606

PART ONE

THE RAID

one

The mill stood in a narrow side-street in the heart of a district characterized by squalor and the numerous streets of a similar sort, as well as by the number of houses crammed in those streets and the multitude of human beings herded in those drab dwellings. It was the third largest linen factory in the world, and it rose like the awful, sheer wall of a canyon along the entire length of one side of the street. Towering above the houses opposite, it confronted the rays of afternoon sunlight which shone in reflection from its upper windows and which gave a rosy hue to the brickwork. That pink blush seemed to pour down the walls and permeate the air between the mill and the row of tiny houses on the opposite side of the street. It was the reflected glory of a sinking sun on a November afternoon, and for a little while it gave a splendid light to that place of murk.

Shortly before half-past three, when it was the habit of the Cashier to pass a considerable sum of money to the Wages Clerk, a saloon car entered the deserted street and halted at the curb below the wide flight of steps leading to the mill's entrance.

Four men were in the car. They were of about twenty-eight or thirty years and were dressed smartly in the style of managers of departments. Three of them alighted slowly; the two who had occupied the rear seats waiting for the third man who had sat beside the driver. All three crossed the pavement and ascended the steps, their cheerful conversation sounding pleasantly on the quiet air of the street and ending abruptly when the heavy door swung to behind them.

The man who remained at the wheel listened anxiously to the steady beat of the car's engine, which was running softly. The car had been stolen earlier in the afternoon; and although he was expert in the handling of vehicles, he had not yet tested the capabilities of this one or discovered its possible faults. He glanced over his shoulder to make certain that the doors were open, after which he peered along the length of the street behind and ahead of him. Except for two women in shawls passing in the distance, and three small children playing on a doorstep at the far end of the street, the place was deserted. He asked himself fearfully how long it would remain so; and he waited with increasing impatience for his comrades to return.

When he had been assigned his part in this raid, he was pleased that he was ordered to drive the car, for he had driven cars on two expeditions similar to this one. Both had been successful. Planned cunningly after weeks of observation, they had yielded much plunder; and thereafter he had remembered only the swift journey from peril to safety and the considerable sum of money which he and his associates had stolen. But now, waiting in the car, his nervous thoughts remembered former occasions when he had sat like this; and some strange remnant of the hideous tension of those moments returned and attached itself to him like a recurrent malady which he suffered.

Anxiety grew again in him, as before, and found a weakness in his nerves. The anxiety was like a pain which increased to such a degree that he knew he could endure it only for a little while longer. His heart began to beat thunderously from fear that he would be unable to sustain that pain. Time swelled around him, slowly, heavily. His senses became unbearably acute, registering sounds, odors, and the taste of the cold air and the smell of petrol and oil fumes and the metalwork and upholstery of the car, assembling all these impressions into a hard mass that weighed intolerably upon his mind and weakened him. And although he knew that he would recover from this weakness at the moment when his companions appeared again at the door of the mill, he knew, too, that if they did not come soon something in his mind would fracture and admit impulsive, hysterical factors which were already advancing from indefinable sources in his spirit.

He glanced fearfully towards the mill's big entrance and wondered impatiently what was happening. His breath fluttered in and out of his dry, parted lips. His hands on the wheel were clammy and weak. And he remembered that this had been his experience on two previous occasions.

A sense of horror and despair welled like a spasm of sickness in him. His abdomen suddenly contracted as though a blow had struck it. And at that moment it seemed to him that a dread, indescribable factor had entered the affair and ruined it.

8

two

The man who had sat beside him was the Chief of the militant Revolutionary Organization to which the others belonged. He was twenty-nine. His name was Aloysius John Murtah. He was known throughout the land as Johnny.

Fourteen months previously, he had been arrested by the police in Belfast while organizing the establishment of arms and explosives in secret dumps within the city boundaries. For years prior to that he had led an outlawed existence. Brought to trial for his activities as a member of the Organization, he was given a sentence of seventeen years penal servitude, four months of which he had served before making a daring escape and going into hiding. A large reward had been offered for information which would result in his capture, and an intensive search had been made for him. All without success.

Actually, he was living less than two miles from the city's heart. The net which was to ensnare him was cast far beyond the city, across bog and mountain, border and sea, as though he were a legendary hero able to traverse vast distances without being recognized. He was living all the time in the home of a sympathizer; and in that tiny dwelling he planned this robbery in order to obtain funds for the Organization.

Except for an hour late on a June evening, and one wild afternoon in September when he had taken a walk along the mountains surrounding the city, this was the first occasion on which he had ventured far into the city itself. He had anticipated this excursion. His body and soul had longed for this activity. Yet during this rapid journey to the mill, he was silent and very troubled; for his senses which had been confined for so long by the walls of the little house in which he had hidden himself were unaccustomed to the width and space which now expanded around him in great ripples of light and color, movement and noise. Something in him flinched from contact with it all. And his body was weak from months of physical inactivity. And his will could not conquer the subtle influences of that long period of hiding during which his spirit had been nurtured more by idealistic dreams than by the vast actuality of life which now rose on all sides and showed its immense face to him.

His weakness increased. He could not find the old

confidence, the former strength of his fine body, the old belief in it. Something in him was impaired. Nevertheless, he went on trying to resurrect it, although at the moment when he left the car and walked round to join his companions on the pavement and begin the hearty conversation which was part of their ruse, he felt a new and terrible weakness encompass him, as though he were no longer attached to the wide reality of life but belonged only to the tiny, silent room in which he had been concealed for so long.

When he and his companions entered the spacious hall of the mill, the movement towards which his plans had been projected for the past seven months suddenly enveloped him. And it was like the onrush of something tangible which overwhelmed him. Not only had it the smell of the cold stone floors and walls, and the warm air which gushed from the offices, but the sounds of the pulsating machinery as well, as they echoed and thudded from other floors. It tasted cold, then warm in a sickly deluge.

A fussy, frowning little man holding a sheaf of papers in one hand and fingering a watch chain across his waistcoat with the other, was standing near the corridor leading to the Cashier's office. He was addressing in sharp tones a young man who was listening with a deferential, abashed air. He stopped speaking when Johnny and his comrades hurried past; and fastening a stern, pompous stare on them, he waited with that exasperating air of interrogation cultivated by factory executives of senior rank. His stiff, mean little face horrified Johnny, for its expression was that of the mill's life which was about to be attacked, as well as the face of reality which thundered and frowned and threatened Johnny at that moment.

It had a strange effect. It focussed in itself all the impressions which Johnny's mind had felt since he had alighted from the car. It became like the fantastic, awful face of a nightmare. He struggled to forget it, to ignore it, to erase it from his sensibilities as he advanced with his two companions. But it remained.

The actions which he and the others took had been planned and decided months before. They were exact. But they did not produce the result which had been expected. It was like trying to fashion a dream from the substance of another dream. It would not develop. The three men hurried along a corridor and burst their way swiftly into a large office where they

10

pointed revolvers at the clerks who were working there. But instead of rising abruptly and standing apart along one wall, as Johnny and the others told them to do, the clerks gaped at the intruders and flushed and then went pale and looked at one another, and turned to the strangers and started to utter curious exclamations and make idiotic little gestures. Then all at once two of them sped from the office by a rear door. The door slammed behind them. Another clerk shuddered back behind a cupboard.

At once, the three raiders went through the counter and hustled the clerks into a little group in a corner. The clerks stared at them with the eyes of men confronted by something which they could not quite believe was real. One of the armed men kept them in the corner while the other intruders crossed to the safe.

Johnny saw the safe door standing open slightly, with a bunch of keys dangling from the lock. He drew it wide open and saw stacks of notes and bags of silver coins. Now the dream became actuality for the few seconds during which he snatched the notes and little bags and thrust them into the canvas sacks which his companion held ready for him. Once, he glanced at the third man who was standing before the clerks and pointing his revolver at them. Johnny saw the big office and the little storeroom into which the two terrified clerks had rushed, and the furniture, and the windows through which the pink flush of departing day shone.

"Yes," he thought, as one dimly recognizes a familiar figure in a dream, "that is Murphy, and he is holding them in the corner. But this is a strange thing I am doing . . . in this office . . . in here . . . and that dreadful little face. . . ." And momentarily he felt again the loss of some vital, indefinable power in himself.

He continued to thrust the money into the three canvas sacks. He experienced neither fear nor tension as he continued; but he could not understand why that was so.

"It is like a dream . . . like the things happening in a dream," he thought.

Then he remembered that for months he had let his mind dwell upon this raid and all the details of it. And the only factor which he had not calculated was his peculiar weakness and the odd effect upon him of the frowning little executive in the hall.

"It is all in," he muttered, turning from the safe.

He took one of the sacks, while his companion gathered the others and handed one of them to Murphy who was backing away from the clerks in the corner. All three came together at the door which, at that moment, opened quickly behind them.

A typist entered. She halted a little way inside the office and stood gaping around. Her lips parted suddenly and she frowned. Before she could scream, Johnny and the others pushed past her into the corridor and hurried towards the hall. They put away their revolvers in the straps below their jackets, still holding their hands upon them in readiness. As they walked, their feet made sounds which echoed in the vaulted corridor.

Johnny hesitated when they reached the hall. His hands and legs were touched by an insidious weakness, like the limp, light feeling which possesses the body in a dream. The others were at the door, and he hastened towards them because a curious sense of detachment was beginning to envelop him. He overtook them and passed through the heavy swing door with them. They were excited and in a hurry. They were in front of him and already at the top of the flight of steps when he halted again.

As soon as he emerged from the building, and at the instant when he saw the saloon car and the tense expression on the driver's face, some vast, impalpable force rose from the daylight, the houses opposite the mill, the pavements, the roar of traffic in the city, and struck his mind.

It was the actual impacting with the dream which he had reenacted in the Cashier's office. It dazed him. He halted. To descend the steps would be like attempting to plunge into a turbulent ocean. Already, his two companions were half-way down the steps. He tried to follow them, but at that instant he heard an outburst of voices behind him. He turned and saw two men. The foremost was a robust, resolute individual whose face had an angry, ferocious expression. He shouted something as he pushed open the door and came out brandishing a revolver. Behind him came a lithe little fellow in a grey suit, and he, too, had an expression of anger and violence on his face. Both men rushed at Johnny and seized him, and for a moment the three of them made a panting, scuffling mass.

"It is a dream!" Johnny thought, struggling to throw them off. He felt neither fear nor surprise; and because of this strange fact he was bewildered.

"It is like a dream . . ." he thought, again.

He dropped the canvas bag and tried to mass all his strength in his efforts to release himself from his opponents. In the unconscious movement of defence, he drew his revolver. He heard other voices behind him. Suddenly, he found himself prone on the top step, and he could not understand where he was or what was happening to him. The men struck him, but the blows were like those in a dream and did not hurt him. Even when there was an explosion and a flash and his hand which gripped his revolver was jerked violently, he still did not realize what had happened. His body rolled down the steps. The Cashier's big body made a huge, warm, immobile weight on him until he thrust it away. Now there were loud shouts sounding so close to his ears that he jerked his head aside to escape them. There was another explosion and another flash which momentarily blinded him. He felt pain begin in his left hand and travel like a flame scorching his arm and his body. He screamed because he was afraid and hurt and terrified that the flame would fold on him again. Hands grabbed him and lifted him. He struggled to release himself from them because he imagined that they were those of the two pursuers. As he struggled, the noise of the city, and the pinkish light of the afternoon wheeled across his senses and dazed him. Voices shouted to him, and he recognized them.

"It is Murphy and Nolan!" he thought.

Then he remembered the whole of the dream: how he and the other officers of the Organization had planned to raid this mill, and how the junior officers and members of the Organization, together with women supporters, had spent months obtaining precise information about the offices, the employees in the Cashier's department, the time of collection of the money from the bank and its delivery from one department to another, and so on. And he remembered, as well, how the senior officers of the Organization had planned to steal a car and drive to the mill and there alight and enter the premises.

"Yes," he thought, "we decided . . ."

But he could not be certain that it had all happened. Had he dreamed it? Or had it all actually happened? And what was he doing here? Why were there voices shouting at him? Hadn't he been sentenced to seventeen years penal servitude? Then what was this hard ground . . . and whose voices . . . and whose arms? . . .

He scrambled to his feet, swaying. Hands grabbed at him and rushed him towards the car, and voices screamed at him to get in for Christ's sake, and other voices shouted that the fellow was killed . . . was killed . . . the fellow was . . . hurry for Christ's sake there is an alarm . . . can't you . . . can't you . . . Christ, he is hurt he is . . . well, drag him in . . . drag him in. . . .

"It is the dream," he thought, "it is awful."

He saw his companions scramble into the car.

"Come on, come on!" they panted, leaning out and grabbing him.

"Yes," he thought, "now I must get into the car. . . ."

Then again he remembered the dream which he had yielded to for so many weeks, and which had recurred again.

"Yes, it is what I dreamed," he told himself. "After we have made the haul from the safe, we are to drive back to the place I was hiding in. But . . . something has happened. . . ."

He put out his arms to grip the car and get in. Again the fierce pain swept through his left hand and arm. He shrieked with agony, and stumbled, gasping and blinking and staring about him like someone recently wakened from a nightmare.

One of his companions got out of the car and dragged him to the running-board. Johnny saw contorted faces and heard wild shouts.

"They are inside the car. . . ."

It had started. Already it was travelling at great speed and bumping over the cobbles. It turned the corner at such a pace and so sharply that it rose on the pavement. He swayed. He made efforts to get inside the car, but the pain scorched him again, while the wind rushing past him burst like a flood upon his bare head.

"What is it . . . what is happening. . . ?" he thought.

Everything wheeled in a swift curve which confused his senses. He closed his eyes. His body was struck violently with such force that the breath was driven from him. He opened his mouth and struggled to breathe, whereupon he tasted dust and smelled the cold stone of the roadway. He lay quite still, panting, looking up at a vast expanse of pink sky.

"Morning . . ." he thought. "This is the hard bed, and I am waking from a dream I have had."

He sat up. Looking about him, he saw houses and some women clustered together and all watching him. He felt afraid.

"Something has happened to me!" he exclaimed. "There

was the car . . . and Pat and Murphy and Nolan . . . and . . ."

Huge visions stormed through his mind. Shooting, screams, faces contorted by fear, two men pursuing him. He got to his feet and stumbled across the road and leaned against a wall. The women were still watching him. And others were running towards them and making a little crowd and chattering and shouting incoherently at him.

"I was dreaming . . ." he thought.

Because he was confused and afraid, he hurried along the street. Cunning guided him, tracing a way for him. He turned the corner and saw a short, empty street ahead of him. He went on as fast as his weak limbs could carry him; and when he had traversed it, he sped down others, striking deeper into the heart of that bleak locality until he saw ahead of him a little row of air-raid shelters. Some of them had wooden doors that were closed. Others were open, with the doors leaning back. He hesitated. He felt shocked and confused and in great pain. Glancing wildly around him, he saw that the street was empty. He lurched quickly into one of the shelters, stumbling against the door which, presently, he dragged upright after him with his sound hand and set in place.

Only a thin light from departing daylight remained inside. He stood quite still, breathing painfully. Now dream and actuality were irretrievably mingled together in his consciousness. Nevertheless, he distinguished certain features of the normal world: the damp, fusty smell of the inactive air of the shelter; the glimmer of daylight; the sounds from the city. And they were like thin strands which his senses groped to retain. He sat down, lowering his bruised body, trying to resurrect reason and comprehension upon the slender threads which his senses clutched to themselves. He kept his eyes wide open and did not yield to the dreadful weariness which brimmed from his body. He tried to struggle through the mists of dream. Pain began again in his left arm. Looking down at the hand, he saw that from the fingertip of the third finger to the wrist there was a raw line through which the bones and ligaments showed. And higher up his arm, the overcoat was soaked and discolored with blood.

"Then I am wounded!" he exclaimed.

He remembered that part of the dream where he had scuffled with the two pursuers and rolled down the steps and felt the ponderous, lifeless weight of that big body upon him, as well as the subsequent moment when his companions in the car had screamed that the fellow was killed, was killed.

Most vividly and terribly it all recurred to him, finding within his mind its source from which it rose anew to remark that he was wounded, that it had all happened in reality, the robbery, the scuffle, the killing . . .

His eyes closed and he fell limply to one side. He had fainted.

three

As soon as the man at the wheel of the car saw the two employees come rushing out in pursuit, a terrible hysteria broke across his mind. He saw the whole plan which Johnny and the rest of them had formed so patiently during the past six months crack and admit failure. He saw Johnny hesitate as though he were dazed, and he detected the fear which suddenly made the others scramble into the car. Shots sounded, and the big man who had rushed after Johnny lay perfectly still on the pavement.

The hysteria broke in a wild scream from his lips. Fear trickled into it. He kept accelerating the engine and making ready to let in the clutch. Every particle of his trembling body longed to slip in that clutch, but he was obliged to wait.

"Johnny! Johnny!" he yelled, then his dry throat could no longer make the words. They slipped soundlessly over the membranes. He swallowed. He became ferociously angry when he saw Murphy and Nolan desert Johnny. He swore and tried to shout again.

"Get him in you bloody fools you. Get him in!" he cried.

It was like trying to fuse two powerful forces into a unity. One was represented by the clutch of the car, while the other was represented by his three companions. He groaned. They were so slow, so clumsy. Time grew like a menacing cloud about them, and he heard the mill's alarm break into a loud jangle.

At the moment when Johnny was dragged to the running-board, the man at the wheel thrust in the clutch and drove the car at full speed along the street. He saw horrified faces of women staring at him from doorways. He heard his companions yelling at him to stop, to stop, for God's sake

16

stop, and he knew that the two forces which he had wanted to knit had not come together. They had touched each other and then parted slightly.

"Drag him in then, can't you, drag him in and shut the door!" he screamed, over his shoulder.

He was approaching the end of the street. He gripped the wheel and hunched his shoulders as he prepared to make the turn. A hand pressed his shoulder. He shook it off angrily and threw his whole weight into his arm as he shot the wheel over. The car shuddered, leaping over the curb and mounting the pavement. The springs creaked. The car lurched. But it was round and speeding down the street.

Murphy shrieked. Pat slackened speed slightly because he knew that something calamitous had occurred.

". . . dropped off he has, dropped off! Stop her and turn. . . ."

He drove on. A blow bashed his hat over his ears, but still he drove on. Hands reached over and wrenched at his arm and voices yelled in his ears. He stopped then. He was weak and terrified.

"All of us!" he moaned, turning his body. "Now they will lift the lot of us! How can I turn?"

"Turn her, turn her, you fool, quick!" Nolan shouted.

"Go and bring him to us!" he retorted.

He saw for an instant the little distant mass of Johnny's body at the crown of the road where they had turned.

"Bring him!" he shouted.

"He is dead!" Murphy cried.

"Drive on, drive on, then!" Nolan exclaimed. "He killed the fellow, I think, he killed him, and there is an alarm!"

The argument became a vociferous whirlpool of words that ceased abruptly when all three of them in the car saw Johnny rise and stagger away out of sight.

"God help us, he has gone!" Murphy said.

"Shall we go back for him? Shall we? Could we turn the car, could we?" Pat said.

And shall we, they all exclaimed at the same time, shall we, would we make it, or has he cut on to the next corner, and is he waiting there — yes, you know he might be so that's the thing, Pat. That is it, so go ahead for Christ's sake, man, he is waiting there and taking a quick cut through.

But they knew that he had not. They knew that he was badly wounded and dazed and unable to make a cunning plan like that. Nevertheless, they kept shouting at one another that he would be there. Look out, look out, Pat, take it easy. Can you see him? Is he there? No, he isn't, no. Go on, go on!

Pat straightened his battered hat and drove faster.

"He has made it all right," Nolan said, tensely. "He has! He will take the straight road back to where we came from. He will be where we said we would meet the others."

Pat and Murphy were silent. Nolan said: "He killed him, did you see? He pulled on the big fellow . . . and the big fellow shot just when he was done for. . . ."

His voice was soft and strained, and the others could scarcely recognize its tone.

"No!" Murphy said. "The fellow fired first! Then Johnny pulled on him!"

"But . . . but . . . the big fellow was . . ."

"He shot the big fellow in self-defence!" Murphy cried.

"Shut up now, shut up, for God's sake!" Pat exclaimed.

"But he killed him, my God, he killed him!" Nolan went on, fearfully. "They will be coming after us like hell for that now. My God, they will tear the city open to get at us now, they will. Oh, my God, my God, I saw the big fellow go down and it was through the head, through the head. . . ."

The hysteria suddenly welled up in Pat again.

"Shut up, shut up!" he screamed.

He was rushing the car at great speed through the dusk and murk of the narrow streets, driving on the crown of the road. Fear was a solid, deadly thing poised in menace in his mind, its whole mass waiting to leap upon his consciousness and abolish sanity and life in him.

"Johnny . . . Johnny!" Murphy sobbed. "Poor Johnny!"

"We did the best for him all we could. We did so!" Pat exclaimed.

The others panted, saying yes, we did the best for him, poor Johnny. So we did. We obeyed the orders, didn't we now? Sure we did. We have two sacks here, and he'll be at Agnes's place where we have to meet the others. He will so.

Pat at the wheel caught his breath. Tears gushed from his eyes.

"God help us, it was hell, hell, it was!" he sighed. "It was hell waiting and seeing . . ."

The others groaned, and again they began all of them to say yes, it was hell; what the hell though, we all obeyed the orders, so we did, and we have two sacks.

They spoke as though they were addressing a fourth person whose reproaches penetrated to their consciences and accused them of having deserted a wounded comrade. At last, all were silent. Pat slackened speed, for he had come swiftly through the district of narrow streets and was about to enter the main road leading through the city. He glanced at the clock on the dashboard.

"It has stopped," he thought, and he called out: "What time is it?"

"It is ten past four," Murphy said.

Pat looked again at the clock. It showed the correct time. But it told him, as well, that barely six minutes had elapsed since the disaster on the mill's steps.

"Get down now!" he shouted.

Murphy and Nolan obeyed him, crouching in the well of the car and covering themselves with a dark travelling rug. Now Pat was alone. Terror touched him, massing itself in him at the fringes of his thoughts, waiting and moving slyly towards him as though it were searching for a weakness in his will through which it could pour and possess his entire mind.

He drove on, along Royal Avenue and Donegall Place and into Donegall Square, and past the City Hall, towards the Dublin Road. He travelled at a leisurely speed, stopping punctiliously at the traffic signals, joining the little press of traffic and moving on again, all the time giving the appropriate signals to other drivers, and even making a gesture of thanks to a policeman at a curb who signalled to him to proceed at a cross-road. But his terror was a thread which had entered his pulse and coursed through the living tissues of his body. He knew that the car's pace could not outstrip the words that were spoken by now over telephones, nor leap beyond time and escape the awful consequences that by now must have accrued against himself and Murphy and Nolan, as well as against that unfortunate figure stumbling across the end of the turning. He drove on as before.

Within seven minutes of emerging from the streets in the murky district about the mill, the car entered a sedate residential district which had been designated for a rendezvous. There it turned into a quiet road and came to a halt halfway along that place.

Two young women were approaching. One was slowly wheeling a large pram in which a baby was sleeping. The other carried a shopping bag. Both women were in animated conversation. As they drew near the car, a third woman approached from the opposite direction. She, too, was wheeling a pram in which a baby was sleeping. The three women met on the pavement near the car and stopped to talk. The driver came from the car, and at once the women greeted him. He raised his hat politely and bent over the prams to look at the babies. After a brief conversation, he returned to the car and opened the rear door.

From beneath the big, black rug which covered his companions he took the two sacks and handed them to the women. They quickly bestowed the sacks beneath the coverlets of the prams, and after bidding goodbye to him they moved slowly away. He stood back, smiled, and raised his hat.

Instead of returning to the car, he walked in the opposite direction, all the time examining the numbers on the gates, as though he were a stranger searching for the residence of an old friend. And he continued thus until he reached the end of the road, after which he walked briskly towards the nearest tram stage and boarded the first tram. Soon, he was far away from the place where he had left the car.

He had not been gone a minute before his two companions rose cautiously from under the rug. It was twilight. They put on their hats and stepped from the car and sauntered slowly away in the direction which the women had taken. They were chatting together, and presently they stopped and lit cigarettes. The little road was very quiet. Nobody was in sight. When they entered the main road, they walked faster and crossed to a tram stage. Presently a tramcar appeared. They boarded it with other persons who were waiting, and soon they were far away from the district.

The stolen car remained in that quiet road until it was discovered several hours later by a constable on patrol. He walked slowly past it, noticing that it was empty, that its rear light was extinguished, and that the rear nearside door was not quite closed. He stopped at a little distance and remained motionless in the darkness. He was watching the car. He waited for the owner to return to it, so that he could question him. Several minutes passed. He became impatient and suspicious. Suddenly, he loosened his revolver in its holster and approached the car rapidly and shone his torch into it. His suspicions were aroused. He got into the car and examined the instrument panel. He got out again quickly and noted the car's number, after which he hurried to the nearest telephone booth and reported to the District Headquarters.

Within a few minutes a mobile patrol arrived in a police car. The constables and plain clothes officers alighted and examined the abandoned car quickly, then one of them got in and drove off. The police car followed.

It was not until next morning that the inhabitants of that quiet place learned what had happened outside their homes on the previous day. Several of them had seen the car drive in and come to a halt, and others had seen the men and women; but none of them spoke about it to friends or neighbors. And none of them volunteered information to the Police.

"It's safer to say nothing about a business like that," they remarked to their families.

four

At a few minutes before five o'clock of that November afternoon, the driver of the car reached a house in the Falls Ward. He was so exhausted that when he was admitted to the little front room whose windows were shuttered on the inside, he was unable to speak. His eyes had a fixed, distraught look, and he breathed swiftly through his tight, pale lips. His whole body was trembling violently, and even when he sat down before the fire he still shook with nervous spasms and still had a wild, strange look in his eyes like an epileptic returning to consciousness after a prolonged attack.

A stern little man, fair-haired and about thirty, was waiting in the room with a handsome, dark woman of about twenty-five. He pushed the chair to the fire for Pat to sit on, and he rested a hand on Pat's shoulder.

"Take it easy, now, Pat! Take it easy!" he said.

His voice had a stiff edge of command mingled with its gentle quality. He looked at the woman who stood proudly and with an immobile expression on her splendid features. She gave him an expressive glance which he answered with an anxious pout. Then he turned once again to the shuddering figure at the fire.

"What happened, man? Was it all right?" he asked.

Pat did not answer. His stringy body shook violently.

"All right," the other said. "Take it easy."

The door opened, and Murphy and Nolan entered. They, too, were in great physical and mental distress. One of them leaned against the wall, with his face averted and one hand moving to and fro across his brow. His hat was crushed against the wall, and presently it slid from his head and fell to the floor. His dishevelled hair — brown and in long, greasy strands — streaked over his hand and his eyes. The other man stumbled across the room and threw himself face downwards on the shabby settee, groaning.

The small fair man watched them in silence for several seconds, waiting for them to speak. But the whole tale of the disaster was written so plainly in their distress that he had no need to hear words. Nevertheless, he spoke.

"What has happened?" he said anxiously.

The man near the door leaned against the jamb, hiding his face, his breath shuddering loudly from his loose lips. He slid into the little chair in the corner near the door, and sat with his arm hanging loosely over the back. With his other hand he wiped the spittle which drooled from his parted lips. He swallowed, as if he were about to speak. His right hand kept passing over his face, sometimes with the back of it against his cheeks, sometimes with the grimy palm wiping his lips. His chest rose in little shudders, as though a huge wave were mounting in him. His feet were turned in a strange way. At last, he dropped his head on his arm and cried in a squeezed, hysterical voice:

"Johnny! It was poor Johnny!"

The man on the settee heaved himself upright and upbraided him furiously.

"Whose bloody fault was it? What is the sense in crying now, when if you had . . . if you had done what I said . . ."

His voice was like steel clanging in the confined space of the room and making deafening echoes.

"Be quiet!" exclaimed the fair man. "Let us have the facts! Where is Johnny?"

But the hysterical outburst from the man on the settee had infected the others. They turned to him and shouted, calling him a liar, accusing him of trying to excuse himself for what had happened, cursing him. Their shouts made a babel which only accentuated the tragedy.

"God help us!" the fair man groaned, through the uproar.

The door opened and the three women entered. Two of them dropped the sacks of money on the table and then stood staring at the rest of the company.

"... and we could have picked him up ..." Pat was shouting.

Again there was pandemonium. Pat sprang from his chair and rushed to the man on the settee. A chair toppled.

"God help us!" one of the women gasped, recoiling.

"I stopped, so I did!" Pat shouted, trying to force his way past the fair man.

"You would not!" the man near the door yelled.

Pat turned in his direction.

"So I did stop! I pulled up ..."

He turned to the fair man who had hold of him in a strong grip, and speaking in a tense, trembling tone, he said:

"I pulled up but they would not get out, and we saw him get up and cut for it, and we thought he would be at the next corner, but he was not there!"

The man on the settee pointed a stiff arm at him.

"You raced the bloody car so. ..."

"Those were the orders."

"That was why he fell off at the turn! You would not slow down, and but for that we had him, but he fell off!"

"They let go of him, they did!" Pat said, addressing the fair man. "They let him drop off. ..."

The fair man pushed Pat back into the chair before the fire.

"Sit down now," he said, imperatively; and over his shoulder he addressed the man on the settee.

"That is enough, Nolan! I want a proper report. Now then!"

He seated himself at the table on which the two sacks lay.

"Do you mean to say," exclaimed one of the women in a horrified, piercing voice, "do you sit there, the three of you, and tell us that you came back without Johnny?"

"Be quiet!" said the fair man, angrily, slapping his open hand on the table, "I am handling this!"

"Without your Chief!" the woman continued, addressing Pat.

The fair man made an abrupt sign to her. Pat swore.

"You have no right to go at us for what could not be helped!" he shouted. "You were not in the party. You have no notion what it was like down there. ..."

"I would not desert my Chief!" she retorted.

"Now would I," exclaimed Murphy, "and him wounded. ..."

Pat made a gesture and began to shudder again.

"Jesus!" he moaned, swaying. "Will you not leave us be?"

He jumped to his feet and confronted the three women. They recoiled sullenly as he made a furious gesture and gritted his teeth.

"Be quiet, all of you! You don't know what happened! It was hell . . . hell! There was shooting. Johnny fired, and there was more of it, and he was wounded, and we could not get him into the car! There was something happened to him. . . ."

"Look at them!" one of the women exclaimed, beginning to sob hysterically. "The officers who left their Chief in distress!"

"Leave us be!" Pat sighed, sinking into the chair. "We did the best."

His glance went round the room like the face of catastrophe confronting all of them, and meeting only their reproaches and contempt.

"Is there not one of you with the decency to give us a drink of something?" he cried.

The fair man at the table made a sign to the women, whereupon two of them went towards the door.

"A drink, is it?" one of them said bitterly. "A dose of poison. . . ."

Murphy pushed her violently through the door, slamming it after her and throwing out an appealing hand to the fair man.

"Dennis!" he exclaimed, shaking his head. "It happened like lightning! There were two fellows came after us, and Johnny was last out when one of the fellows got hold of him and then the two of them rolled down the steps and, my God, there was screaming and yelling and the alarm was on, and after that there was shooting and . . ."

His voice became shrill and his words came faster until they melted into a confusion of sound into which Nolan and Pat joined their voices until the atmosphere of the little room was saturated with a tension which seemed to Dennis to constitute something dangerous for all of them.

"All right, now, all right!" he said loudly. "Take your time! Stop the shouting and let us have the facts, quickly. If Johnny is still down there . . ."

"Are you still throwing that up at us?" Pat exclaimed.

"Maybe you forget that I am Johnny's Deputy," said Dennis. "And another thing: there will be a court martial for the three of you . . ."

"To hell with that!" shouted Nolan.

". . . to establish responsibility for your failure to carry out . . ." Dennis went on, looking sternly at him.

"Failure, is it?" Nolan demanded, pointing to the sacks on the table.

"Be careful what you are saying!" Dennis said.

Nolan sank back, burying his head on the cushions.

"Now," said Dennis, "let us hear what happened."

There was silence for almost a minute. The dark, proud woman who had stood behind Dennis and not uttered a word throughout the dreadful minutes, folded her arms on her fine breast and sighed softly.

"I am waiting!" Dennis said.

It came slowly, at first from Pat in a faltering pulse of words that presently gathered momentum which the others augmented until the whole rose in the same kind of shrill uproar as before. Hysteria shot out abuse, reproaches, curses, taunts. Contradictions became furious arguments. At that juncture three men entered the room. They were Adjutants from other Companies of the Organization. Hearing the commotion, they stood in silence, realizing the disaster, and waiting until Dennis spoke before they ventured to remark anything.

"All right, all right!" Dennis said, making a gesture for silence at Pat, Murphy and Nolan. "That's enough! I will take your reports separately, later on."

He spread a large map of the city on the table. The three Adjutants gathered round him and examined the locality on which his forefinger rested.

"The police will have a cordon round the place by now," one of them said.

The three women returned with trays on which cups and saucers and a big teapot stood. They set down the trays on the table, pushing aside the sacks containing the money and setting the cups, which they filled and handed round. All drank thirstily.

"Yes, there will be a hell of a cordon," one of the Adjutants said.

Another laughed sardonically. "They will tear this city from the roots to get us this night," he said, sniffing.

Someone tapped on the door. At once, all were silent. Revolvers appeared in hands. All eyes turned to the door.

"Open it," Dennis said.

One of the women opened the door cautiously. A boy's hand was thrust in holding a copy of the *Belfast Telegraph.*

The door was closed again, and the newspaper was passed to Dennis. He unfolded it and spread it above the map. All except Pat, Murphy and Nolan gathered round him to peer over his shoulders while he read in a flat monotone. First, the dark headlines above three columns:

ARMED RAID ON MILL.
CASHIER KILLED IN DESPERATE STRUGGLE.
THIEVES MAKE BIG HAUL.

He read the columns after that and then was silent with his strong, thin hands outspread on the paper.

"Killed!" exclaimed one of the women in a quavering voice.

It was like a taut wire giving forth a vibrating note. All were silent. All except Pat, Murphy and Nolan exchanged significant glances.

"Killed!" the woman said, sobbing.

"Jesus, Mary and Joseph, help him!" another woman said.

They crossed themselves and joined their hands. One of the Adjutants glanced at the three women, and then at the dark, proud, imperturbable one. He mumbled fervently, first of all making the sign of the cross on his breast:

"Holy Mary, Mother of God, intercede for him!"

The three men who had been with Johnny on the raid did not join in the prayer. They drank tea thirstily, not looking at the others, but burying their lips in the cups which now and then rattled in the saucers and made a curious accompaniment to the muttered prayers and the hysterical sobs of two of the women.

"Holy Mary, Mother of God, help us we beseech thee. . . ."

They were not praying for the cashier who had been killed. Instead, their prayers were for Johnny, who was wounded and still in hiding somewhere in the district about the mill, and whose plight seemed to them to be extreme and tragic.

Presently Dennis spoke.

five

"Listen now! Listen!"

Except for the proud, taciturn woman who had remained throughout, the room was cleared of all but the officers of the Organization. Pat, Murphy and Nolan remained where they had been since their return. All were smoking quickly and nervously, dragging smoke from the cigarettes with taut, pale lips, and then removing the cigarettes with trembling fingers and blowing out noxious clouds of smoke and spitting. Pat at the fire kept flicking the ash from his cigarette and spitting out fragments of tobacco. Soon, he threw the butt into the fire, but almost immediately he lit another which he produced from a small pocket in his jacket, and with which he fidgeted as nervously as before. Fumes of horror kept surging into his mind as his thoughts burned with recollections of the raid. His emotional soul that had never been stable or directed by reason or the temperature influences of truth or tolerance swayed like a towering thing on a loose foundation as his hysteria raged about it. He smoked quicker than ever and tried to forget what happened; but the events of the afternoon seemed to have their source more in his body than in something external to him. And all at once they overwhelmed him again. He spun round and shouted at Dennis:

"A court martial, is it? So you think you will hold a court martial on us!"

"For failure to carry out the orders!" Nolan shouted scornfully at Dennis.

The three Adjutants and Dennis lifted their heads from the map and stared angrily at Pat and Nolan. One of the Adjutants spoke to Dennis:

"Go ahead and never mind them, Dennis. Poor devils! They had bad luck, you know."

Dennis looked down again at the map. He pointed to the district about the mill.

"I am going down there," he said tersely.

The three officers — Seamus, Sean and Robert — glanced at him.

"The three of you will follow me," he continued. "I am going there with my hand bandaged. I will get past the cordons and make a search for Johnny. Or better still," he went on, finding a sounder plan, "better still, I will draw off the cordons by letting the police see me . . ."

Sean whistled softly and shook his head.

"They will cut you to pieces at sight! If they think you are Johnny, they will blaze at you!"

". . . and as soon as you hear my signal — three short blasts — you will enter through the gap in the cordon and not come out until you have found Johnny," Dennis went on.

Sean laughed nervously. He had a long, narrow face and a flat skull over whose narrow brow a few greasy little wisps of black hair fell near the center above the curve of his big, hooked nose. His eyes widened as he laughed, giving him a malicious appearance and opening to view all the things of his character for which he was renowned in the Organization.

"It is going to be slaughter, Dennis!" he said excitedly.

Pointing his finger at the map, Dennis showed them the streets where the three of them were to take positions.

"Be there at seven-fifteen," he said. "I am going there for seven. Now! Any questions?"

He looked up at them. All three were curious individuals. Robert especially so. He had the austere, rapt air of a fervent young priest. His face was thin, with the yellow, blotchy skin stretched tightly over the jutting cheekbones and the pointed chin. He wore a broad-brimmed black hat similar to those worn by young clerics in the days just after their ordination, and when they have recently purchased a complete, new outfit. It was too large for him and gave him a slightly ridiculous appearance, probably because he wore it low over his forehead in the romantic style of desperadoes and high at the back of his big head, which was out of proportion to his narrow shoulders. Indeed, everything about him seemed to lack harmony and proportion. His austere expression did not suit the ungainly attitudes of his odd-shaped body, which was clad in a curious assortment of badly fitting garments. His legs were long, but his arms were short and plump. His shoulders were narrow and soft like a young girl's, and his hips were broad and fleshy like those of a mature woman. And feminine, too, was his habit of joining his hands in a gesture which was inimical to his deep voice and his reputed physical strength and the amazing powers of physical endurance of which his body was capable.

"So we wait until you have drawn off the police before we close in?" he said.

His tone was fastidious, as though he were trying to give the orders the romantic flavor which inspired him and which Dennis had not rendered to them.

"I have told you," Dennis said curtly.

"This fellow wants a battle," Seamus said, pointing to Robert.

"I believe in action," Robert said, half-closing his eyes and nodding his head.

"Any more questions?" Dennis said, interrupting him.

They shook their heads. He got up from the chair.

"Very well, now. You have the orders," he said.

He indicated Pat, Murphy and Nolan.

"Take them with you quickly to Company Headquarters and let them rest a bit," he said. "They are to remain under arrest. . . ."

"It is poor thanks!" Nolan said.

"Thanks!" exclaimed Dennis, folding the map. "Will I thank you for leaving Johnny down there and giving us a hard night's work?"

"It was not our fault!" Murphy declared. "It was the luck turning against us!"

Pat jumped from his chair. "I am ready to go down there this minute!" he said vehemently.

He thrust Robert aside, and standing with his hands outspread and gesticulating, he confronted Dennis.

"So I am, now!" he said.

Dennis gave him a bland glance.

"You are as nervous as a wee pig going to market," he said; and he turned a thin smile to the rest as he added:

"You can rest yourself instead."

He jerked his head towards Nolan and Murphy.

"Take them away!" he said, addressing the three Adjutants.

Murphy got up from his chair again and gathered his trodden hat from the floor. With an abashed, shamefaced air he punched it out and put it on. Pat and Nolan followed him, with the three Adjutants behind them. Then the door closed.

six

Dennis sat down again at the table and rolled back the sleeve of his jacket and unbuttoned the cuff of his shirt and bared his arm a little way above the wrist.

"Agnes," he said, addressing the dark, silent woman who had remained all the time, "bring the bandages and things."

She had removed her fur coat and hat. Dennis glanced up at her as she spoke. She turned towards the cupboard in the recess of the wall behind him. She was a handsome woman of twenty-four. Her hair was black and heavy. It hung in massive tresses that framed her face and poured in a cascade to her shoulders, like a mane, like something of a separate vitality, full of its own feeling and color. It accentuated the sheen and perfection of her white skin and the delicate bloom below that sheen. Her brow was wide and clear; and her hair, parted in the center and drawn evenly to each temple, made a sharp contrast of color against the pallor of that forehead below which her large dark eyes were brimming with color and expression that were disturbing to look at. Those eyes held such impressive reflections of the deep, personal moods of her proud spirit that people could never sustain their gaze for long. The secret things of her passionate nature were there, and it was as though one were beholding sometime intimate and nude. And her whole beauty — the authentic Celtic beauty — was full, like a rare, rich fruit for which the senses were unprepared and to which they could never quite accustom themselves. It brimmed in her eyes; and it seemed to melt the garments of her body so that to be near her was to experience some indefinable yet potent physical intimacy.

She brought the dressings from the cupboard and put them on the table and sat down. She was wearing a red woollen jumper and a tweed skirt. The jumper was cut low about her neck and breast, so that the firm white column of her neck was visible where it flowed smoothly to her shoulders and breast. She was seated no more than a foot from Dennis, and as he moved his hand across the baize cloth of the table, her own smaller, lithe hand touched his. Her magnificent body was so near him. The great bloom of her beauty possessed the air about him. Her hands — always like the subtle ends of tendrils, always so suggestive of something intimate — touched his hard hand as she began to bandage it. And yet all this had no effect upon his sensibilities. He was like Johnny in that respect.

She knew why it was. He was pledged already. His whole nature was submitted to his ideals, submerged beneath the purpose of the Organization. Looking at his hard, fair features, and touching his hard flesh, she felt only the coldness of him.

Yet below that coldness there was heat. The immeasurable heat of courage, resource, patience and unyielding resolve.

He had been a member of the Organization since his seventeenth year. Since then, his life had been a fantastic record of illegal exploits, arrest, trial, imprisonment, escape, flight and pursuit, murderous forays against the Police, and successful enterprises similar to the one which had occurred this afternoon. She knew his story, and she admired and respected him for it. In almost every detail it was similar to that of his great friend, Johnny. But in Dennis hardly anything of that tale was perceptible or expressed by his appearance. Whereas in Johnny it was alive, radiant, vivid.

She knew them both intimately. She saw them daily, for she was an active, trusted supporter of the Organization, and had worked under Dennis's orders for several years, and had been closely concerned with many of his more daring exploits. She had heard of Johnny long before she had met him. And when at last she came face to face with him, she saw the whole of his life in all its romantic details inscribed in his manner and appearance.

It excited her and altered the whole course of her personal life. It became a secret of which she was not ashamed in herself when her dreams held her, but which she was fearful of others discovering. She never divulged this secret, not even to Johnny. It was difficult to screen. Her proud nature gradually assumed a curious austerity which only softened whenever she was with Johnny.

Dennis watched her. He trusted her with important missions. Had she been a man, she would have been on the Staff hnny and himself. But she was a woman. He looked at her magnificent head and body, and the fact that she was a beautiful woman indicated one profound condition.

She was pledged to her body: to her great beauty; to all the splendor of her hair, her exquisite countenance, her flesh in its woman's form; and to the passions and emotions and impulses which that body dictated to her. And because of this condition, which he imagined was authentic, he never trusted her with the innermost secrets of the Organization, nor with missions of a particular confidential kind. And never would.

His eyes watched her hands and slowly lifted their gaze to her face. She glanced at him then as though she were aware not only of his scrutiny of her, but of his thoughts as well. Motion died slowly out of her hands and her eyes rested on his.

"You know it is hopeless, don't you?" she said; and she added slowly, still with her fine eyes on him: "The police will have cordons everywhere the night."

"Finish it, finish it!" he said peremptorily, thrusting his hand against hers.

"They will lift him this time," she continued. "They will search the whole city this time. . . ."

"Come on!" he said sullenly, interrupting her and frowning.

Her voice rose in reply, and the whole turbulent force of her nature was audible.

"Do you think you will fool them with a trick like this?" she asked.

He continued to frown, but he was silent, waiting for her to finish what she had to say.

"They know you well enough," she went on. "They will recognize you as soon as they see you. You are smaller than Johnny. You are fair. He is dark. . . ."

"They will not have time to see me," he interjected angrily. "I intend to keep at a distance. They will see this white bandage in the dark, that is all."

"Then they will shoot," she said.

He shook his head. "They will come after me. They will think I am Johnny."

His thin, cruel lips opened in a smile. "They will have a run for it, Agnes!" he said. "Out they will come after me, and in will go Sean and Seamus and Robert; and by God they will get Johnny out of that. . . ."

"You think the police are such fools?" she demanded.

His smile passed, and his keen features resumed their taut expression.

"Is that the foolish way you are thinking, Dennis?" she said.

He lowered his gaze from her and sighed.

"If he had got away we would have had word by now," he said. "And if they had lifted him we would have heard of that, too, by this time. So he is somewhere down there yet, and we must find him."

"Four of you?" she said, shaking her head. "Why, you would need the whole Organization!"

He frowned irritably and merely pushed his hand against hers. She was silent for several seconds. Then she resumed the bandaging.

"It is hopeless, and you know it," she said.

"I have given the orders," he retorted.

"And the police have been given their orders, too! The cashier was killed, and for that they will muster all over this city. If you and the rest go down there, it is only more shooting, and then trouble and the curfew again, and the police searching the place here every five minutes!"

She tied the end of the bandage and thrust his hand away as she finished speaking.

"Then what else are we to do?" he demanded, flushing.

She rose from the table and stood at the hearth with her arms folded over her breast and her gaze averted.

"It is the only thing," he said, as angrily as before, snatching his overcoat from one of the chairs and jerking his arms into it.

"Isn't it now?" he added. "Can you not see that?"

Still she was silent, with her back towards him. He glanced repeatedly at her as he moved about the little room and put away the map in its hiding place behind the skirting, and took his revolver from his pocket and examined it before placing it in the strap beneath his left arm. Her silence was indicative of something to which her thoughts clung stubbornly, and it challenged him, although he was unwilling to answer the challenge and betray the fact that his plan was the only one which he could devise in this emergency.

"I have given the orders," he murmured, putting on his cap and tying a woollen scarf about his neck. As he lefted his chin to fold the scarf, he glanced again at her and saw her turn slowly and, still with folded arms and a pensive air, come back to the table.

She sat down slowly, and at the moment when her body took that new posture something in her proud spirit collapsed. She lowered her head, as though in resignation.

He was pleased. He went to the door.

"Goodbye now!" he said, curtly.

"Dennis!"

She spoke the word in a level, slow tone which intrigued him. He was inquisitive about the mood which held her and the thoughts which seemed to assemble behind the word. Because he had time and the inclination, he came back to her.

"What is it?" he said.

She rested her hand lightly on his arm. He saw her exquisite face with its dark crown of hair pouring to her shoulders. And all its beauty and expressiveness was lifted to him in appeal.

"Dennis," she said, speaking in a low, vibrant voice, "don't go! Go to Company Headquarters now and cancel the orders. The police will be out in hundreds near the mill, and they will have the tommy-guns. There will be battles. You know they will not let you have a chance to get near Johnny. You know he killed the cashier, and they will stop at nothing to put their hands on him for that. You know it is hopeless for four of you to go down there. Cancel the orders."

He looked down at her and struggled to detach himself from the conclusion which all her passionate nature was forcing upon him.

"And leave him?" he asked, quietly but incisively. "Is that it? Leave him to be lifted?" His words quickened and something broke in him and a new tone infiltrated into his words. "Leave my best friend, my Chief. . . ."

"You know you will never get near him," she said.

He was startled. "Are you telling me I must leave him to make his own way when he is surrounded by hundreds of police all out to put hands on him?" he demanded.

"Yes!" she retorted. "Yes!" her voice rising and her features blazing. "Yes!"

It horrified him because it was incomprehensible to his soul that knew little of life except his friendship with Johnny and his fervent attachment to the ideals of the Organization.

"What is this?" he exclaimed. "What are you saying?"

Her expression in all the force of her passionate spirit was uplifted to him.

"He is doomed," she said, "and you know it!"

He made a furious gesture. "Cancel the orders!" he exclaimed contemptuously. "And leave him! Leave my best friend, my Chief!"

"Yes! Leave him!"

"To what?" he asked, leaning over the table.

"To me!" she retorted. "Let me have him!"

His anger and impatience, and all the forces of his character were frozen under the sudden passage across his soul of jealousy. He was weak and unready before this invasion. Never before had he experienced jealousy. Within an instant it took possession of him, igniting dreadful suspicions which touched the core of his friendship with Johnny so that he felt mocked, excluded from something which he imagined Johnny shared in secret with this beautiful woman.

34

He struggled to escape it. "No!" he shouted.

"Let me go to him!" she said. "Let me find him!"

"No!" he repeated.

Then in anger he gripped her chin, holding it fiercely in his hard hand and forcing back her head and looking down into the great shapes of her eyes while he submitted her to this jealous probing.

She sustained it for a proud instant, trying to fling into his hard eyes all the passion of her love for Johnny, all the exasperation which her soul had suffered for so long. She met only his jealous stare. An immeasurable despair increased in her and poured from its source in her heart.

And that was what he saw. Not the pride and faith of love which was fulfilled, but only the shadow of unrequited passion which, as he stared, glimmered its reflection in her features. It was bare to his sight, this unutterable despair of love, this hopelessness and failure and shame from bruised pride. Until tears drowned it, obliterating it for an instant and then presenting a more poignant expression of it all.

It was his triumph. Something in him was restored. His jealousy subsided, for in her failure he read Johnny's absolute loyalty to the Organization and to himself and their friendship. Her forlorn expression related it all, and he was glad of her defeat.

His hand left her face. He buttoned his overcoat, still watching her and seeing the tears glistening on her cheeks. For a moment, he was touched. Obviously, she loved Johnny perhaps as much as he did, but in her woman's way: to possess; to distract; to inveigle from the Organization. He smiled from triumph; but he had nothing to say in sympathy, for as he watched her he imagined that a sullen resolve was reflected in her features.

He paused at the door.

"I forbid you to leave this house tonight," he said curtly; and he added: "You are to remain here, in case Johnny comes."

She remained as before, with her face uptilted and the expression of resolve flowing over her features.

"Those are the orders," he said, going out.

seven

When the Adjutants — Sean, Robert and Seamus — left the house with Pat, Murphy and Nolan, they walked in pairs at some distance from one another as they proceeded to Company Headquarters in a house situated about a quarter of a mile away. By this time it was quite dark. A high wind was harassing the night and driving heavy clouds across the sky with great gusts that had the odor of the sea in them. Seamus, who was a heavy man of thirty-four, was walking with Pat, while Robert followed with Murphy. Sean and Nolan were on the opposite side of the road, some distance behind the others.

"What happened at all?" Seamus asked Pat, nudging him with his big elbow and thrusting his heavy face towards him. "What in the name of God went wrong?"

He had heard it all before, when Pat and the others had reported it to Dennis; yet his inquisitive nature sought some small, additional details which he imagined had been omitted because of fear of deceit.

Pat's breath shuddered between his teeth.

"I was waiting for them, you know," he began, feeling for the first time the kind of sympathy which his shocked nerves desired, "sitting at the wheel and waiting, and when the three of them came out with the sacks . . ."

His voice was lowered to a sibilant, tremulous whisper. He stopped, gasping, and broke into a swift nervous laugh which sounded almost like a sob.

"So it was when the three of them came out?" Seamus said.

"And with the three sacks . . ." Pat said, his voice alternating swiftly between laughter and sobbing.

"Was it then . . . was that when the shooting was?"

"It was fierce!" Pat said. "Out of the door . . . two of them . . . the big fellow and a wee chap. . . ."

"But, you know," Seamus said, nudging him again, "you had guns. Why did you not use them? Always draw first and get in the first shot!"

He thrust his face closer to Pat's and kept lunging at him with his elbow.

"That is the way to settle interference, Pat!" he said. "That is what a gun is for. . . ."

"It was hell . . . hell . . ." Pat murmured, remembering the dreadful suspense while he had waited, and the scene on the mill's steps. The elbow thudded his ribs again.

"Action is the thing!" Seamus said. "Act, shoot, and don't be stopping to feel nervous."

Pat halted. His voice rose to a tight whine.

"Blast you! You are another one criticizing us!"

Rage and exasperation welled in him. He backed against a wall and drew his revolver. His words came loudly in the silence of the street.

"You are like that little swine with his court martial! All of you standing there and criticizing us after we had had hell down there! A court martial for failure! For failure he says!"

"For God's sake, man!" Seamus exclaimed. "I am only saying . . ."

Robert and Murphy came abreast of them.

"What are you shouting for, you mad fool!" Robert muttered at Pat, going past him and dragging Murphy with him. He glanced back and stopped suddenly. Murphy went on a little way and halted, waiting for Robert to come on.

Robert went back to Pat and Seamus.

"Put that away!" he said angrily, indicating the revolver which Pat held. "Be quick! And don't forget that you are under arrest."

Pat went close to him and thrust his face to within a few inches of Robert's angry features.

"Repeat that, you!" he said.

"I will repeat it!" Robert said, "You are under arrest. There is a court martial waiting for you and Murphy and Nolan. If there is more nonsense from you, I will report you. Now put away the gun and come with us sensibly!"

Pat closed his eyes slowly until they were thin slits through which tiny gleams of white showed. Robert pushed him away.

"Stop fooling! We have no time . . ." he said.

Pat drew back. He put away his revolver and sniggered. All at once he turned and went off in the direction from which all of them had come. Sean and Nolan had halted on the other side of the road. Nolan sauntered across, then came Sean.

"My God!" Sean exclaimed in a whisper. "The police are everywhere this night, and you fellows are holding a prayer meeting here."

"The silly fool has gone back!" Seamus said.

"God save us, we have no time to fool about here!" Sean whispered, trying to impel all of them on the way.

Suddenly Murphy came running towards them.

"Look out!" he muttered, rushing past them like a gust of wind and disappearing into the darkness. A loud voice sounded in a challenge which the breeze broke and scattered before the tense little group had time to discern the words.

"By Christ! Peelers!" Sean said. He drew his revolver.

The gesture, and something violent and combative in Sean's behavior, released impulses in the others. They turned at once and fled in a tight, thudding little cluster.

The figure of Pat loomed before them as he came running back from his foolish flight. He stumbled amongst them and threw them all momentarily apart.

"The police . . ." he gasped.

They were silent. They crouched, glancing keenly about them, all of them holding revolvers.

"Hold your fire!" Robert whispered calmly.

Seamus snorted scornfully. "And be shot to pieces by a bunch . . ."

He raised his weapon swiftly and fired.

". . . of blasted peelers, is it?" he asked loudly. He fired again.

There was another flash and another report which the wind seized and carried in a long, slow thunder far away over the little houses. The sound excited him, and standing out in the center of the pavement he fired until the revolver was empty.

"God, man, you have done for us now!" Sean said.

Seamus began to fill the chamber of his revolver with cartridges from his pocket. He laughed softly.

"That will hold them off a bit!" he said.

The others stood stiffly against the wall. Pat, Nolan and Sean were shuddering. Seamus hissed. He knocked on the door of a house behind him.

A monstrous burst of firing came from the far end of the street, the sounds melting into a single roar which the wind seized. The bullets whipped past, and in the far distance there was a crash of glass followed by wild shrieks and the blast from a police whistle at that end.

Seamus said angrily: "They are both ends of this street!"

He banged again on the door. The others were breathing loudly and tremulously through their open mouths. All became tense as a figure came noiselessly towards them. It was Murphy.

"They are at that end, too!" he whispered, panting.

The door behind them was opened a little way by a tall

man in shirt sleeves. At once Seamus pushed past him into the house.

"Let us in here!" he said sternly.

The others followed him swiftly. Then the door closed.

"Mother of God!" whispered the householder.

"Hold your tongue!" Seamus said. "Now, and for the rest of your life!"

A woman recoiled into a room as they hurried through to the scullery.

"Which way?" Murphy asked the householder, dragging him after the others.

"Boys, now, boys . . . it is over the wall is the best way," the man stammered. He was afraid of the police finding him in the act of assisting members of the Organization; and although he sympathized with the Organization, he was afraid of these menacing, desperate men.

He trotted into the yard and put bins and boxes against the old wall at the rear. All of them cleared it swiftly, dropping down into the yard adjoining the other and standing before the locked door of a little kitchen. They banged on the door with their fists and waited.

"Ah, to hell. . . ." Seamus muttered angrily.

He went to the window and crashed the butt of his revolver through the glass above the catch, which he released expertly. He flung up the window and scrambled in.

"This way!"

Pat was last. His trousers caught on a projecting nail. The others were through the house and already moving along the street before he disentangled himself and overtook them. Robert was speaking.

"We have lost time! There is no time for us to escort you three to Company Headquarters. . . ."

"Escort!" Pat exclaimed. "You!"

He frowned with contempt at the ridiculous figure whose big hat seemed too large for the head, and whose body seemed to lack harmony of proportion, and whose character in its curious austerity and authority was rendered pompous by the big hat and the loose overcoat.

"The three of you will report to the senior Adjutant," Robert said, hurrying on.

"I will not take orders from a wee fool!" Pat said.

"Stop that, you!" Robert said angrily. "I will report you to Dennis for that!"

Pat rushed towards him, but before he could strike him Murphy prevented him, seizing him by the arm and marching off with him and dragging Nolan as well.

"Come on!" he said. "Leave the brave Adjutants to get their taste of fun! Come on! Let them get a bit of the music. God help them!"

He walked on. His presence was very comforting to the other two, who were badly in need of someone who understood the agony which their nerves had suffered.

"Good luck to you!" Nolan called back cynically to the Adjutants.

"Pat! Murphy! And you, Nolan!" Seamus called. His voice came clearly through the darkness and breeze. "Come back and obey orders or you will suffer for it!"

The three men ran on without answering. At last Pat touched the others and stopped.

"I am all out," he panted.

Murphy and Nolan had halted.

"Take it easy, then, but for God's sake don't stand about," Murphy said.

"The police have the tommy-guns ... those were tommy-guns fired at us, you know," Pat said.

"Those three ..." Nolan panted, and he broke off to laugh nervously: "I am thinking they should say prayers."

All of them walked on rapidly.

"Maybe masses will be said for them before tomorrow is out," Murphy said.

"They were, you know," Pat said; "those were tommy-guns! By Christ, they would cut you in halves before ..."

He shuddered, as though his body were suddenly plunged into icy water.

"Single file," Murphy said, as they approached a corner. He was leading. He halted. A woman came round the corner. She was walking with her big shawl drawn over her head and face. Murphy put out a hand and waylaid her. She gasped, and stared at him with terrified eyes.

"Sh!" he exclaimed sharply.

She made the sign of the cross on her breast, drawing out a skinny arm which was raw and bare to the elbow, and which held a little purse in its fingers.

"Where is the police?" Murphy asked her.

"Dear help us," she moaned, "the police is infestin' us the

night. They're searchin' all . . ."

"Are they round the corner here at all?" Nolan said.

"Sure, there is a pair of them nearly every breath you she moaned.

She drew her shawl in place again and disappeared quickly.

"It's desperate, you know!" Pat said. "If a couple of them stopped us . . . My God, it would be all up with us!"

"Where are we going?" Nolan asked.

"You know, boys, I am thinking we had better make for Teresa's," Murphy said.

The others were silent. They were listening to the passage of police cars in the neighboring streets. The sounds were lifted by the rising wind and carried over the whole district. Occasionally a shriek ascended like the thin tip of a flame twisting and detaching itself to float away and expire or become obliterated by the noisy passing of a private car or lorry on the main road. From somewhere far distant, the sound of a tramcar speeding along a straight road was audible like the noise of life itself in all its indifference to the personal tragedy. A train's whistle blew for several seconds, and this was followed by the clang of shunting wagons in a marshalling yard. And from the docks came the slow, majestic note of a ship's siren. The three men standing irresolutely in the windswept, empty street heard it. Momentarily, it lifted their sordid lives to the contemplation of life beyond the streets which their own bitter purposes had made deadly. It proclaimed the oceans and wide lands, and rendered small and trivial by comparison the meagre territory and the unrelenting civil strife which were all that these three outlaws had known from earliest infancy. Hatred, fanaticism, and murder, within a tiny island beyond which they had never ventured, and outside of which their stunted imagination could not extend. And yet they had a fleeting vision of that wider, better world at the moment before the echoes subsided and the rattle of police tenders rose from nearby streets.

"Let us get out of this!" Murphy said.

Of the three of them, he was the most positive, the most resolute, but the least imaginative. He had recovered quicker than Pat and Nolan. Now his forthright temperament flared beyond the hard discipline of the Organization, beyond the barriers and into folly and disobedience. He took charge. With his revolver in his fist, he beckoned the others to follow him.

"I am sick of this," he said, pressing down his hat against

the high wind. "Let us get in somewhere and have a bit of kindness. We have had nothing but the black looks. Let us have a sip of something for our share of the work today."

"The police are all around this place," Pat said, holding back. "Go easy, Murphy! Don't forget the tommy-guns!"

"Where the hell are we going?" Nolan whined.

"This way," Murphy whispered, "this way."

He ventured to the corner and edged round it against the wall. The others waited in suspense for what they believed would be the inevitable challenge and outburst. But all was silent, except for the sound of police cars deeper in the Ward.

"It is clear," Nolan whispered.

He and Pat hurried after Murphy and overtook him.

"To Teresa," he whispered, nodding. "She is a good sort."

The others said nothing. The vision of Teresa which his remark evoked was encouraging and yet disquieting as well. They hungered for the kind of sympathy and hospitality which they knew she would give them; but they knew there was a great price to be paid for it all. And the price was disobedience of orders and disloyalty to the Organization; for the widow Teresa's house was out-of-bounds to all members of the Organization. Nevertheless, thither they went, slyly, huddling in narrow doorways, retracing their steps when they heard the Police patrols, once too making a sudden flight and coming under fire when a challenge sounded. It took them half an hour to travel that short distance, and it cost Pat and Nolan a great effort; but it made only a slight demand on Murphy. His mood was resurgent, but his blood was pulsing with vain fancies. He had emerged safely from terrible perils! He had been brave and cunning! He had brought back his sack full of money, and himself as well! He had fulfilled his task!

"She will give us a good fill of whisky, and a bit of something to eat with it, and a decent fire to sit over," he said.

"I am thinking we should report first of all," Pat said anxiously. "Those were the orders. . . ."

"There is plenty of time," Murphy interrupted.

They had reached Teresa's house. He knocked softly on it, and sensing the hesitancy of the others, he said quickly:

"We'll just take a nip or two and a bit of something to eat, and then we'll report at Headquarters."

The door opened with a great rattling of chains and unbolting and clacking of locks. A massive figure confronted them. Instantly, Murphy went in. The others followed him rapidly through the little opening. Then Teresa closed the door and smiled upon them and spoke to them for the first time.

"Is it yourself, Fergus Murphy? And you, Pat, dear; and Nolan, my darling? Is it really yourselves, God bless you?"

Her melodious voice lapped them soothingly. Here at last was warmth and a greeting! Her smile was a caress. Benignity beamed in her huge eyes and coursed through her thick arms and into her big, jewelled hands, which she put gently upon the three men as she urged them into her drawing-room.

"Take off your coats now and sit down, boys! Sit up to the fire. It's a cold, hard night! Pull over the big chairs, my dears, and sit easy now!"

She took their overcoats and was suddenly motionless.

"Maybe," she whispered, sinking her voice to a hoarse bass, "just for your peace of mind, you know, you had better have these things handy."

She tapped the bulky pockets and smiled as the men removed the revolvers and placed them in the holsters beneath their jackets.

"So," she said, resuming her expansive manner and sighing, "so now we are all comfortable. Now!"

She put the garments over a settee on the far side of the room and came back to the hearth. A huge, flowing figure, she dominated the room. Stout she was, and active. Her big body swung its ample skirts, and her massive bosom beneath the black silk of her dress swayed and leaped like a live thing imprisoned there. The big golden cross on her raw breast swayed, too, and the beads of the necklace clicked. Her rings flashed their stones. Her big eyes, dark and expressive, gleamed. And her large lips, crimsoned with cosmetics, opened over her big mouth as she smiled and chattered.

She constituted with others a world which she dominated and which was reported to be concerned with the smuggling of goods to and fro across the border between North and South. She was known to the smugglers as a crafty brain, a hard one, a plunderer. Her house was large, and as gaudy as herself. She lived in that style, ostensibly on an income left her by her husband, who had made a fortune from a dozen little shops in the villages amidst the bogs and in the corners of noisome slums in Dublin. But all her associates knew that she derived a still larger income from the profits of smuggling, from hard dealing, from merciless blackmailing, and other illegal enterprises. She was feared. Yet, often at close quarters her most bitter enemies and victims discovered that she possessed an attractive temperament and a generosity in the way of hospitality which bewildered them.

"Poor Ireland!" she often wailed. "We are oppressed, so we are! We are under the heel of occupying troops who oppress our own people!"

And this glib falsehood was sufficient to cause her neighbors to forget that she and her husband had monstrously oppressed thousands of their poor customers and own countrymen for almost half a century.

"Now," she said, offering cigarettes from a silver box. "Now, what is it to be? You'll take a drop, all of you? You will so. You boys need it and deserve it, for . . ."

She lowered her voice to a purr, ". . . for I have been reading in the *Tele.* of the doings in the city. Great work! Things would make the heart stir with pride!"

She went behind them to bring bottles from the sideboard and set them on a silver tray which she carried to a small table near the fire.

"Here," she said, handing a copy of the *Belfast Telegraph* to them. "Read it now while I bring the glasses and set something ready for you. You'll take something to eat? You'll stay and put your legs under my table? Just sit there now."

She swept out. In the room it was warm. There was a smell of heavy furniture and upholstery and thick, warm carpets. And above all these odors there was the heavier one of the perfume which she used.

"Rich, you know," Murphy said, standing with his back to the fire. "She is worth thousands. . . ."

"It is out of bounds here," Nolan whispered. "There would be hell for us at the court martial if Dennis knew."

Pat and Murphy giggled. "Yes, the court martial!"

Nolan said gravely: "There is no sense in disobeying the orders. . . ."

"Who is disobeying orders?" Murphy said, glaring down at him. "We have come here to avoid encounters with the police! It is a way of getting past trouble, that's all! What else would we do, and the peelers running at our heels and cracking at us with the automatics? Isn't this the only place? I know it is banned to us. I am not forgetting that. When the road is clear, we will make off."

"Sure!" Nolan said.

"She is a good sort, you know," Murphy said in a more

pleasant tone. "There is some have not a decent word for her, but it is jealousy. She is rich, but she is generous as hell. Just see now! It'll be lashings of whisky in a minute, and when it is sitting warm here," and he patted his belly, "she'll give us something to eat."

"Sure," Nolan said, watching him with a sombre air.

"Generous, you know! Hospitable!" Murphy continued, swaying on his heels. "That is the real Teresa! There is scandal about her, but it is not true. She has not had a chance to prove herself."

"Sure!" Nolan said, glancing at Pat and winking.

Pat nodded. He and Nolan were smiling as though each understood what was passing in the mind of the other.

"Well, it is the truth!" Murphy declared angrily. "Why do you not see for yourselves, instead of listening to the bad things said against her?"

"Sure!" Nolan repeated, and this time he laughed with an explosive little whinny which was charged with derision and cynicism. His whole body trembled, as though sudden cold shocks were travelling through it. His nerves were not yet recovered.

"Sure, sure, sure, you keep on!" Murphy exclaimed. "What is wrong with you?"

His voice was sharp. It cut at Nolan. All three of them were touchy, uncertain, mistrustful, and sick with fear.

"You sit there!"

"Don't you know, you fool . . ." Nolan said in a whisper, jumping to his feet and confronting Murphy. "Don't you know who she is and what she is? You have lived in the Falls long enough to know she is only a blasted gombeen woman! Did you ever get something for nothing out of such a one? Can you not realize why the drinks are coming up, and the food, too?"

"It is true, you know," Pat said. "It is so, Murphy! She is that sort! That's the way the fortunes are made. It will be something for something. . . ."

"Ah! You sit here warming your behinds in her chairs, and all you have to say . . ."

Nolan interrupted him. "You will see! There will be drinks and the grub. Plenty! At her price!"

Murphy glanced darkly at him for an instant. His face was creased by a frown of contempt which slowly expired. Then he was pale, and in his eyes there was a gulf, and on his lips a little shudder which grew as the gulf filled with a volume of fear which poured from his eyes and travelled over the whole countenance. He sighed.

"Maybe we should not have come," he whispered, as though he were speaking to himself.

"We'll have the drinks and then off we go," Pat said.

"And . . . if she works round for a bit of information . . ." Nolan whispered, nodding and smiling.

"We say nothing," Pat said.

They all nodded in agreement. A moment later when she stepped noiselessly into the room, they had the mood and manner of three men who had made a decision. She read it accurately in their looks, in their silence and their movements. She smiled. She placed the glasses on the tray.

"Now, boys!" she said, lifting the bottles and tossing back her head and looking round at them with an expression which persuaded their tardy sensibilities and momentarily conquered their resolves.

"Here is Scotch, and this one is Irish, and there is plenty more where these ones came from, so now don't stint yourselves," she said, gaily.

She noticed some degree of diffidence in them. She lifted the four glasses in her wide hands and thrust them in turn to her visitors.

"What is over you? Here!"

She laughed. It was a surging, immoderate spurt of gaiety which they heard, and which convinced them of her sincerity and generosity.

"To look at you," she said boldly, as she tipped the bottles over the rims of the glasses and poured the contents, "I would think you boys had colds on you!"

They were silent, clutching the glasses. She looked at them quickly, in turn, and poured herself a full glass before saying quietly: "So this is it! So . . ."

They exchanged puzzled glances and looked at her as they raised their glasses.

"So it was the three of you!" she exclaimed. "I know! I was only this minute thinking to myself when I read the paper, says I to myself: 'Now who would the other three be? What ones would have gone down there with Johnny?' And . . ."

"Here's your good health, Teresa!" Murphy said.

"Good health!" the others murmured.

She put down her glass and smiled at them.

46

"I am proud to have you round me!" she exclaimed. "I am, so! Three heroes like yourselves! Great deeds, wonderful deeds you have done this day! It is not you should be drinking my health, dears, but myself drinking yours, and so I do! I do, with all my heart!"

She lifted her glass and nodded to the three of them before taking a gulp from its contents.

"It is wonderful whisky, Teresa," Nolan said.

She sank slowly into her chair, relaxing her big body, spreading her arms along the chair's arms. The jewels in the rings twinkled like laughter. But her big face slowly assumed a sad expression.

"Poor Johnny!" she said, sinking her voice. "Poor dear, and him wounded, so it says!"

They were silent, staring at the fire or at the whisky in the glass.

"But what in the name of God happened at all?" she said softly. "Such a stroke of bad luck to hit you!"

"There it is," Murphy said, sighing and giving her a quick glance. "Just the bad luck. . . ."

"Was it now?" she murmured.

"It was hell!" Pat said, passing a hand over his face.

She leaned forward as though she were actually drawing closer amongst them.

"What happened at all?" she said, her voice taking a softer tone. "Sure, when four such fine boys take a hand in things everything goes well! What was it turned against you?"

"It was when the fellow came rushing out after us," Nolan said. "The big fellow . . . and there was a little chap with him . . . but the big fellow was the one. Johnny was last, you know. And the fellow was on him before we had a chance to turn and let him have it. Murphy and myself were down the steps when it happened. Johnny . . . you know, Teresa, we did not know he was hanging back so . . . there was something holding him . . . and quick as hell the big fellow was on him, and then the shooting starts . . . and the little chap rushes about raising hell and giving the alarm . . . and . . . but you know, they can say what they damn well like and hold us to blame for not getting Johnny into the car, and say there will be a court martial on us for failure to carry out orders and . . . but . . . but they can say what they like, but for . . . for . . ."

His speech became thick and incoherent. He felt Teresa's eyes upon 'him and the implacable weight of her inquisitive, forceful nature probing him. And he saw Murphy's glance of horror and Pat's distraught look.

"But you know . . . you know . . ." he stumbled on.

Teresa sighed and, lowering her eyes, she flicked from her vast bosom a little spot of face powder.

"And have they found Johnny, tell me?" she said. "Have the police got him, or is he safe and well amongst friends? I know I should not be asking these questions of you, but there is no sleep for a patriot like myself this night if that poor boy is down there in the cold or arrested!"

Tears misted her huge eyes and her lips drooped. She dabbed her eyes and nose with a tiny handkerchief.

"And him wounded, too!" she cried.

"They will get him out," Nolan said swiftly.

He swallowed a mouthful of whisky.

"God help him, poor darling!" Teresa moaned, looking at the three of them.

"But are you not going down to give a bit of help?" she asked. Then she chuckled excitedly; laughter sounded in her deep bosom; the golden crucifix shook and the necklace rustled.

"The police is all around here, up and down, so you would think the whole lot of you was out this night, so you would," she whispered. "There has been searches already. There is hell going on. Says I to myself when I heard the racket: 'The boys is mustering! There will be trouble this night. All the boys of the Organization will be moving out. . . !'"

Pat remained with his left hand covering his face. Murphy was taciturn. Only Nolan spoke. He gasped as he smiled.

"Slaughter!" he exclaimed, in a constricted tone.

Pat stood up quickly. His elbows were pressed against his ribs, and the hand holding his glass shook so violently that the liquid spurted out. His face worked spasmodically.

"Jof Jesus' sake . . . can we not take a drink in peace and forget the . . . the . . . the . . ."

Murphy and Nolan were on their feet, trembling, pale, tense. It was Teresa who snatched them into control.

"Ah, now! Sit down now and drink up, dear; and when we have had the drink we will go in for a bite of something hot!"

Her hands fell softly and tenderly upon them: big, warm paws touching the bodies whose nerves were still raw and exposed, and whose fibres still retained impressions of the car's motion and the echoes of shouts, screams, shots; and whose hearts were swollen with a sense of grievance and insult.

"And all the bitches would give us with a cup of tea and not even a warm bite to fill us after!" Pat cried. "And Dennis sitting there and promising us a court martial — and the two sacks not a yard from his nose the whole time — and then putting us under arrest and letting Sean and Robert and Seamus march us . . ."

"Sure, it is all right now," Murphy said, patting his shoulder. He laughed nervously, adding: "Maybe there will be no court martial! Maybe there will be nobody to preside at it!"

"Drink up now, Pat dear," Teresa said.

She crossed to the radio and tuned it to dance music. The sound purred out, flowing across the carpet, rippling through the air.

"Have some music. That'll cheer you. And her . . ."

She replenished their glasses.

"Now, get that inside you, boys, while I see about something to eat. The maid is having her evening off."

She left them sitting on the edges of their chairs: three big men shattered by a dream, not yet fully awakened, perhaps never to achieve complete consciousness of themselves and the deeds which they committed. Standing outside the room and listening, she heard Pat say:

"The thing is torture! I have it in my guts! It is like a thing filling my stomach!"

And then Nolan: "Ah, take a good pull of whisky! Wash it away! The thing will go when your nerves are rested. Don't think about it!"

"The whisky is prime," Murphy said. "She has good stuff! Drink up, and it will bring ou round. It is the same with all of us."

"But you know," Nolan said, lowering his voice, "she is after information. Be careful. It is no good trusting her, you know."

"It was you told her!" Pat exclaimed. "You spilled the news to her! You sat there and told her . . ."

"Oh, my God, my God!" Murphy said. "Can you not let up for a bit and take a drink and . . ."

"I am only saying we must all be careful, now the drink is flowing," Nolan said.

She heard the suspicion and mistrust and fear in their voices, and she frowned. They were so abject, like pitiable things that were defeated in themselves and had come to her for shelter and succour, despite their fear and contempt for her. She understood them. She knew that normally they would not have come here. They hated her for her riches and success, and because her activities sometimes conflicted with theirs, or because her agents should have been members of the Organization. They threatened her, but she was too well protected to injure. Often the police visited her and questioned her. She swore, knowing that the Organization had informed against her. It was a feud. But now . . . now, with three of the leaders in her power . . .

She crossed the hall noiselessly and entered the little cloakroom in which the telephone was affixed. Drawing the door close behind her she lifted the receiver. Dialling a number, she waited. A brusque voice answered her, whereupon she asked for a district Police Headquarters. When, after a considerable delay, the connection was made and a voice spoke, she asked to be put through to the Inspector or Head Constable on duty. She gave her name.

Presently another voice spoke.

"Inspector," she whispered quickly, simulating alarm, "they are here . . . three of them . . . three who were on the raid! They are here and they are threatening me! God help me, I don't know what'll happen to me if you don't send someone to protect me! They are saying I must let them hide in my house because it is the only place this night. I am afraid, I am!"

The voice asked her for the names of the three men. She gave them in a tone of distress and terror, adding:

"Be quick, Inspector . . . these fellows are desperate! I am terrified! I have come away from them to the telephone, but they are after me to put up a meal for them."

The voice told her to keep calm and wait for assistance.

In the room they heard the single note which the bell emitted when she replaced the receiver. It was louder than the music which purred and slopped unctuously from the radio.

"Someone is at the street door!" Pat said, fearfully.

Murphy had risen. His hand was thrust under his jacket and was gripping his revolver. Nolan laughed softly and remained with his legs outstretched to the fire's blaze.

"Do you not know a telephone bell when you hear it?" he said.

"What is she at the telephone for?" Pat said.

"Ah, for heaven's sake take it easy!" Nolan said, making an angry gesture. "You are giving us all hell with your nerves! Let us have a drink in peace!"

But the soft, single note of the bell had had a furtive quality which encouraged the dread suspicions that were active in the minds of all three visitors. It was like something sly that suggested a ruse which that big, florid woman was spreading like a net about them.

"Turn down the radio," Murphy said, jerking his head towards it.

His rigid body made a tense column from which terror spread like an infection to Pat and Nolan. For an instant, they resisted it, making little gestures, breathing little murmurs of confidence.

"Ah, sit down, sit down!"

"Drink up, Murphy! Sure, you wanted to come here."

But soon the fact that Murphy's suspicions were aroused swept away the weak little attempts to resist him. The last foundations of safety seemed to Pat to dissolve. His hands shook. Fear burst in his mind, exploding throughout his body, disrupting the subtle bonds which held him to life. Now he felt alone, separate, a fragment of living tissue lost in a welter of terrors from which there was no escape. He realized the dangers which involved him. He stood up, swaying, holding his full glass to his lips and trying to tip the whisky into his mouth. It spilled down him, and the glass dropped from his twitching hands, bursting in fragments on the carpet and slopping its contents all about.

"What the hell is wrong with you?" Nolan whispered.

He turned very pale. "Pat, what is it?" he said.

Staring at the others, Nolan saw their tortured eyes. A sense of doom began in him like the silent course of a falling star: small and hot and silent in himself as it coursed through his blood and his broken nerves, until he knew that his span of life was as short as his painful gasps of breath, and only as broad and as deep as the lungs which inhaled and exhaled air.

"What is it?" he said. "Is she . . . is . . ."

His hand flew to his jacket and came out with his revolver in the unconscious movement of defence. To kill before he himself was killed. The ancient, final retort, the terrible expedient, the final threat.

"What is she doing?" he whispered.

They were tense, listening. Life was outside this house,

beyond the night, beyond the Falls Ward, which they had turned into a town full of dread activities, beyond the land, a broad world with voices of warfare, but still a wider world, free of the tiny dreams that drove them to hatred and murder. A wide, flowing scene into which they would never enter. Only doom encompassed them. They felt it flowing soundlessly about them.

"Let us get out of here," Nolan whispered.

"Sh! For heaven's sake . . ." Pat said.

"I am off!" Nolan said.

The others turned on him. "Shut up! Don't move!"

The dance music whined and gurgled softly about them; but outside the room, like an outer skin, the house was silent with the hush of evil intentions. They felt it instinctively.

Murphy crept to the door. He stood there with his ear to the jamb. The others followed him and stood at a little distance. All three held their revolvers at the ready. Murphy stood back.

"Put away the guns," he said, "and let her come in. Then we will settle the nonsense. Make her take that chair."

He pointed to the chair farthest from the door. He returned his revolver to his holster. The others put up their weapons. Then all returned to the hearth. The whisky was on the tray. Pat leaned down and gathered the broken pieces of his glass and hid them behind the fender.

"Here! Take a drink from mine," Murphy said, holding out his glass.

They drank heavily. In a little while the whisky began to warm them.

"She is a long time," Nolan said.

"Get the coats and things," Murphy said. "Come on! We might have to get out of here quickly."

They put on their overcoats and hats and stood in a compact group. The minutes passed. Time grew like a barrier between themselves and the outside world, and between themselves and Teresa's hospitality. She was entrenched behind it.

"Where is she?" Pat said, impatiently.

"Maybe she is gone out," Nolan said.

The whisky gave them a momentary courage.

"If she starts mischief I will give her a dose of lead!" Pat said, tapping his revolver. "I will! I will not spare her if she tries anything. . . ."

Nolan frowned. "Let her try!"

Murphy emptied his glass and smacked his lips.

"Pass the bottle, boys! Fill up! It is a cold night, you know!"

Nolan handed him the bottle. As he poured whisky into the glasses, he looked towards the door with a swift, mocking glance.

"We will be the first to have something for nothing out of the old doll, you know! Here's health!"

They tipped down the whisky in foolish gulps. Caution was swept aside. They sniggered amongst themselves.

"When she opens that door," Murphy said, "I will give her the biggest fright she is likely to have ever!"

Nolan giggled. "No, you know, for Christ's sake, go easy! No, look here, Murphy. . . ."

"Ah, to hell!"

"Sh!" Pat said, winking. His face was flushed. "Easy boys, easy now! Lay off the drink now!"

They winked at one another.

eight

Teresa went noiselessly from the cloak-room to the kitchen. There she made a pretence of setting crockery for a meal. She put plates and dishes and cutlery on a tray, and even brought from the pantry a big, home-made meat pasty, which she set in the oven to warm.

"But I am thinking I will have to eat it myself," she whispered. "The foolish boys!"

She sighed and shook her head.

"Sure, they are very stupid when it comes to the bit!" she murmured to herself. "Sure, they just come storming into danger, and think they will get a fine warm welcome and drinks all round out of me, just because the police is at their heels, or they are in a nervy way. And any other time it is only curses and abuse for poor Teresa! Oh, I know them! Pullin' the guns on decent ones like myself and trying to threaten me their way, and interfering with my important private business. Well, they deserve all they get if that is the way they do go on. Sure, it is a battle all the time, and I am only a poor weak woman with no man to protect me since himself passed away, God rest his soul!"

Five minutes passed. She bustled about the neat kitchen, setting out bread, and making a show so that if any of her visitors came to the kitchen she might melt their suspicions with the array of cutlery and crockery and food. But she was wondering how long the police would take to send an armed squad from the local barracks, and she tried to calculate how many minutes would elapse before the squad surrounded the house and the shooting started. And she wondered if the squad would come from another district, or from the barracks nearer her house. And she wondered, too, if the police would thank her for presenting these three prizes to them.

"They are full of whisky, in there," she thought. "Full to the eyes with it, and it seems a shame to give them over like that, and the three of them a bit tired and nervy after the brave things they have done this day. Three very brave ones, and clever, too. Clever as the devil himself. But done for now, and spoiled with the drink now, and . . . God help us, there will be shooting."

She was glad that her maid was out and that there were no friends in the house to witness this monstrous event. And she was nervous. She feared that the evidence of her treachery would be discovered by the Organization, and that they would take reprisals and vengeance on her.

Her hard brow knitted.

"No," she whispered, "it must be in the street."

She went towards the kitchen door. Hanging behind the door, there was a little mirror which the maid used; and as she went out she paused for an instant and saw her reflection. She gave a touch to her hair and settled the golden crucifix on her bosom. Then she entered the hall. Noiselessly, she tiptoed across the thick rugs to the house door and stood there, listening. It was dark here. Her senses were alert. Only the wind sounded outside, and the occasional patter of a child's running feet; but her acute sense of hearing extended beyond the pavements, beyond the nearby corner. Still she detected nothing but the rising wind puffing at the house and whirling through the streets.

Anxiety began in her, but her powerful nerves controlled it. Fear was far away, at some remote horizon of her thoughts, along with vague visions of vengeance, death, horror, all of which she soon quenched. But she had no intention of admitting the police to her home, or of permitting her visitors to remain. She took a deep breath.

She knew what had happened. She assembled the truth from the shreds of it which the men had given her. The three of them returning from the raid and reporting to Dennis, and being reprimanded for leaving Johnny in peril, for failure, for losing their nerve. A court martial threatened them; and the three of them being told to report to their headquarters. But all three of them coming here, on the way, or purposely. And nobody in the Organization knowing of that disobedience. Thus, for her, there was safety. As much safety as she had ever enjoyed.

"Although precious little it is," she thought.

Then an instinct moved her. She left her place at the door of the house and crept to the door of the room. For a few seconds she was motionless. Then her face assumed a tense expression. She opened the door and went in.

In her grand, imperturbable way she ignored the attitudes of the three men, and the fact that they were wearing their overcoats and hats.

"Boys! Listen!" she exclaimed in a soft whisper, raising the palms of her hands towards them. "A friend has just given me word on the 'phone — maybe you heard the bell — and she says the police are headin' this way. Don't wait now. I am thinking of your own safety, dears. Go now! Don't be waiting here for them to surround this place and murder the lot of you. Cut now, while there is time! It is very dark outside and you have plenty of room. Don't be waiting!"

She swept her authoritative, compelling glance upon them. It was less a glance than an expression of the powerful nerves and the majestic, crafty will behind her bold eyes.

Tattered, terrified nerves flared up against it.

"It is a trap!" Nolan shrieked, fumbling for his revolver.

"Yes!" Pat shouted.

Murphy's mouth opened and he breathed heavily.

Teresa threw back her head and made a scornful gesture as she drew in a great rustling breath of exasperation.

"It will be worse for you if you stand there like fools and ignore the advice of a good friend!" she shouted. "Will you be sensible men now and go while there is time?" she added, bawling.

She encircled their senses with her forceful personality. She encompassed the air about them with her vigorous gestures.

"Come, now!"

Drawing them to the door, she ushered them out: three exhausted men, already half-fuddled with drink.

"Don't be showing those things!" she whispered, pointing to the revolvers. "Dear God, must I tell you what to do?"

They hid the weapons in their pockets.

"Quiet now!" she whispered.

She took her time as she crossed the dark hall and pretended to grope her way to the street door. She was certain the the police squad had not yet arrived.

"Where are you, my dears? Pat, is this you? It is. Now, listen! I am going to open the door, and when I have it ready, out you go, and God bless you!"

She fumbled with the chain which was always upon the door, and with the lock as well. She heard sounds of cars approaching. They were faint from the distance. At once, she spoke loudly in a quick sentence which drowned that distant rumble.

"Quick, now! All of you! And don't wait, but make a run for it, and the dark will hide you. God keep you, now!"

She flung wide the door. They went out cautiously, the darkness rising before them like an ocean of danger into which they must plunge. They hesitated.

"For God's sake . . ." she whispered.

A gust of wind bursting through the street struck them coldly and violently as they moved out to the top of the step.

"There are three steps!" she cautioned them.

Three deep steps . . . again steps and peril and the horror of a dream . . . the vast, bewildering dream which was life. . . .

A that moment all three of them heard the approaching police cars, one of which had halted and from which a loud, clear order sounded as feet rushed towards the house. They heard the door slam behind them. Then the chain rattled into place and the heavy bolts shot into position.

It was the sound of doom from betrayal. They leaped down the steps and started to run, tripping over one another in the darkness, stumbling, rising again, panting. A challenge came loudly from the pursuing police, whereupon all three halted, drawing in and standing stiffly against the wall.

The challenge roared again. Suddenly, they began to run again. A figure loomed before them. They tried to stop, their feet slithering as their bodies collided with one another. A blinding beam of light shone full into their faces, stabbing at

56

them like steel piercing their eyes, and expiring and leaving their sight impaired. They were dazzled. They saw in the darkness only the horrid, hard light lifting across their vision. At once, all three fired and ran on. They shouted in rage, in defiance.

The fumes of the whisky were torn down at last in this final moment. Courage welled in them in a last flame. All three halted, hearing shouts of challenge ahead of them. Now at last they were calm, resolute, fatalistic, for the darkness was suddenly rent by a monstrous burst of firing. They shouted wildly into the night a single oath of rage, of defiance, for the guns were on them at close range.

There was a second roar which swept through the air of the street and echoed to the mountains in a great solemn explosion which was gently rejected by the sky and the wind. The bullets ripped brickwork and glass. Murphy gave a strange whimper and coughed, his body toppling. Pat and Nolan stumbled and fired again. To fire was to live, to act with a last, despairing spark of life from a dream which had been born far back in time when an ugly, embittered teacher had spoken to a class of little boys.

"We must never resign, never give up this struggle against the hateful English and their tools. . . ."

They fired until the bursts from the automatic rifles snatched the weapons from their sundered fingers and tore open their bodies and ended the dream and the evil and bitterness and stupidity. Three sodden, shattered shapes were upon the cold pavement.

"It is Murphy!" said an armed constable, bending over one of them. His comrades spoke the names of the other two. Someone threw a big ground-sheet over the three bodies, while a Head Constable gave orders and called up a tender. Beams of torches shone about as the constables searched for and found the three revolvers. A door opened furitvely some distance from the scene, and Teresa in a fur coat came out.

She hurried forward and reached the fringe of the excited groups of constables.

"Mother of God!" she wailed. "What has happened?"

Before they could prevent her, she rushed forward and gazed at the mound from which feet in strange attitudes protruded.

"Dear God, it is three of them!" she shrieked.

She recoiled, the constables tapping her shoulders and

impelling her away. A neighbor met her.

"Is it killed they are?" she whispered.

Teresa moaned. "It was three fellows was running," she gasped. "I heard them running past . . . then there was shooting and . . . now . . ."

"God have mercy on them!" the neighbor murmured.

"Away out of this now," said the Head Constable, signing them away. The neighbor scuttled off at once. Teresa loitered. The Head Constable recognized her. He knew her as a rogue, a smuggler, a thief and worse, and now an informer.

"I have some questions to ask you," he said coldly. "Later on."

She sustained his hard stare for an instant and then returned to her house. There she hastily removed the glasses and the bottles of whisky. She lifted the cushions of the armchairs and set them back, after which she quickly swept away the cigarette butts from the grate and emptied the ashtrays. The inane purr and scoop of the dance music was still beating its monotonous measure. She sighed tremulously as she crossed the carpet and turned the dial so that the sound became louder. The music ceased and a voice spoke.

"Our next, ladies and gentlemen, is a l'il number entitled . . ."

The music began again. Teresa stood quite still before the fire and assembled her thoughts. Her left hand gripped the golden crucifix on her bosom, while her right hand patted her hair which had been tossed by the wind. She was examining her reflection in the big mirror above the mantelpiece. She saw the iron grey hair streaked with ugly strands of black, and the eyes that formerly had been full and dark but which were now hard and wide and as coarse as her heavy lips, that always seemed to have lurking behind them the laugh of derision, the explosive threat, the coarse oath, or the soft tongue of blarney. She saw, too, the heavy jaw under its fat, which was that of self-indulgence and all the selfish complacency of a tyrant. And on the big hands were the jewelled rings. Now they flashed again at her and excited her cruel instincts, for they were the visible things of success which her savage, pagan soul had always lusted after.

But the face was what attracted her principally, for it had enormous secrets which she alone discerned. It bore the whole record of her life in a valley celebrated for centuries by the poets of Ireland. First, the lithe peasant girl, then the shrewd woman, then the driving spirit making its way to riches and power above the hearts and trampled lives of hundreds of her poorer neighbors. . . .

It was all there. And suddenly she smiled. It was the soft, benign glow which had deluded saints and scholars and tourists. She knew it, and in her deep bosom, far below her clamped lips that treasured their evil, a laugh began. It shook her big body and burst at last from her mouth.

"God help us all, you're a great woman, Teresa, my girl, and a great sinner as well, so you are!" she exclaimed.

She chuckled again, and this time there was a tinge of guilt in the laugh, for she knew what she was looking at. It was the reflection of treachery in its age-old expression. That same monstrous treachery which had touched so many of the great leaders of her native land. It was the sow's face — she had read the words somewhere — the sow which devoured its young.

She shrugged her massive shoulders and turned away. Today was Friday. Tomorrow night Confessions would be heard. She would go to the chapel and kneel in her pew, and after a little while had elapsed, she would rise and enter the dark, wooden cubicle and sink awkwardly to her knees at the grill behind which the patient priest was seated.

"Pray, Father, give me your blessing, for I have sinned!"

And then, after the blessing, and when she had said the Act of Contrition:

"I was deceitful, Father. . . ."

nine

The three Adjutants — Robert, Sean and Seamus — continued cautiously in the direction of the city after they had given orders to Pat, Murphy and Nolan. They were worried. The night was gathering its dark garments about itself and storming across the land in a flurry of cold wind from the southeast; and in the darkness stood the police, in pairs, in extra patrols, armed and on the alert. They were the known factors, and the three men did not minimize their ability. Often in the past they had had short, fierce conflicts with them at street corners; and they knew that these constables were well-trained, swift and courageous.

But tonight's activities were much more than an unexpected brush with the forces of law and order. This afternoon a cashier had been killed by a member of the Organization; and tonight the police were mustered in strength to find Johnny, to oppose all attempts to rescue him. There was a tense, angry note in the air, and the Adjutants heard at least one expression of it whenever the police cars raced past in the darkness. Yet they did not fear the police as much as the possibility of treachery.

Unlike the officers of the law, whose plans and operations were decided by reputable authorities, and whose lives were disciplined by the corporate life of the Constabulary, they lived a furtive, outlawed existence amongst citizens to whom their every movement was visible. The force of this circumstance necessitated an implicit faith in those willing and sometimes unwilling supporters and neighbors who were obscure people, often poor, often harassed as much by visits from the members of the Organization collecting for funds as by visits from the constables searching for concealed arms and explosives.

Thus, from the very foundations, as well as from every other quarter, the possibility of a word escaping in chatter, in anger, in folly or spite, was always present. These men knew their contemporaries, their own countrymen, and all the pitiable flaws at the root of their characters and temperaments: the smile hiding the guile; the sworn promise from the weak will which could never implement it; the blind madness of anger; and the hysteria which loosened secrets. And they were perturbed.

In three houses in different streets they met their runners and issued certain orders. Peril encompassed them, like the darkness itself or the wind which blew about them. It had done so for years, but tonight it had a more terrible aspect. It had additional eyes and ears tonight. How sentient it had become they knew already, yet as they moved into its currents they discovered that it was not only alert but full of purpose. They moved cunningly through the streets of the Ward where many of the inhabitants remained indoors under the influence of portentous rumors. At last they emerged in the main roads where the traffic and the crowds characterized the great outer stream of the city's life.

About that time the darkness in the Ward was touched by

the patter of feet, the whispering of youths who met in groups of three or four and moved down to the police patrols at the corners of streets joining main roads. There, having gone safely past without being stopped and without having aroused suspicion, they proceeded towards the borders of the district in which the mill stood. And there, singly, they loitered amidst the inquisitive persons who approached the district.

A single individual coming through the Ward and entering the main road stood but a poor chance of passing without being swiftly scrutinized, and perhaps stopped that night by the vigilant constables on duty at numerous points that night. But a man on a cycle passing at a leisurely speed and perhaps whistling softly aroused no suspicion. Even a second might pass thus, and a third as well, when the cordons began to form. The ruse succeeded.

But the will and the heart which had made that swift passage through extreme peril were conscious now of greater perils. Even to run that little gauntlet left a horrid impression on the mind. For ahead were larger dangers. The night was full of them. A glance might loosen them. A voice suddenly calling might be a shout of challenge, or the first indication of recognition. And if the request to halt were not obeyed, death itself might come as swift as the bullet. But ahead, in the district where Johnny lay wounded — there, indeed, issues would be decided. And they knew it, those three Adjutants following each other and Dennis, those hearts touched already by dread anxieties and morbid ideas from centuries of fanatical extensions of the will into regions of darkness and insurrection. They knew that the police were there, in force.

There were youths waiting to receive the cycles and wheel or ride them to points where they might be used again by those officers. There were many ardent youths. There were voices muttering in the darkness, uttering fervent remarks.

The furtive figures merged themselves into the shadows and the darkness and went into the district. They went by different routes and met at an appointed street. A wrist showed for an instant, and a face — that of Sean — bent above the luminous dial of a wrist-watch.

"What time is it?" Robert whispered.

"The quarter," Sean said.

Robert made a sign to Sean and Seamus. "I am going now," he said.

"Best of luck! Goodbye, now!" the others whispered.

They saw him go noiselessly and without hesitation to the corner and flatten himself against the wall there. Next moment he had disappeared. It was uncanny and even exciting and beautiful in some indescribable way.

Seamus nudged Sean.

"It is queer, you know," he whispered. "Have you noticed? There is not a peeler anywhere! I am thinking they have a big plan."

There was a tinge of alarm in his remark which ripped off the protective surface from Sean's courage and left him afraid. He became angry. He thrust his hawk-like countenance towards the thick face of the other.

"What is queer about that?" he whispered. "Do you think they would make a show of themselves for us?"

Seamus was not afraid. What he experienced in his slow, unimaginative mind was a sense of alarm because neither he nor his companions had anticipated this absence of the police from the district. He nudged Sean with his elbow.

"You will see," he said, whispering. "It is an ambush!"

Sean knew him and understood how his mind worked. He knew that he made hasty surmises that were invariably wrong. And he knew that his one and only virtue was his aggressive courage.

"Don't be silly," he retorted.

Seamus went on: "It is my opinion Johnny is not here at all. Maybe he got away. Maybe the police have him and are just letting us come in so that . . ."

"What are you saying?" Sean exclaimed angrily, making a gesture.

". . . letting us come in so they can lift us when they have closed round us," Seamus said.

"Well, it is past the quarter," Sean said; and although he was reluctant to part from Seamus, he added: "It is time you went to your post where Dennis told you."

"I am going," Seamus said. "But I am telling you: they are not down there," and he pointed to the heart of the locality. "Dennis is in there, but there will be no whistle from him. I am thinking he has been lifted. The police will come this way," and he jerked his head towards the borders of the district.

"Then we ought to find Dennis now," Sean suggested.

Fear began in him again. It was difficult to subdue. It pulsated through his body with every beat of his heart.

"We will give him five minutes," Seamus said. Then, like Robert, he disappeared silently in the darkness, going in the opposite direction and leaving Sean alone in the windswept, empty street.

Sean stood rigidly in that place of narrow alleys and silent storeyards. His hands were thrust deeply into his overcoat pockets. Not far away there was a tall telegraph post whose wires hummed loudly in the high wind, sending out a note which the staunch post echoed, too. He heard it and did not like it. He kept lifting his shoulders as though to fold the collar closer about his ears and neck where the freezing wind struck him and carried the post's note to him. Fear was moving like a live thing in him. He forced his senses to remain alert so that he might see anyone approaching him, and hear them, and hear too, Dennis's whistle. But through the medium of those acute senses fear was travelling. It made little deadly rushes towards his will, herding his thoughts and threatening them. For a little while it was quiescent. It seemed to have retreated or diminished. He drew a deep breath.

He looked about him with wide, quick glances. Now he achieved a sudden, clear realization of his position. He recalled what had happened this afternoon. An armed robbery and the killing of the cashier. And he knew that those crimes were matters which had roused the full, angry attention of public opinion, as well as the resolute forces of authority. Squads of armed police! Hundreds of them, all directed by trained, clever officers, who had a plan which was surely larger and better and more comprehensive than the one which Dennis had formulated. And he knew that the police were somewhere in this district, and that soon ... soon ... the big, resolute figures ... and the challenge ... and the deadly bullets ... and the darkness ... and perhaps death! The cold air was pregnant with it, and the single, vibrating note from the great post nearby proclaimed it.

He felt lonely and tense. His abdomen contracted and his breath gasped. His whole body trembled, so that he wondered how he would be able to move, to raise his arm and use his revolver and think, if and when the moment came. He closed his lips tightly and tried to subdue the ripples of cold and fear that travelled over his body. Waiting was the worst aspect of the whole affair.

His lips parted. "It would ...," he gasped, in a moaning whisper, ". . . it would cut the heart out of you!"

And that was how they found him. In a thunderous rush of big bodies they were upon him, all round him, their shouts of challenge ringing in his ears, their weapons aimed at him, their strong hands seizing him before he could bring his hands from his pockets and aim his revolver or ward off their grip as he attempted to run. The police! A squad of them!

He flung his body violently to and fro. His fears were gone, melted by the hot pulse of anger and shame. He worked an arm free and dealt a cracking blow to one of the constables which sent the man crashing back against the wooden door of a builder's yard. He contrived to draw his revolver, and he clenched his teeth and bent his whole body as he struggled to aim it. For several seconds there were only the sounds of scuffling feet and blows and muttered exclamations. An arm was raised. It came down swiftly, and the baton cracked sharply upon Sean's hand. The revolver dropped from his fingers, and in the next moment he was pinioned. A constable pounced on the revolver and handed it back to a comrade. Now they had Sean firmly. He held them all rigidly for an instant while he exerted his remaining strength. Suddenly he went slack. His shout of anger and pain ended abruptly. The Head Constable in charge of the squad shone a torch in his face, whereupon Sean winced and lowered his head sullenly.

"This fellow is one of them!" the Head said. "Hold up your head!" he went on, jerking his big hand under Sean's chin. "Yes, he is one of them, right enough!"

He spoke Sean's name. Then he chuckled tersely.

"Take him away and put him in the truck!" he said.

A huge sense of humiliation filled the prisoner's mind. His right hand was numb where the baton had struck it, and his arm was throbbing with a dull, drenching pain. But the shame which he felt was worse than the pain and the numbness. To be taken like this! To have them pounce on him unaware! And not a single shot fired!

It quenched everything in him which had supported his fanaticism. It revealed him to himself for the first time, stripping off the crust of vanity, violence and bitter ideas that had always bolstered his belief in himself, and revealing to him his fruitless life which, as he now appreciated for a single wretched moment, was nothing but an instrument for the sour idealists who, from his infancy, had preached to him and urged him to this fanaticism. But it did not end there.

Soon, it gave place to dread conjectures. Then he looked

sullen and dangerous, although all the fight had gone from him, and he was thinking behind his malicious mask: the trial . . . the sentence . . . the long years of penal servitude . . . the whole of it looming before him in a tedious, dull vista . . . for what? . . . for a dream which clerics and small-souled teachers fostered in their festered minds! He knew it . . . the dreams and the evil glances backwards to a past which lay far off and which their monstrous hearts would not let lapse.

They put handcuffs on him.

"Get in now!" a sergeant of police said to him: an aging man with a slow, almost paternal air.

The police truck was wide open before Sean. As he got in he caught its cold, steely odor. It struck his senses like a blow.

"Now," said the sergeant, climbing in after him and sitting down facing him with a revolver in his hairy fist. "This is number one! All right! Go ahead!"

The doors were closed and bolted. The engine started.

ten

Dennis had come down alone. He wore a dark overcoat and a black cap. The woollen scarf was about his neck and chin. He entered the district quickly and adroitly, believing that everything would happen swiftly, and for this reason he glanced from side to side as he advanced. Until he had proceeded for a distance of a hundred yards and had reached a point at which he expected to encounter the police. There he halted. He drew his cap deeper over his head and lifted the edges of the scarf higher about his neck and face. In his right hand in the pocket of his overcoat there was a revolver and a whistle. He held his left hand plunged deeply into the other pocket. He waited for five minutes, a motionless figure, part of the intense darkness of that region. He was listening and watching.

He heard only the noises of the nearby streets: the barking of dogs; the voices of the inhabitants. And the low, incessant rumble of the city's life flowing upwards to the sky's immense vault and pouring down in slow echoes. Nothing else. No movement of patrols. No whispering or sounds of footsteps. No sounds of police cars. And he knew that he could trust his ears.

He became anxious. He could not understand why the police were not in this district. Without pondering this fact, he moved on. Now he was like the wind which flowed swiftly and then in slow, meandering little gusts. He hurried for a few paces and then stopped and stood motionless in the shelter of doorways and embrasures. He skirted the meagre radiance from the "star-light" lamps, and went on, his body full of a momentum and rhythm which he could control without losing an essential quality of it. And in that way he penetrated deeply into the heart of the district, passing men and women and vociferous children without being accosted or recognized.

He halted at last on the corner of the street in which the mill stood. A piece of heavy wrapping paper, torn and stained, lifted in the wind and was blown along a few feet. Further on, some children were at play, running to and fro and making sounds suggestive of gun bursts. Dennis halted. They were playing on the mill's broad steps. Three of them came down the steps, whereupon two from behind rushed upon them, pretended to fire, to call an alarm. There was even a mock scuffle.

"By geez!" yelled one of the children. "I'm hit! He's got me!" He reeled about and finally got down at full length on the pavement.

There began a furious argument.

"Away out of that! I am Johnny, and youse is the others!"

"Och, no! Sure, we said . . ."

Dennis passed by swiftly. He came back a minute or two later and followed the route which the car had taken before Johnny had fallen off. He moved most cautiously, on tiptoe, staring all around. Reaching the narrow cross-roads where Johnny had fallen, he looked about for a clue, for some fortunate indication of the way his friend had gone. He found nothing. Presently he set off down the street through which the others said Johnny had gone. Children were playing thereabouts, and in other streets through which Dennis travelled. Presently, one of them padded softly beside him.

"Mister, mister!" he called, seeing a stranger, seeing yet another stranger in a locality which this afternoon had been visited by many strangers: plain-clothes men, reporters and others. "Mister, give's a pahny . . . a pahny, mister!"

Dennis stopped and glanced quickly about before he grinned down at the boy.

"I will call the police," he said.

The child repeated his request. ". . . a pahny . . ."

"I will have the police on you," Dennis said.

The child watched him with the astute, critical stare of a little old man.

"A big, big peeler, like the ones is up and down here," Dennis said.

The boy smiled, and watched with curiosity and anticipation this intriguing person whose presence seemed to hold promise of liberality.

"Have you not seen them?" Dennis said. "The big police . . ."

The little one grinned and shook his head, drawing in his nether lip under teeth which were broken and dirty.

"What?" Dennis exclaimed. "You have not seen the police looking for the fellow who killed the man at the mill?"

Again the child smiled as he shook his head. His playmates had ceased their game and come up to listen.

"Here is a wee boy," Dennis said, addressing the newcomers, "who has not seen all the big police up at the end of the street!"

A small, hoarse-voiced youngster of seven pushed forward. Here was the natural leader, the little one with a frown, the pusher, the embryo tyrant jealous of other children. He sniffed and ran his dirty hand under his steaming nostrils.

"Where is the police, mister?" he demanded.

"Have you not seen them?" Dennis exclaimed softly. "All the police and the Heads, looking for the fellow who killed the man at the mill! Hundreds of them!"

The children looked at one another and then at this man of fabulous tales.

"Och, away out of that!" the little leader shouted. The others giggled. "There is no police! Sure, you are a cod!" he declared.

"Honest to God, there is hundreds of them!" Dennis said. "Maybe you have not seen them, but there is hundreds a fellow was after telling me."

They looked at him and broke into a chorus of derision at his credulity.

"Sure, sure, there is no police now," the bold one said.

"Is that a fact now?" Dennis said.

"Sure, the police was round where the fellow was killed!"

"Is that so?"

"And then they went away."

"The whole lot of them?" Dennis asked.

"Sure."

"And did they find the fellow who shot the man at the mill?"

"Sure, they found him!" the leader said.

But the rest were laughing at this lie. They broke away in a restless little flight from which they returned to study again the man, and to hear their leader lie to him.

"They did not!" Dennis said. "Did they now?"

"My dad saw him," a small girl said.

The leader frowned at her. "Quit your blether!"

"I seen him," a boy said. "I seen him runnin'!"

Their voices surged like little leaps of foam. They had all seen him, the fugitive in flight from the police, the murderer, the gangster, the fantastic figure of the cinema come to life in their streets. All of them . . . he had a gun . . . sure, he had two guns . . . and was blazing hell . . . he had a tommy-gun, it was . . . he fired . . . he killed one of the police . . . away out of that, he killed all the police . . . the police ran away . . . the man ran away . . .

They clung to Dennis, tugging at his coat and sleeves, trying to sell news to him. The facts were snatches from films which they remembered only for the violent scenes and which they augmented by their childish talent for the dramatic. They vied with one another, hoping for reward, these shrill souls born in this squalid district and growing up amidst its murk which the awful, indifferent face of the mill dominated like a symbol.

But one child, a timid girl, moved away, remained apart from the rest, on the fringe. The truth was in her, for she had seen Johnny. She was the witness who had seen and heard; and it had impressed the whole of her budding sensibilities. It had startled her. It had been strange and terrible and even mysterious. And now that there was untruth and many words, she withdrew to ponder and preserve her secret, as she had thus far kept it silent and intact within her mind.

Dennis saw her. She watched him with special intent, for he was some kind of link between that seift, panting, bleeding figure of dusk, and all the subsequent events that had throbbed in the district. He was clad like that stumbling figure. She saw him give money to the others, and she crept a little way towards him.

"Did you see him?" he asked her. "Did you? The man."

She came forward timidly, as much because he was someone to whom she might impart the burden of her secret as for the pennies which were coming from him. He had, besides, a mood and manner which she found pleasant. She nodded shyly.

"Where was he?" he asked her.

She raised a hand and made a little gesture.

"It was there," she breathed.

It might have been anywhere within a radius of thirty or forty yards, for she had not yet acquired a sense of accuracy in direction.

Dennis looked about cautiously. The other children had sped off with their pennies.

"In a house?" Dennis asked.

"No. There," she said, making the same gesture as before.

Opposite, there was a row of little brick air-raid shelters.

"In the shelters?" Dennis said.

She nodded.

"Which one?" he asked, giving her his hand. "Show me."

At once she edged back a little.

"It was there . . ." she whispered, pointing to the second one from the left in the line.

Something was beginning to subside in her, and the ancient instinct of her people was becoming active in her: the fear of informing; the unwillingness to give evidence. He caught swiftly at the ebbing tide of her secret, holding out a shilling to her.

"Did the police find him and take him?" he said, giving her the coin.

She clasped the shilling in a tight, dirty fist and shook her head.

"Did the man run away?"

She seemed bewildered, and breathed as though making an effort at recollection. The truth was fading; the facts were no longer clear for her childish mind to assemble into words.

"He . . . it was there . . . I seen 'im . . ." she contrived to say.

"And the police never came?"

She shook her head. Questions occurred to him, so many of them that he was obliged to restrain them and select what was easiest for her to answer. But in that little interval he lost her. Her secret was divulged, and she was released at last from the strange, unfamiliar weight of it. As though it had been a physical burden as well as a mental one, she suddenly sped away, lightly, free, a child again, without care or responsibility.

Dennis cut across the road and entered the shelter. He halted cautiously, then he struck a match. Holding the light high, he saw it—the evidence of Johnny's sojourn there. He stared down at the bloodstains in the corner, seeing the drops of them, and the mark of a hand, and the horrid dried spatter stretching across the cement floor. The match expired. He did not light another. He hurried out.

He sped through the street, not daring to blow his whistle and give the signal that would bring in the Adjutants, for in his anxious mind he feared an ambush. Johnny was gone, was arrested perhaps, and the police might be approaching from the rim of a strong cordon through which he and his comrades had been allowed to pass only so that they might be trapped.

As he ran, the conviction that he and the others had fallen into this snare increased in his agitated mind where the idea developed, raising all manner of minor anxieties. He asked himself how he intended to warn his comrades, and how he would extricate them from this quandary.

He halted, trying to conceive a good plan. In the darkness, shadowy forms seemed to be moving silently towards him. The wind carried all sorts of sounds—vague and difficult to trace to their source—which he could not recognize. A loose gutter tapping against a wall was like the patter of advancing footsteps; and hearing it he swung round, crouching, with his revolver drawn and his eyes straining to pierce the darkness.

Suddenly he heard footsteps and saw two figures closing on him. He drew back at the moment when he heard his name called in a sibilant whisper.

He recognized Seamus and Robert. The momentary feeling of relief was succeeded by anger.

"What are you doing here?" he hissed. "Why are you not at your posts?"

They crowded close to him. "Listen, Dennis, listen!" Seamus said. "They have lifted Sean! There are dozens of them, dozens! We had better get out of this now!"

"Where is Johnny?" Robert asked Dennis. "Have you found him?"

"I saw where he was," Dennis said. "He was in one of the air-raid shelters. . . ."

"Was he, was he?" Seamus said. "What has happened to

him?"

"He was not there. God knows where he is," Dennis said.

"Well, what are the orders?" Robert asked.

"They are all around us!" Seamus said. "The police are all around. There is a cordon would encircle a whole army!"

He was voluble from excitement. He longed for action, perhaps for shooting.

". . . the orders?" Robert asked again.

Seamus took Dennis by the arm and tried to drag him on. "Orders . . . my God, hark at him! Orders, he says! Let us cut out of here while the chance is ours!"

Dennis jerked his arm free and pushed Seamus against the wall.

"You fool!" he whispered, "behaving like an old doll! The two of you deserting your posts and running about like this!"

Robert said stiffly: "We waited for your signal, and we thought . . ."

Dennis touched his arm and gave a warning exclamation. All three were silent, for all had heard it: a murmur followed by a scuffled step on the pavement. They waited tensely, staring into the darkness about them, not daring to move.

Out of the darkness and the flurry of wind at that spot came the rush of oncoming feet, swelling to a thunder of charging bodies. The three men hesitated. To run, or to fight it out? Seamus shouted a warning and fired twice in quick succession. Then he fled. In the next instant, three big figures hurled themselves upon Dennis and Robert.

eleven

All five went down in a sprawling mass of tangled arms and legs, rolling over and over, with sometimes an arm lifting and delivering a blow or a leg kicking out. A helmet rolled away and swayed in the gutter. A baton whirled off and clattered on the pavement. A shot sounded in the distance, the bullet whistling briefly in the wind. At once, one of the constables wriggled free from the fight and fired rapidly in the direction from which the shot had sounded.

"Get after him!" one of the other constables shouted, heaving his massive bulk above Dennis and Robert. A sharp blow on the face smothered his next word. Then the mass rolled over again.

Dennis was half buried beneath thrashing legs and knees. He heard the peeler fire and set off in pursuit of Seamus, and he had a sudden impulse to laugh, for he was certain that the man had gone in the wrong direction.

"Dennis!" Robert gasped, speaking in Gaelic. "Go, you! I will hold these fellows!"

"We will finish them off first!" Dennis shouted, in the same tongue.

"We will see about that!" shouted one of the peelers, lifting himself and giving Robert a blow in the face. The other loosened his hold of Dennis's leg and sought a better grip on his arms. He was too late. The moment of release was a tiny aperture through which all Dennis's strength poured, bursting the clutching hands and enabling him to get to his feet.

The constable drew his revolver. Before he could aim it, Dennis kicked it from his hand and fled. At once the constable threw his whole weight upon Robert.

Robert let them grip him firmly, then he exerted his strength. He clenched his teeth and got to his feet. For a moment the constables were awed by this amazing action, for Robert stood quite still, with his arms about them, holding them, even moving off with them in the opposite direction to that in which Dennis had gone.

The constables realized what his plan was. They pitted themselves against him in a burst of ferocity which sent all three of them swaying and reeling in a compact group to and fro across the narrow roadway and the pavements.

Some men and women who had come from neighboring houses were making a wild uproar, shouting at the police, screeching curses at Robert and exhortations to his assailants. The hubbub increased, for the onlookers were afraid that the constables would be overpowered and shot.

All at once a cry of relief and satisfaction rose, for the ridiculous man who had been struggling with the police went down in a sudden flat spread of limbs. The police raised their batons. There was a dull, thumping sound followed by a groan.

The two constables stood slightly back from the prone figure. Around them, the onlookers were cheering and pressing forward.

"Back now! Stand back!" the constables shouted.

They stooped and dragged Robert to his feet. He was dazed. His body swayed. The constables rushed him away very quickly, the crowd running behind them for a short distance and jeering at Robert, whose feet made ridiculous attempts to walk. They were quick, mincing little steps which ended in a stumble from which he never recovered, for by then he was being borne off into the darkness so rapidly that his legs trailed behind him like those of a dummy. His overcoat was bunched at the shoulders, and he looked more ludicrous than ever.

The crowd laughed. Lying in the roadway was Robert's hat, and not far from it—with the wind already blowing it through the dirt in the gutters—was a length of bandage which Dennis had stripped from his hand and thrown away. A woman clad in a voluminous black shawl and an old tweed skirt ran out and snatched up the hat. Soon she was the center of a vociferous mob. Hands lifted and grabbed at the hat to clap it on heads, to examine it, to strike it. It became a trophy, a valuable relic of the events of afternoon and evening.

"Give it! Let us have it, youse!"

They began to fight for possession of it, pushing one another, cursing, shouting and laughing, snatching the hat and throwing it about, kicking it, setting it on the pavement and stamping on it, until within a few minutes it was so battered and torn that it no longer resembled a hat but had become a ragged, filthy thing which had no visible relation to its owner. Somebody threw it high into the air. It lodged on one of the little low eaves of the houses, just above reach of hands. They let it stay there and dispersed.

From a blackened pile of ruins of houses that had been shattered during the recent air-raids on the city, Dennis and Seamus heard them. When all was comparatively quiet, Dennis spoke.

"It is time we moved out of this," he said.

"Which way?" Seamus said.

Dennis did not answer immediately. He knew the district thoroughly; and he knew that every exit from it would be cordoned by the police.

"Not far," he said, and his tone was unhurried, calm.

He saw Seamus peer out, and he heard him breathing in slow, strong inhalations.

"The peelers are everywhere, you know," Seamus said.

He nudged Dennis, who seemed to come alive and look at him as though from the distance of a decision which was going to separate them.

"I am wondering where Johnny is," Dennis said.

Seamus nudged him again with this thick elbow.

"If we are going . . . if we are to make it . . . there is no sense in staying here and letting them come at us again," he said.

Dennis was silent. In his soul there was a great envy of Johnny. He had a vision of his friend and saw him now as a man whose whole existence represented the expression of certain ideals. The fact that he had killed the cashier, and that he would be charged with that crime if arrested, seemed more like a misfortune rather than a sin. It was a mere stroke of bad luck, in Dennis's opinion. Yet it rendered Johnny in a particular aspect. It would raise him into the ranks of the martyrs for the cause. And in those ranks were Sean and Robert. He envied them, for he was excluded.

In them, the ideals of the Organization were symbolized. Johnny would be executed. The others would be tried and sentenced to long terms of penal servitude. But for himself there remained only the incessant furtive existence amidst the streets of the city, the dark places, the little rooms in little houses, and the endless opposition to the officers of the constabulary, and the straining against Governments which he knew he and his associates could never overthrow.

It all offered him only a prospect of loneliness and exclusion from what he imagined was the glorious fate of his friends. It placed them all much higher than himself. They were fulfilled, whereas he was still a mere fugitive, outlawed, doomed to failure.

He felt suddenly lost and apart, rejected by fate. In his soul he was very lonely and jealous.

"I am not afraid!" he said loudly.

"For God's sake . . ." Seamus whispered, dragging at his sleeve.

"I have never been afraid of the peelers!" Dennis said.

"What is on you, man?" Seamus said, frowning and drawing back.

"Will I creep about? Will I crawl at their feet for the rest of my life?" Dennis shouted.

Seamus dragged him back into the ruined sockets of the houses. He was trembling.

"My God, what is wrong with you, Dennis? They will hear you, man!"

Dennis pushed him away. "Let them! I am going to find

Johnny!" he said loudly.

"Don't shout, Dennis! They will hear you! Listen, Dennis!" Seamus said. "We will take our time and slip out of this place. Maybe Johnny has got away and is at Headquarters, waiting for us. We will get out of here, and find my runner and send him back for news."

"I am not sneaking about in fear of the bloody police," Dennis declared.

He stood out of the ruins, his little body erect, his head thrown back. Voices were audible in the distance, and he laughed swiftly as he heard them.

"Shut up making a show of yourself, Dennis!" Seamus said, taking hold of him and pulling him back.

"Go back to Headquarters," Dennis said.

"Not without you," Seamus said, shaking his head.

"I am giving you an order, Seamus!"

"I am disobeying it, Dennis, until I know you are in your senses," Seamus said.

Dennis shook himself from the other's grip and began to mutter angrily. He drew his revolver.

"Hide that thing, man!" Seamus said.

Words gibbered in rage on Dennis's tongue as he pushed Seamus aside and walked out to the pavement.

"Dennis!" Seamus whispered.

"I am going to Johnny and the others!" Dennis said. He started to walk along the street.

"You know Johnny is lifted!" Seamus said, taking hold of him again. "You know the police have him, like they have Sean and Robert! Blast it, let us get out of here before they get us!"

Dennis shook him off.

"I will not crawl away from them!" he said loudly. "I am not afraid of them. I am going to the others!"

He walked on swiftly, leaving Seamus alone in the windy darkness. The voices in the distance rose to an excited hubbub as Dennis approached them.

"It's the police!" Seamus called softly. "Look out, Dennis!"

He started out after him. He saw him distinctly as he passed below the dim light of one of the standards.

"Dennis, Dennis! Come back!"

Suddenly he sped towards him and overtook him.

"Dennis," he moaned, "what'll the rest of us do if they lift you? Dennis, think of that!"

The other went on as before. Then Seamus exploded in fury.

"Blast you! Is it mad you are?"

He drew his revolver and stood in front of Dennis, barring his way and jabbing the muzzle of the weapon against his chest.

"Have some sense, you fool! Stop this, and remember you are Johnny's Deputy!" he exclaimed.

Dennis pushed the weapon aside and went on. Seamus let him go. He stood baffled and helpless, his body suddenly very cold after the heat of that moment. His mind, too, was cold, full of slow, drifting mists of collapse and despair that clouded his resolution and courage. Ahead, the police were shouting at the crowd to disperse. Suddenly there was silence, except for the faint sound of Dennis's feet.

"Christ save him!" Seamus muttered. "They will kill him! He is done for now!"

He hesitated a moment. Then he walked quickly after Dennis. He drew within twenty feet of him and walked in step with him, holding his revolver ready. When his keen sight saw the dim forms of the constables at the corner, he moved a little to one side.

He heard the police shout at Dennis to halt, to stand where he was and put up his hands. Dennis continued in the same pace as before. Seamus halted and drew back flat against the wall of a house. Now he could see four constables standing with their revolvers raised. At once, he took swift aim and fired almost at the instant when Dennis fired, and the shots from the four revolvers which the police held ripped the fabric of the night. Voices screamed. Seamus kept his eyes on the four constables and fired again, twice, in rapid succession.

Silence followed the sounds. It grew around him with a curious intensity which horrified him. He stared into the darkness and fancied that he saw four black figures crouched near the corner. He blinked, holding his revolver ready. When his sight cleared, he saw only four prone shapes lying apart from one another. His eyes winced. Then he saw Dennis lying not far away.

He knew what had happened, and his terrified soul moaned as he stood there swaying and panting. The silence seemed to embed him in its heavy substance. He stared wildly about him trying to accustom his senses to all that had occurred. Moving forward, he looked down at the motionless body of Dennis. He bent down and put his hand on the shoulder and turned the limp body so that he might see the face.

He saw nothing but an obliterated mass from which his sight recoiled. Gasping, he drew himself upright, seeing the big bodies of the constables lying a little way ahead. So still! He began to breathe very quickly. His twitching fingers groped in his pockets and found cartridges which he inserted into the chamber of his revolver. He stood there, hesitant, shocked, wondering what to do. He was alone . . . to run . . . to fight it out . . .

Suddenly he turned and fled, running faster than he had ever done before. To escape . . . to elude the oncoming police whose steps he heard . . . to save himself from the same fate which had befallen Dennis, and Sean and Robert, and Johnny . . . to escape a fate whose horror threatened to overwhelm his mind . . . to find people, to see traffic, to attach his senses to the normality of life and to sink his sensibilities upon it all before reason was ruined irreparably.

He fled through the streets, crossing roads, rushing round corners. He was challenged, fired at. Once speeding towards a corner, he collided with three constables and stumbled amongst their tumbled bodies. His knees gave way and he went down. For a dreadful instant, a sense of defeat touched him. He got painfully to his feet. Then he ran. The bullets whipped past him. But he was faster than his pursuers. He hid in another blackened mass of gutted houses, shifting cunningly there as the constables entered and followed him. Tiptoeing out, he sped on. He reached the last barrier, and burst through it. It was the thin outer rim of the cordon, and he was through it after a last outburst of firing. Three minutes later, he was in the main road, amongst traffic and people. He walked at a leisurely pace. Soon, he crossed the road. Five minutes later he boarded a crowded tramcar proceeding from the city's center to the Shankill Road.

twelve

The tramcar was full. Inside, there were men and women from the day-shifts in the factories and shipyards, together with housewives returning from an afternoon in the cinemas or late shopping. Besides these, there were youths and girls going to dance halls or cinemas in the locality.

Seamus was inside, standing between two girls styled fantastically in the manner of screen actresses and a stout man smelling of spirits. The air was putrid, for ever since the car had left the shed earlier in the day, and perhaps as long as a week or even a month, the tiny windows and little ventilation shafts had remained closed. Sometimes passengers who were almost overcome by the acrid atmosphere would attempt to open one of the little flaps, but at once some stout man or woman would complain.

"Sure, the draught is terr'ble! Do you want us all destroyed with the influenza?"

"This tram stinks!" the passenger asserted.

"Och, away out of that!" someone retorted. "Stop lettin' in the draughts on us!"

Or the little conductor would heed the complaint about the atmosphere of his car and come in and try to open the ventilators.

"Some people," he muttered, closing his eyes and slightly jerking his head upwards, "you would think some people lives in fields! This window has come stuck!"

About every hundred yards the tram halted at the stops. A few passengers alighted. Many more pushed and scrambled aboard. Somebody on the platform tugged the bell rope and the vehicle jerked forward, jostling the passengers violently together. The little conductor came clattering down from upstairs; and pushing aside the passengers who were crowded on the platform, he seized his way bill and began to enter the particulars of his takings. When the car stopped he returned the bill to its place and regulated the outflow and inflow of passengers. His voice was crisp and authoritative, and all the actions of his little limbs and body were vigorous; yet nobody seemed to take any notice of him, imagining him to be only a person who collected fares and gave them a ticket which, at the end of the journey, the majority of them dropped in the roadway. Swarms of boisterous, vigorous youths stormed the vehicle, pushing the alighting passengers roughly aside, shouting, laughing, filling the stairs, the platform, and the doorway. One of them tugged the bell-rope. Then again the car jerked forward, flinging everybody about. The imperturbable conductor rattled the coins in his hand and shouted:

"Fares! All fares! Fares, please!"

Pushing his way inside, he wriggled under arms, over knees, squirming past big bodies, pushing aside slender ones, all the time clipping tickets, collecting coins and giving change. From time to time the bell rang and the car stopped. More youths pushed their way aboard, shoving aside the other passengers who were trying to alight. The little conductor wriggled his way to the platform and planted himself at the doorway so that it was almost impossible for anyone to come out.

"Hurry along, there! Pass along quickly, please!" he bawled; and again he snatched his way bill and contrived to finish a little more bookkeeping before attending to the passengers.

"Plenty of seats on top! Pass up the stairs, please! Full up inside now!"

The laden vehicle jerked forward again. He hurried inside and collected more fares.

Presently the car stopped. A crowd of raucous, panting youths and men poured towards it and filled the platform.

"Now then! What's goin' on here?" shouted the conductor, working his way to the platform and grabbing his way bill. "Fares, please! All fares!"

He pulled the bell-rope, signalling the car to proceed. Nothing happened. The overloaded vehicle remained motionless, with many more noisy passengers pushing wildly aboard. The little conductor frowned, and muttering to himself he wriggled along the interior of the car towards the driver.

A great current of sweet, cold air was gushing through the tram and causing many of the passengers to shudder and exclaim angrily.

"Shut the door, there!" they shouted to the driver. "Sure, you'll have us all killed with the draught!"

"This car is overloaded!" the driver retorted, glaring in at them.

"Whose fault is that?" somebody shouted back. "Take your face outside and let us have a bit of comfort in here!"

"I'm sayin' this car can't proceed!" declared the driver.

"What the hell have we paid our two dee for then?"

The conductor bobbed up not far from the driver.

"What's holdin' us, Billy?" he asked.

"Sure, I'm telling you! The car is overloaded!" his mate shouted.

A passenger called: "Och, away out of that, man! Go back

to the wheels and things and do your best!"

"Fares, please!" shouted the little conductor.

"Ernie, clear them fellows off the platform!" the driver said, angrily.

The conductor looked at him and laughed.

"Them's fixtures, Billy!" he said. "Them's the things you can't move!"

The stout, tipsy man next to Seamus laughed loudly.

"No Surrender!" he shouted.

The two young girls next to him giggled. He lurched around and grinned at them.

"Them fellows is true blue! They won't budge! Not an inch!"

The passengers laughed or became angry according to their temperaments. The rowdy youths clustered on the platform and stairs and, pushing into the tram, tugged the bell-rope and kept bawling in a vociferous chorus.

"Start her up! Go ahead, in front!"

"Clear that platform!" the driver shouted back. "This car is overloaded."

A great chorus of banging and whistling greeted his request.

"No Surrender! Not an inch!" hiccuped the fat man.

Laughter and angry chatter came from all sides.

"Fares, please! All fares!" called the imperturbable little conductor, reaping his harvest of pennies.

Suddenly the driver unfastened the chain across the steps of his platform and disappeared into the darkness. Seamus had been watching him. He knew what was going to happen. He became perturbed. Glancing around in the direction of the conductor's platform, he saw the driver come aboard with a constable.

The latter began to clear the platform of passengers.

"Away off this, now! The lot of you! Step off and let the car proceed!"

Several passengers inside had lost patience and were leaving the car by the driver's open platform. Seamus followed them, slowly, fearful of appearing in flight from the constable who was already moving down the inside of the car and thinning out the passengers there.

"Leave the car! Come on, now!"

Seamus turned to make his way past other standing passengers. For an instant his profile was visible to the constable, who was a tall man towering above the others in the car. Seamus saw him peer quickly and crane his neck. At that instant a cheeky boy tipped the constable's hat over his face.

Seamus edged out very quickly, past the standing passengers and through the front platform. Without glancing back, he crossed the road and sped off rapidly towards the nearest turning.

The constable no longer troubled about the crowded tram. He, too, worked his way along the interior and swung off the vehicle. There was no sign of Seamus in the darkness. Nevertheless, he did not hesitate. He loosened his revolver in its holster and ran round the car.

Seeing the vehicle cleared of its crowd and the driver back again on his platform, the little conductor sang out cheerfully:

"Are you all clear that end, Billy?"

The driver shouted something and closed the door.

"Go ahead, Billy!" the conductor said, ringing the bell.

The vehicle jerked forward, flinging the fat man against the two girls. There were cheers from upstairs.

"Fares! Fares, please!" shouted the conductor, disappearing upstairs.

The constable who had set off in pursuit of Seamus had not gone a dozen paces before he realized the futility of his errand. Ahead of him, as well as to right and left, were the young ruffians he had ejected. They were scattering from his threatening presence, laughing and shouting amongst one another at a distance.

The constable cursed under his breath and felt a great anger against these yelling boys. He resumed his patrol. In imagination, he appreciated what would have happened had he apprehended Seamus. He had heard terrible facts regarding the trouble in the district around the mill and elsewhere in the city this night. Constables had been killed and wounded in fierce encounters with members of the Organization who had attempted to rescue Johnny. Elsewhere, several members of the Organization had been killed in other encounters. Had he been able to slip the handcuffs on Seamus, there would have been commendation and perhaps promotion for himself.

He felt frustrated and exasperated. He raged inwardly, and suddenly hastening his pace he overtook two of the youths.

"Let's see your identity cards!" he demanded.

They looked saucily at him. Taking their time, they began to search their pockets. Only one card was produced. The other boy said insolently:

"Mine's home."

A feeling of immoderate satisfaction began in the constable. He took the boy by the arm:

"You can explain that at the Barracks," he said.

thirteen

Seamus reached the turning and walked quickly around the corner. There the wind which was blowing from the southeast in gusts which were increasing to gale force met him and resisted him. He tried to maintain his swift pace, but he made little headway until the wind momentarily subsided. He sped on then, hearing the wild gust passing into the distance while from its source another rose.

The sound of the mournful wind roused a sense of doom in his mind. He felt isolated. Yesterday, and for many years before that, his life had been characterized by perils to which he had become so accustomed that when, for periods as long as a fortnight or a month, no dangers seemed to threaten his existence, he was often perturbed. For then it was as though he were returned to the everyday world from which he had been a renegade for so long; and he discovered that the rest of mankind was progressing towards visible goals, all jostling and fighting forward as they had done for thousands of centuries, while he was left behind and rooted in a cause which was lost unless it was opposed. Now his sense of isolation was at the other extreme. And this time and for the first time, he knew that his actions and those of his associates in the Organization had aroused a terrible exasperation in the rest of mankind in the city, and that those citizens had halted in their journey towards personal goals and were all demanding vengeance. He felt himself to be one of the objects of that anger and exasperation, more particularly since Johnny was gone, and Dennis was killed, and the other Adjutants were arrested. And the sudden terrible recollection of that tragedy in the heart of the district visited him like a monstrous nightmare. He groaned. His body trembled.

In this mood and condition he arrived at a modest house in a street deeper in the locality. He knocked on the door and glanced cautiously around and walked on a few paces. After a little while, he returned to the door, which by this time had been opened and left ajar for him. Looking furtively about, he admitted himself swiftly and closed the door quickly and noiselessly behind him. He entered a room at the end of the narrow hall.

Several men and women of his own age were assembled there. They were sitting at the little hearth and on the arms of the settee and armchair. All were very tense and taciturn, and as he entered they turned to him in silence and watched him with a forlorn expectancy which he sensed at once and which he answered with silence. Still they waited, their sombre eyes heavy with hope and directed to him as he stood with his back to the door and his shocked gaze dragging itself over them and his trembling hands unfastening his overcoat. Then his glance curved from theirs and he sank heavily into a little chair which one of the women pushed forward. He let his head rest on his arms along the back of the chair. He heard the soft sounds made by the flames in the fire and the gas jets in the brackets on the wall above. Below those sounds there were others: the breathing of his associates; the scratching of a match when one of the men lit a cigarette and handed cigarettes to the others; and the long, harsh whistle of the wind in the street. A window rattled in the room above.

"Give us a cigarette," he muttered.

He lifted his head and accepted the cigarette and the light which one of the women gave him. He inhaled the smoke and then exhaled it in a sigh.

"Did you find Johnny?" one of the men asked, softly.

Seamus lifted his head and let his gaze linger on the expectant features. He shook his head. At once the others began to ask questions in a babel of anxiety and alarm.

"What has happened?"

"Where is he at all?"

"What about . . ."

He groaned and put up a hand in a gesture of distress as the others clamoured at him for news. Closing his eyes, he swayed slowly.

". . . desperate . . ." he moaned, "it was desperate. . . ."

The voices passed to silence again, and he was left like a soul submitted to a single burning question whose probing he could not bear. He did not know what to say, for the whole tragic event, as well as his sense of doom and isolation, seemed too huge, too portentous to convey in words. Yet words rose and trickled to his tongue and increased there; and he uttered them, suddenly overwhelmed by an emotion which carried the words on vibrating chords of despair and grief.

"They are all gone!" he exclaimed. "Sean and Robert are arrested. And Dennis . . ."

He sobbed, his voice choking. His eyes swept their gaze over the company in a single frantic glance. One of the women gasped and then buried her face in her hands and began to sob in long, poignant cries. The full horror of the events of afternoon and evening swept into his mind.

"Dead!" he cried loudly. "Dead!"

For an instant his mind achieved complete realization of the meaning of the word as it applied to Dennis, and perhaps to Johnny and to the man Johnny had killed. Then a kind of stupor touched his thoughts.

"For Christ's sake . . . give me a drink!" he said brokenly.

Many minutes passed. Somebody had given him a glass of whisky, which he sipped and then gulped while the women sighed and moaned and kept murmuring snatches of prayers and making the sign of the cross. The men murmured to them and smoked nervously and whispered questions to Seamus which he did not answer.

"And, you know, Seamus . . . did you know . . ." one of the men ventured presently. "Did you know? Pat and Murphy and Nolan . . . gone, too!"

One of the women sniffed as the tears drowned her eyes and poured down her cheeks. Seamus bowed his head.

"God help us all!" he whispered thickly.

He stood up, throwing away his cigarette with a quick, tense movement and trying to assemble the news into control in his mind as the voices related it to him.

"All three of them . . . killed . . . outside Teresa's!"

"Outside!"

Seamus put his hands to his ears.

"Don't tell me; don't speak! I want to think!" he cried. He was trembling. His mind was confused beneath an immense mist of horror which he could not dispel.

"What are we to do, Seamus? There is no news of Johnny," one of the men asked gently.

Seamus could not answer him. He flopped down on the settee and buried his face in his hands.

"Leave him now," one of the women said. "He is tired. Say no more now, but let him rest, poor soul! He has had a bad time, God help him! Leave him be now."

They lit cigarettes and went out to the kitchen to make tea.

The men who remained in the room were silent but restless and perturbed. Soon they began to murmur amongst themselves, discussing the tragic events of the afternoon and evening, while Seamus rested.

He heard their words, but the sense of them did not penetrate the immense confused mass of his thoughts. He detected only the note of horror, the quality of fear and resolve and fanaticism which the voices held and which roused in him only a vast sense of tragedy.

"Seamus!" one of the company said gently. "Seamus!"

He lifted his head and looked at the man.

"Seamus, you know, if Johnny is lifted . . . you are the Chief now. It means . . ."

"Sh! Leave him be!" one of the women said, entering with a tray on which cups and a teapot stood.

"I was only saying, you know . . ." the man explained.

"I hear you," Seamus said brokenly, "I hear you," he went on. "If we don't find poor Johnny, or if the peelers have taken him and are not letting on, then I am Chief of Staff."

He lifted his head and confronted them and said in a wild voice which sent echoes through the house:

"And if they lift me or finish me, there will be someone else. And if the bullets finish him . . . but, God help us all, what is going to happen to us? When are we going to be free of it all and win through and . . ."

His voice broke and he emitted a great, tremulous sigh.

"It will go on, Seamus!" one of the women said. "Until they listen to us and hear what we want to say! It will, so!"

She handed him a cup of tea. He sighed again and was silent.

fourteen

When Dennis left Agnes she rose from the table and began to tidy the room. She emptied the ashtrays into the fire and swept the hearth clean of ash and butts. The chairs which stood about the room clearly indicated the recent gathering, as did the fire which had dwindled for lack of fuel. She set the chairs straight and attended to the fire. When the room was quite neat again she went to the kitchen.

There she noticed that the other women had washed the cups and replaced them on the hooks of the dresser and left everything in order. Nothing which would be likely to reveal the recent presence in the house of the officers of the Organization was visible. The sacks containing the stolen money had been removed, and the women had left the house.

She returned to the room and stood before the fire, whose small, leaping flames made sounds suggestive of tranquillity and comfort. Above the mantelpiece, the two gas brackets made a faint hissing which, like the pleasant sounds of the fire, did not disturb the room's silence. About her, the hush gathered more intensely now that the men were gone and the tedious, anxious hours of the night opened to her turbulent imagination.

She sat down in the little wicker armchair by the fire. Here, in this room of her father's house, her passionate spirit had developed from childhood to womanhood. Here, in the small house in the confined Ward, she had developed the ability to dream, to turn from the drab actual world and look towards an inner one which her emotions formulated in all the terms of her temperament. Here, patiently, she had lived more on the belief in her intense personal world than on the fabric of reality. She had dreamed; she had come from childhood to girlhood and at last to maturity with a belief in herself which was like a singular plant cultivated in secret by the power and scope of her imagination.

She looked up quickly from the fire and saw the wallpaper, the table and little cupboards, the chairs and the sagging settee, the curtains drawn close across the shutters; and she knew that these things were the drab porperties of a scene in which she had always been the principal figure until the advent of Johnny. It had been a tiny, circumscribed scene, filled only by herself, her mother who was now dead, and her father who was seldom at home. Here, in this little house, her life had started; and here at this moment her belief in herself was failing.

Long before Johnny's advent in this house, echoes of his life had reached her and enlivened her imagination with visions of his daring and courage and enterprise. Romance attached to him. To her he represented the perfection of the manhood of her race. She carried in her handbag several newspaper reproductions of his photograph. In her mind she held an image of him which she possessed completely. In all the subtle, profound moods of her spirit he was hers, at the source of her dreams, like an inspiration that abolished the walls of the tiny house and enlarged her personal world and gave it hope and horizons that were immeasurable.

Then one night he broke from prison and came to her father's house and was given shelter.

A great happiness dawned in her life. Her proud spirit was convinced that his fate was merged with hers, and that she had effected this by the intensity of some force in her will. His room was but a few feet from hers. He sat at the table with her. He worked all day in the room upstairs, issuing long reports and orders to the Organization of which he was Chief. He read books which she brought for him from the libraries. Often, she spent hours with him, talking about the ideals of the Organization of which she became a trusted sympathizer, and for which she undertook many dangerous missions.

But her happiness was because he was a prisoner in the house where her forceful spirit had for so long been confined. The great taunt which his romantic life had made to her thwarted spirit in its restricted environment had been answered by her fate in this way. Now he belonged to the same meagre space in which she dwelt. He dared not venture from the house. But she was free! She could go out when she wished, visit friends, shop, go to cinemas, in absolute safety. And be certain that when she returned he would be there.

It was her soul's secret which she herself hardly dared to admit, but which she relished with all the passionate pride and jealousy of her nature. Until the terrible sense of triumph and possession was touched by pity for him. Then she longed to express her remorse, her pity for him, to love, to be loved in return. In secret, she was willing to relent in her possession of him.

But nothing of all her love for him reached his sensibilities. He was beyond her. He was a prisoner here. As much hers as he was the prisoner of circumstance. But her remarkable beauty—the full bloom of it, intimate and impressive—passed over him like a shaft of radiance which evoked no reflection of itself from the sombre substance of his soul. Her triumph had not been conceded by his spirit, which was utterly possessed by his fanaticism.

And yet to find him, to yield to him, had become the whole purpose of her life. Her whole life was committed to the passion which she recognized only when she appreciated its hopelessness. He was virgin and celibate, and would be so always. He was the Organization, its Chief, and the least member of its staff was nearer to him than she could ever be.

But he was there, day after day, before her eyes, a taunt to her pride and her emotions. He was at the source of her dreams which would never be fulfilled. She confessed it to herself: this terrible predicament! This bitter triumph which she had wanted but which she could not savor! And if this were love, then how bitter was the truth of it, and how terrible and significant were its sources! How extensive were its currents that invaded the entire consciousness so that there remained no territory into which the thoughts might shut themselves and find release from their wounds! This shameful defeat of all her beauty and pride and the desires of her body and soul! This thing to have happened to her! And the anguish from it all!

She rose and walked about the room, touching the chairs and the table, her senses withdrawn, overwhelmed by a rage of despair. To have to endure this defeat! To know that Dennis knew what had happened to her! To be so exposed in her shame! To have to suffer this terrible anxiety now that Johnny was in peril and wounded!

Her imagination completed the picture for her, so that she saw herself submitted to an agony which Dennis would observe as, day by day, Johnny's fate developed. The arrest. The trial and sentence. . . .

To have to live for weeks, months perhaps, throughout that period! And to have to endure every moment of the last days, and the last minutes before his execution! And afterwards, for a lifetime! To be challenged thus and thwarted, and finally defeated in her beauty, her pride and her pity!

Police cars had entered the street and halted outside the house. She did not hear them. Orders were shouted; and houses opposite, as well as those on terraces adjoining her own, were entered and searched. She did not hear the loud knocking on the door, until a crescendo of sound from the passage outside the room interrupted the long flight of her thoughts.

A voice shouted: "Open up here!"

She went noiselessly from the room to the door of the house and heard them, constables, stamping and murmuring outside. Tiptoeing back to the room, she stood with her hands on the door jambs and glanced quickly about at the furniture, the floor and the table. So much had happened here within the past hour that it was inconceivable that some evidence of the brief sojourn of the men would not be obvious, or that some essence of the air which had surely been impregnated with disaster would not communicate itself. Or that upstairs Johnny's room would not reveal his existence there, although she knew that it was always prepared by him for a possible search and was kept empty of evidence.

The knocking sounded again, and peremptory voices called. "Do you want us to break this door open for you? Open up here!"

She went to the door and opened it wide and confronted them. Four big constables, all of them armed with automatic rifles. The cold night air rushed into the house, bringing on its current the cries from the street where all was bustle and shouting across which the sounds of doors slamming and men shouting and women tirading whipped to and fro. Dark figures passed in groups. Feet thudded. Several youths suspected of membership of the Organization, and others upon whom arms and ammunition had been found, were being led away under arrest. In a house opposite, dumps of arms and explosives had been discovered beneath the floor of a small room on the ground level. A strong guard was stationed at the door, and the occupants were being taken away. In a single second, she saw or surmised it all.

"What is it?" she demanded of the constables.

A sergeant of police spoke. "We have orders to search this house, miss!"

A Head Constable was approaching from the opposite side of the road. She turned her back on all of them and went to the room, hearing them come noisily into the house and run quickly upstairs as well as to the kitchen and the yard. The yard door was opened. At once the wind burst into the house in swift currents which emitted shrill sounds that subsided only to rise again. The thud of feet overhead shook the little gas brackets on the wall above the fireplace. The mantles trembled and the flames around them wavered for an instant.

She stood with her arms folded across her breast and her head turned towards the door. Suddenly, in rage, she took a step and swung the door fast, slamming it loudly, and thereafter going to the table and facing about, waiting.

The door opened slowly and the Head Constable appeared in the doorway. He glanced at her and then about the room.

Entering slowly, he closed the door without turning from her, and stood leaning back against it. In the quietness, she could hear his heavy, measured breathing through his nose.

He was about thirty-seven, in his prime, a tall, splendid body, filling almost the whole space of the door. His hat was level on his head. His sharp but pleasantly blue eyes regarded her without animosity from beneath the peak. She saw only his face. It was handsome from its natural shapeliness as well as from the consciousness of authority and the factors of that authority coming into his life when he relished success. It had reflections of happiness, amiability, across which the purpose of his visit gleamed like something which he sought to soften. The truth was that he and she were two handsome beings. Each knew it. But only he acknowledged it. Her glance fell momentarily from him so that she saw the uniform: the smooth dark cloth fitting tightly over his wide shoulders and magnificent torso and limbs. And the dark leather of the Sam Browne with the holster. And on his big hands the gloves. And in the left hand his black stick. And in his right hand the big revolver.

Her eyes rose again to challenge him. He was the representative of the Law, and he stood in this room where so recently there had been officers of the Organization who had disclosed facts of the raid and the disaster, and who had made fresh plans to rescue Johnny. It was like a fusion. She feared that he would be conscious of it and realize what had occurred here. The exhausted, hysterical presences; the shouting; the tale of disaster and tragedy; the plans. Only her silence was the inadequate curtain before it all. Absolute silence.

"Where is he?" the Head Constable said slowly and firmly, speaking in a quiet, almost intimate tone.

Her heart beat faster. Surely, if he had senses he would see in the still air of the room the shadows of those recent figures: Pat, Murphy, Nolan from the raid; and Dennis, Robert, Sean, Seamus. And the women. And hear echoes of those despairing cries, and the rage and hysteria, and the plans. And the prayers for Johnny.

He came forward slowly, a great male figure filling the room with impressive indications of everything which his uniform and his personality represented.

"I am asking you where he is?" he said.

Her silence answered him but told nothing of Johnny. He stood before her looking full at her dark eyes, watching them for what she knew might be the reflection of her thoughts as his words raised them.

"This room is full of cigarette smoke," he said. "They have all been here!"

He waited an instant before uttering their names, as though he were reciting them not so much from memory as from accurate knowledge of the presence of the men in the room within the last hour.

"They have been here," he repeated.

It was less a question than a statement of fact; and as he uttered it he studied her as closely as before, his undeviating gaze watching her eyes for an acknowledgment.

"They were here, the whole bunch of them!" he asserted. "Sitting in this room, pulling away at the cigarettes and drinking the tea!"

And he went on, speaking slowly, the words coming quietly from between his taut lips, as though he were drawing nearer to something which her silence guarded and which would presently reveal itself to him.

"Dennis, and the rest," he added.

She was quite still. She subtracted from her features the substance of mood, the reflection of thought and the indication of what lay so heavily in her mind as he went on speaking. Overhead, in the little room, heavy feet were thudding on the boards. On the stairs and in the kitchen the same heavy sounds rose as the constables searched the house. Anger flooded her mind, but she restrained all the impulses which resulted, holding them under the impassive weight of her silence. The tall, uniformed body remained before her, his eyes probing her until everything of her being seemed to be touched by the mild, blue stare of them and to become a part of the silence and stillness into which both of them were merged. Until she saw a smile begin on his face and waver and expire.

A peculiar weakness possessed her. She knew that he had guessed all that she had tried to conceal from him in the depths of silence. She sat down slowly at the table; and as her gaze returned to his, she saw him smile again and shake his head.

"That's the truth of it now," he said. "The whole bunch of them, after the raid, after the killing, the lot of you all talking about Johnny."

As he spoke he brought the long barrel of the revolver like a finger to her chin, resting its cold metal lightly on her skin and running it slowly to and fro, pensively, almost caressingly, as though he were attempting to cajole information from her.

His keen sight saw the stain of tears about her eyes and upon her cheeks. They were like the little, gleaming pools left by a stormy, receding tide; and he knew what had engendered that tempest in her. The chilly barrel of the revolver ceased to move under her chin. He coaxed her head back with an insistent pressure of the barrel while he leaned against the table's edge and stared down at her.

She let him do that. She was not afraid of what he might see in her eyes, nor was she ashamed of the tears. But she was afraid of herself and her fury, which was mounting in her to answer him with words that might betray her resolve.

He spoke quietly. "This time, it is manslaughter, killing," he said, without bitterness or rancour, but with a quiet intimacy. "This time it is not for taking a smack at the police, or for trying to blow out the windows of a police barracks, or for bringing in arms and explosives and making dumps of them in the city. It is because he has killed a man. That's the truth, this time. Now he has gone too far, and there will be no wriggling him out of it this time. Not even if the whole lot of you with Dennis and the others try it. The fellow has killed a civilian. It is murder."

The cold barrel left her chin, but her face remained uplifted because the impress of the steel's chilly length had not yet subsided from her skin. She knew that the Head Constable had seen her tears and that he had guessed for whom they had fallen. Shame began in her proud spirit but passed quickly to terror. She remembered his words.

"It is murder."

She remained rigid at the table, the terror streaming through her heart and her limbs. She hardly heard the Head Constable open the door and call an abrupt command. The men came from upstairs and noisily entered the room where she was seated. She rose then and moved aside and stood against the wall, watching the Sergeant and the others as they drew out the furniture, turned up the chairs, lifted back the linoleum from the floor near the door, and drew up a loose floorboard to flash torches below. They tapped the walls, lifted off the pictures and examined the walls beneath. At any other time, it would have roused a cold, scornful fury in her. Now she was indifferent to what they were doing. She sat down near the fire and stared at the flames.

It was all finished within a few minutes. They replaced everything and went out quickly, leaving the Head Constable with her.

He gave a last look around the room, as though he were not willing for anything to be left in disorder after the search. Then he stood facing her. He nodded.

"Well, good-night, now," he said. He added quickly: "Stay out of this business," and lingered for an instant as if to add something more to what he had said. Then he nodded again and went out quickly.

She heard the house door close loudly and heard, too, the muffled thud of feet passing along the pavement outside. Minutes elapsed. The silence resumed timidly, slowly, like her thoughts that were rising in a flood of despair as she remembered again the words: "It is murder."

She rose and put on her hat and her fur coat. Crossing to a little cupboard in one of the corners, she stopped down and groped beneath it with her palm uppermost. When her hand came up it was clutching a small revolver which she hid in the folds of her coat.

Her face had the same rigid expression which the Head Constable had seen upon it; and her movements as she turned out the little gas jets and passed from the room to the yard had a curious economy which suggested her purpose.

fifteen

In the yard there were several empty wooden boxes. She put one of them on top of another, and with a third in her hand she climbed on them. She got astride the wall, and using the third box as a step, she let herself down in a yard of a house in the street next to the one in which her father's house stood. She crossed the yard and entered the tiny kitchen and closed the door softly behind her before going noiselessly towards the door of the room facing the street. There she stopped. She listened at the door before tapping softly upon it and opening it.

A mongrel dog came to her feet and began to wag its tail and looked up expectantly at her, whining softly. She opened the door wider and peered around the room.

An old woman was seated in a decrepit armchair beside the fire. Her small, stringy hands with the fingers bent and roughened by time, disease, and work were empty in her lap. Empty, too, were her dim eyes and the soft, almost senile features. Only the lines of age showed on the pale flesh. She was dressed in an old black skirt and faded blouse over which she was wearing a red cardigan which was darned coarsely in several places with badly-matched wool. Around her body was a heavy black shawl whose folds swathed her shoulders and arms, and which had evidently fallen from her head which it had recently covered, for the grey hair was disordered in untidy strands, and the little comb at the back of her head was hanging loosely.

When she saw Agnes, comprehension began in her. First of all, her hands parted from each other and began to move slowly up and down her thighs. Next, her misted eyes filled with a soft light which increased like a candle flame rising steadily. A smile gathered on her features, and her head started to nod and to tilt towards one shoulder. At last, a gentle effulgence grew in her face and became a look of benignity. Her smile was suddenly beautiful as her old hand lifted and extended itself towards Agnes.

"Sit you down," she said softly. "Come. . . ."

Agnes took the hand. Instantly the old, hard fingers closed fiercely about the young white hand and drew the fine body towards the chair with a surprising strength. The smile increased, claiming back from time what had been cruelly stolen and spoiled and offering it all to Agnes in a swift, remarkable brilliance. Upon the foundation of the bones the former beauty of the old woman glimmered for a moment, perhaps from the old pride which the lovely presence of the younger woman had awakened in the old heart. It shone there like an apparition, like a memory in the mind of Agnes who had grown from infancy to womanhood in its light.

"Ah, now . . . now . . ." the soft voice whispered.

The left hand folded over Agnes's and stroked it. The old body began to rock. The head nodded, and the beauty passed from the features and time resumed its possession of them more cruelly than before. The smile lost its lovely quality and became a leer, with the tongue's tip moving across the few stained teeth behind the lips from which words gibbered.

"Ah . . . you know," she said, as though to herself, "I had

eleven childer . . . eleven . . . so I had. And . . . there was seventeen side-cars at my wedding . . . and poor Hugh . . . poor Hughie Fitzpatrick that wanted to marry me runnin' away and never seen again . . . and great times I had, glory be to God, so I did . . . and Frankie and all of them saying I was an angel of God . . . so . . ."

She breathed in a harsh rustle through her mouth and laughed in a quick, tinkling cackle.

"That's the way of it!" she exclaimed with extraordinary vehemence. "The coming up and the going down of the sun!"

She relapsed into a murmurous, incoherent monologue, communing with herself over her lost beauty, which the advent of Agnes had recalled to her former pride. Vanity and jealousy flamed briefly from their smouldering cinders from contact with the yound woman. And pride struck its sudden chords and broke into a discord of babbled words.

Agnes smiled as she gently removed her hands and moved aside. On the wall to the old woman's left was a large framed photograph of her taken many years previously when she had been in the noon of her beauty. To the right of it there hung a mirror in which Agnes saw herself reflected. For an instant, she was quite still, seeing herself framed in the mirror beside the large photograph, seeing the two beautiful faces side by side. She turned away, and instantly it seemed that the old woman's eyes were waiting for her with a smile of mockery which passed quickly, as a lifetime might pass in the memory, as beauty itself might bloom and then wither. Agnes was silent, but the old woman was speaking clearly again.

"Ah, my dear, Agnes my chick, God help us all for the bullets are flyin' again and the boys are on the run! Jesus, Mary and Joseph help them!" she cried. "Mary, Mother of God, intercede for them!"

Agnes glanced down at her. The old woman met her gaze and held it and was silent for a moment. Something lit in her wandering thoughts and gave them coherence.

"Have the peelers taken him, Agnes, dear?" she whispered.

"What one, Granny?" Agnes said.

"Ah, glory to God, you know," the old woman said sharply. "There is only one does be in your heart, girl! Johnny, I am saying. The lovely boy!" Her tone became a moan again as she continued: "Have they found him, dear? Con and Larry was sayin' . . . poor Johnny! God help him this night! God help us all, for the bullets are flyin' again!"

She drew breath and expelled it with a loud groan which her own ears seemed to await, and which encouraged a mood of sorrow in her which she wrapped around her spirit as warmly and as soothingly as a cloak.

"Oh, God and the holy saints look down on us this night and protect us!" she cried.

Her body rocked. Her old hands moved slowly over her thighs, while her eyes that were misted as much by all the reflection of memory intermingling in them as by time, stared at the fire that gleamed softly upon her dry, pale skin. She hardly felt Agnes's gentle touch of farewell on her, or heard her move to the door or leave the house. She heard in imagination only the thud of running feet and the shouts of the pursuing peelers followed by the fierce crack which the revolvers made in the night. Those sounds were the frequent accompaniment to many of her thoughts; and although they were often faint and remote, they were always moving in some part of her memory. Often, she summoned them by a conscious effort, and then she was silent and never quite sure whether they were actual or imaginary. She recalled the living and the dead who participated in those wild encounters with the police.

But sometimes the noises rose of their own volition in her mind, violently, rending her thoughts, shattering the slow, delicate patterns of her dreams and causing her to moan and to sway her body in the little chair at the fireside. Then her son, Con, and his wife and the children were irritated.

"Ah, stop your racket, Granny!" they exclaimed.

Yet, when the feet actually thudded along the pavement outside the house, and the police banged on all the doors and made searches for arms and explosives, and the firing sounded in nearby streets, she laughed excitedly and shook like a marionette in her chair.

"The bullets are flying!" she cackled. "The boys are givin' the bloody peelers hell!"

Then the old mongrel dog at her feet stopped scratching itself and got up and began to yelp and prance about, upsetting the teapot on the hob in the grate and the kettle beside it, and the tongs jutting from the bucket.

"Ah, for Jesus' sake!" her son shouted, throwing down his newspaper.

The uproar delighted the old woman because it broke the monotony of her life in the house. She cackled louder than

96

ever as she waved her arms above her ears and heard the dog barking and her son bawling. The children laughed and yelled excitedly until their father cuffed them.

"That's enough out of youse!"

sixteen

The wind was blowing furiously from the southeast. It was bitter with the salt of the sea in its volume. It poured along the main roads and filled the side streets with its freezing currents and its disquiet. It streamed down from the heavy clouds that it swept through the darkness, and fluttered at street corners, blowing all the ways. Its voices were shrill, and in their volume the sounds of the city were audible: an incessant beating of a wave; a murmurous din full of the unending clamour of mankind.

Agnes heard it as she entered North Street and stood on the corner where that street enters Royal Avenue. She heard, too, the topic which was upon so many tongues that night. Sometimes the words were in a monotone which brushed her sense of hearing like some low note of the wind. And often the remarks were sudden and violent and explosive, as though driven up by some terrible force in the human breast which had been disturbed and outraged by the events of the afternoon. And again, she heard the topic and heard, too, the dull, brutish call for vengeance which was in the blood or the stupid mind of some noisy man or shrill woman. But no matter in what tone the words came and the topic was discussed, it was not so much an individual expression as one from the mass which, like a flame, was inclined in varying degrees by the force of air. And the force in this case was from traditional feeling.

It rendered the city in a new mood to her, showing her men and women in streets, and showing, too, the familiar scene disclosed merely as a place wherein Johnny was a fugitive, was lying wounded and in peril under the same clouds that sped above her and in the path of the same harsh wind which buffeted her.

Standing on that corner, she had a feeling that the voices claimed Johnny as theirs. Their malefactor, their outlaw, the man who had killed one of their citizens and outraged one of their laws. But in her heart she made her own vehement claim to him, and she believed that hers was the better one. It brought her strangely nearer to him. He was here, in the city which in the vastness of space was but a small area whose mile or two which separated her from him was no more than the distance which two souls could never diminish in their eternal duality.

She felt strengthened and comforted by the idea. She walked slowly towards York Street, past the scarred Library and the *Telegraph* office, and on towards the district in which she believed he was hiding. What she trusted now was not the word which would reveal his whereabouts to her, nor her own eyes that might discern him were she to wander deep into that district, but a more subtle sense, indefinable and yet very active in her at this moment when distance seemed so diminished.

Pausing again, she looked about her and wondered what had befallen Dennis and the rest. The patrols of police were doubled and trebled hereabouts. Nearby were groups of men and women, watching, wating, talking in tense murmurs, for this was the rim of a strong cordon, and all who passed into the side streets were stopped and questioned. She walked to the opposite side of the road and went nearer to the cordon. And it was then that she knew she was being followed. She was slightly startled, and then fatalistic, realizing that in view of what the police knew or surmised had happened in her home they would not be likely to let her wander unobserved.

She saw him stop and give her a slow, intent look and then put a cigarette to his lips: the big peeler in plain clothes. Cupping his hands over the lighter he lit the cigarette and exhaled, lifting his head as he put away the lighter, and gave her a long scrutiny. Her gaze met his. He looked away and pursed his lips, first of all removing the cigarette. She turned away and walked on, past the little inquisitive groups, not caring in what direction she went. Until in the pool of darkness at the corner a single figure confronted her.

She recognized him immediately. He was the Head Constable who had conducted the search of her home. His gaze was full upon her, and she imagined that about his lips a smile of recognition and even pleasantry wavered for an instant before he nodded. But whether the nod, too, was one of recognition and was friendly, or merely an indication of some suspicion confirmed in his thoughts by this encounter with her, she could not tell.

"Just out for a bit of a walk?" he said in his quiet tone.

She made no reply. He smiled broadly and assumed a serious expression.

"I would advise you to keep out of it," he said. And he went on: "I can tell you, miss, you won't find him, if that's what you are down here for."

He was silent, as though his keen, probing sight had at last penetrated to the depths of her mind and conveyed a new and startling suspicion to him. Something in his pleasant, authoritative expression was changed for an instant, and he seemed taken aback.

For the first time, she flinched. It was as though he had discovered her resolve. Her eyes wavered and their gaze fell from his. She heard him address her again, telling her to go home, to keep out of this trouble and not to interfere. Then she hurried on past him, afraid of her secret now that he had discovered it, anxious to commit herself completely to her purpose before he or others might prevent her.

She crossed the road and stood at a tram stage. Opposite was the tall newspaper office.

"In there," she thought, remembering the brevity which in itself conveyed the cold horror of fact, "they print it." And she saw the words again: "ARMED RAID ON MILL. CASHIER KILLED IN DESPERATE STRUGGLE. WOUNDED ASSAILANT AT LARGE."

Something more freezing than the wind which blew so furiously through the city settled upon her heart and gave her a sense of foreboding, raising in her a belief that the forces which possessed her and which had dictated her errand were greater than her will, more powerful than anything else in the city, and more potent at this moment to help her than to satisfy Justice.

Standing there, she heard women about her whispering of the topic. Two tramcars approached. The women boarded the first. She took the second, which was proceeding to a terminus in the suburbs. Inside the big peeler in plain clothes was seated.

It did not seem a coincidence to her. It was inevitable, after her encounter with the Head Constable. She gave him a quick glance. His legs were crossed and he sat half-turned with an arm resting along the narrow ledge of the window and the ticket which the conductor had just given him gripped in his big fingers. He stared at Agnes as she sat down amidst four other passengers. As her eyes met his, he slowly shook his head, as though he knew whither she was going.

She averted her head at once, withdrawing her senses from contact with the scene and people about her, hearing as from a great distance the rumbling of the car as it crossed the city and travelled towards the terminus, seeing nothing but her gloved hands holding her bag. Yet all the time she was aware of that detective nearby.

His presence made a statement of some kind to her, like an admonishment or a threat. And when at last she glanced up and encountered again his heavy gaze, she saw what she imagined to be an expression of pity in those features which, as she knew, were incapable of expressing any such emotion. And pity at that moment was as merciless as the conditions that raised it.

She turned her head and heard the conductor call the name of the Square near which was the house she intended to visit. Rising to alight, she saw that the detective had risen, too. He came out to the platform where the conductor spoke to him.

"Cold night!"

"Aye, you're right!"

"Snow," said the conductor, "blowin' up for a taste of snow."

"Aye, looks like it," the other said, alighting.

He followed Agnes, at first closely, then at a distance, which she increased until she imagined that he was far behind her. She halted and looked quickly about, seeing Father Tom's little house on the corner some distance to her right. She hurried on through the thrash and whine of the wind.

He was already there. His tall body was lounging against the wall from which he came quickly when he saw her. He stepped towards her. She walked past him. He overtook her and kept pace with her.

"You know," he said, speaking in a persuasive tone, "it's a waste of time. Old Father Tom can't help you. You might think he'll be able to do something for you, but I'm telling you you'd save yourself a lot of trouble and disappointment if you gave the old fellow a miss. Why don't you go home?"

She gave him a quick glance. He shrugged his shoulders.

"You're going in then?" he said.

"Yes," she answered.

He stepped forward and lifted the knocker and banged twice with it.

"There you are now," he said, stepping back and smiling. He nodded. His face assumed a serious expression and he leaned his head slightly towards her.

"But I'm telling you you're too late. Johnny belongs to us."

He went away quickly at the moment when the door was opened and the housekeeper peered out.

seventeen

"Is Father Tom at home?" Agnes said.

The housekeeper's pale face showed with a soft clarity in the dim light of the hall. Her right hand came up and slowly touched her hair, which was dark and drawn smoothly from the center of her head towards the back of her neck.

"There is someone with him just now," she said. "Maybe you would like to come in and wait."

Her voice had a natural hush suggestive of a world of detachment and quietude.

"What name will I tell him?" she asked, admitting Agnes and closing the door after her.

"If you say it is Agnes, he will understand perhaps."

"I will, so," the woman said, opening the door of a small reception room. "Please sit down."

The room was of a severe character, sparsely furnished, without a fire, and with a cold odor. There was a table covered with a heavy blue cloth standing against the wall and holding between book-ends a few books of a religious character. Agnes sat down on one of the hard, small wooden chairs. Opposite her, above the table, was a picture of the Sacred Heart on a wall whose paper was faded and slightly stained where a sideboard had formerly stood. The little black grate to the left was empty, and in the fireplace the tiny fan of paper trembled in the draught of wind which echoed with a hollow, boiling sound in the chimney. Elsewhere in that silent room were some flowers in a vase. Things of life and color, of nature, they seemed to flourish there after severance from the plant and the soil, as though their life had discovered a new and more vitalizing soil in the hushed atmosphere of the old man's home.

There was a tapping on the door. A little old man, slightly bowed, entered. He had a head of snowy hair which was as abundant and brushed in the same hasty fashion as that of a young boy. His blue eyes, misted with age, observed her with gentle interest as he advanced with his hand extended.

She rose at once, seeing him for the first time in her life: the old priest, the old man called a saint and rendered a legendary being by the tales told of him. A saint, they said, beyond evil, and existing in his own tiny world of solitude and prayer; for he was old, so old that fathers declared that he had been old when they were youngsters, so old that he had long ago retired from parish work. A great man, they said, in whom life had dwindled only to assume a strange energy of an unearthly quality. An old man who was reputed by some to have performed miracles. One to whom the most active critics oof the Church relented, seeing a soul which was said to be pure in the sight of God. A singular old man who, when he wrote or telephoned or visited. Authority on behalf of the poor and wayward who were in trouble, was accorded the deference and respect due to princes and other great ones of the earth. Because he was old and gentle? Because he belonged to God? Because the things of the world had long ago expired in him and he had become the embodiment of wisdom, truth, goodness, and was ready to intercede, to uphold the law, to interpret wisely what might seem harsh? Or because of his legend which, with mingled fact and fantasy, related strange things of his power? Or merely because his wisdom touched the secret chords of the heart? This old man who, when all was said and done, was merely a being who loved his fellow men.

His pale eyes saw her, and his old hand held her young, firm fingers while with his left hand he twiddled with the thread of a loose button on his soutane.

"Father Tom . . ." she said.

He looked at her fine eyes and saw therein much that was troubled, much that seemed to his keen sensibilities for such conditions to be sharp and tragic.

"I expected you, my child," he said.

And when she seemed surprised and became silent because her introduction of herself no longer seemed necessary, he went on: "I have another visitor. A poor man whose little bird is sick. He is telling me . . ."

Then he seemed to lose the way of his thoughts and to

lapse into a dim world as he fingered the long thread of the loose button and smiled and murmured.

"Ah, yes . . . now . . . now, let's go and hear what he has to tell us. Yes . . . and there's a good fire upstairs."

And opening the door, he led her to his room above, walking beside her on the stairs, slowly, and saying: "Yes, I expected you."

"Father Tom," she said, "you are not mistaking me for someone else?"

"No, no, no," he declared, smiling at her to reassure her. "You have come to ask me about Johnny, is it?" he whispered.

A great sense of happiness flooded her heart.

"Yes, Father!"

"Although, mind you, I did not know your name," he said. "But never mind! The thing is that someone was sure to come to me about him. Maybe more than one person. Maybe many. But one of them has a just claim to him. But first of all," he went on, halting outside his room, "first of all, there is the man whose bird is sick. We must listen to what he has to say."

The room was much larger than the little reception room downstairs. A fire burned in its big grate, the flames adding to the radiance from a shaded lamp on a table near the hearth, at which chairs were placed. Above the mantelpiece was a large oil painting from which the faces of biblical figures were visible dimly. On the floor was a thick carpet on which a few chairs, a single table and a bookcase stood. He drew her in towards the fireplace and pointed to a thin little man of indeterminate age sitting hugging a brilliant bird-cage in which a budgerigar was huddled in a corner.

"This is my visitor," he said, "and his name is Shell. And this young woman," he said, addressing Shell, "is Agnes."

Shell half rose as he smiled and nodded.

"How are you, miss?"

She smiled at him and took an armchair opposite him, seeing in a single swift glance the simple furnishings and the little book open on the table on which the lamp stood.

The old priest composed himself slowly in his chair, and it was as though something of the room resumed about his small figure at that moment: the tranquil atmosphere which was not of the normal world but of himself.

"Loosen your fur coat," he murmured to Agnes, "and be quite comfortable. Shell was telling me he is having a wee bit

103

of trouble with the bird."

Shell had a large head on which the hair was sparse and black. His features were small, except for the eyes, which suffered a defect that rendered them abnormally prominent. Combined with his habit of thrusting forward his head when he spoke, this gave his soft words and his timid manner a curious vehemance. But the rest of him, from his tiny features to the depth of his soul, was small and circumscribed in a meagre compass determined by the attributes of his character. Wispish altogether, he was, suggestive of all the forms of life that are minute, fearful, and yet possessed proportionately by the same compelling desire for existence and self-expression as are the mighty beasts of the field and the forceful personalities of city life.

"Yes, Father!" he breathed, and turning to Agnes he said:

"Do you see this wee creature?" and he pointed to the vivid bird standing subdued in the bottom of the cage. It was huddled there amongst the scatter of seed and droppings near a water cup.

"Would you believe me if I was to tell you that this bird is a rare one?" he said.

"It is a budgy," Agnes said indifferently. "There are thousands of them."

Shell said quickly: "I'll not deny it, miss! I'll not dispute the truth of it! There are millions of them, like there are millions of men and women. But there are rare ones amongst us, like this bird. Queer and bad ones."

Her eyes came towards Shell in their gaze. Shell's eyes were waiting for her. He pointed again to the bird.

"A king, I would say! A chief, you know. A devil of a fellow, sort of. Always piercing the air with his tricks. Like . . . just like some fellows there is."

His eyes held hers with a cruel compulsion which she resisted by turning to the old priest. But Father Tom's hands were in his lap, and his expression was that of a spirit lapsed into lethargy.

"What is his name?" Agnes asked Shell, indicating the bird.

Shell smiled. He was slow to answer.

"Me and Lukey and Tober—them's the friends I live with—the three of us call him Johnny," he said, his eyes holding her in the same implacable stare as before.

There was silence for almost a minute. Agnes looked at the fire and then at Father Tom's placid figure in which there was infinite patience. His glance went to Shell, who looked down quickly at the bird and then lifted his eyes again to Agnes.

"I was tellin' you, miss," he continued, "Johnny is fierce! He is what you would call a bit of a menace to society. The bird society, I mean. On account of that, me and Lukey and Tober has a rule saying the door of this cage is not to be opened, for in my room there is other birds, and Johnny can't thole 'em. Two or three times when the door has been open for him to sort of take a trip around his street, he has done mischief, gettin' in at them other ones and layin' about him something cruel; for some bad blood is between him and them other budgies, although you could hardly put a name to it."

"It is just a matter of pride, perhaps," the old priest suggested.

"Ah, no, Father Tom," Shell said, shaking his head. "I'm thinkin' it is because he is in the minority. That's queer and hard to put up with."

Father Tom's furrowed face assumed a smile.

"Yes . . . yes . . . I'm sure!" he agreed. "And when the other rascals up and toot their bit of a song it annoys him. Is that the way of it?"

"The very thing!" Shell said, emphatically.

"There now!" the priest said, turning to Agnes. "Would you believe that now? The wee bird is almost human!"

"Human!" Shell exclaimed, pointing to the bird. "I have seen this fellow bursting with the rage when them others is havin' a bit of a song amongst them! I have seen him pushing against these bars and bursting his wee throat with the wild song he sings! That's why me and Lukey and Tober keep the door closed on him."

He leaned back and sighed and relaxed, as though he had established the identity of the bird to them and reached the end of a chapter of his story.

Agnes gave him a cold look. "Well, what is wrong with him?" she said.

Shell drew breath. He appeared to relish the chance to continue the next part of his tale.

"I'll tell you," he said, leaning forward. "He gets out of his prison . . . this cage, I mean . . . and away he goes!"

"But now he is back!" Agnes said.

Shell stopped her with a gesture. But Father Tom leaned forward and spoke.

"Tell us what happened when he got out," he said

imperatively.

Shell grimaced. "Murder!" he whispered.

Agnes winced and looked at the priest with imploring eyes. Father Tom sat back in his chair and did not appear to notice her expression. He was listening to Shell, who continued:

"He gets out and then he goes to the big cages where there is other birds, and he flings the seed about right, left and center, and begins to fight the other birds. In the battle, he slays one, and gets hurt himself!"

Neither he nor the priest seemed to hear Agnes's sudden exclamation or notice how she averted her head.

"Do you see, Father?" Shell said, lifting the cage and holding it towards the old man. "Do you see that wee spot of blood on his left wing, near his body?"

"The foolish fellow!" Father Tom whispered, peering at the bird.

"That's where the one he killed gave him a dig," Shell said.

"And how did you succeed in capturing him again?" Father Tom said.

"Capturing?" Shell asked.

". . . getting him back into the cage."

"Oh, aye! I see what you mean. Oh, dear help us! There was a riot, I'm tellin' you! Me and Lukey rushed into the room. Out goes Johnny all over the house. And not a sign of him for two hours. Not a sound, although the lot of us in the house was lookin' for him. . . ."

"Now when would that be?" Father Tom said.

"It would be . ." Shell said, pensively, looking at Agnes, "it would be about four, this evening."

"Four," murmured the priest.

Shell was making little sounds to encourage the bird.

"You see, Father? See? He is awful distressed."

"How did you get him back?" Father Tom asked again.

"We searched the whole house. Not a bit of him anywhere! Back we go to the room, and there he is lyin' in the bottom of the cage, near his end—spent, you know!"

"Crept to his home," said the priest.

"Lyin' up in the corner, so as you could scarcely see him," Shell said. "Wounded! And all of us lookin' for him everywhere!"

"And what . . . what would you say the state of his health is now?" the priest asked.

Shell pondered the question, and at last he spoke.

106

"Well. I don't rightly know," he said. "The corner he is lyin' in is not the place for him to sort of sit up proper."

"Perhaps," sighed the priest, "he is not long for this world."

"Oh, I wouldn't say that," Shell said, "the fellow has great strength, although there is not a sound out of him."

"But he seems to be badly wounded," Father Tom said. "Maybe the best thing you could do would be to let nature take its course, seeing that things have gone so far. . . ."

"Father Tom!" Shell whined. "I would hate to let him slip out of my grasp now."

The priest glanced at Agnes and smiled slowly and rested his hands on his knees, drumming lightly with his fingers.

"Father," Shell moaned, "it's a hard world, you know. It's no use of pretendin' it isn't. The best thing for me to tell you that I want the bird because there is money in him."

The old man rested his gaze gently on Shell.

"Yes . . . yes . . . my son . . . it is hard . . ." he murmured.

"Fierce!" Shell said. "It's fierce! There's prayin' and all that, but sure that doesn't make any difference to the way things are. And the way is that if you don't take what comes in the way of chances you're finished, and there's nothin' for you. Sure, I have to live. . . ."

"Poor fellow!" the priest said, sighing, and lowering his head and gently moving his hands to and fro over his knees. But his pity was not only for Shell, for Johnny, but for himself and for all mankind. And his vision extended beyond Shell, who was trying to sell a fugitive, and included men and women everywhere selling, buying, bartering, threatening one another in all the terms of character and temperament, gaining advantages, taking revenge, squabbling over issues which would die when they died. While beyond, in Time, was God who had given them a world crammed with such plenty and so fruitful that it was the simplest thing for the cunning to gather immense harvests and reap cruel profits. And besides the plenty there were other gifts: consciousness, free-will; and, best of all, a soul. But consciousness and free-will were all that they prized. The third gift was not understood, never appreciated or considered, except when the body was in extremity or dying. And the other two gifts had not gained them much, for they had taken them only as weapons wherewith to ravage the world and afflict one another with terrible wars. Strange creatures! Weak and strong, bold and timid, uncertain, never constant, and yet lovable!

He heard Agnes talking to Shell.

"What will you do with him?" she asked. "Where is he?"

"Sure, I'm telling you," Shell whined. "I want to get him out of the corner like and give him something to sort of put him right. . . ."

"And after that?" she asked.

His mood changed abruptly, and he leaned towards her as though he were conscious of his importance.

"Maybe you don't believe me," he said, "but I'm telling you there are lots of people would pay me a grand price for Johnny!"

Her retort came swiftly.

"It would not be to let him live!" she reminded him.

He made a contemptuous gesture as he answered her.

"Hold on, hold on! I'm not thinkin' of them ones! I was thinkin' of the ones he has for friends. Maybe they would have him. I had it in mind to ask Father Tom here . . ."

"Yes, yes, that's a good thing to do," the priest interjected.

"Selling him!" Agnes exclaimed. "Where is he?"

"Now, please!" Father Tom said gently. "Don't blame him! Let him live! That's the way he has to travel . . ."

"But asking a price for him!" she cried, "and not saying where he is!"

"Sure, I told you where he is!" Shell whined. "In the corner!"

"Sh!" said the priest. "If you know where he is we must trust you. Now, tell us. What price? What price are you wanting for him?"

Shell sniffed and sat back in his chair. He felt insulted and humiliated.

"I could get two thousand for him," he muttered truculently.

Father Tom smiled and slowly shook his head. He glanced at Agnes and then back at Shell.

"Foolish man!" he said gently. "It would not make you happy! You would not eat better bread than you do now!"

"I'm only sort of telling you what I could raise on him if I had a mind to," Shell said.

"Oh, is that it?" Father Tom replied. "Oh, I understand now. Well, we will find a little something for you, Shell, my son. But not the thousands," he said, turning his misty eyes to the hard little face. "For the thousands would become a dreadful load on you, a dreadful load. . . ."

"Sure, I know that!" Shell exclaimed, flinging out an angry hand. "I was only sort of saying . . . sor of puttin' the thing fair to you. . . ."

"Yes, yes, of course! So you were," Father Tom said.

Agnes rose and stood over Shell. Her passionate presence seemed to threaten everything in his cruel, determined little spirit. It quenched an essential flame in him and left him cold and afraid so that he flinched, cowering back in his chair and shielding himself with his hand.

"Where is he?" she demanded.

"Sure, I will bring him to you!" he whined. "He is in a wee corner. . . ."

"Where?"

The words cut at him like a whip about his ears. He saw the priest rise and interpose himself between Agnes and the chair in which he was cowering.

"Now . . . my child . . . he is somewhere in this city, and Shell has seen him, so let us be content with that."

He turned to Shell.

"Go and bring him to us," he said.

"Sure!" Shell said, rising with alacrity. "That's what I was sort of wantin' to hear from you and the young lady. Only it'll be no easy job, I'm tellin' you, Father."

"Of course not, but you will try," the priest said, resting a hand on his arm and gently urging him to the door.

"Aye, I'll try," Shell said, "for I know where he is. I know rightly. Only I'm still thinkin', Father, and sort of wondering how much . . ."

He grinned and then looked at the priest in a shamefaced manner and hung his head. His big eyes swivelled a sly glance at the old countenance, which was set in an invariable, gentle expression.

"I am poor," Father Tom whispered. "I have no money put past me. None at all."

"Ah, that's bad," Shell murmured, pursing his lips. "Maybe the young lady could help you out, so as the thing could be squared off properly."

"I am sure she could not," Father Tom said.

"But I have heard tell," Shell went on, "a fellah was tellin' me that his reverence the Pope is queer and rich," he whispered.

Father Tom smiled. "Blether!" he whispered, in a

confidential tone.

Shell frowned. "Is that a fact?"

"Just blether."

"Well, now, how do you suggest we could settle the matter decent like?" Shell said.

"Oh, you know," Father Tom said, "there are riches and riches, and maybe I could find something . . ."

"What like?"

"If you would accept it, I would try to inspire in your soul a precious particle of faith. . . ."

"What's this you're saying, Father? Faith?"

"That, or something. Something for the soul, my son."

Shell demurred. "Ah, you know, Father, I'm not disputin' such things are worth a bit to ones like yourself and the rest of you. But I could not live comfortable on that. It wouldn't sort of pay the rent and the grocer and give you the cash for a pint or get you far. And that's plain honest to God sense."

Father Tom smiled and, looking intently at him, poked a forefinger at his belly and winked.

"Go along now, Shell," he whispered. "Bring him to this house by midnight at the latest. Do that, and there will be a fine reward for you."

Shell blinked and seemed bewildered and troubled. He was loth to go.

"Is it still the bit of faith?" he softly asked.

"I am afraid it is," Father Tom admitted. "You and I are poor men, Shell. We live as best we can. I have been poor longer than you have. Come back to me, and I will show you the great riches you can find. Come back with Johnny, and you and I will talk about the way to live."

Still Shell loitered and was loth to go without a promise of something tangible for reward. His sly spirit, constrained and educated and clothed by what he saw, heard, touched, tasted and smelled, could not accept the possibility of reward in any form but the tangible and perceptible. For beyond was a world of values which he mistrusted and scorned. There was talk of God and Truth and the Christian way of life; but he had never met one who lived by it. There was bread in that way of life. There was God and Heaven, Redemption and peace. He had never seen or heard it applied to anything but hatred and political differences in his native city. He shook his head, being suspicious of it. His own sinful, precarious existence seemed founded on something more clean and more firm.

immeasurable power and purpose which it represented. But after a little while had elapsed, he felt calm again, realizing that no matter how evil and cruel mankind was, it was still circumscribed by what was eternal and known only to the Creator. But no sooner had he admitted that much than he felt troubled, for he could not admit that the Creator who was Goodness and Truth and Beauty could give to the world creatures who were evil and merciless to one another. Yet, as soon as he remarked to himself that men and women were evil and merciless, he felt that he had been harsh and unjust, for he was a man and he understood his fellows because he was apart from their ambitions and desires, and had come to love them for their strange and sometimes exquisite hopes and vanities.

"Yes," he thought, "no matter in what way they behave, they remain the creations of the Divine Will. In all of them there is the fire of that Will. Sometimes it becomes a glorious flame which sends its rays like sunlight across centuries of human history. Mostly though, it barely suffices to light the darkness into which man crushes his soul. For in spite of the beauty of the natural world and its lovely seasons and fruits and colors, mankind has fashioned another world upon it: huge buildings, huge schemes, huge systems which crack and bring disaster. There is evil in that world that is super-imposed upon the natural one. Why is that? Why is it that evil and bestiality come so readily to the fore in mankind? If they are creations of the Divine Will—and that is true—why have they this energy and ability for evil? There is free-will, but that is only our excuse for what we do. Or is it not evil after all when we nourish hatred and anger in our hearts and kill one another? Is it all within the scope of what the Divine Will permits us, and is it acceptable to the Will which regards us as imperfect things making our way slowly forward to perfection from the gradual-consciousness of our sins? Or are we not of God at all, but just embodied forces of evil, filling the earth with our clamour?"

He made a little gesture as though he were impelling something away from him.

"No . . . no . . ." he thought. "We are expressions of the Creative Will: the Will which created everything of life and the multitudes of universes out in space. The truth is that we are that Will, we are God, and that we dare not yet believe it, but are compelled by our fear to project our godhead into an external, invisible god, a man, a personality like ourselves, we fear it, although in our secret selves we rejoice in it without realizing why we do so. We rejoice because life is ours and because we do exactly as we wish. We have the power to procreate life and to destroy it. We are the lords of the earth. We dream, and in a little while the dream becomes reality; and in this way we have risen from the surface of the earth and gone into the sky; and we have made the forces in the ether the agents of our words to one another across vast distances. But we are still afraid or unwilling to admit that we are the Will; and the cause of our hesitancy is that if we were to admit our Divinity and our divine destiny, it would impose restraints upon us and command us to be gentle, merciful, unselfish and kind, and to renounce all evil, And we are too fond of indulging our power to bridle it willingly, for first of all we wish to taste the full extent of that power, even if it takes us millions of years more to experience to the utmost that power before we admit that the time has come for us to take upon ourselves the godhead which is ours. And another reason why we hesitate is that we have not yet discovered Faith. But soon . . . soon . . . a spark of it will light in a human soul, and then . . . then will come Godhead . . . and it will not be insulted by the mob and hung upon a Cross, as He who was the first to receive the spark was expelled from amongst the living!"

He heard Agnes speaking to him, but he was so immersed in his thoughts that he failed to extract the meaning of her words from the sounds which her lips made. But he saw the earnest expression in her beautiful eyes, and he knew that she was pleading with him for something.

"Why does she come to me?" he thought sadly. "If she wishes to make her claim to this fugitive, why does she not do it before all mankind, instead of asking me to do it for her? They all believe that I am able to work miracles, or that I am able to divert the laws for them. But I do nothing except encourage Faith in them."

Under the compulsion of her expression, he suddenly withdrew himself from his thoughts and spoke to her.

"What is it you want of me, my child? Is it to help you rescue this man from the power of the law which he has offended? So that you can restore him to your comrades in the Organization, and begin shooting policemen and defying the Government and exasperating those who are loyal to that Government?"

"No, Father," she said, "not to take him back! But to take him away from all of them . . . and be with him. . . ."

"His crime has condemned him," he reminded her.

"I know, Father."

"He must make the journey from life . . ."

"With me," she said.

He stared at her in silence, unable to believe what he had heard, fearful of believing it.

"With me, Father," she repeated.

"Do you know what you are saying, my child?" he asked, horrified, for she was the first being to share his secret beliefs and to stand before him like a witness of the things which both of them believed.

"Let me have him, Father," she said, "so that I can take him from all of them and make the journey with him."

"Why do you want to do this?" he asked gently.

"Because I love him," she said.

"Love," he thought, looking into her eyes and seeing the anguish and hurt pride and unrequited desire. "Here at last is a woman who is not ashamed to tell me the truth of love. Here is a woman who will not tolerate the humiliation of it, but who rejects the bondage of it, the intolerable physical bondage, and who seeks a union beyond this life!"

And he rejoiced in his ancient heart that had long since appreciated what was true of love.

"Yes," he thought, remembering the poignant voices of men and women who had confessed to him when he had been a parish priest. "Yes, a long time ago, when I knew scarcely anything of human beings, they confessed to me that they loved what their senses discovered in one another. But they lied! Actually, they did not love. They lusted only to possess, to taste, to destroy. They have had poets for thousands of years who have persuaded them to believe that the jealousy, lust, fear, vanity, envy and hatred which they experience when they encounter one another is love. But if they were honest in their souls they would confess that there is hardly any authentic love in their relations with one another."

And he who for many years had loved mankind and grown beyond dogma and creed and all worldly things except a little food to sustain his body and clean clothes to protect it from cold, and a fire at which to dream, turned to Agnes and said:

"Tell me about that love."

She gazed at him with the look of someone discovered in

evil. But there was neither shame nor contrition in her expression.

"I am waiting," he said.

But she was silent, until he said compassionately, as though he were opening a door through which she could pass to freedom: "It was jealousy, after all, wasn't it? He spoiled your world? He ruined your belief in yourself. He was free and had done so many so-called brave things. He lived what you imagined was a full life. By comparison, your life seemed small and trivial?"

"Yes," she admitted, wondering at his knowledge of the secret things of her life.

"Of course," he said gently, "you were entitled to your belief in yourself. . . ."

"I was happy until he came," she said pensively.

"You mean you were whole, until you discovered that he had qualities or capabilities which, because they were glowing in him, seemed wonderful because you lacked them?"

"Yes, Father."

"Then you were envious of him?"

"I was."

"But before that?"

She smiled. "I dreamed of him. I dreamed he was brave and fine."

"Was he?"

"Oh, he had courage and daring . . ."

"And you had not?"

"I had," she said, "but I had not had my chance to use it."

"So you were jealous of him?"

"Yes," she whispered.

"But did you never stop to think that you had qualities which he lacked? My child, you had your beauty, your soul."

"Yes, I had, Father," she said, "but he never acknowledged those things."

"Although you had acknowledged his qualities?"

"He must have known that," she said.

Father Tom smiled. "So you were jealous of him?"

"A little thing and I would have hated him, perhaps," she confessed.

"So your love for him was . . ."

"It is the name for disappointment and jealousy and fear," she said; and at that moment she had such an expression of shame that the old man smiled to comfort her.

116

"I understand," he said. "Don't be troubled. Only tell me what remains in you. Is it all of those things or only one of them, or something else?"

"It is all of them, and pity," she said.

"But why is there fear?" he asked.

"It used to be because he might love another woman, or tell me that he could never love me," she confessed.

"Did he love you?" he asked.

"For him, there was only the Organization," she said. "I knew it. But I was afraid he would tell me. That was when he was hiding in my father's house. And that was when I loved him, for then he was near me and a captive in the house because he dared not be seen outside, while I could do the things that I had done for a long time and not feel imprisoned any longer. But now there is the fear again."

"Why?"

"Because they might find him this night, and heal him and try him and execute him."

"But inevitably he will die . . . at some time. . . ."

"But if they take him . . ." she exclaimed, ". . . and if I must live while he is on trial, and while he is being executed, and afterwards for all the years of my life . . ."

"Yes, yes," he murmured, appreciating the great challenge which that man's destiny had made to hers.

"And the pity?" he asked, after a pause.

"Because he was my captive, and because he has failed and has never been free."

"But that is not all," he said, shaking his head.

She was silent until he cajoled her with his patient look.

"It is because he will die," she whispered.

And looking at her, he knew what she wished to convey to him in those words. He was alarmed by the enormity of her intention. Yet when he encountered her gaze he saw only the composure of her belief. He was awed.

"You realize what you intend doing?" he said.

"I do, Father," she said. And she continued:

"He will die . . . if the police find him, or if the Organization takes him. But if I take him the little while he might live yet, I go with him and he will not be alone ever again."

"But afterwards?" the old priest exclaimed, not being fully aware of the whole of her intention, although at that moment it began to filter into his mind.

117

"I am with him," she said simply. "I shall go with him."

The old priest seemed suddenly stricken with terror. He lowered his trembling hands and stared at her to penetrate the proud look in her eyes.

"To go with him . . ." he exclaimed.

"Yes," she said.

"Have you . . ." he whispered, in awe, "have you such ferocity?"

"I love him," she said quietly.

He thought again: "Love . . . the great wound, the name for envy, jealousy, fear, lust." And struggling to control his thoughts, he asked her: "But to take so much from him, for a wound . . . for a hurt which will heal in time!"

"There is more than that, Father," she explained. "I take him from all of them. They, too, will kill him if they find him. He has hurt them, and they will demand his life. My hurt is greater than theirs. If I take his life, I recompense him. I go with him."

He rose to his feet and made a gesture of denial.

"You have neither the right nor the power!" he declared.

"I have the belief that what I do is good, Father," she retorted.

"It is evil, my child," he said, standing before her and looking down at her uplifted countenance.

She smiled up at him and shook her head, and was no longer proud or vengeful, but was the embodiment of faith.

"No, Father, it is good," she said.

He covered his old face with his hands and sighed, thinking of what he believed of men and women, that they were divine, that they were the Creative Will, that they were God, and wondering if at last one soul had reached the infinite frontier to stand there and claim the confirmation of godhead.

Taking his hands from his face, he cupped them slowly about the soft chalice of her face and said:

"Have you—tell me truthfully; search your heart and tell me—have you this faith?"

"I have, Father," she said.

"Be sure of it!" he warned her. "Be so sure of it that afterwards you will not hear the baying hounds of remorse following you to eternity! The faith . . . the belief that our souls are God, and that because the Will made us in its own image and likeness we are the Will in all its expression."

"I have faith," she whispered.

"It must endure," he warned her again, "beyond life, beyond time. . . ."

"It will," she said.

". . . into eternity," he added.

"Yes," she said.

He sat down again and joined his hands in his lap and let his eyes rest upon her as he thought:

"I don't know whether it is a great sin or a great moment. I don't know whether I am a heretic, forgotten by God, now that I have come to have so much belief in Man, or whether God has given me so many years in which to let me discover things. I only know that she has this boundless faith in the goodness of what she intends to do."

He sighed, and turning his gaze from her for a while he stared at the fire and was silent until a loud knocking sounded on the door of the house.

"There it is," he said equably, "that is Authority, come to make its claim for the body of Johnny."

He rose quickly and bade Agnes follow him. There was a small room adjoining the large one. It was a little study, a place of tranquillity whose odor was of linoleum and floor polish.

"It will soon be warm," he said, drawing out a little electric fire which he switched on. He hurried away, drawing the door behind him.

Agnes glanced about her at the small bookcase with its rows of old volumes, and the tall, brass fender with its battery of large tongs and pokers. The walls were bare except for a crucifix of ivory above the bookcase beside the little settee whose indented surface was evidence of much usage. At the small circular table which was covered with an ink-stained green baize cloth there was a chair, pushed back as though from the task which the old priest had not yet completed, for the pen was there still, together with the pad of paper. Everywhere in the room there was the indefinable impress of his character: a harmony in the inactive air: a quietude as of rejection of commonplace things: and the thin strings of extreme age, stretched subtly in the air to give forth notes which his presence echoed and evoked.

She drew the portable fire to the settee and sat down. Voices were audible: the housekeeper's saying:

"It is the Inspector from the police, Father Tom."

And the old man's: "Yes . . . well . . . ask him to come up, please."

The thud of hard, determined footsteps sounded on the stairs and was followed by the housekeeper's little rap on the door and the murmur of her voice as she showed the visitor in. At the moment before the door closed and the housekeeper returned to her room, there was a swift impact of voices from which Father Tom's rose clearly.

A saint, they said always, an old saint. But actually he was merely an old man who had travelled to strange frontiers.

nineteen

He was seated opposite the Inspector of Police.

"I know what you have come to talk about," he said.

The Inspector sat on the edge of the armchair which Agnes had recently occupied. His hat was on his left knee. His black stick lay against his left side and his gloved hands were folded around the cap. He was a heavy man, once tall, but now a thick body bowed by the slight corpulence which was beginning to weigh his bones and muscles under the long overcoat which was buttoned closely under his chin so that only his face and head were visible. The head was small and round and thinly covered with dark hair cut very short. The face showed more of the marks of daily shaving than the reflection of thought, for its lines were those of the rigid mask of authority. Commonplace and unprepossessing, the features seemed to have long ago accepted that mask and to have taken it deeply into the immobile substance of the skin.

"Father Tom," he said, "this is a serious matter."

"Yes, of course," the priest said. "But why have you come to me?"

The grey eyes gradually settled their gaze on the priest as the answer came.

"Because the woman was seen to enter this house."

"But surely, now, surely there is nothing against her?" Father Tom said.

"She is an active supporter of the Organization," the Inspector said. "It has been established that the man Johnny has been hiding in her father's house since he broke jail some months back. And we know that there was a meeting of officers of the Organization took place in the house just this night. I'm telling you, Father Tom, the woman is dangerous."

Father Tom smiled. "So are we all . . . all of us . . . all very dangerous, Inspector! Think of the potentialities in the nature of most of us!"

"We have evidence . . ."

"I have listened to her," the priest interrupted.

"She has been after you to help get Johnny away from us!"

Father Tom made no comment on this remark. Instead, he seemed very pensive, looking up eventually at the stiff mask of the Inspector's features.

"She is a good woman," he said.

A frown rippled across the Inspector's face.

"I have evidence to the contrary," he said.

"Have you?" Father Tom said, "and what is it? Tell me."

"I have told you already, Father. She is one of them, right in the heart of all their schemes. And she is trying to get Johnny to safety."

"Yes, I suppose so," the priest murmured.

"And I am telling you, Father, that's a serious matter," the Inspector repeated, shifting his position and assuming a pose which was intended to emphasize his words.

"A crime, I'm sure," the priest said.

"A very grave one."

"Tell me now," Father Tom said, leaning forward, "would you say from all your experience of men and women that they are a bad lot? Looking at them in the mass, and perhaps in the particular, would you admit that there is a terrible lot of badness in them, Inspector?"

The man of authority nodded. "A terrible lot."

"Much real badness? Evil . . ."

"From the cradle to the grave, some of them."

"But would you say that they are fundamentally evil?"

"There is some good in them, I suppose," the Inspector admitted, shifting uneasily under this conversation.

"What like?"

"Somewhere," the other said impatiently; "it is somewhere in them, I suppose."

"Is it now? Is that a fact, Inspector?" Father Tom said, with the air of a man who was learning much and who did not notice what demands this conversation was making upon the time and patience of his visitor. "I am asking you this because I daresay you must know that I myself have had a little experience of the badness of them. And I am often wondering to myself where in the name of heaven is the goodness in them."

"You might well ask," the Inspector muttered, tersely.

"I suppose so," Father Tom remarked. "But now tell me this, please. If there is some good in them, we would recognize it when we saw it, would we not?"

"There is precious little of it, I am telling you!" the Inspector declared, loudly and angrily. "Look at this business at the mill! Look at the trouble there is in the city . . . look at it! All badness, because . . ."

"But we would recognize the goodness at once because of the contrast it would make with what is cruel and evil," the priest persisted.

"Maybe," the other grunted, warily.

"And then what?" Father Tom said, extending his hands. "What do we do and think when we see something which is evidence of the good in them?"

The Inspector smiled slightly and shook his head.

"Then," he said sardonically, "then you can expect the seven other devils to come into the house! For you can take my word for it, Father, there is a price to be paid for goodness and badness and everything else!"

"Yes, of course," the old man admitted, as though the Inspector had gained an advantage, "but I was only going to say that we ought to commend the good that comes from the human heart, particularly when it is something particularly beautiful." And lifting his eyes to the younger man he added: "It happens sometimes, Inspector. Something completely good. . . ."

The Inspector narrowed his eyes and nodded slowly.

"I know rightly, Father, what you are going to tell me," he said.

"Do you?"

"Aye, about the woman who is here."

"Yes, well, it is about her. . . ."

The Inspector smiled vainly. He had the momentary animation of the man who discovers in himself an ability for sharp discussion.

"Aye, I thought so," he said. "She loves this fellow, Johnny. And she comes to you for help. And you think it is a good thing that she wants to save him from the consequences of his crimes!"

122

"Yes," said Father Tom, bowing his head.

"And you think a bit of devilry like that is a fine thing?" exclaimed the other harshly. "Is that it?"

"Yes," the old man said. But now his glance lifted, and the Inspector saw in it the whole shining light of conviction. He was awed by that light.

"Yes," Father Tom continued, "it is a lovely thing. For don't you realize, man, dear, you are out in force everywhere in this city to look for the fellow and exact the full penalty from him in the end. You'll arrest him and—if he isn't dead from his wounds before that—he'll go forward for trial and be sentenced to death. But it is not his body the woman wants. It is his soul! And if you sit there and tell me that is not a good thing she intends to do, then you are no Christian."

The Inspector pressed his lips together and rose.

"His soul is the concern of God and maybe ministers such as yourself, Father Tom," he said. "I have my duty. I am here to ask you where is this man!"

Father Tom rose, too. He went to the door and turned off the electric light switches. Then, crossing to the window, he parted the heavy curtains with two vigorous movements. He beckoned the Inspector to him.

"You ask me where he is," he said, taking the Inspector by the arm and bringing him close to the window. "I will show you," he went on. He raised the window. The wind burst into the room, rushing past the two of them and swirling about the curtains and the rest of the room. On its harsh current the hollow roar of the city's life was audible, lifting its volume like a wave which poured forward to an invisible, undetermined shore which it would never reach.

"Out there," Father Tom said, shuddering in the bitter cold, "down there amongst the stones of the city. Somewhere in the streets, in the cold and darkness beneath the clouds."

He closed the window and drew over the heavy curtains.

"Is that all you can tell me, Father?" the Inspector said, turning towards Father Tom, who had hurried first to the light switches and then to the fire.

"Why do you ask me where he is?" Father Tom retorted, as he stood chafing his cold hands at the fire. "Do you mean to tell me that you don't know where Johnny is?"

"I would not be here if I did know," the Inspector said. "It is no secret that he has slipped us."

Father Tom sat down and sighed.

"I would have been happier had you and your men found him," he confessed, "for it's a poor chance and a hard way he will have on this wild night."

"Well, you can give us the information and be the happier for it," the Inspector said.

Father Tom looked up at him and said: "I know no more than you do."

The stout man of authority stood before him, a big uniformed figure, the symbol of the law.

"I am telling you, Father Tom, there will be terrible trouble if this man is concealed or assisted to escape from us. We are not in the mood to have him pulled out of our reach. There will be a public outcry if the fellow gets away," he said.

"I know; oh, I know, well enough," Father Tom said. "We heard it, the two of us, when we were at the window. There was the voice in the air, saying that Johnny must be brought to justice."

"Then maybe you will take heed of it and let us get the thing over and done with, before there is trouble."

"I can do nothing for you, Inspector," Father Tom said.

The Inspector put on his cap.

"Maybe you said the same to the woman," he remarked.

"No, I said nothing like that," Father Tom said.

"The fact of the matter is that she would not have come here if she thought you could not help her!"

Father Tom smiled. "Oh, you know, you know what they think," he said. "They think I will perform miracles."

"Do you tell me, Father, that you are not willing to help this woman find Johnny?" the Inspector asked.

Father Tom was silent for a few seconds.

"You and I are both looking for Johnny," he said at last. "You want his body. I want his soul."

"It's one and the same thing," the Inspector said.

"Then maybe we could join forces," the priest said.

"I have no power to make bargains with you," the Inspector said. "I am here to do my duty. Johnny belongs to the Law, body and soul . . . the man who killed another."

"I acknowledge that," the priest said.

"Then obey the law. Support the officers of the law in their duty, and don't interfere!"

"It is not to interfere, but . . . oh, only to believe that there is Faith in at least one of us, and some good in at least one of us!" Father Tom said. "Not to flout the law, but to claim a little something out of mercy."

The Inspector squared his shoulders and walked towards the door.

"It is a game you are always at, Father! This time, we say no!"

Father Tom bowed his head as though in disappointment. When he spoke it was in the tone of a suppliant.

"Would you grant me one favor, Inspector?"

The Inspector shook his head.

"No, Father Tom. Not one! Not half a one! I have my duty to perform."

"Oh, it would not interfere with your duty, Inspector!" the priest hastened to assure him.

"What is it?"

Father Tom raised his eyes to him.

"If I say that Johnny will be at the Square or somewhere about these streets towards midnight, will you let me say that the woman can be there as well, Inspector?"

The man of authority nodded with satisfaction.

"You can say that fifty women will be there as well, as long as you promise to deliver Johnny . . ." he began.

"Oh, but I am not able to promise!" Father Tom exclaimed. "I only hope that he will be somewhere hereabouts at that hour. That is all. The woman hopes so, too."

"You believe there is a strong likelihood?"

"I do, Inspector."

"We'll leave it like that then," the Inspector said.

Father Tom accompanied him down the stairs and into the dimly lit hall.

"You will allow the woman to be with him?" he asked, whispering.

The Inspector smiled faintly.

"About midnight," he said quietly. "We'll be on the lookout."

"Thank you," Father Tom whispered gratefully.

He closed the door softly behind the departing figure and came shuddering back to the hall. He ascended the stairs slowly and reached the landing outside the little room adjoining the large one. Tapping softly on the door, he went in.

Agnes was asleep on the settee.

He looked down at the perfect composure of her features and thought of the peculiar state called sleep which is the strange necessity of the living body. And thinking of the mysterious force which is the living body, and the wonderful thing which is the soul, he withdrew silently, closing the door after him and returning to his room to stir the fire a little and muse.

PART TWO

JOHNNY

one

When Johnny recovered consciousness in the shelter in which he had run, he could not recognize his surroundings. The short November day had passed to twilight. Darkness was falling, and the shelter was so cold and so dark that at first he imagined that he was sitting on the floor of the prison cell from which he had escaped earlier in the year. The air was harsh with the odor of brick and cement and dampness. He was so sure that he was in the prison cell that he made no effort to rise, but allowed his thoughts to move slowly of their own volition.

They began to assemble about a strange dream whose details recurred vividly and whose atmosphere had so impressed him that all his sub-conscious mind was still possessed by it. Thus, he remembered the smell of the office into which he had gone to plunder the safe, and the sounds of shrill voices, and the motion of the car, and the face of the mill manager who had been in the hall, and the warm weight of the cashier's body when the two of them had rolled down the steps of the mill. And the smell of the pavement. And the sounds of the revolvers. And much more.

"Yes," he thought, with sudden clarity. "In the dream I killed him and he wounded me! He plugged me in the left arm, and the pain was so bad I could not get into the car with Pat and Murphy and Nolan."

He felt an impulse to laugh at the absurd dream, At that moment he heard the thunder of traffic reverberating in the earth and rising from the stone floor on which he was sitting.

"It is traffic in the Crumlin Road, outside the jail," he thought. Then the volume of his thoughts returned once more to the dream which he had experienced; and again and again the terrible events recurred to him, not in an ordered progression but in a rapid presentation of confused detail. And now he remembered as well how he had sat around a little table with Dennis, Sean, Seamus, Pat, Murphy, Nolan and others and planned a raid on the mill. Also, his mind presented recollections of the journey in the car to the mill; and he remembered the strange weakness and baffling sense of datachment which he had felt throughout the journey, and in a heightened degree when he had left the car and entered the mill. He recalled, too, the curious fact that a certain quality of fear had been absent from his mind throughout the whole time which he had spent in the mill. And yet, now, when he remembered the part of the dream during which he had grappled with the big cashier and toppled down the steps with him and fired at him and had been fired at, he experienced not only intense horror but fear as well.

"What an awful dream," he mumbled aloud. And he tried to expel it from his memory.

"I have never had such a nightmare before," he said, trying to sit upright.

He wondered what time it was, and he listened intently for the familiar sounds of the prison during the evening. He heard only the echoes of traffic and the puff and thrash of the wind outside the shelter.

"I can hear the trams," he said. "It is morning. Or is it evening?"

He tried to remember what had happened before he had slept and had the nightmare; but the dream interposed itself between the present and the past like a huge curtain enveloping him and holding him suspended in the present. He tried to rise, but at once he felt pain in his left arm and hand.

"Just like the pain in the dream," he thought. Then from a remote region of consciousness a curious host of fears began to advance upon him, gathering into a great, menacing force which approached and from which his mind tried to escape.

"What is happening to me?" he exclaimed aloud; and now he struggled to rise, whereupon the pain clawed at him, rending his whole body and driving the breath from his lungs.

He submitted to it and lay quite still.

". . . sleep again," he thought, "better sleep again. It is still the dream. . ."

But he was afraid, and instead of sleeping he made another attempt to rise and discover his surroundings. He put out his hands to the cold stone of the floor. Pain crashed at his left hand and bruised his whole body. And as his right hand moved swiftly to touch his left hand and ease the agonly, his fingers encountered the cloth of his overcoat.

130

He sat quite still then, thinking frantically:

"I am wearing an overcoat! What is this? Why am I dressed like this? Where am I? What has happened to me?"

He made immense efforts of will. He gasped. He remembered what had happened, and it no longer had the character of a dream. It was actuality, breaking across his mind in a flood and reminding him that he had made the raid, and killed a man, and been wounded, and that he was a fugitive, alone.

He scrambled to his feet and took a few tottering steps towards the source of the draught which was blowing in the shelter. He swayed, and his body struck the wall, whereupon his head flopped forward and the skull crashed against the brickwork. He was slightly stunned. His eyes closed and he groped with his hands and clung to the wall where it jutted at the exit. And because there was now that imperative impulse in his mind to leave the shelter, to make for the house where he had lived since his escape from jail, to elude the police, to save his life, he guided his weak body with his hands and presently emerged from the shelter.

It was quite dark outside. The night had come down and it was full of darkness and a high wind. He stared about him with wide, fixed eyes. The darkness flowed about him and seemed to him to penetrate his sense of sight. Running his hand across his eyes, he kept peering around and thrusting forward his head to discern his surroundings. And soon he was able to see houses and the pale strip of the pavement, as well as chinks of light which showed at the edges of windows. Those thin strips of light proclaimed the fact that there were men and women in the houses, and at once his terrible thirst bade him knock on one of the doors and ask for water and a place to rest his agonized body for a little while until . . . until . . .

But fear interposed itself, riding across his mind. The normal world was at a distance, beyond an impassable gulf. It was quick, noisy, teeming, bounded by laws, protected by those laws, encouraged by its own purposes. But those purposes were no longer shared by him. He saw the houses and knew that they were inhabited. He heard the traffic sounding in the air about him. It was life. But it raised no response in him. The things which had held him to life and given him purpose were expired in him. His thoughts flowed in terror because he had killed, because he was a fugitive, and wounded.

"I am finished," he thought. "It is all up with me. . . ."

He lurched quickly away, realizing with a sense of relief that he was on the fringe of the district in which the mill stood, and was moment by moment making his painful way still farther from it.

And at last he sought only a place where he could rest and be alone. He feared to encounter the police, who would arrest him and take him first to hospital and then, when he was healed, send him to trial. He drowned the thought of it. He admitted that everything in him was fulfilled. He had accepted the task which his fanatical spirit had imposed on him. He had existed for years upon a dream which was ended at last. He had obeyed passionate impulses and resolved himself. Now he shuddered with horror and agony. He had committed murder. And he was seriously wounded.

He tried to hurry. Often, he stumbled. The wind struck him and thrust him about. His hand and arm pained him, and weakness possessed him so that he was obliged to stop and lean against walls and doors where he longed to yield to a desire for rest, for silence. But he was afraid of being seen by people, by the police, and of being dragged back to a life which he had rejected. He went on.

He had no goal. He wanted only a place where he might first of all slake his thirst and then yield everything of himself to rest. In the darkness he passed many people who glanced at him but did not identify him. His appearance did not suggest the fugitive, the violent slayer, the figure which popular imagination had drawn of him. He looked like a hatless young man waiting for someone, walking slowly for a few paces, stumbling in the darkness, and then halting. A man lost in thought, half hidden by the night, waiting, and then trudging on again, a little unsteady, and afraid in himself, and cautious.

He loitered near the empty ruins of houses, wondering if within those sockets there was a corner sheltered from the icy wind, and a tap at which he might drink. But children were playing amidst the stark shapes of those shattered walls. He gathered his strength and went on, trying to avoid the dim pools of light below some of the lamp standards, moving out of sight of men and women returning from the day-shifts in the factories and shipyards, until opposite him he saw on the far side of the road the wide gate leading to a contractor's yard. It was open a few feet. He halted, seeing beyond the gate the dark stacks of building material—timber, bricks, salvaged perhaps from ruins—and telling himself that in that extensive place there were corners, places where he might hide his painful body and rest his fearful spirit.

He stepped to the edge of the pavement and moved into the roadway. A military lorry was approaching. He saw it and tried to hurry. But somewhere along the line of his limbs, his strength dribbled away in a futile little rush. He hesitated, swaying in the center of the road, seeing the big vehicle swerve to avoid him and slacken its speed. Its headlights held him. He groaned, closing his eyes.

The lorry swept past him, with someone leaning from its cab and shouting incoherently at him. The big side almost touched him. He stumbled, trying to move backwards, putting out his hands and trying to thrust himself backwards. His sleeves caught on a projection and he was dragged a few feet and then dropped like a mere loose thing thrown off. He tottered backwards and fell headlong across the crown of the road.

Two passing women saw him. They cried loudly, but his own shriek of pain was louder than their cry, for he had fallen on his left side and torn open the wounded flesh and admitted pain into his body.

He was quite still. The two women ran out and stooped over him and lifted him. He had fainted. For a few seconds they seemed nonplussed. Then leaning down over his lowered form they made another effort, rousing him to momentary consciousness and walking slowly with him to one of the houses opposite.

They shoved open the door. At once his senses had an impression of warmth and quietude. He yielded to it.

two

They were two married women, two sisters, Rosie and Maud, who lived in two houses adjoining each other and who were known throughout the locality for their positive temperaments and forthright, bold characters.

When they reached the pavement with Johnny, Rosie exclaimed softly:

"He has gone over again! Get on the other side of him, Maudie!"

She heaved Johnny's limp body from her massive bosom across which he had slumped, and edged her way through the doorway into the house, with Maudie following her and holding Johnny by his wounded arm. Maudie closed the door by giving it an adroit kick. Then she and Rosie entered the little parlor and moved forward to the settee.

"Hold him," Rosie murmered, while she lit the gas mantle above the fireplace.

Coming back she took hold of Johnny and gently lowered him to the settee.

"Put up his feet," she said, while she settled cushions beneath his head.

"Take a look at him!" she said in her gruff, broad voice. "This fellow has had a bad knock! That lorry gave him an awful crack!"

"His arm is broke!" Maudie exclaimed.

"Ouch, away out of that!" Rosie retorted. "You're talkin' daft! Fetch a basin, and the kettle of water. And take a look and make sure the water is boilin' hot. And . . . "

"It's broke, I'm tellin' you!" Maudie said, thrusting her big face towards her sister. "Anybody could see that!"

Rosie sighed with exasperation and closed her eyes as she swayed angrily.

"Listen here!" she blazed. "Who has done the first aid? Me or you?"

"I'm not talkin' about the first aid!" Maudie retorted. "Only for wee Billy comin' home on leave, I would have got me badge, same as you. Sure, I did all the learnin', same as yourself, and I'm tellin' you his arm is broke!"

"You know damn fine you failed in your practicals!" Rosie shouted. "So shut your trap while there's practical things to be done, and fetch the basin and the boilin' water and them other things!"

"You'll see, when you strip his arm," Maudie said, rising from her knees and hurrying into the kitchen.

Rosie gently eased off the overcoat from Johnny's shoulders. It came a little way, and then she could do no more without assistance. She sat back on her haunches, shaking her head, a frown of pity and horror on her big features.

She saw the raw wound which ran from the tip of the finger of the left hand to the wrist; and she slowly turned back the sleeve and saw how the blood which had streamed from the wound in the arm had dried in a crust across which a thin, new trickle was flowing. Vague suspicions began in her, but she did not ponder them.

"God help 'im," she murmured, leaning forward and lightly parting the dark hair from his forehead. Then again she saw the dirt staining his face, and the blood that had drenched his jacket and overcoat, and the rime of mucus about his eyes and lips.

"Maudie!" she called loudly, and there was a note of alarm in her voice.

"I'm comin' as fast as my two legs can carry me!" Maudie shouted. "What's wrong?"

"This fellah is hurt bad," Rosie said, lowering her voice.

"Sure, I was tellin' you!" Maudie said, coming to the door for an instant and then returning to the kitchen. "It's his arm is broke, and what you want is one of them imp... impoverish splints."

"Impoverished!" Rosie bawled back to her, gently running her fingers over Johnny's dirty face.

"That's what you should apply," Maudie said, coming in with a bowl of boiling water.

She set it down on the floor beside Rosie and helped her remove the overcoat. Johnny groaned. His eyelids flickered.

"It's a pity of him," Maudie said.

The overcoat was tossed to a chair.

"For goodness sake!" Rosie sighed, in horror, seeing the sodden sleeve of the jacket. "Did you ever see a young fellah in such a state?"

Maudie screwed up her big features in an expression of pity and horror.

"Oh, dear help 'im," she murmured, turning away for an instant.

When she looked down again at Johnny, she saw Rosie gently feeling the arm.

"There's no bones broke," Rosie said. "Give's the scissors."

"What's this you're doing?" Maudie said, handing her a pair of scissors from the mantelpiece.

"Take a hold of his shoulders while I rip up this sleeve," Rosie said.

Maudie drew back and frowned. Her big body had a swirl of rage.

"Cuttin' a good jacket like that!" she exclaimed. "Sure you have no right to do that, without askin' him first!"

Rosie turned her huge, vehement countenance to him. The

dark hair with its streaks of grey swung with the movement. Her big, capable right hand swept the locks from her brow. She flung down the scissors.

"It's what they told us up at the First Aid, and you know it!" she said.

"Maybe," Maudie retorted. "Whose coat is it but? Yours or his?"

"It's his, sure!"

"Well, then."

Rosie flushed angrily. "You're that aggravatin' in the face of difficulties. Nobody would think you was a woman of forty-eight, with five grown children, and a man of your own. Standin' there and tellin' me . . .

"So I am," Maudie rejoined, squatting down beside her and tearing open a large packet of lint from which she took a big portion to place ready for her sister. "I'm only warnin' you that it's his jacket. . . "

"Hold on a wee bit," Rosie interrupted. "Will you take a look at our hands!"

"What's wrong now?" Maudie asked.

"Germs!" Rosie said, thrusting out her big calloused hands and rising heavily.

"Should have scrubbed them with carbolic soap," she said.

"Oh, all the fuss," Maudie muttered. "Sure, didn't they tell us the air is full of germs?"

"Listen here," Rosie said, nudging her and going towards the door, "I'm not takin' the risk of givin' this fellah septics!"

She nodded her head emphatically and hurried into the little kitchen, where she first of all untied a packet of sausages which she emptied into a frying-pan and set on a slow gas-ring, and then began to wash her hands with carbolic soap.

She was a large woman, the mother of two adult sons and one daughter, all of whom were in the Services. Her character was positive, expressive, developed by innate wit and perception to a degree which often plunged her into opposition to the smaller, less informed spirits of her neighbors. There was a quality of progression in her nature. She did not root herself upon tradition, upon the unchanging life of the district, but went her way boldly, a thinking woman, a vehement clear-sighted soul, quick, forthright, kind, generous. And in all her plans and pursuits, Maudie was beside her, a smaller counterpart of herself, like an echo or reflection, faithful to her in her heart, yet always giving the impression of

136

a critic, seldom completely in agreement with her, yet never quite in opposition to her. The two of them were local arbiters, the pillars to which the weak went and against which the bitter pitted themselves.

"Go you out now," Rosie said, returning to the patient, "and get the germs off, same as myself."

She got to her knees beside the prone figure on the settee and began to bathe the wound on the hand.

"Maudie!" she called softly, after a few minutes.

"What is it?"

"I'm thinkin' this fellah should go to hospital."

"Aye, you're right!"

Rosie unbuttoned the jacket and parted it.

"Dear help us!" she gasped.

Maudie returned quickly, hearing that ejaculation. Standing beside her sister and leaning forward with her wispish hair falling over her brow, her heavy face assumed a look of pity and curiosity as she saw the dull stain on the waistcoat and shirt.

"I wouldn't like to interfere with that," Rosie said, leaning back. "I'm not all that skilled yet."

"Aye, you're right," Maudie said. "That's work for the high-up ones at the hospital."

"I could do a wee bit for the hand, you know," Rosie went on, "but there is awful damage on it. You can near see the ligaments and them things."

"Aye, you can."

Their voices became softer and slower and empty of urgency. They resounded peacefully in the cleanly comfort of the little room, touching Johnny's sense of hearing and drawing his spirit into calm. Something was restored in him. He opened his eyes.

He saw first of all the ceiling which had been whitewashed recently by Rosie and her husband, and then the picture of soldiers in old-fashioned uniforms making a line before an oncoming mob of ferocious tribesmen. The wallpaper was pink, with little bunches of flowers printed on it. Below the picture was a mantelpiece with many vases and several photographs of smiling youths and a girl in unform. He saw these things and heard the soft hiss of the gas jets. Then he saw two faces, with the eyes softly regarding him, and he knew that the spirit which gave life to those eyes was kindly and would not disrupt his peace at this moment. In this room with the two women, and the familiar sound of the gas in the mantles, and the odor of warm water and lint and soap impregnating the air about him, he felt an immeasurable peace which eased at last the troubled things in him.

"How are you, son?" Rosie murmured.

"You took an awful crack from that lorry," Maudie said, in the same tone.

"You'll be fine soon," Rosie said, "for we'll get the ambulance for you, and have you took to hospital. . . "

He heard it and tried to sit upright, saying painfully:

"No. . . no. . . " and panting. And moving his head as though to escape a burden. Distress was in his tone.

"Oh, now, sure you'll be better there," Rosie said, cajoling him.

He groaned, and sinking back he repeated the words with an intensity of emotion which indicated something more than a mere unwillingness to go to hospital.

"Maybe," Maudie said, "you would like for us to send for your Ma or Dad or someone."

He shook his head, dragging it painfully from side to side.

"Have you somebody . . . your wife, maybe?" Rosie suggested.

In reply his head moved as before and the negative broke loudly from his dry lips.

"Sure, it's all right, sure, then," Rosie said. "Sure, we wouldn't send you off to hospital if you're not wantin to go."

But his head continued its movement and the agonized word was repeated until movement and articulation betrayed a particular fear which both women sensed, and which their ponderous glances remarked to each other.

"But listen here," Rosie said gently, caressing his right hand, "the thing is I am not so well up in the first aid to see what's wrong with you. You've had a bad accident, and I'm thinkin' maybe we should send for a doctor."

He moved his head as before and said, "No, no!"

"He's queer an' bad," Rosie said to Maudie. "What am I to do?" she whispered.

"It's gettin' late. Alfie and Sammy'll be home soon."

Rosie frowned and made a gesture of scorn.

"I'm not worryin' my head off about them!" she said. "It's him I'm thinkin' about."

"He's awful thirsty," Maudie said.

"Aye, he is. Go and fetch him a taste of water."

Rosie spread her big hand gently on his breast and tried to discover his pulse. His chest rose in swift, shallow shudders as he breathed; but of the pulse there seemed only an elusive flutter. His dim eyes watched her.

"What's your name son?" she said, removing her hand from him and taking his right wrist between her thunb and two fingers.

He was silent now, watching her and finding relief in the mere presence of that ample body with its rhythms of calm, kindness and wisdom. He trusted himself to her, yielding in himself, so that his pulse, when she found it at last, was a diminished thing, lapsing, fading, so distant, so faint.

She was much perturbed. His injuries were obviously more serious than her limited skill could define and repair. She smoothed the tangled strands of his hair.

"Son, you've been in queer trouble. You're queer and bad. Is there somebody we could fetch for you?"

"What's he say?" Maudie said, bringing a tumbler of cold water.

"Nothin'," Rosie said simply, putting another cushion beneath his head to facilitate his drinking. He moved eagerly to take the water. His shoulders rose. His eyes opened wider and a sudden reflection of all the swift, violent things of his life swept into them with an alien glimmer and travelled over his features, bringing a hard expression. His body shuddered. His hand reached for the glass and clutched it.

Rosie and Mudie exchanged glances but said nothing. He was gulping the water.

"Oh, take your time!" Rosie said, taking the glass and holding it to his lips.

He plunged his lips into it. His brow contracted. Violence dwelt for an instant on his countenance and declared itself in the attitude of his body as he heaved himself upright and drank.

"It's some row he was in," Rosie thought. She said: "Slow . . . take it slow, son!"

He pushed his face upon the rim of the glass and sought with his right hand to lift the tumbler from her. He tipped it for an instant. Then the contents spurted from the glass and streamed down his face, over his garments, over his trembling hand.

"Take and fill it again for him," Rosie said, removing the glass from his hands and passing it to Maudie. "I know it's bad for him, but he wants it."

She waited until Maudie was in the kitchen before she leaned towards Johnny and spoke.

"What happened?" she said, looking full at him.

The echoes and reflections of violent things had expired in him, and again his eyes were filmed and weak.

"Was it someone took a cut at you?" she said.

He was silent. There was a peace and ease in his body. The big, square, glistening face which leaned towards him was brimming with kindliness, was full of virtues that touched his sensibilities and composed his spirit. There remained only pain and weakness. But they were of life which he had renounced because he knew that he could never again taste it completely. He wanted only this calm which he had found and upon which he reclined his soul.

Maudie returned with the glass, which she handed to her sister, who held it to his lips.

"Give it to him while I run in and set something for Sammy's tea," Maudie said.

Again Johnny lifted himself to drink. This time Rosie's firm hand restrained him.

"Take it slow, else it'll come back on you and you'll not get the good of it," she said.

He saw Maudie depart. Now he was alone with Rosie and he was glad. He wanted to savour the great vitalizing calm of her spirit. As he moved, the pain returned. He dropped back heavily on the cushions.

"I'm thinking . . ." Rosie began, anxiously; and even in her bewilderment her voice was still soothing to him.

Their eyes met again in a long glance.

"What's your name son?" she asked.

He shook his head. His name—everything of his life—no longer seemed relevant or important.

"You're not telling me, then?" she said.

Again he shook his head, making between himslef and all the things of the past a great act of rejection.

"I won't ask you then," she said, "But I can see with my own eyes you're hurt bad."

As she spoke she deftly bandaged his left hand. Often her big eyes lifted their glance to him. Once he smiled.

"Tell me this," she said, not looking at him, "what am I do do with you?"

She finished binding his hand and gently composed hand

140

and arm and rose from her knees sighing. Looking down at him and presently drawing a chair close to him, she sat down.

"You know you're in a bad way and should have the doctor to dress your arm," she said.

His eyes upon her had a remote look; but he heard her and smiled.

"I'm finished," he whispered hoarsely.

Except for the frantic negative, they were the first words he had uttered to her, and they confirmed something which had settled in her thoughts when she had attempted to remove his jacket. For a little while she was silent, holding his right hand and finding the faint pulse. She was too much of a realist to delude him about himself when it was so plain to her, and obvious to himself as well, that he was dying.

"I'm thinkin' I must send for somebody," she said, adding, "Don't you want to see anybody? Sure, there must be someone?"

His eyes flickered their lids. He spoke than as though from a distance which was beyond life.

"I'm finished," he cried, on a groan of pain. "It's all done. . ."

She stroked his right hand. "Then let me send for someone belonging to you."

His eyes opened and fastened their gaze on her. He saw the big, plain face full of an expression of kindliness and natural wisdom.

"There is nobody . . ." he said. "Give me peace here . . . let me stay a bit. . ."

His eyes closed again.

"Sure, son," she whispered.

She rose after a few seconds and stood with her feet wide apart and her big body in an attitude indicative of indecision. Her hands moved slowly together. Maudie returned.

"He's sleepin'," Rosie said, going into a little passage and waylaying her. "Listen here," she went, whispering. "One of us ones better run down to the Warden's post and get one of them fellahs to come up and take a look at him, and maybe bring a doctor. He's awful bad. I'm thinkin' he's passin' out."

"Dear help 'im," Maudie murmured, peering in at him.

"Take a run down to the Post and tell them."

"Aye, I will."

"Say there is a young fella here knocked down by a lorry and wantin' a doctor quick."

"Aye, I will, I'll just nip in and put on me, first."

"I'm thinkin' I'll maybe give him a wee drop of that whisky Alfie has put by for when the boys comes home," Rosie said, turning back into the room.

"Aye, it might hold him up a wee while," Maudie said.

"I think I'll try him with a taste of it but."

"Aye, give him a wee sip of it in a spoon while I take a run down to the post."

"Aye, I reckon I will," Rosie said.

She heard her sister pad heavily to the house next door. Standing irresolutely, as before, and looking down at the pallid face and the dark stain on the garments and the marks that had appeared on the cushions, she began to question herself about him. Who was he? What had happened to him? The wounds . . . certainly not knife wounds or from falling in the roadway or being knocked down. From bullets? And why was he determined not to tell her anything of himself? From whence was he, and who and where were his family, his friends? What kind of life . . .?

She could have found the answer to some of these questions had she opened his pockets and examined the contents. She knew why she refrained from doing that. It was not because of any particular delicacy of her nature, for she never considered such decencies when they obstructed her good purpose. Looking at him and at the torn, stained overcoat which she had removed from him and thrown over a chiar, she realized that deeply within her mind she had accurately assessed his character, correctly discovered his whole way of life, and the sort of associates with whom he spent that life. And it needed only a few trivial revelations to confirm what was in her mind.

Yet there was nothing which he would disclose. She stook looking at his pale face from which the sudden reflections of his violent, fanatical life had subsided and given place to an expression of calm.

It was as though he had surrendered to her, yielded his life with all its faults and purposes and problems, and all its tragic conclusion, to her safekeeping. It was a responsibility greater and more profound than any which she had yet accepted, and it raised misgivings in her.

She sighed as she moved aimlessly about the room. Seeing his overcoat, she took it and held it at arm's length and then closely examined its texture. And it was inevitable that she should presently notice the slight bulge in one of the pockets, and then slip in her hand and feel the cold weapon and realize that the little strap which she had noticed under his left arm was not part of his braces but a holster.

"Holy God!" she exclaimed, withdrawing her hand quickly, for the chill contact which it had made with the weapon was the fusion of surmise with truth; and at that moment she remembered rumors which she had heard from neighbors of a raid somewhere in the city. A raid on a mill followed by shooting and the killing of the cashier. And . . . so the rumors said . . . one of the raiders had escaped. He was the Chief of the Organization, and they said he was wounded. And, of course, you just did not suppose that you would find him wandering about and knocked down by a lorry and bring him into your own house.

She sat down with the overcoat over her knees. Now, suddenly and unaccountably, her pity for that doomed soul in its stained and wounded body increased to an unbearable degree, overwhelming the defences of her formidable character and exposing her to strange intimations.

"God help him!" she muttered, and staring at him and realizing that he would die either from loss of blood or from the hanging which awaited him after trial, it seemed to her that his tragedy was inexplicably hers as well. His terrible fate afflicted her, as though he were curiously bound to her by ties which were as deep and as profound as those of blood relationship, and which had sprung from his obvious faith in her pity.

It overwhelmed her. Tears began to fill her eyes and trickle down her cheeks. She dropped the overcoat and stood over him, conquering her tears and sobs, frowning, swaying a little.

"God help you," she cried, "what am I to do with you? What did you come here for?"

She sighed heavily, sniffed, and dried her eyes quickly. He was nothing more than a figure of tragedy and pain. The whole tale of his life with its furious challenge to authority was inscribed on his body where it was ending in a thin trickle of blood from a wound. He was nothing but a shattered, weak thing, alone, with nowhere to rest, lost from all the things which had supported the hot impulses of his being.

"And what'll my man say when he sees you?" she exclaimed. "What'll Alfie say, and Sammy, too?"

Her big body was suddenly active. Snatching up her

voluminous shawl and flinging it over her head and shoulders, she ran to the door and sped out, in time to see her sister going rapidly in the direction of the post.

"Maudie! Maudie!"

She was panting. She did not often run or exert herself or have cause for alarm.

"Maudie! Come here till I tell you!"

She overtook her sister.

"Listen, here . . ."

She drew Maudie back to the house and closed the door. She told her.

"This fellah . . ." she began.

She beckoned Maudie into the room and took up the overcoat and drew out the revolver.

"See? See that thing?"

"For God's sake . . ."

"Look at him! He's the one that killed the fellah in the mill! They was saying he was wounded and got away. They was all sayin' . . ."

"Right enough," Maudie exclaimed. "You've only got to look. . ."

"Chief of the Organization!" Rosie said.

"My God, it's awful, Rosie!"

"But he's finished. He's lost an awful lot of blood."

"Rosie, what'll we do with him?"

"Maudie," Rosie confessed, "I can't . . . I can't just fetch the police and turn him over to them. I can't. Not with him just lyin' there near dead, and nowhere to go to die, and the police out lookin' for him maybe, and . . . I just can't . . ."

"No more can I, Rosie," Maudie said.

"But I'm thinkin' what Alfie'll say when he comes in."

"Aye, Alfie'll say a lot."

"Alfie won't let him stay here."

"Aye, you're right. Alfie won't. Sammy might, but. Sammy's awful tender like with dumb animals and things."

"There's a reward for information about this fellah," Rosie said, biting her lower lip.

"Aye, for before he was on this day's work. For the time when he got out of prison."

"Two thousand pounds."

Maudie covered her face with her hands.

"I'd die if I laid a finger on it!"

"I'm afraid," Rosie said, "I'm afraid Alfie'll do his duty and maybe go to the police, not thinkin' of the reward or anything, but sort of puttin' himself in the way of gettin' it."

"You would never sleep easy for the rest of your days," Maudie said.

"Aye, I know."

"You'll have to tell Alfie but."

They heard footsteps at the house door.

"What'll you tell him?" Maudie whispered.

They exchanged glances. Rosie sniffed and went to the door of the room.

"Alfie," she said, when the house door opened; and her tone was deferential and yet firm and persuasive, "there's something I've got to tell you."

She confronted a man of fifty dressed in overalls under a shabby overcoat. His features were large, fixed in an expression of unvarying dourness and solemnity. The eyes were brown below tufted eyebrows, and his moustache was bushy above his lips. It was a face into which little expression of thought might be expected to flow; and yet, as now, when suspicion or apprehension was reflected in it, it assumed a kind of simplicity and frankness which belied the harshness of its customary look.

"What's this you're sayin', Rosie?" he said, gruffly, staring at her and then at Maudie and beyond them to the prone figure on the settee.

"Come here," Rosie said, drawing him into the kitchen.

"What's wrong?" he asked. "That fellah . . "

His manner was angry, but it was only a defence against his sudden fears, as well as something which would evoke the familiar resources of Rosie's character upon which, at this moment, he felt inclined to trust himself.

"I'm tellin' you," she retorted in a similar tone.

"Go ahead, then!" he rejoined, following her and flinging his cap on one of the chairs.

"It's about that young fellah in there, Alfie," she said.

"What's wrong with him? Who is he? What . . ." he began. She cut him short.

"Alfie, he's not long for this world."

He looked solemnly at her and spoke quietly.

"Is that a fact? What's happened to him? What's his name? Who brought him here?"

She was silent. Her big eyes were upon him, heavy with communication, ponderous with the import of her news. And seeing her thus, with so much that was eloquent of disaster filling her expressive features, his suspicions were inflamed.

"I'm askin' you: who is he?" he demanded.

She did not answer him. Instead, her gaze wavered from his, and lifted once more to him with the same troubled look as before.

He made a rapid gesture of anger and rushed from the kitchen to the door of the parlor. Maudie drew aside and watched him fearfully as he stood on the threshold staring at Johnny, at the overcoat, and at the revolver lying on the garment. He spun round.

"It's him!" he exclaimed. "That's him, right enough! That's Johnny, the fellah the police are lookin' for!"

His voice was strident with anger and alarm. His manner suddenly admitted all the issues which pity and kindliness had so far delayed. And as he rushed back to the kitchen and stood confronting Rosie, she felt those issues blow up to a tempest which whirled and confused her. Her troubled eyes assumed an expression of guilt.

"Bringin' him in here!" Alfie shouted.

Maudie slipped quickly away and entered her own home. A thin, greying man was in the kitchen. The light shone on his ruddy, rotund face which, as ever, was full of an expression of surprise.

"Where's my tea? Where you been?" he began.

"Sammy, Sammy!"

"What's wrong with you?"

She was panting. "In Rosie's . . ."

She tried to drag him towards the door. He threw off her hand and stook back, cautious as ever, unwilling to be drawn into trouble.

"Leave hold of me! Blargin' at me! What's wrong?"

She drew closer to him and told him, lowering her voice to a whisper.

"That fellah . . ."

"What fellah?"

His voice was loud for an instant until Maudie interrupted his mood and speech with a single word. She stood back and saw horror begin and expand on his little face.

"It's him, Sammy," she added.

"I'm keepin' right out of this!" he said, softly but emphatically. He sat down again.

"I'm stayin' right here, Maudie! I'm not takin' anything to

146

do with a thing like that!"

She understood him thoroughly in every inflection of his weak, obtuse character; and she knew, too, her own influence on him.

"It's him, Sammy," she said. "And Rosie is tellin' Alfie about him. The fellah is near dead, and Rosie wants for him to stay and be easy, I'm going back. I'm standin' by Rosie for what's decent like!"

He put up a grimy hand in an emphatic gesture.

"I told you. I'm takin' no part in things like that," he said.

But an instant later he followed here, venturing in and standing at the door of the little room and staring at Johnny, and presently going towards the kitchen, to listen, to weigh the drift of the issues before rendering his word to the strong side. Always the spectator, the timid little soul, hovering on the fringe of events, he was confronted at last with a circumstance which he knew he could not escape and into which he knew he must proceed and declare himself truthfully in a positive fashion, courageously, without duplicity.

"You can take and put the fellah out of here!" he heard Alfie tell Rosie.

"Alfie," he said, entering the discussion, "it wouldn't be human!"

three

Johnny heard them distinctly. Previously, there had been peace into which he had let himself sink. He believed in the humanity of the two women, and he trusted them not to disturb him when he ventured into the regions of mysterious quietude which were the outer districts of a greater and more mysterious territory beyond. He wanted to enter that outlying region and venture his spirit there in order to accustom it to the solitude and to find courage with which to make the passage into the territory beyond. He longed to slough off all the broken fragments of life which remained in him and on him. But it was difficult and agonizing. His body was a crust of pain beneath which his soul huddled in fear. And he required time and calm in which to make that effort and accept his fate.

147

No sooner had Maudie departed than he mistrusted Rosie, realizing that despite her innate kindness she was apprehensive. By then, he was some distance on his journey from life. Now it was necessary to struggle back to consciousness, to resume control of his weak body, to gather it under the reins of his will and leave this house. He groaned at the terrible effort which this demanded; and when he attempted to rise, pain struck him, tearing his flesh and confusing his mind.

He was dimly aware of an additional presence in the house, and he heard a man's voice.

"It's the fellah ... it's Johnny, the Chief of the Organization! The police is combin' the city for him!" Alfie said.

"I'm not sayin' it isn't Johnny," Rosie said.

"Then you can take and put him back where he was fetched from!"

Rosie spoke gently in reply. "Alfie! You're not speakin' from what you know is right!"

Alfie snorted. "I am but!" he said crisply.

"Alfie! And him nigh dead!"

"That fellah was on the raid! Think of that! That's Johnny, lyin' in our parlor. That's the Chief of the Organization, and the police wants him bad!"

"I'm not sayin' he isn't, Alfie. It's what he is now that I'm thinkin' about."

"Aye, and I'm thinkin' of the decent man he killed!"

"That's his sin. His God will judge him for that."

"What the hell are you askin' me to do, then?"

Rosie was silent. She waited until anger and all manner of attendant emotions had subsided a little in Alfie's mind.

"Man, dear, I'm only askin' you to remember he's nigh dead," she said, softly.

"I have no pity for them fellahs," Alfie retorted. "Shootin' at the police. Murderin' innocent men at their work. Robbing and all that and callin' it . . ."

"But he's dying now, Alfie. You wouldn't treat a dying dog like that!"

"A dog is the friend of man, Rosie! Is them fellahs our friends?"

She sighed. "I don't know, Alfie. Maybe not. All I know is he's not long for this world, and I don't like to be hard on him."

"Take and call the police then! Or send up to the post and

148

tell the wardens to fetch an ambulance," Alfie said.

"It's awful hard like," she said. "Not lettin' a dying man have a bit of peace and quiet."

"Maybe it is hard. But it's sense, it is!"

"Sense is cruel sometimes. You can't live like that. You have to . . ."

"Have to what?" Alfie demanded.

"There's more than sense."

"I won't deny it, Rosie."

"Then let him rest where he is."

"Aye, and maybe die there. Is that it?"

"It's the least you can do for the dying. Alfie."

His voice rose. "You're askin' too much, Rosie! You can take and put the fellah out of here!"

Sammy was standing at the kitchen door, and he was shaking his little round head and pursing his thick lips.

"Alfie," he said, "it wouldn't be human!"

Alfie did not look at him. He sat down and stretched out his legs and swung his feet on his heels. A look of determination was on his face.

"I've said. I've told you," he remarked.

The others were silent. He glanced quickly at them. He was afraid of them in their unity and of the arguments which he knew he had not quenched in Rosie or Sammy. He said quietly:

"I'm thinkin' of the law, too."

"There's more laws than one," Rosie said.

"She's right," Sammy said.

Maudie touched his arm. "Here, you! Quit your blether!"

"I'm choosin' the right side and I'm standin' firm on it," Alfie said.

Again the others were silent. Again he supplemented his remark.

"Listen, here!" he added. "What'll the police say if us ones let this fellah stay here, and us not lettin' on to the police?"

"Oh, the police!" Rosie exclaimed, flashing a scornful glance at him. "You're not all that feared of them so sudden, are you?"

"I'm feared of no man, while I'm doin' what's right," Alfie said.

"You could say you found the fellah on the doorstep and brought him in and seen he was dead," Sammy said.

Nobody appeared to have heard him.

"I respect the law," Alfie said to Rosie.

"There's no law says you must not give peace to the dying," Rosie said.

She sat down and put her hands on her knees.

"Alfie, if he has killed someone, that's his trouble. God help me, I'm not one for attendin' church and all that, but there's Christian feelings in me. I've got children of my own, grown children like that one in there . . ."

"Let his people take care of him!"

"My conscience says for to let him rest where he is," Rosie said.

"And my conscience says for me to put him out of here quick and not have him dyin' on us and makin' this house a marked house for evermore!" Alfie said. "That's what my conscience says. I'll tell you why," he went on. "I'm a decent Protestant man . . ."

"So am I," Sammy interjected.

"Quit you . . ." Maudie whispered.

". . . and I know what folks round here would say if we was to let this fellah stay here," Alfie continued. "And I know what the police would think. And another thing, Rosie: I know what the men in our shed would think."

Rosie sighed. "Aye, I know, I know!"

"And I'm thinkin' of you and the boys and young Rosie and myself," Alfie went on. "That fellah will die. But us ones will go on livin', and there's problems. My sympathies is with the law . . ."

Rosie looked at him with a hard expression.

"Go you then and put him out," she said. "You are the master here. And if you can't do it, run tell the police, and then maybe you will get the big reward the police is offering for information about him."

He rose slowly to confront all of them. Something wavered in him.

"I am not a hard one," he said. His voice trembled.

Rosie looked up at him and smiled.

"Alfie, you can't do it, can you?"

Sammy spoke. "It's a thing I could not do."

Maudie nudged him with her elbow. "Sure, nobody is askin' you!"

"To tell you the God's honest truth," Alfie confessed, "it goes against me to lift a hand against him."

"And who is wantin' you to lift a hand against anyone?"

Rosie asked.

"I'm thinkin' of the neighbors, and the men I am workin' with these twenty years, and the police I know; and I'm wonderin' what they'll be sayin' if I don't put this fellah out," he said.

"Listen, here!" Rosie said. "Let them ask theirselves in cold sober sense—forgettin' politics and such like—what they would do! Let them as likes to think and talk violent do the violent things and not expect others to do it."

"But there is the right and wrong of it, Rosie," Alfie persisted.

"We are harborin' a murderer and the Chief of the Organization. God help us, that's a load of mischief you can't hold. We ought to go to the police."

"Go you then and tell the police," she exclaimed.

He frowned. His hand scratched his neck.

"I am not one for runnin' to the police," he said, in dismay.

"You had better say what you are going to do," Rosie advised him.

He sat down, frowning, running his knuckles over the thin stubble of his beard.

"I have never had such hard things to decide," he remarked in a soft, troubled tone.

Rosie snorted contemptuously. "Hard things? It is only hard because of the politics and all that in you! Sayin' hard things all your life and callin' them politics, and knowing all the time that they's bad and against Christian feelings. And then findin', like now, that your true heart was never in the hard words, but was only stirred by the bad blood was raised up in you . . . ."

"That's treason, and you know it!" Alfie said.

She met his horrified glance boldly.

"Is it?" she exclaimed. "I am loyal to king and country and I fear God. My sons and my daughter is in the Services. I'm actin' on what my conscience tells me is human and kind when I see a dyin' man, and I don't want no politics or religion to tell me I must put him out. I hold nothin' against anyone on this earth, except the king's enemies. Maybe this fellah Johnny is one of the king's enemies; but he is dyin' and that's what matters now. Let the ones who like living at daggers drawn with their neighbors come in and put him out!"

She was panting. Her big face and her neck and bosom were flushed. Suddenly, she was silent. The others stared at her in awe.

"Them's awful sentiments in a loyal house," Alfie said sadly.

Rosie stepped heavily towards him.

"I want to live at peace with other people," she said. And she added: "Have I ever done you wrong, Alfie?"

"I can't say that you have."

"Have I ever failed in my duty to you or others?"

"No, Rosie, you have not."

"Have I ever done anything out of badness, or asked you to do a bad thing?" she went on.

"Never," he admitted.

She nodded with satisfaction. "I speak the truth, Alfie, and I don't listen to ones who talk with two tongues."

She turned round and went to the little gas-ring on the stove and began to move the sausages to and fro in the frying-pan.

"She's right," Sammy said to Alfie. "Rosie is a woman who speaks the truth and acts decent to all. You could walk a good bit from here and meet a lot of people, Christian and otherwise, and they would all tell you the same about Rosie."

Alfie sighed. "Aye, I know rightly, Sammy, man. But I don't know what to do about that fellah lyin' in there."

He moved his hands restlessly together.

"You know, right enough," Rosie said, over her massive shoulder as she spread crockery and cutlery on the table.

"It's cruel and hard," Alfie murmered. "Either way, we're let in for something that's going to make things hard for us."

Glancing at Rosie and seeing her big body and realizing the direction of her positive character and temperament, it seemed to him that this moment with its grave problem was the culmination of something which had been steadily approaching for years. It had all started years ago, when she had been a young woman of independent mind and character, whose wit and courage and other qualities had attracted him. And for years she had lived her life, freely, going her own good way, slightly apart from him, never sharing his violent ideas or the phrases which he uttered, and which were forever in the air and in the lives of their neighbors in the city. The things which he discussed had governed his life, yet underneath them all there was his heart, which Rosie had influenced with her temperament that was governed naturally by things that were boldly and majestically eloquent at last. And at this crisis he could not escape that influence.

He knew that the others were waiting for him to make a decision. He saw Rosie glance at him in pity and understanding. Maudie, too, gave him a glance from time to time as she helped Rosie arrange the tea things. Sammy watched him as though he shared his inner predicament.

In the other room, Johnny had heard them. The voices came from the vast circumference beyond his core of peace. He knew what was going to happen, for the voices indicated it all to him, disclosing Alfie's inability to accept the problem. Therefore he struggled to rise from the settee.

It took him many minutes. He returned to consciousness from the regions of coma and calm, accepting the heavy garment of pain. He rose unsteadily and took a step forward. His feet tripped over the basin of water and he stumbled heavily across the room, falling against the door.

He groaned. They heard him and hurried in to him. He stood back slightly and drew himself erect and regarded them with a look of bewilderment which slowly changed to an expression of determination. He moved towards the door, unsteadily at first, then firmly but slowly, with his head erect and an exultant gleam in his eyes.

They made way for him in silence as he went through the little passage and approached the door.

"Ah, God help him! He's took and gone!" Maudie said.

"Here! Hold on, hold on a wee moment," Alfie called.

He took a little flat bottle of whisky from a china vase on the mantelpiece.

"Take a hold of this," he said, handing it to Johnny. "Here!" He unscrewed the stopper and put the bottle to Johnny's lips.

"Put the whole of it inside you, man! It'll do you a power of good!"

Johnny clenched his teeth on the neck of the bottle and tipped the contents into his mouth. In a few seconds the bottle was empty. He gulped. It fell from his lips.

"Put this on you, son," Rosie said, folding his overcoat about his shoulders and bringing it together over his chest. As her hands moved over his shoulders she felt his body trembling with pain and the effort of movement.

He heard her speaking to him, but between himself and the normal world of which she and the others were a part, great mists were drifting, obscuring his vision, blotting out sounds and amplifying others and admitting curious echoes to his mind.

His hand lifted and groped for the door handle. Behind him the last impacting words of the argument lifted and passed to silence. Alfie came forward with his grim face set in a hard expression from which the eyes peered out as though he were suffering grief. He unfastened the door. A wild gust of wind blew into the little passage and tore a picture from the wall and sent it hurtling to the floor.

Johnny felt the icy wind on his face and heard it whistling through the house. The black night was full of its sounds as it loomed before him. He faltered. He flinched from the clamoring gale and the sounds of the city which it whirled into the heavens, and the great black wave of darkness which it massed before him. Behind him was the warmth and comfort of the little house; but in it were men and women, the creatures of life, uncertain, unpredictable. Soft, kindly things were in their glances for an instant, but he was no longer beguiled by them. He understood that he would not be allowed to stay.

He lifted his right foot and stepped out, seeing nothing but the darkness. He took another step and stumbled headlong across the threshold, out into the street, lurching as he recovered himself. He heard the door slam loudly behind him, whereupon all the things of life seemed to withdraw from him, leaving him suspended and terribly alone. Until he recollected that he was still a fugitive, a criminal, a murderer, a dangerous revolutionary, outlawed, wounded, dying.

The fumes of the whisky rose to his mind, and the warmth of the liquid afforded him a tiny access of strength. He stood erect, lifting his head, staring about him with eyes which scarcely discerned the dim objects which the night grudgingly permitted to the sight. His senses were withdrawn into themselves, to the core of consciousness where the profound essence of his spirit had its source. A babble of ridiculous, incoherent words broke from his lips. They were the final expression of all the ideals which had given purpose to his life. The exultation which he intended to pour into them at that moment was brief. It ended in a brutish sound, loud and fierce, terrible and audible. Then it ceased. But it made clamour still within his mind. in the depths of his being. It was the full, spiritual ecstasy, beyond the pettiness of mortal affairs, and he savoured it sweetly before it dwindled rapidly from him and left him empty and aimless. He mustered his remaining strength and stumbled on.

Hands touched him, placing a cap on his head. Halting, he stood to facilitate the action.

"Here! Put this on you! Quick! There y'are now! God help you!" Maudie said.

He went on while she sped back to the house. The others were in the kitchen when she returned. Alfie was holding Johnny's revolver and facing Rosie.

"What did you keep this thing for? Isn't there trouble enough . . ."

"You could get seven years for bein' in possession of that," Sammy exclaimed.

"Sure, I held it from the poor fellah, to stop more killing," Rosie said. "Give's it here!"

She snatched it from Alfie's hand and thrust it towards Sammy and Maudie.

"Take it, youse!"

"I will not!" Sammy exclaimed, backing away. "The thing has done murder this evening. Seven years . . ."

Maudie took it.

"What'll I do with it?" she asked Rosie.

"Take and drop it into the drain along a bit."

"Come on!" Maudie said, beckoning to Sammy.

When they were gone, Rosie served the sausages and sat down opposite Alfie at the little table drawn up before the tiny stove. Her vehemence, her vigorous spirit, her magnificent and distinctive temperament, were subdued. Her chin trembled and her features shuddered. Then came the tears. Big, slow, ponderous as her words in their sad stream.

"Oh, the pity of him, the pity of him! Shootin' and killin', and livin' for trouble, and on the way to the gallows all the time, poor lad!"

"Aye, you're right," Alfie said. "Them fellahs is fierce! There's nothin' you could do for them ones. We acted charitable . . . ."

It did not console Rosie. Her wise vision penetrated beyond the immediate moment and the environment into which that tragic figure had strayed.

"There's plenty could be done . . . there's always a remedy, Alfie, for bad things," she said.

He was silent. The affair had ended, as far as he was concerned; and he had gained his way without a drastic act.

But Rosie was perturbed.

"What'll happen to him? Why do them fellahs behave like that, Alfie? Shootin' and killin' . . . ."

"It's queer and bad, in a Christian country," she said.

Alfie munched his food hungrily. He emptied his cup and passed it to Rosie for her to fill again.

"We acted for the best. He took and went, and that's the best thing," he said.

four

In a deep doorway in Corporation Street, Johnny was huddled. A big cloth cap covered his head and concealed his face. His overcoat was draped over his shoulders and buttoned over his arms. One of his hands was wrapped in a long bandage which had come loose. The bandage was not visible, for he was standing with his face pressed against the door. His attitude was so unnatural that passing pedestrians imagined that he was drunk. They glanced at him and were amused, contemptuous, revolted, according to their opinions of drunkenness. None of them stopped. They were soldiers, civilians of both sexes and various ages; but despite their degrees of intelligence and perception, they all believed that the figure in the doorway was nothing but a drunk man.

Whereas it was an immortal soul in its raiment of flesh and bone. This was the curious phenomenon which has emerged from aeons of life on the world. The body was sustained by certain known processes. But the forces which supported the soul were secret and unfathomable. It was a mystery that it was there, in the body which was merged into the darkness in that doorway.

Because the body had lost much blood through a wound in the hand and arm, its life was ebbing. The soul in that body knew this and no longer submitted itself to the things of earthly existence, but prepared itself for departure from the body which was no longer able to sustain it. It became aware of itself as a glorious, immortal thing; and remembering the ages of civilization which had impressed it, and the beautiful and evil things which had lit upon it to mold and develop it, it was conscious of its strength that would enable it to traverse a

156

new territory towards which it peered with hope, and which was to be its next experience. It communed with itself, appreciating the journey which was before it. Then it felt upon itself a great burden which it could not escape and which would hinder its progress towards a new life.

It remembered that it had killed a man. The facts of that sin were of the sordid, of the evil of certain aspects of existence. The soul had forgotten them because almost all of the things of life had lapsed into triviality. But the huge sense of sin remained like a weight which terrified the soul and suddenly rendered the journey hazardous and even convinced the soul that it could not attempt that journey. Consequently, it became fearful; and shuddering back into its wounded body it remained there, hesitant, horrified by the fact that soon the body would die, which meant that there would no longer be a place for itself and that it would have to venture forth on that perilous passage.

Nobody who observed Johnny suspected what mysterious forces were moving and cogitating in him; for only when human eyes see the body's dead husk is its emptiness eloquent of the mysterious powers that have departed forever from it. And only then is the mind compelled to consider the soul whose symbol nowadays is more a dead body than a living quick being. In that dark, windswept place along the street, Johnny was still a living being. And had anyone stopped and considered the plight of that body and recognized who it was, it would have been only to appreciate that he was a criminal sought by the officers of the law.

Thus, he remained until an ancient cab drawn by a thin yet strong old mare drew up at the curb opposite him. The driver slowly draped the reins over the rail before him and got down from his box. He was a tall, thin old man of rakish appearance. A bowler hat was set ajaunt on his head, which was large and balanced neatly on his thin neck, which rose from his shoulders like the wooden neck of a dummy. The rest of his body was clad in an old overcoat, very long and held together by a belt, a muffler, a few buttons and several devices such as hooks and safety pins. He walked stiffly but with a swagger which had a quality of truculence, independence and mischief. He patted the mare's neck and made a single exclamation of affection and then stood nearby on the pavement. He was waiting for four fares who had booked him and arranged with him to meet them at this spot.

His name was James Prescot. For years, he had almost forgotten it. It seemed unfamiliar to him when he signed it on official forms that registered him as a person permitted to drive taxi, carriage, etc., in the public thoroughfares. He signed it slowly, squinting at the paper, pressing his wide lips together, all the time conscious of a sense of impersonation. For James Prescot was the slim youth, the jaunty fellow, the roisterer, the violent Orangeman, hero of the troubled times. And the man whose awkward fingers signed the name had been known for years to the public, to the linen merchants who sometimes hired his taxi in lavish days before the war, to the police with whom he had a black record, as "Gin" Jimmy.

He stood quite still on the pavement. His hands were thrust deeply into the pockets of the overcoat. His eyes were the only part of him that moved. They were small and grey under grey, tufted eyebrows, and they shifted their gaze swiftly from point to point of the roadway, the commercial houses, and the warehouses and turnings opposite him. His head scarcely ever moved. He was like a tall scarecrow, with his overcoat flapping in the high wind.

But soon he took a few steps along the pavement and halted opposite Johnny. He stood with his back to him, and glanced to right and left. A few people passed. Then there was a momentary emptiness in the scene. He knew that it would not last long. Soon, more people would pass. Soon, the patrols of police would reach this spot. He had seen them coming this way only two minutes previously when he had passed them with his cab. He gave another glance to his right, then he spat loudly and strolled to Johnny.

He had seen him. With his keen eyes, he had seen him when he had driven up on his cab. Hardly anything eluded his sharp vision: faces of friends and acquaintances, rivals and enemies; faces of detectives, prostitutes, merchants, lords, ladies, the Lord Mayor, the Prime Minister, Cabinet Ministers, The Moderator, judges, solicitors. He knew them all. He knew the city in its streets and its moods. And he cherished a curious sense of possession over all of it: the streets; the moods and events that made news; the fortunes and lives of its famous figures. He saw much, and he heard much. This evening he had heard of a raid, of a killing, of a man wounded and in flight . . . .

He put a hand on Johnny's shoulder and turned him. And stooping and peering into his face, he chuckled, letting go of

Johnny and saying aloud:

"Look at him now! Take a look at him! Two thousand quids' worth of mischief! Just strollin' round for anybody to pick up! Just about goin' beggin', you would say!"

His wide lips curved in a great grin from one ear to the other. His long, thin nose above them pointed sharply. He sniffed. He heard footsteps, and his keen sense knew that they were those of the police patrols.

In one slow, strong movement he put his arms about Johnny and lifted him as easily as one would lift a light bolster and carried him to the cab. He opened the door and settled him quickly on the seats and closed the door again. Then he stood waiting as before, standing back from his cab and humming a tune.

Two constables approached. They recognized him: the old miscreant; the old drunkard; the eyes and the ears of the city; the old character beloved of famous men, feared by his enemies, always under suspicicion with the police, sometimes their ally, often their opponent. He greeted them.

"Good-night! Cold!"

They nodded curtly. "Good night," one of them murmured.

He turned round. "I am keepin' watch," he whispered hoarsely, "and if I get as much as a wee glimpse of him I'll let you know, boys!"

"That's right," one of them said.

Neither of them stopped their patrol. Jimmy fell into pace beside them.

"A desperate business," he said.

The one nearest him nodded.

"I'm thinkin' he is away out of it by now, you know. Taken away by his friends. Sure, when youse fellows is on the look-out, he would not walk ten steps without being lifted!" Jimmy said.

The constable nearest him grinned under his helmet.

"I suppose, 'Gin,' you have not seen him?"

Jimmy chuckled. "I would not like to mix myself up with the business, you know. If I did, it would be a bullet from his friends, or seven days' hard, or maybe ten years' hard, from youse fellows I would get. Sure, you know me but. A decent Protestant man, loyal. The friend of the police."

The constables grinned and were silent.

"Well, good-night now, boys!" Jimmy said, halting.

They passed on. Now he was afraid and wished that he had not spoken to the police, for he knew what would happen now. Soon, one of them would come strolling back. He would stand well back against the wall, or in the doorway, opposite the cab. He would stand there for hours if he imagined that by doing so he would discover a clue to Johnny's whereabouts. Or he might approach the cab and open its door and peer inside.

Jimmy hurried back to the cab and climbed swiftly to the box. He whipped up the mare and turned the vehicle round and drove it some distance away, where he halted it again. He climbed down and drew from the depths of his garments a silver watch. He examined it, sniffed with satisfaction when he saw that he still had time to keep his appointment with the four fares, and spat.

He waited for five minutes before turning the horse and driving back to the spot at which he was to meet his fares. He approached slowly, letting the mare walk. At last, he halted her. He did not climb down immediately from the box. Instead, he gazed about him, his sharp eyes probing the darkness and seeing various people moving along the pavement. The two constables were not amongst them.

Jimmy got down and threw a rug over the mare's back before going to the cab door. He glanced cautiously around. When he peered inside the cab it was no more than an inconsequent movement, a mere glance. He gazed along the pavement, which was deserted again. Suddenly he got into the cab and closed the door after him and sat down beside Johnny.

"That's that!" he muttered.

He looked at Johnny, whose head was sunken on his chest.

"Now, my boy," he said, tapping Johnny's thigh, "now we'll take and consider what I'll do with you!"

He folded his arms across his chest.

"Now!" he murmured. "The first consideration is the fortune. Two thousand. A nice wee taste of money for Mister James Prescot, after a life of hard work spent in the service of the public. A nice little shop somewhere . . . sweets, cigarettes, matches, ginger beer and a corner in periodicals, and a little 'book' on the quiet. Or . . . or . . ." he went on, cocking his head to one side and spreading a hand, ". . . or an extension of my present profession. Half a dozen carriages, bringin' in, say, three quid a day each in these times. Not bad! Or . . . or a partnership like, with due references from both parties. Very

160

nice! Very nice!"

He chuckled. Turning to Johnny, he said softly:

"Johnny, my boy!'

Johnny groaned.

"Can you hear me, Johnny?" Jimmy said, gently touching his thigh and shaking him.

"Ah, God help you, man!" Jimmy said, shaking his head. "You're not long for the joys of life, either way. I've seen 'em sober, and I've seen 'em so bad with drink taken that they were ready to sleep under the naked sky. And I'm thinkin' you're worse than any livin' mortal. You're lost, my son! The game is finished for you. And it wouldn't be fair on you in your present condition to sell you. And if I did, I know rightly what it would be for Mister James Prescot, coachman in ordinary to the great Belfast public! It would be two thousand quid for informing on you like, and a bullet in me backside or some other vulnerable area of my defences from the members of the Organization. So that's that! But it was nice to indulge the dreams for a wee while, Johnny, man. It was that! Dreamin' is fine, but the real thing is at a price, and maybe you know that yourself. There's a price on everything. Maybe you don't see it at first. But when you turn up the edge of it, there's the wee ticket with the writing on it, or maybe there's no ticket, but the bill comin' in with the letters on the mat. Always the price! So I'll tell you what I'll do, Johnny, boy!"

He got up and opened the cab door and peered out. He waited until the pavement was once more deserted; then, lifting Johnny with the same ease with which he had deposited him in the cab, he brought him out gently. He carried him back to the doorway and stood him there in the same attitude as before.

"There y'are now," he whispered, propping him there. "You've been took for a ride, and maybe I've saved you from the police and put you in the way of gettin' clear. The price is nothin'! Nothin'! Do you hear that? You don't? I'm not mindin', Johnny! The odds is all against you, except 'Gin' Jimmy. So good-bye now, and the best of luck!"

He went back to his cab and removed the rug from the mare's back and climbed to the box. He hummed a tune, and felt happy in his murky soul. He was conscious of having done something good, for nothing. His generosity surprised him more than anything else, and the sense of it glimmered pleasantly for several minutes until his fares arrived. Four young naval officers.

He climbed down and opened the door of the cab and greeted them.

"There y're, gentlemen! The smartest vessel in the city! Captain 'Gin' Jimmy!"

The officers gave him the name of the hotel at which they were dining. Jimmy saluted and closed the door.

He got back to his box and drove off, jamming his bowler hat against the wind, which was rising to stiffer gusts with freezing edges on them. He had not gone more than a quarter of a mile before he overtook an acquaintance.

He was a thin little figure, a mere wisp of a thing in the great ocean of darkness through which the wind surged. But "Gin's" keen sight saw him at that moment when he emerged from a sidestreet and stood at the curb waiting to cross the road. He was holding under his arm a covered bird-cage.

"Gin" Jimmy reined in the mare and hailed him.

"Shell!"

The little man looked up.

"Oh, hullo, Jimmy! Hullo!"

Jimmy glanced cautiously about and then leaned down from the box and cupped one side of his lips with his hand as he said hoarsely:

"Away back a bit! You can't miss it, Shell!"

"Is that a fact, Jimmy?" Shell exclaimed.

"Sure! I've just this minute seen it!"

"Is that so! You're not coddin' me?"

"It's the God's honest truth!" Jimmy said, giving the reins a tug and waving his hand at Shell. The vehicle rolled on, with the mare clopping at an easy pace and Shell staring after it and softly murmuring.

"Aye, it might be, it might be but," he said.

Johnny remained propped in the angle between the wall and the broad door. When he had been in the cab he had tasted ease. Now his body was once again the prey of pain which clawed at him like a beast which had driven its fangs into him. The pain increased whenever he moved, stirring angrily and settling deeper into his body. To escape it, he remained very still.

It became a terrible condition between himself and the thing that had settled upon him so sharply. It was as though the pain were a separate, sentient thing, something fantastic yet actual which held him and was content to remain so, but

162

which became ferocious whenever he moved. He accepted this condition, although in his soul he was afraid. His lips moved and little soft, barely audible whimpers of pain and terror suspired from them.

So he remained quite still, with the wind flapping the overcoat's empty sleeves. His senses that had been roused by his encounter with "Gin" Jimmy tasted the dirt and mucus on his lips and caught the keen odor of the wind and the dust which the wind lifted and flung into this deep corner.

"What is happening to me?" he thought. "What is it all for? I was in a cab . . . ."

He closed his eyes, whereupon the sounds of the city diminished and the darkness of night seemed to cloud his consciousness.

"It is a dream . . ." he whispered. "There were two good women . . . and two men . . . all talking . . . and the fellow taking me into the cab . . . ."

The words made a faint sound, whereupon the monstrous beast of pain was roused. It stirred and sank its fangs deeper into him.

He shuddered. Then he closed his lips tightly and held his breath and was quite motionless until the monster was once again fallen into lethargy. A sly idea took form in his mind.

He drew a slow breath and filled his lungs and then cautiously exhaled and drew another breath. He waited. The beast was only a dull, inert weight upon him. He was encouraged by this slight initial success of his plan. He imagined that the beast had fallen asleep, for only the faintest ripples of pain travelled over his body, and they were subsiding quickly. He waited a little longer before he ventured to lift his right foot and alter the cramped attitude of his body. With much caution he moved the foot slightly and lowered it and transferred the whole weight of his body to it while with the same patience and furtiveness he changed the position of his left leg. His eyes remained closed all the time. The beast did not stir.

Now he was so excited that he bagan to move his right hand. At once he encountered a curious obstruction which he could not overcome or understand. His hand was held fast by something.

He felt despair begin in him. Fear made his heart beat faster. He imagined that the beast detected this and was watching him and waiting in anger and impatience to destroy him as soon as he moved again. To outwit it, he held his breath and remained motionless for several seconds. After that, he attempted again to raise his right hand. As before, he discovered that it was held by something.

He became quite still again, presently repeating his furtive movements. His fingers encountered a strip of material. This was the bandage which Rosie had bound about his left hand. and which had come loose and entangled itself with his right hand. He caught the bandage in the fingers of his right hand and tugged.

The material loosened. He imagined that it was a bond of some kind which had been put upon him. Very slyly, he drew on it until he supposed that it was loose. His right hand was now free of it; but the long bandage trailed loosely from his left hand, where it was held fast by its end which adhered to the wound over which there remained a sodden piece of lint.

But he was satisfied and encouraged. He felt the pulse of the slumbering beast upon him, and he imagined that soon he would completely outwit that beast.

He rested and lapsed into a swift sleep which was actually a coma. When he came to consciousness after two or three minutes, he opened his eyes. The darkness and high wind assailed him and confused him. He remembered only the dreams that had had their passage through his mind. Then he recollected not only that he was attempting to escape from a monstrous beast, but that upon his soul there was the huge weight of a mortal sin. And as he remembered these things, they became a unity which terrified him.

He blinked his crusted eyes and tried to discern his surroundings. He saw the dark corner in which he was standing, with the high wooden door, and the wall and the pavement leading away from the cobbles on which he stood. Then again he began his attempts to elude the beast of pain and sin.

He made strange movements, lifting his feet slowly, high, in turn, moving forward in a ludicrous fashion, his right hand guiding him along the wall of that big commercial building, his eyes closed to exclude the darkness and to permit his mind to concentrate upon its fantastic ideas.

After many minutes, during which he covered about twenty feet, he increased his pace slightly. The beast upon him was a deadly weight which caused him to stagger and stumble. He wondered how he might contrive to escape it altogether.

He moved even faster, discovering a better method of walking. Men and women who passed that weird figure and saw its ludicrous steps laughed explosively, for he seemed to be quite a drunk, with his cap fallen low over his nose and his overcoat buttoned over his arms, and his feet making those high, slow steps and touching the pavement with a slithering, cautious movement.

Some soldiers passing him stopped at a little distance. One of them—a young man of sensitive temperament—went back to him.

"You hurt, chum?" he said.

Johnny stopped. He remained rigid, with his eyes closed and his lips clenched. The young soldier stared at him and saw the terrible pallor of that face, and the trailing bandage blowing in the wind.

"Come on, Harry!" his friends shouted. "Come on! We'll be late!"

"This chap's hurt!" Harry shouted.

"He's tight!" the others retorted.

Harry hesitated. At that moment, Johnny lurched towards him, whereupon a faint taint of whisky came to Harry.

"He's had a drop . . ." he called.

His comrades laughed. "A drop? He's had a bucketful! Come on!"

"You all right, chum? Are you?" Harry asked Johnny.

The voices rose in the darkness.

"Oh, come on, Harry! He's all right. Leave him alone!"

Johnny lurched forward past Harry, who stared after him for an instant before rejoining his friends. His heavy boots clattered loudly on the pavement.

All at once, Johnny halted with his right foot suspended a few inches above the pavement. The echo of those vital voices whirled in his ears. He was confused, afraid, imagining that the beast would re-awaken and destroy him. He resolved to gather his breath in his lungs and mass his strength and make a swift rush from beneath the brute.

He drew the breath and expelled a little of it. Steadying himself with his right hand, he felt the wall and assembled his mind in an impulse. But instead of running, he walked quickly.

He achieved only a futile, shambling gait which, instead of carrying him in a swift burst far out of reach of the beast, had only taken him to a little distance. Nevertheless, he had slipped from beneath its terrible and oppressive bulk and was free. He drew a full breath and tried to run.

He found himself in the center of the pavement, where he collided with a woman. She spun round and gave him an indignant tirade. He stopped. His body swayed and he extended his right arm and slithered helplessly back to the wall. Then he ran on, for the beast had awakened and was pursuing him, and already he could feel its tentacles touching him and scratching him as he sped on. He cried out in a gibber of fear, panting. Summoning his strength, he ran faster, achieving nothing but a lurch, like a man running down a steep incline and taking swift little steps. He felt the beast overtake him and leap upon him to settle its horrible claws deeply into his body and rend him. Still he did not stop. He continued until the weight overpowered his limbs.

He discovered that he had entered a turning and stopped a few feet from the entrance to a large public house. The street was empty, and the doorway with its windows full of bottles of beer and spirits offered him comparative shelter. His eyes closed and he panted to recover his breath. Then for the last time he struggled to escape from the weight of the beast. His hands lifted and he lowered his head and made wild movements, as though he were grappling with a ferocious animal. The bandage on his left hand finally parted from the wound and trailed out on the wind, which soon wrenched it from beneath his overcoat and sent it whirling along the pavement. The pain drove deeply into his body. He closed his eyes. The door of the public house behind him opened and light flooded out. A man and woman came from the bar, drawing back when they saw that figure before them.

He heard voices in what seemed a great tumult, and he spun round to seek safety amongst that company. The man and woman drew aside, the woman edging from proximity to Johnny and hurrying away so quickly that the man had no time to draw the door close behind him.

The door remained wide open. Johnny lurched towards it. He went in. The crib at the end of the bar and next the door was empty, with its door open. His first step took him across the threshold, and his second carried him into the crib. It happened so swiftly that the customers standing in ranks at the bar counter and clamouring for drinks did not notice him. Certainly, in that instant of his advent, he was no more than a dark shadow, unrecognizable, a mere shuffling presence visible at the edge of sight, but arousing no particular attention in that place where his arrival was not an event which stood within the realm of possibility in the minds of the numerous customers.

Extending his hands, he steadied himself at the little table which protruded from the wall between the two benches built against the partitions. He fell heavily on one of the benches, flopping forward at once over the table and remaining thus with his left hand exposed and a trickle of blood glistening on the wound and down the fingers. The wound in his upper arm had also broken open again and was making a fresh stain on his garments. On his body, the beast had driven its sharp talons, which were reaching down to the final source of life.

"I am finished now," he told himself. "The thing is killing me . . . it is . . ."

Then his soul cried out in horror, because the body was dying and the great burden of sin prevented the soul from taking flight across the territory beyond life. It was lost, threatened with extinction.

five

His entry had been so sudden that the customers had not seen or recognized him. But Fencie, the proprietor, standing behind the counter at the far end of the bar, and superintending the barmen and the bar-boys who came from the saloons on the floors above, saw him and recognized him. He saw the door of the bar swing to behind him, and the door of the crib close upon that terrible figure. And it was like the invasion of his life by something fantastic and calamitous.

Fencie was a thick, florid person of fifty-two. All his life as a publican in this quarter of the city near the docks and at the end of numerous small and large streets had been a kind of journey through perils which had arisen only because of the particular course into which he urged all his affairs. He was thoroughly dishonest, a notable scoundrel who sailed close to illegal exploits and then darted through them before he could be caught. But recently, probably because the hue and odor of the place had become rank and somehow reflective of his crimes, he had effected some structural alterations to his premises and had the whole place repainted. Also, he had commissioned an eccentric young artist to paint several frescoes on the walls of the various saloons. Luke Mulquin was the name of this artist. He was known locally as Lukey. During the execution of the commission he had suggested to Fencie that the house should be re-named.

Fencie considered the suggestion seriously. When at last the place was opened again its new name was resplendent above the door, "The Four Winds." And inside, on the walls, were the frescoes painted by Lukey and depicting the four winds, the four seasons of the year, the four quarters of the globe. A new class of customer began to frequent the house: artists, poets, writers, journalists, politicians. They sat in the cribs in the big bar or upstairs in the lounges, rendering a leaven of respectability and quaintness to the noisy, garish air of the place in which several famous ladies of the town and their consorts of touts, idle racing fans, loungers and old men had formerly dominated. Fencie was delighted. He was reformed. He had emerged from a long period of vice and crime and could look forward to a successful old age.

Now, suddenly, a terrible misfortune lodged itself in his affairs. Standing motionlessly and watching the door behind which Johnny was seated, he flushed a deeper red and then turned pale. Big pink blotches showed on the muddy pallor of his skin. His hands trembled. One of the barmen—a tall, sour-faced man of thirty—who had seen Johnny come in, stood in an arrested attitude and looked helplessly at Fencie, waiting for instructions.

"Leave him be," Fencie muttered.

The barman looked surprised. For several seconds he seemed unable to comprehend Fencie's words. He stared at the boss, and then at the crib near the door, and finally at the other barmen. They were drawing drinks, giving change, exchanging greetings with the regular patrons. But all of them had seen that terrible figure enter the bar and lurch into the crib. And two of them had recognized him.

"Who is he?" one of them asked another, as they came together at the till.

Fencie was watching them closely now. A bell rang. The indicator above the cribs showed a red number.

"Number seven!" Fencie roared.

He came along the counter.

"It is Johnny!" whispered the barman to his colleague.

"God help us!" the other whispered in terror.

And all at once there seemed to be a great rush of orders. The pot-boys clattered from the lounges upstairs and shouted for pints, for glasses, for half-ones, for bottles, slamming money on the wet counter beside the pile of trays. All was bustle and clamor, behind which Fencie strutted roaring orders, greeting customers, watching the crib near the door, and seeing the barmen whispering together as the news travelled amongst them that it was Johnny, it was, away at the top there in number one.

Fencie watched that crib with especial interest, wondering what Johnny would do, what dreadful scenes would occur before the bar closed. His heart boomed in his breast and filled his arteries with a furious pulse. He breathed loudly and painfully. Terror deluged his mind, and despair filled his heart. The night was early yet, and before him the hours stretched like a protracted agony which he must endure. More customers entered the place, hovering outside the first crib and even putting their hands on the door and pushing it open a little way and then going off to another crib along the bar. As they passed Fencie they shouted a greeting to him.

He tried to smile. His lips wavered. His big bulbous nose appeared to jut more prominently than ever from the bulk of his face. His grey eyes, small and sharp and set closely under thick brows above which his forehead curved and his grey hair rose in a stiff bush, had a curious, wild expression.

"Hullo, hullo!" he exclaimed abruptly. "How are you?"

"It's queer and cold the night, Larry!" the customers exclaimed.

"Aye, you're right," he said from habit.

His nervous thoughts took the words and considered them. Queer and cold. He had heard them so often that they had no particular meaning for him until this moment, when they had a ghastly aptitude. He trembled. More customers entered, whereupon he turned anxiously towards the door. They came laughing and shouting along the bar. Again, greetings were exchanged and orders given. Now the big bar was rapidly filling. Upstairs, the lounges were packed with customers. Soon, from floor to topmost lounge, the place would be crammed with a crowd of customers. Bells would ring. The cribs would be full of noisy men. Other customers would line the counter and lean against the crib doors. The pot-boys would come clattering down the stairs and stand shouting at the service flap. The barmen working the cribs would push their way to and from the counter and roar orders. The till would clang. Trays loaded with bottles and glasses would be

169

lifted from the counter and taken to the customers upstairs and in the cribs. Change would have to be given rapidly while other orders were shouted and memorized.

"Four pints, one Scotch!"

"Two by the neck! Three glasses!"

"Five and nine off!"

"Number six!"

And Fencie knew that he would have to be attentive to it all, to urge and maintain it, to keep order, to keep his eyes and ears open, to greet old customers and welcome new ones. His spirit flagged when he contemplated the effort which, at other times, was a normal feature of his day's work and which pleased him. Now he would have to watch the first crib and be prepared for all manner of possibilities: the arrival of the police; fights, a riot, shooting; perhaps worse. He sighed. Drops of perspiration formed on his forehead and trickled into the furrows. He asked himself what he could do to prevent a row, a disaster, his ruin, the loss of custom.

First of all, he felt inclined to go unobtrusively to that crib and lift its occupant to his feet and run him out so swiftly that nobody would have time to recognize Johnny. But he rejected this idea, fearing that some sharp-sighted fellow amongst the company in the bar would recognize Johnny and either give the alarm to the men around him, or else slip out and inform the police. Next, Fencie considered leaving Johnny undisturbed in the crib until closing time. Yet, although that seemed the only course remaining to him, he began to worry about all sorts of possibilities that might arise. He feared Johnny. And he feared his customers, who might discover that wretched fugitive, and the police who might accuse him of harboring him, and the Organization who might imagine that he had held Johnny only to hand him over to the police and reap the reward.

He groaned inwardly and lamented his misfortune that had planted the fugitive on him. His expression deepened and became a glare of pain and anxiety which customers observed. They began to tease him, asking him what had put him out, what was on his mind, what was getting at him. He grinned and said the weather would cut the heart out of you, and he had a touch of lumbago from the cold, don't you know, all down the back.

But he heard them. They were discussing events in the city this evening. The raid; the shooting and killing; the shooting of members of the Organization; the killing and shooting and activity all over the city; and the anger and hatred and rancor; and the cordons everywhere; and Johnny still free. And he saw the barmen with their heads together at the till and at the big casks of porter along the counter. He guessed what they were saying.

"Who is he?"

"Did you not see? It's Johnny!"

"Holy God!"

"There is going to be trouble!"

"Shooting!"

"I am getting out of here. . . ."

"You're right! I am going, too! Shooting. . . ."

"There will be a riot when they see him!"

"They will tear this place to pieces!"

"I am getting out!"

Mistakes were made in the orders and in the giving of change. There was nervousness everywhere. It came like a subtle tide which flowed from the loud talk along the counter and seeped behind to where the barmen worked. It was angry, violent, revengeful. It created a fracture which Fencie could not repair, although he hurried along the bar and exhorted his employees.

"My God, Mr. Fencie, sir," one of the nervous barmen murmured to him, "would you not think of putting him out before there is trouble!"

Fencie glared at the man. "What? Eh? What's that?"

"There will be shooting . . . they will wreck this place if they find him sitting here! Just listen to them, Mr. Fencie! My God, sir, they would kill him! And . . . for goodness sake, Mr. Fencie . . ."

"I am attending to everything here," Fencie said, sharply.

He shouted an order. His loud voice cut through the vociferous roar of conversation, laughter, and shouting. His thick body was at one end of the counter one moment and at the till the next. Presently the barmen saw him draw a double whisky. They murmured together.

"Fortifyin' himself against the wrath to come!"

"Maybe he will give us ones a drop each!"

"Sure, it's us that'll take the knocks when the trouble starts! It'll be the bottles and the bullets for us!"

"Go you and ask him then!"

"Look at him!"

Fencie put the little glass on a tray and carried it to the crib near the door.

The barman exchanged rapid glances as he went in and drew the door fast behind him.

"I heard a fellah . . ." one of them whispered to the others, ". . . a fellah was sayin' there is dozens shot . . . dozens of police . . . in a big battle with the Organization!"

"Is that a fact?"

"And hundreds of members of the Organization killed and arrested. A big sweep. Another fellah was sayin' they have called out the whole police force and put cordons everywhere."

"And himself sittin' over there!"

"My God, keep your mouth shut, Billy!"

"Aye, don't be lettin' on . . ."

All were afraid. They kept glancing nervously at the crib into which Fencie had gone.

six

As soon as Fencie was inside, he closed the door quickly and set down the tray on the table. The partition dividing the crib from the adjoining one was so high that only a very tall man could look over. And the din of voices in the bar was so loud that nothing which Fencie intended to utter would be audible beyond the confines of the crib.

His first glance at Johnny convinced him that it would be futile to expect that appalling being to understand him. Johnny was sprawled across the narrow table. His cap had tipped back on his head and lay over the back of his skull. The button of the overcoat had ripped off, leaving the arms exposed as well as the broad stains of blood across the breast and down the sleeves of the jacket. The left arm lay across the table. Fencie leaned a little to one side and saw the raw hand.

He drew back involuntarily, and for an instant his cruel nature was softened by the sight of that bedraggled, hunted man lost from all the violent, combative purposes of the Organization, and now nothing more than a doomed, wounded thing seeking any haven, a mere rag of humanity impelled by the last errant currents of life in him. Next moment, all the sly features of his own character urged Fencie: caution, fear, an implacable selfishness and mercilessness. He put out his huge hand and shook Johnny by the shoulder.

A groan escaped that figure lying over the table. Fencie heard it. It was only a sign to his hard nature that there was life in Johnny.

"Come on, now!" he said, lowering his voice and thrusting his head towards Johnny. "You are in your senses, right enough! Listen! Listen, do you hear?"

He sat down beside him and dragged the limp body upright and leaned it against the wooden partition. Then he saw the big, bright drops of blood on the table and gleaming on the garments. He became silent and horrified. The blood was life—rich, vivid, the precious liquid of the body—all trickling from the flesh and foretelling the death of the body.

"Dear help us," he murmured, "you're in a desperate state! You're not long for this world, I'm thinking!"

And again, something in his harsh nature was supplicated by the awful condition of the man before him. He saw Johnny as someone brought by Fate to him. For an instant, he felt as though this were an opportunity for him to display a little charity and kindliness. But at the touch of that gentle sentiment on his brutal heart, everything of his nature retreated. He shook his head. There was no sense in being soft! There was nothing to be gained by helping this wretch!

His own circumstances came into first place, and he frowned as he shook the limp body and saw the eyelids open tremulously and then close once more.

"Listen here, now! Listen. I'm telling you. . . I'm telling you straight, you're not going to sleep here! Pull yourself out of that sleep! Wake up! D'you hear? Come on, now! Get a hold of this!"

He gave Johnny a nudge with his big fist and then lifted the glass of whisky. He put it in the right hand whose fingers closed at once upon it. Lifting the hand, he conveyed the glass to the pallid lips.

Nothing happened. Johnny's hand was lifeless. Fencie lowered it to the table. He went red with fear and impatience. Clutching the glass, he thrust it against the lips, tilted back the head and poured the whisky into the mouth.

"Swallow it!" he said, sharply, putting aside the glass and rubbing the throat. "Get it inside of you!"

It dribbled out down the chin and shone its drops over the waistcoat and the dirty overcoat.

"Oh, blast you!" Fencie grumbled. "Lettin' it go to waste like that!"

He drew away and pursed his lips and stared helplessly at Johnny. He lifted the cap and put it on the head with a single quick movement. Again, he nudged and shook the limp body. The eyelids trembled, and this time they lifted wide over the eyes. But the eyes were dim, with the pupils almost invisible in their tiny points beneath a great wash of delirium. Dried mucus and dirt rimed the eyes and clung to the lashes and had gathered in tiny white clots in the corners of the eyes. Life had ebbed from the face, and only a fleeting ripple of vitality touched that void countenance.

Fencie sighed and got up. He propped the body in the corner, bringing down the peak of the cap like a visor hiding the eyes. He folded the overcoat callously over the raw hand. From the floor he lifted an empty cigarette carton and folded it into a thick wedge. When, a moment later, he came from the crib and drew the door close behind him, he inserted the wedge deftly between the door and its lintel. It acted as a lock. After that, he had only one fear: that the police or the members of the Organization would trace that forlorn man to "The Four Winds."

He returned to his place behind the counter. The barmen watched him, wondering what he had said to Johnny and what he proposed to do with him.

"God help us," they murmured, whenever they came together at the till or the big casks, "he is just lettin' him sit there! It's askin' for murder! There is going to be trouble, right enough!"

"He has lost his nerve. Look at him!"

Fencie had gone round the counter amongst the customers. He was standing near the door of the first crib at which he kept glancing as though he expected its occupant to appear suddenly at the door. And although he was laughing and conversing with several old patrons, it was plain to the barmen that he was nervous and apprehensive.

"Maybe he is after the big reward," one of them suggested.

"I wouldn't put it past him," the other whispered. "He would think of money first of all."

"It's desperate," another said, drawing change from the till. "There will be a battle here, pretty soon!"

"Number nine!" Fencie yelled, coming along the counter and taking a tray. Presently he appeared behind the counter.

"He is all right in there," he murmured to the senior barman. "When we close I will put him out."

The barman was a slow, dour man in middle-age.

"Maybe there will be bullets and bottles before that," he said. "Let three or four of us run him out before there is murder."

"Oh, leave him," Fencie said. "He is half-dead. Let him sit quiet there. Then I will put him out."

The barman gave him a cynical grin before he turned away to serve a customer.

seven

In a large untidy room of an old house on the opposite side of the river, Shell sat before the fire with his cage on his knees and his arms encircling it. Behind him a sombre man of about twenty-eight, who was dressed in flannel trousers, a tweed jacket, and red shirt, was cleaning a clutch of artist's brushes and wiping them in a rag dipped in turpentine.

The room was lofty. From the ceiling there hung an old gas-fitting long since disused and broken, and now discolored with dust and verdigris. A length of thick string twisted around it supported the flex leading from a point on the picture rail above an electric plug and brought over to hang from the old gas pipe. At the end of the flex there was a powerful, screened bulb which shed a trumpet of light upon the objects beneath. Beyond that area of light, the rest of the room showed dimly: the couch against the far wall, and the lumpish mass of bedding on the couch; the walls hung with strange paintings of heads; the easels and mirrors; the small tables littered with jam-pots holding brushes; the trays containing tubes of paint; the tattered pieces of rugs and carpets; the chipped and stained crockery and cheap cutlery; the books stacked against the wall and in home-made bookshelves. And vivid pieces of drapery thrown over the old chairs or lying about the floor amidst boots and shoes and garments and old newspapers. And on the vacant chair opposite him, the evening newspaper at which Shell pointed.

"Lukey," he said, "is there anything about him? Does it say?"

"Ah, quit bletherin' about him!" Lukey exclaimed, frowning as he flung down the rag and stuck the brushes into an empty vase.

"Sure, it's a very natural question," Shell whined.

"It is not a question!" Lukey retorted. "You know damn fine there is news of him in the paper. But you just want to blether about him . . . ."

"I have great sympathy for him," Shell protested.

Lukey faced him. "Then . . . well, then, quit talking about him and asking whether he is found yet!"

His voice was loud. It vibrated in the room. And his lean, strong body seemed to send it forth as though from some tense source in his spirit that was rendered strangely restless and disquieted by the news which was flying about the city from mouth to mouth.

"But it is on my mind, Lukey!" Shell complained.

"Let it stay there and don't talk about it!" Lukey shouted angrily. "Or else clear out and leave me alone!"

He sat down heavily in the old, sagging armchair opposite Shell. Thereabouts, the flames of the fire made a ruddy radiance which threw the shadows of the men against the ceiling in grotesque shapes that loomed over them and stirred with fantastic movements at their least change of attitude. Lukey sat with his thighs spread and his hands resting on them. The frayed sleeves of his jacket had shrunk, leaving exposed his strong, flowing wrists that terminated in lithe hands that were suggestive of his curious temperament and the peculiar ideas which often massed themselves in a formidable, straining intensity in his mind. He stared at the fire which was burning the dried logs of wood which he had recently thrown upon it. The flames leaped and crackled, transmuting the wood into peculiar shapes that composed the red heart of the mass. Ideas grew in his turgid mind as he watched the process. Fire, heat, a consuming and changing into smaller and different shapes.

"He is away for good and all now, I am thinking, Lukey," Shell whined. "He took and died on me," he added, pointing to the empty cage.

"It was your own fault," Lukey mumbled. "Fussing with the thing . . . ."

"Sure, I thought I could do a bit of good to him," Shell

said, sighing.

"The thing was all right where it was, in the corner of the cage."

"Aye, but he was dying, and when a wee budgy is in that state you want to be doing something to help it like."

"Well, it is dead now, and so there is no point in yammering about it now," Lukey said. Then again he stared at the fire.

Interesting visions grew in the flames. He saw a face moulded by the red core thrust itself forward and mouth words before it was swallowed into the confused mass of shapes. Almost instantly another countenance formed, an urgent thing, with taut lips behind which terrible secrets pressed. The lips struggled to restrain the words. The dark eyes flashed in agony for an instant before the flames obliterated the face. Other forms arose, faces of agony, of hope and desire, of joy and passion, of evil. All of them looked at Lukey and spoke to him in words which were soundless but which his sensitive spirit understood. And he laughed swiftly, imagining that he was listening to the tale of the great journey through time and space which human beings call life.

Shell watched him and saw his handsome face brimming with happiness and wonder.

"Oh, you are away in the head!" he exclaimed. "You are nuts, so you are! Crackers, bats!"

"What? What's this you are saying?" Lukey asked, turning to him.

"I am thinking, you know . . ." Shell began, and he pointed again to the newspaper which Lukey had thrown to the floor when he sat down.

"Go and listen to your budgies!" Lukey said.

He looked at the fire and forgot Shell's presence, for at that moment more faces assembled in the flames and burning embers, crowds of them, an urgent multitude pressing forward to peer at him and laugh, and jeer, and shout at him in soundless warning, or to regard him with pity. Wonderful faces full of mystery and dreams and knowledge. Men and women, and amongst the latter, at the fringe of the foremost faces, one gentle grave spirit, persistent, disturbing, who watched him with soft eyes in her proud, subtle face until she, too, disappeared in the inferno which had created her. A log sank deeply into the red heart of the fire, whereupon all the faces were obliterated without any of them having imparted their secret.

"Lukey!" Shell was whispering, and his shadow on the ceiling moved slyly towards that of the artist whose own shadow was proud and detached and motionless.

"Lukey, I had a bit of advice given me about the bird."

"Blast you and your budgies!" Lukey said, flinging himself back in his chair and folding his hands behind his head.

"I told him I could sell the bird for a couple of thousand quid, you know," Shell said. And now he lifted his mean little face in all its terrible cunning and its miserable evidence of his hunger for existence. Seeing it, Lukey saw the glimmer of its tiny soul which existed upon the awful scraps of life which Shell contrived to gain for himself. Small and evil and wronged by other souls that collided with it and thrust it aside, it had found its place in this wretched clay amidst the violent concourse of humanity making its passage across time. And that seemed good and even a little beautiful to Lukey, who smiled pensively.

The smile came slowly to his features, and it pleased Shell, who imagined that it was a retort to what he had said. He saw Lukey's broad, white brow with the raven hair framing it, and the expressive eyes alight with vitality and dreams, and the long, sensitive nose over lips that were mobile and fashioned by the words that sometimes poured from them. And he thought that this man Lukey was a fine fellow, sometimes terrible in his fits of anger and frustration, sometimes vicious from that frustration, but often generous and oddly gentle, and sometimes silent and dismayed as though he knew what thoughts and evil projects were shaping in the minds of other people.

"And I told him I could find the bird. And there was a grand young lady there, and she was after the bird, too. So I held my ground like, and the old fellow agrees that the best thing would be for me to bring him along till him," Shell said.

Lukey was not attentive to the words. He saw Shell and he considered him, thinking that soon he would begin another portrait of him which would be more penetrative, more profound than the shallow sketch of him which he had completed recently.

"So that's how the business stands at present," Shell continued. "After what 'Gin' Jimmy told me . . ."

He waited for a retort from Lukey, not daring to venture into this project until he had mentioned it to him. But Lukey Malquin was not listening. He saw the mouth making

178

movements, and the eyes reflecting the weight and mood of thoughts, and he considered the peculiar processes of thought which emerged in the audible sounds of words. He believed that thoughts sprang from something which was more subtle than the mind, more sensitive; for the mind was merely the instrument across which the five strings of the senses were stretched. And with only five inadequate strings, little of the immense music of life and space could be expressed. But the soul which created the profound movements of thought was as comprehensive as a great orchestra. It was more interesting than the body, which was only the medium whereby it had existence.

Considering the soul, he wondered what was its purpose, its source, its final goal. Such questions were often in his mind, and he developed them avidly with all the energy of will which he could concentrate. But from this point his thoughts moved to consider the predicament of one soul in particular; and, as before, he became uneasy and tense and even afraid, because the vision of that soul in its suffering was so vivid in his mind.

"And so I told him I would do my best," Shell continued. "He said I was to bring him back to him when I had sort of perked him up a bit. But that's not all of it, Lukey. I know where I can set hands on him. The thing is to sort of deliver him to the old fellow. And I'm thinkin', Lukey, I'm sort of wondering . . ."

Lukey emerged from his thoughts.

"What's this? What are you talking about?" he demanded.

His face assumed a frown. Something of the sense of all Shell's chatter had reached him.

"I'm telling you, Lukey," Shell said timidly, watching the effect of his words on the other. "I know where he is sittin' at this moment, and I know where I can take him." Then he nodded his head and winked; and removing his hands from the cage he held out a cupped palm and made the motion of trickling money into it.

"Hundreds!" he whispered hoarsely. He chuckled. "Hundreds, Lukey!"

"Do you mean to tell me . . ." Lukey exclaimed, rising.

He stood over him. "Where have you been?" he demanded.

"Sure, I only took and went to old Father Tom!" Shell said.

"What for?" Lukey said.

He took hold of the lapels of Shell's jacket and half lifted that cringing being from the chair.

"What for, I am asking you?" he shouted, shaking him.

"Sure ... sure, now, Lukey, listen, man dear!" Shell exclaimed tremulously.

"You wee sneakin' rat, you!" Lukey shouted.

"Listen, listen, Lukey!" Shell whined. "Sure, there was no harm in it but! Sure, there's hundreds of police out after him to get a hold of him to put him up for trial and the gallows. Sure, when the way is clear to lift him out of such troubles and hand him over to the hand of mercy ..."

Lukey dragged Shell from the chair and rushed him towards the door. There, the two of them panted and scuffled. Shell kept whining in a high-pitched voice, while his hands grabbed at chairs which toppled to the floor as Lukey dragged him away, and at easels that swung with him, and finally at the lintels of the door itself.

"Lukey, listen! Listen while I tell you, Lukey! There's great money in it! There's hundreds. Me and you and Tober could live decent like for years ..."

"You rotten little sneak! You dirty wee rat!"

"Listen, but! I was askin' old Father Tom ..."

"Selling a human being!"

"Aye, but he goes to the right buyer!"

Shell broke free and he whimpered the remark. Lukey backed against the door for an instant and then made a swift rush at him, cornering him and seizing him by the arms.

"How much did the old priest promise you?" he asked.

"Sure, there was no exact figure mentioned, Lukey!"

There was the sound of a blow. Shell cried out.

"How much?" Lukey said loudly.

"Lukey, there was no figure named. The old fellah sort of left it open, sort of hinted there was something good in the way of a reward ...."

"What sort of reward?" Lukey demanded inexorably.

"Sure, it was what them old fellahs give for rewards!"

"What?" Lukey persisted.

Shell groaned. "Lukey, he held out no promises, but says something about faith. A great mystery he will sort of explain ...."

Again Lukey hustled him towards the door.

"You damned wee liar, you! I am going to hit you, Shell ... for trying to sell a fellow who is on the run!"

"Listen, Lukey," Shell panted. "Father Tom will likely

hand him back to the Organization. And the young lady . . ."

"I am going to knock hell out of you, Shell!" Lukey said again, pushing him towards the door.

"Don't, Lukey! Let me go! Sure, I know where poor Johnny is at this moment! Let me just whisk him over to old Father Tom's now . . . ."

Lukey held Shell with his left hand, very firmly. With the other he threatened him.

"I am going to hit you hard, unless . . ."

"Unless what?" Shell whispered.

Lukey's arm drew back slowly. Shell flinched, watching it with blinking eyes.

"You are not to take him to Father Tom's," Lukey said, speaking slowly and in a level tone. "You are not to sell him like that. You are to get hold of him and bring him to me, here, and let me have him for two hours to make a study of him. Two or three hours. Do you hear me?"

"Do you mean . . ." Shell exclaimed.

"You heard," Lukey said. "I want him here, to paint a portrait of him."

Shell looked into the dark, vital eyes. He gasped.

"Lukey, that's a desperate thing you're askin' me to do!"

"I want him," Lukey said. "He is the man I must paint. Bring him here, and afterwards you can take him to the old fellow."

Shell watched the arm poised to strike him.

"I don't rightly know, Lukey . . ."

"You are to bring him here, to me, and let me make a portrait of him . . . ."

"Ah, now, Lukey," Shell said, "you know it would take you ten or twenty hours maybe to make a picture of him. So how would you do the job in two or three hours?"

"It will be just the head," Lukey said. "It will be something in his eyes . . . in two hours I will have time enough to find it and paint it . . . ."

"Lukey, I don't know . . . I don't . . ."

"Then I will just knock hell out of you, Shell, and lock you in your room," Lukey said. A menacing look grew on his face. His arm was flexed, ready to strike.

"Lukey, let go of me while I think!"

"Yes or no?"

"I sort of want to think over my plans for gettin' him here," Shell said.

"I'm asking you: yes or no?"

Shell sighed. "It s yes, Lukey," he said.

Lukey released him and pushed him towards the center of the room and advanced towards him.

"You have promised, Shell. Don't forget that. If you don't bring him here within the half-hour, I will hit you when I see you again. I will hit you hard, where it will hurt you, because you are a dirty little rat, sneaking about looking for crumbs to steal and rewards and things like that. But if you bring him to me, you will be doing the only good thing you have ever done or are likely to do. Then I will think you are not such a bad wee fellow after all."

Shell sat down on the arm of a chair and appeared to be pondering what Lukey had said. He lifted the bird-cage from the floor and nursed it on his knees. Lukey crossed to the fireplace and sat down.

"Ah, you know . . ." Shell murmured, rising and walking about the room with his head hanging pensively. "You know, Lukey, it'll be difficult . . . ."

He walked to and fro, slyly drawing nearer to the door. At last he made a little rush, grasping the handle and wrenching open the door. He stumbled in his haste, scrambling to his feet again and casting a fearful backward glance at Lukey, who had risen and rushed in pursuit of him. Shell's intention not to bring Johnny to the house was obvious in the way in which he had tried to bolt from the room. Now it became even clearer as he tried to draw the door fast behind him.

Suddenly, he let go. Lukey, who had hold of the handle, stumbled backwards. Shell sped on through the wide, dark hall. By the time Lukey had recovered himself and rushed after him, Shell was drawing the house door behind him. His sharp voice lifted in a shout of defiance.

"I am not taking rists for the fun of putting up models for you, Lukey! And you needn't be thinkin' I am that kind of fool!"

Lukey followed him in a spurt of speed, but the door slammed. He knew that by the time he opened it Shell's rapid little body would have disappeared in the darkness.

He returned to the big studio and sat down before the fire. Again, he watched the flames, but the heart of the fire no longer offered spectres and fantastic visions to him. Instead, all was flame through which an occasional ember collapsed and was soon disintegrated. Lukey's glance wandered to his easel, where the portrait at which he had been working earlier in the day was hanging. He got up and approached it and stared critically at it. A single glance at it convinced him that the face of the model—a young, dark-haired woman from the locality—held tides and secrets in its depths which his urgent, yearning talent had not been able to express on the canvas. He had seen so much in that subtle, living tissue; yet the face depicted on the canvas was a void, a mere shape empty of the light and flowing reflection of thought and mood and character which so filled the original. He turned away in an attitude of doubt and frustration, moving aimlessly about the studio, touching the brushes in the pots, the tubes of paint in the trays, the litter and disorder of things everywhere.

The fire had lost its flames. The logs were almost consumed, merged into a red mass. And in his mind where all day there had been the heat and flame of creative fancy, there was now only darkness and a mist where everything of his impetuous ideas had expired under the cold rain of doubt. And in his heart there rose the dread, familiar fear of failure and want and personal shame. He sat down before the fire and yawned.

He was twenty-eight. He had been a laborer, a ship's fireman, an assistant in a grocery store, a barman, a waiter. Since his fifteenth year he had been an orphan, living first of all with friends who were almost as poor as himself, and then in the slums of the city, in cheap lodgings, in sordid rooms and appalling shakedowns in corners. It was a curious, wayward existence, led amongst acquaintances who were of the same heedless temperament as himself. Yet through it all there was a thread of his fate which gave him individuality. He was like a rare flame amongst those other beings. He had acute sensibilities, a sensitive and alert mind. He saw and heard, tasted, touched, caught delicate odors of beauty and grace and liveliness, and was informed by experience. He formed his own beliefs which grew and developed in him like a vision of life which was new and not yet related. Then he longed to express those beliefs and all the amazing patterns of thought that fashioned them, and all the wonderful, individual threads that composed the whole vision of life. He had some slight talent for drawing. Now at last he began to extend it. He bought paints and materials. He saved a little money and gave up his work as a laborer.

Since his twenty-third year he had lived the life of an artist in the lower rooms of a house in which his two friends, Tober and Shell, shared existence.

He painted portraits of men and women: heads, which the models could scarcely recognize, which they frowned at, which aroused guffaws of laughter.

He became notorious in the locality. Artists came to see his work. They saw the walls covered with startling portraits of men and women of various ages. They hardly knew what to say, for their own talent was so gracefully composed in their minds that they could not understand the disorder and crudeness of this young man's genius, which seemed to them to rush at their senses like a yelling thing, violent, terrible with power, awful with its vision of life, insurgent, mocking, intractable. They themselves painted charming landscapes in which the sun was always shining and in which no such thing as a lowering mist or vexed sea was ever allowed to show. They loved life and all its color and change; but this idea of life horrified them. They could not accept it. Moreover, in answer to Lukey's modest questions, they confessed that they doubted if the public would ever become interested in such work. They purchased for a few pounds each some of his better and more formal canvases. Then they went away. They were perturbed. They recognized that this man was a genius, was gifted. Yet there was no place for him amongst themselves or in the city. And they wondered why Griffin had so much encouraged Lukey.

Griffin was a man of Lukey's age. He was employed as a senior assistant in a local firm of antique dealers. Tall, thin, and of an incisive temperament, humorous, kindly, he was an established authority not only on painting, but on literature, the drama, religion, politics, and many other diversions by which the public sought an outlet for energies which were hemmed in by the sea which divides them from England and by their temperament which separates them from the outer world. There was hardly a platform which he could prevent himself from taking, and from all of them he theorized in a robust, crisp fashion. There was scarcely a stranger to the city who, coming to the North for information regarding its history, literature, drama, painting, politics, commerce, hopes, was not swiftly and adroitly contacted by Griffin and as swiftly loaded with facts. And, similarly, when a new artist or novelist, poet, politician, playwright, appeared from amongst the population, Griffin was there to study him from some vantage point and thereafter applaud him or dismiss him in a few theorizing remarks.

In that way he had encountered Lukey Mulquin. It did not occur to Griffin that, in the past, he had sometimes exalted fools or made little mistakes regarding men of talent. What mattered to him was the fact that he had to safeguard certain principles and defend the gateways of art from charlatans. Face to face with Lukey, he knew that at last he had encountered a genius. He examined his pictures closely, studying them to discover their form, their style and subject, putting his face close to them and dissecting them stroke by stroke. They were original in every sense of the word, and their effect on him was to disclose the chaotic world in which Lukey's spirit had its source and from which his frantic ideas poured.

In order to compose that world and afford the unregulated ideas a better chance of expression, he lent Lukey books, bought his pictures, introduced him to writers and other artists, lent him money, and gave him much encouragement. Something like a dawn began for Lukey from this friendship. He became ambitious, impetuous, convinced of his destiny, satisfied with himself. A month passed. His bright dawn made no difference to his material prospects, for he was as poor as ever. He sold very few pictures. And when he took several canvases to dealers he was greeted with abrupt refusals.

One morning he appeared at Griffin's office.

"Mr. Griffin," he said, hurrying into the room and leaning across the desk with his hands resting on the edge, "there is something wrong!"

"Is there?" Griffin said, leaning back in his chair and bursting into laughter.

He had a very keen sense of humor which gave a saving proportion to all his own enthusiasms.

"It's no laughing matter!" Lukey exclaimed angrily.

"I suppose you have come to tell me that you are not selling any pictures," Griffin said.

"Mr. Griffin, everybody laughs at them," Lukey said.

He related a long story: somebody had told him that the other artists said that his work was crude, false, without depth; he had no money; he was losing hope.

"Now, listen, Lukey!" Griffin said, rising and coming round and sitting on the edge of the desk. "I have told you this before: your function in life is not to make a fortune from the sales of your pictures, or to live a life of extreme comfort. You have never had much money, and so you would not know what to do with a lot of it. You would go drinking and philandering and ruin your life as an artist. So forget about such idiotic things as success. Just continue to paint in your own way. Nothing else must matter to you. You must find all your happiness and all your hope in developing your ideas."

"But how am I to live?" Lukey said. "I need some money!"

Griffin made an angry gesture. "Don't bother yourself with such things! Concern yourself with work!"

"What is the good if the things don't sell?"

"The good is that you are creating something!" Griffin shouted.

"It is a dog's life," Lukey grumbled.

"That's a lie!" Griffin said. "You know you are happy when you are working . . . ."

"Yes, but afterwards . . . my God, what is to happen to me? I am not thirty. Suppose I live to seventy and have no money and . . ."

"Stop talking like that!" Griffin said. "Your job is to create a body of work from your own ideas. Go back to your easel and do some work. And don't come here talking like a shopkeeper or thinking whether you are a success or not. There is no such thing as success for people like you . . . ."

"When are you going to arrange an exhibition for me?" Lukey said.

Griffin laughed. "Oh, maybe next year, or perhaps in ten years' time, when your work is mature! Say, when you are able to discern more and express what you see . . . ."

"God help us!" Lukey sighed.

Whichever way he turned there was Griffin waving him back to his easel. He obeyed him. Lukey knew what he wished to express in his work, but the result seldom satisfied him; or if it did, it soon seemed to lose its initial brilliance and to dwindle away into mediocrity. Then he doubted himself and his delicate talent and all his ideas. And no sooner had he admitted these doubts and misgivings than his work appeared futile and without anything of the subtlety which he imagined he had expressed in it, and which it seemed to have when his mind was full of confidence.

Doubts were the great enemies of his existence and his work as an artist. They appeared to him to stand in mighty ranks on the fringe of all his beliefs, waiting to advance and utterly destroy everything by which he lived. Then he was afraid, for his beliefs were nowhere else existent. They were his, having their source in him, so that if they were destroyed he would never again be able to live by them.

"There is no such thing as a soul," the doubts said. "It cannot be proved that there is anything in the body but the processes of life. All reason is from the mind, which is the seat of nerves that convey impressions of the external things. And the brain is active only because of the blood which circulates through it and gives it heat. The mind is complex and subtle, and often profound and beautiful; but it does not contain the soul. The soul is said to be immortal. Therefore, how can it be of the body, which is mortal?"

Lukey admitted these doubts as he stared at his most recent work. He saw the head of a young girl who lived in a nearby street. She was quick, vital, brimming with impulses. And he discerned in her something more than the expression of that vitality and its impulses. His own quick sensitivity was attentive to the lively yet inaudible pulses and stirrings of exquisite emotions and desires which were the source of all the life of her young body at that time.

"It is her soul in her," he thought. "It is older than her body, and her senses know it and wish to discover everything about it. She is in a hurry to taste everything."

He wanted to express those desires that gave brilliance and harmony to her attitudes and expressions. He imagined that he heard and saw the soul in her as it bloomed and assumed color and form in all the joy of existence. But he could not understand why it was that despite his belief in what he experienced, he achieved so little of the expression of those experiences. He imagined that his failure was because he required a more profound encounter than any which he had yet had. He had sought it by painting the evil, the merciless, the fanatics, people like Shell and Tober and young prostitutes, and others: vagrants; lost souls; the pessimists and optimists. But they clung to life, to habits which obscured the soul.

Returning to the fireplace, he saw the evening newspaper lying beside the chair. It told of a man who had killed another and who was wounded and in flight from the police. His imagination revolved around that news. Then again, as he had done since the late afternoon, he saw with eyes of that fugitive, and heard with his ears, and touched with his hands,

187

and tasted the harsh odors of the city. And he knew that were he to encounter that man he would discover at last the full light, the great mystery which he sought.

He remained at the fire for several minutes. He was restless and disturbed. Presently he replenished the fire. Then, yawning and stretching his limbs, he put on an overcoat and scarf and left the house.

eight

He walked in a westerly direction, crossing the river by the Queen's Bridge and entering Ann Street from which he turned in the direction of Victoria Street. The wind was blowing in stiff gusts from the south-east. It was very cold. He hunched his lean shoulders to heave the overcoat higher and shelter his head and neck from the keen edge of the wind. His gait was long and rapid, attuned more to his urgent thoughts than to the ability of his body to maintain it evenly through the darkness and the hurrying pedestrians. Often he stumbled at the curbs and collided with people, whereupon he came from his thoughts with a peculiar abruptness which caused people to stare at him as he jerked himself to one side and recovered his pace. Both hands were thrust deeply into his overcoat pocket. His hunched shoulders, and his head set against the wind, gave him a furtive appearance. But there was something positive, singular and forthright about him as he swung along. And in his mind which pursued its visions of that hunted soul there was a weight and momentum which carried him as though upon an errand.

Yet he was going to "The Four Winds" only to satisfy a desire for company and diversion. If his appearance suggested an errand, it was merely a fortuitous aspect. He had that positive air; nevertheless, his long thoughts and his vehement expression of them always suggested their possession of him rather than his control of them.

When he entered Victoria Street he became aware for the first time of a new note in the city's voice. He stopped and glanced quickly about him. Ever since he had entered the larger streets, where there were many people passing, he had been vaguely aware of a new, quickened tempo. He had not considered it. It made echoes in him which he did not ponder. But now that he was fully aware of them, he seemed to hear them from all sides in a volume which poured noisily and harshly into his ears. And as he stood there he heard a little crowd come stamping towards him. Two constables were at its head. Behind them, the voices made an angry, menacing uproar. He drew back, hesitated, had a sudden awful impulse to run. Before he could act the constables were beside him, holding him, peering at him.

"Show your identity card!" one of them said, sharply.

Lukey fumbled in his jacket pocket and produced it. The excited little mob stood at a distance, restless, chattering in voices of rage and vengeance, shouting threats, telling the constables that he was the fellah, he was Johnny right enough.

"The name is there," Lukey said. "It is Luke Mulquin."

One of the constables shone a torch on the card as he examined it.

"It is Luke Mulquin," he said, passing the card to his comrade.

"Aye, that's right," said the other, handing the card back to Lukey.

Lukey returned it to his pocket. The crowd had swelled. It pressed forward, its leaders panting, making furious gestures and shouting in hoarse voices that they would settle the score and make it even.

One of the constables turned towards them.

"Move off! He is not Johnny! If you don't clear off now and disperse it'll be the cells for you!"

They began to shout in a fury of frustration. Lukey stood watching them.

"Sure, he has not hurted them, has he?" he asked one of the constables.

The officer spoke briefly to him. "You had better be off now, before there is trouble. It is bad enough, all over the place, without a bit more."

The crowd loitered there for an instant longer and then broke and fled as the constables drew batons and moved forward. Lukey was momentarily afraid.

"They would tear him to pieces!" he exclaimed.

The constables were driving the crowd all ways along the street. Shouts sounded in brutish outbursts and died away in the distance. Lukey turned away and continued his journey.

"Suppose I was Johnny," he thought. "They would have

killed me!"

The thought drove him deeply into him and shocked him. He halted. Looking about him, he saw patrols of constables at corners. They were halting men and women and examining identity cards. Further off, another small crowd was gathered, with little clusters of noisy youths watching and talking excitedly in loud, harsh tones which rolled on the wind's current and thrust upwards into the night. Everywhere, people were moving, coming to a halt to look at the patrols, to exchange information, rumors, anger.

"My God!" Lukey exclaimed. "It is about Johnny . . . they are talking about Johnny! They are waiting to see if he will come this way. They are waiting to see the police lift him."

And when he muttered that it seemed to him that the night itself with its icy wind and its furious voices stirred darkly over the city and probed the streets and the alleys and noisome entries. Its bitter fingers fumbled and tore at the darkness, to dispel the shadows, to rip wide the black curtains which might conceal Johnny. Its voices mumbled across the cobbles and whispered along the faces of huge, silent buildings. At corners, they broke into shrill chatter; and parting, they sped off to dart into deserted entrances or to pour wildly into the gutters or the dank foundations of walls oozing with slime and guarding a hollow silence into which the incessant breathing roar of the city dropped occasionally as the wind veered. Elsewhere, the greater currents drove harshly, never at rest, menacing and mominous, snatching words from the lips of people and merging them into a single sound.

"They are hunting him!" Lukey muttered. "They are getting the trail of him and yelling at his heels!"

Then his imagination sharpened, and he understood at what final frontier of mortal existence the man Johnny was now poised with his remaining particle of consciousness. He appreciated the dreadful extremity of that soul, and felt pity for him.

He could not understand at first why he felt pity.

"He shot and killed the cashier," he reminded himself, as he walked on. "He took a human life."

But although he continued to apply reason and justice to Johnny, he could not dispel the pity and sympathy. And he became afraid again, wondering what would have happened had the heedless finger of fate touched him instead of Johnny, chosen him, giving his life that impulse. He trembled. Then he

190

knew why he felt pity for Johnny.

"Yes," he thought, "it might have been me. It could easily have been me!"

He let his swift imagination accept the condition. He let his thoughts weave and tower over him and accept the crime and the sense of guilt and terror. And he appreciated how easy it was for such an experience to alight upon any being. The great calendar of crimes was not specified against one man or woman, but against all mankind. All were potential criminals. The sunlight which poured upon the world, and the rain which deluged the lands, and the winds that blew, touched all men. And the impulses which flared in one mind had their source in emotions that were common to all.

"If I had done it!" Lukey thought.

Then the sound of the city terrified him, and when he saw the robust, armed constables on patrol his heart pounded and his limbs became suddenly weak as though the blood was withdrawn from them. Nor could he sustain the normal glances which met his own. He lowered his head and turned aside. A horrible, inexplicable sense of guilt possessed him. He saw men and youths loitering in narrow side streets and entrances, and because he knew that they were waiting to pounce on Johnny, should he appear, he shuddered, hesitated, and went on only after nerving himself to pass them. He despised them for their revolting anger, which drove them to wait there. But as soon as he was safely past them, he pitied them, realizing that in their minds there was an emotion which they did not understand. But he knew what it was.

They, too, felt guilty, as afraid and as guilty as he himself was. In their souls there was the same terror and responsibility; and they waited for Johnny only to fasten the guilt on him, to hasten him to the constables and escape the mysterious burden which was on their souls.

Lukey hastened on. When he reached "The Four Winds" and pushed open the heavy door and went in, the violent clamor of voices in that place struck his ears like a blow from something savage and elemental. His sensitive spirit recoiled, and his body hesitated to enter that throng whose voices were a single roar about one topic. He hesitated. The smell of the beer and spirits, of human breath, of garments warmed by the air of the place, swept about him as the door swung to behind him. He was confused. Suddenly, Fencie appeared, coming towards him with a curiously deliberate air and standing with his back to the door of the first crib on whose handle Lukey's hand was resting.

"That one is full up," he said. "Try along a bit."

He made a wild gesture, indicating the long line of cribs extending to the far end of the bar.

Lukey took a few steps. Around him were many faces. His glance swept over them, and again he was afraid. He saw red faces, dull and commonplace. Sharp ones, ugly ones, others with the noses plunged into big pint glasses around whose rims flabby lips were fastened. He saw the necks moving as the liquid was swallowed. He heard bursts of shouting, snatches of sentences from arguments, oaths. Then again he hesitated. Fear poured into his mind and set in motion a terrible panic. He turned and pushed his way back towards the door.

Fencie confronted him with an angry look.

"Did you not hear what I told you?" he exclaimed. "That one is full up!"

He spun Lukey round and gave him a shove. Lukey stumbled towards the far end of the bar, tilting beer from a glass clutched by a thick hand which was lifting towards ready lips. The liquid spurted over the face and down the coat. An oath exploded from the lips.

"Sorry!" Lukey mumbled, hurrying on.

The abuse was extinguished by the roar from all sides. A barman, recognizing Lukey, opened the door of a crib for him and jerked a thumb towards its single occupant. Lukey slunk in and sat down. He saw Griffin sitting in the corner.

"Fetch us a pint," he muttered to the barman.

The latter withdrew, slamming the door. His shout rose above the general din.

"Pint!"

Lukey lifted his head and stared at Griffin. He could not remember an occasion when he had been more pleased than now to see that genial presence.

nine

Griffin was accustomed to Lukey's peculiar behavior when a fantastic notion took form in his mind; yet when the door opened and Lukey stumbled awkwardly in and flopped down with his head bowed and an expression of fear and bewilderment in his eyes, he was momentarily startled. He removed his pipe from his mouth and stared at the visitor, who sat with his hands on his knees and his whole body bent under what seemed to be an oppressive load.

"What's the matter with you?" he said.

Lukey was listening to the noise. He heard the roar of conversation and shouting and laughter, and it seemed to him that it made a challenge to reason, to mercy, to civilization itself. Arguments were joined like waves weltering and seething aimlessly at the foot of a massive cliff. Single words lifted with an alarming violence, like the baleful gleam of light on baldes drawn in murderous anger. Idiotic laughter whirled, coming as though from a source of chaos or lunacy into which the power of reasonable influences could never penetrate. Indescribably brutal noises exploded in the clamor, which never for a moment abated, but which continued to resound to the limit of an indefinable region which Lukey imagined to be threatened by this uproar.

Watching him, Griffin was perturbed. He had encouraged this curious being to such a degree that he wondered if he had been wise to do so. He had set Lukey upon such a course, such a lonely journey, that he felt a grave sense of responsibility to him.

"What is on your mind?" he asked, leaning forward.

Lukey suddenly imagined that instead of being informed by temperate things of beauty and truth, the human will was ruled by implacable forces of hatred, fear stupidity, lust, cruelty. This idea fell swiftly into his mind and increased, installing itself like a monstrous intruder. It whispered to him, telling him that if mankind were persuaded by what was good and beautiful instead of by what was evil and ugly, its expressions would be mild and full of harmony.

"Mr. Griffin!" he exclaimed, rising and sitting close to the other. "Suppose we are not civilized after all! Suppose it is all boloney, and we are still bloody brutes fighting each other!"

Griffin laughed heartily from sheer relief. Tucking his wreathed chin against his chest he emitted a shattering guffaw.

"I thought you were going to tell me something else!" he exclaimed.

"Mr. Griffin!" Lukey continued, touching Griffin's arm. "Suppose there is no God, but only man! And suppose man is . . . well, suppose he is like he is out there!" He jerked his head towards the bar.

"Think of that, Mr. Griffin! Suppose there is no such thing as civilization or God or anything like that, but only the cruel things which were in man from the time when he was a brute and living with the brutes of the field and forest!"

Griffin shook his head. "It is essentially a progressive universe! Its whole nature is progressive development. And cannot escape that development."

"I don't believe it!" Lukey declared. "The laws of Moses and the Commandments are still the necessary laws. If we have become civilized since the time when those laws were made, why do we still break them? No! We are still savage and evil! There are terrible things in us that don't alter in spite of civilization! Civilization is only the wearing of better clothes, reading and writing for the masses, better conditions of labor perhaps, music and art for the people, and more science. And what does science do? Helps mankind to slaughter more efficiently! By comparison with the savages of prehistoric times, we are devils! In one night we can see as many people killed as would satisfy the bloody jaws of old Moloch or Baal! Is that your progressive universe?"

Griffin smiled optimistically. "It is a poor outlook, at present, but it will improve! You must remember that mankind has been on this world a very short time in all the aeons which have passed since the earth was formed. Nature is slow in its processes . . . ."

Lukey shook his head. "The world is only a damned big ball floating in space!"

"But subject to certain factors . . . ."

Lukey shook his head again. "It is subject to blind forces, terrible conditions, awful chances and such like!"

"Oh, not as bad as that!" Griffin said.

Lukey leaned nearer to the other.

"Mr. Griffin!" he continued. "I don't believe that man believes in God after all. God is only an invention of man, so that man can feel safe and can pretend to be sorry for the evil and badness in him. I believe that man only pretends he believes in God. And all the time there is free-will. And there are terrible things done by that will. Look at the way Nazi Germany has denied the belief in God! Think of what has been done by civilized man in Europe! My God, don't tell me it is reasonable! And now listen! Do you hear that racket out there?"

"It's healthy!" Griffin declared. "I like it!" He cocked his head on one side and jerked it back quickly. "Man is a lusty animal and he makes a noise! He loves to express himself!"

"Listen to them," Lukey said. "They are talking about Johnny. That is what the racket is about. It is the same all over the city tonight. There is a man who has offended the laws. He has killed a man. They are afraid, because it is a thing that any of them could have done. Instead of being Johnny, it might have been any of them. They are afraid. And they want to find Johnny and be sure that he pays the penalty. They want to be sure that the guilt is loaded on him and not on them!"

Griffin smoked his pipe and was silent. Lukey's strange ideas and convictions impressed him and admitted to his own mind a new vision of the world. It was as though the whole fabric of his own inner world were rent and some majestic tempest of actuality were now raging over what had been only a false representation of life. He smiled pensively.

"I wonder," he murmured, looking at Lukey.

"Mr. Griffin!" Lukey said earnestly, tapping him on the arm. "If I could find Johnny! Suppose I found him! Then I could look into his eyes and I would see the truth there. I would find the whole truth, and I could make a great portrait of him and it would be there . . . ."

"Yes," Griffin admitted, "you would discover terrible things . . . ."

"They would not frighten me," Lukey said. "I would nerve myself and face them. It would be a terrible experience, but I would express it all in the portrait." Then he lowered his voice and whispered: "Shell says he is still alive. He had news of him from 'Gin' Jimmy. Just think, Mr. Griffin! If it is true that he is still alive, he must know what there is in the soul of men and in his own soul. He has heard the sound there is in the city. Knowledge of terrible things is in his soul. And if I could have him for a couple of hours, I would paint the portrait of him, and it would be there on the canvas.

ten

While Lukey was talking to Griffin, the door of the bar opened and Shell appeared. At that moment, Fencie was standing halfway along the counter, where he had set down a big tray and called an order to one of the barmen. He saw Shell come in, and he saw him glance in his direction. Their eyes met, whereupon Shell grinned and jerked his head in salutation and turned to enter the first crib.

Fencie rushed towards him with such impetuosity that the customers imagined that he was going to eject that notorious little figure in whose hands there was an empty bird cage. And Shell, too, imagined that that was what Fencie intended to do. He drew back slightly.

Fencie's manner changed immediately. His pace slackened. He grinned amiably as he advanced.

"What's this contraption you have here?" he said jocularly, hurrying past Shell and pretending to examine the black-out blind over the door. Then before Shell had time to speak, Fencie rested a huge hand on his shoulder and impelled him towards the far end of the bar.

"Full up that end, Shell," he said. Then he shouted above the din: "Pint!" And halting at last at the far end of the counter where there was space, he indicated the bird cage.

Shell grinned. "Sure, it's a cage!" he said. "Can you not see that?"

"It's a funny thing to be bringing with you," Fencie said.

"Oh, well, don't you know," Shell said. "I have lost the bird I had in it, and I am looking for him."

His prominent, evil eyes in his little face held Fencie's eyes in a stare which probed and which seemed to Fencie to rummage furtively amidst all the secrets and terrors that now filled his mind.

"Is that a fact?" he mumbled, indicating the pint of porter which a barman had placed on the counter before Shell. The barman waited for the price of the pint, but Shell ignored him. Blinking his eyes and withdrawing their gaze from Fencie, Shell put his hand slowly and firmly around the big glass and lifted it, sinking his thirsty lips on the rim and dipping his nose into the froth. Fencie dismissed the barman with a curt gesture and glanced anxiously towards the first crib.

Shell saw the gesture and the glance which followed it. He watched Fencie slyly and was convinced that something lay heavily on the publican's mind. Then for an instant their glances met again, whereupon without a word Fencie returned to the counter opposite the first crib. Someone nudged Shell.

"What has happened to the bird?"

The man who asked the question began to laugh. So did his three companions who, for the past hour, had been standing at the counter with him. They were strangers to Shell, whose moist, vacant expression seemed to all of them to present him as a person who was a possible diversion for their drunken mood.

"He is dead," Shell said, pursing his lips.

"Just took and died on you?" one of the men said, swaying towards Shell and impregnating the already putrid air with a thick waft of beer fumes. He grimaced slowly at his companions, who broke into another outburst of laughter which was aimed derisively at Shell.

"Aye, that's right," Shell said. "Died in a fit of laughter after drinkin' too much of the porter."

Lifting his glass of porter from the counter, he moved off to the curve of the counter where he stood apart and alone except for the vociferous pot-boys who clattered down from the lounges upstairs. There he stood watching Fencie.

Fencie knew that Shell was waiting for him to come and converse with him. He was afraid. He knew Shell, and he feared him at this moment, not because he was evil, but because in some indescribable degree he and Shell were counterparts. And also because he feared that Shell had discovered his secret.

He kept glancing along the crowded bar, above the heads of the customers, to where Shell stood waiting patiently at the curve of the counter. Sometimes Shell's head was averted and his nose was dipped into a big pint of glass and his lips were closed around the rim. Then suddenly his damp, sly countenance would turn in Fencie's direction, and his eyes shot their gaze with a horrible accuracy and significance at Fencie, who felt it pierce him like something cruel and menacing, whereupon his relentless heart trembled. Fantastic suspicions increased in his heated mind. He felt a morbid curiosity regarding Shell's advent with the bird cage, and could not prevent himself from moving slowly towards him, until fear and curiosity were mingled in dread. Then he came deliberately towards Shell, who quickly drained the big glass and held it in a way which suggested his surprise at its sudden emptiness. Fencie snapped his fingers at a passing barman and indicated the empty glass, which the man lifted at once and carried to one of the big casks.

"So the bird has gone?" Fencie said, leaning against the

counter.

"He has flew," Shell said, making a forlorn grimace.

"Ah, too bad, too bad," Fencie murmured, signing away the barman when he delivered the dripping pint of porter.

Shell lifted the glass and drank deeply.

"Aye, but," he said, returning the glass to the counter and wiping the froth from his lips with the back of his hand, "I am looking for him, you know!"

Fencie smiled, "What sort of a bird is he?"

Shell held him in a hard stare.

"Hurted in the left wing," he said quickly.

"And you think you'll find him in the dark on a wild night like this?" Fencie said.

He threw back his massive shoulders and slowly drew himself to full height, towering above the miserable scrap of life which stood before him. He was striving to impress Shell with the old, elemental things: size, physical strength, the threat of physical violence. In his fearful mind he longed to shatter the bond which Shell seemed to hold upon him. And he tried to impress Shell with a false air of detachment and security.

"How will you see him in the dark;" he said, driving a laugh from his big chest. Shell sniggered as he looked up at him.

"Sure, I will find him, Mr. Fencie. I am half-way to him already!"

"Are you?"

"Aye, I am!" Shell asserted. "I know rightly where he is. At this very minute!"

"Why don't you . . ." Fencie said, glancing with an indifferent air along the bar to the first crib and then returning his gaze to Shell. "Why don't you up and after him?"

Shell stared impudently at him.

"Sure, I am takin' my time like," he said.

"But if you don't take and hurry . . ." Fencie went on.

Shell grinned and made an imperious little gesture which told Fencie to cease lying and making a pretence of ignorance regarding Johnny's whereabouts. At once, Fencie lowered his gaze and looked first at the floor with its drift of spent matches and empty cigarette cartons and pipe droppings and expectorations, all washed in a sticky tide of beer swills and sodden cigarette butts, then at the crowded bar and the clock, which showed ten minutes to nine, and finally back at Shell.

"And what will you do with the bird when you have him?"

He asked, and his tone was humble.

"Sell him!" Shell said swiftly. "He's a prize creature!"

". . . wounded, but," Fencie interjected.

"Worth thousands, wounded or sound," Shell said.

He pegged Fencie with his gaze, and it was like a shaft striking that solid being in all the places of his spirit where his own evil nature had its roots.

Fencie stood away from the counter and fingered a cork which he held in his huge, red hands.

"Suppose you can't lay hands on your bird after all?" he said. "What's to be done then?"

Shell grinned for several seconds. His answer was in that expression, and he supplemented it with a threat.

"I will go to the police, Mr. Fencie," he said, softly but incisively.

Fencie was silent. He looked down at Shell and frowned. Suddenly he sighed and let the cork drop from his fingers. He shrugged his shoulders.

"I wish you luck," he muttered.

"Sure, but you will give me a hand, Mr. Fencie?" Shell said.

A morose expression appeared on Fencie's face. Fear circumscribed his palpitating heart. Fear of Shell whose sly, adroit nature was capable of going to dreadful expedients to enforce its purpose. Fear of the police accusing him of harboring Johnny. Fear of the Organization taking revenge on him for betraying Johnny to Shell or to the police. Fear of his customers discovering him in what they might imagine to be synpathy for Johnny. Everywhere about his flabby heart terror grew and nestled closer against him and possessed him.

At that moment a loud groan sounded from the crib nearest the door. It rose from a low note and dragged itself to a higher pitch of greater volume until it was audible to all in the bar. It swelled into a protracted cry of agony which passed from an expression of physical pain to one of immeasurable despair, which changed slowly until a quality of exultation filled it. And into that vibrating expression of triumph there poured at last a challenge which rose to a yell of defiance. All heard it, and all became so silent that the sound of a window agitated by the wind was audible, as well as the patter of spattering liquid from one of the cask's taps.

Words ceased abruptly on mobile lips. A match about to be applied to a pipe expired and dropped from the arrested hand. Hands bringing glasses to lips became rigid. All eyes were turned in the direction from which the shout was coming. All along the noisy bar sound and movement subsided. The barmen looked up from their work and turned pale and then glanced in fear at Fencie. Then the yell subsided. It was followed by the crash of a glass on the stone floor of one of the cribs. At once everybody started to laugh and exclaim excitedly, the voices merging into a swelling chorus of amusement from which words rose in sentences that told Fencie that somebody was drunk, had passed out, was took bad, was breaking the glasses on him. And beneath that uproar of laughter and derision the bar resumed its activity. Again came the bursts of arguments, the calls for drink, the spurting laughter, the snatches of song, and the shouts of the barmen calling orders.

It was then that the door of the crib in which Griffin and Lukey were seated was flung open and Lukey appeared. He stood there, fixing a sullen stare on the press of customers at the bar. Then he saw Shell talking to Fencie, and at once he rushed out and took hold of him.

The little cage clattered to the floor. The glass of porter which Shell had just lifted to his lips shot out of his hand and struck the counter and fell to the tiled floor with a crash of breaking glass and slopping liquid. He put up his arms and tried to protect his head from the blows which fell heavily on his ears and cheeks. He tugged like a little mule as he tried to wrench himself from Lukey's grip, and for a few seconds the two of them slid across the wet floor, trampling amidst the beer swills and rubbish and the bird cage, and colliding with other customers in that confined space. Shell's whine as the blows fell on him rose for an instant and then became lost amidst the general uproar which spread rapidly from that end of the bar to the press which extended along the counter.

Within half a minute there was pandemonium. Everybody moved forward to see what was happening, and the swarm became so compact that the least movement of those in the forefront sent the mob behind swaying and reeling and thrusting to and fro. Shouts rose. Glasses crashed. Several men climbed to the counter to watch the fight. Heads rose from the tops of cribs. A bottle whirled from the mass and crashed against a mirror at the back of the bar, making a huge crack from which splinters spread. The barmen tried to reach over and grab the culprit. Blows were struck, and one of the barmen reeled back with his face bleeding. And at the far end

Lukey still had hold of Shell and was punching him. Shell was cornered. He had his head lowered and his arms raised. He was kicking and screaming so that it was impossible for anyone to get near him to rescue him. Several men attempted to drag Lukey from him without avail. Lukey merely turned and lunged wildly at them, sending one of them totering back against a shelf on which rows of bottles of stout were ranged. The man's arm plunged amidst the rows, whereupon the bottles were toppled. They fell to the floor and burst open, adding to the ruin. The shouting increased. There were laughter, threats, sudden little brawls and minor arguments that added to the din and confusion through which the barmen tried to scramble. Two of them slipped on the slimy rime on the tiled floor and fell heavily, making a loud slapping sound which caused shouts of derision and amusement. One of the barmen rose quickly and aimed a blow at someone who had laughed at him. The others, coming past him, collided with him and reeled all ways, and finally upset Fencie, sending him to the floor, from which he rose and drew back to a safe distance to bawl in a piercing tone:

"Lukey! Lukey! Stop the fighting! Quit this!"

He lost his balance again and slithered heavily to the floor, from which customers assisted him and stood back from his sodden, stenching garments. He was pale and panting. His eyes had a look of horror, and he held up his right hand which had received a slight scratch which he pretended was a serious injury.

"Call the police! Fetch the police!" somebody shouted, above the uproar. Fencie shook his head and limped to a safer distance and stood there as though dazed and in great pain. He panted heavily and moved his right hand up and down and occasionally covered his face with his left hand, pretending he was suffering. But all the time he was aware of the movement and clamor around him, and of Lukey standing over Shell and battering him while the barmen and customers struck in turn at Lukey.

At the height of this turmoil a woman rushed from one of the cribs. She was fashionably dressed and of about thirty years. Her little red lips, usually set in a tiny bow and always parted to reveal two pearly little teeth, were now wide open and twitching with terror. But no sound came from them. She tried to shake off the grasp of an elderly sedate gentleman who blushed to find himself exposed to such noisy company, and who kept attempting to draw his companion back into the privacy of the crib. His bowler hat suddenly slid over his left eye. His fumbling hands dropped the kid gloves which they held. His silver-mounted walking stick rattled to the floor and got under his feet, causing him to slip heavily and drag the woman with him.

"Oh, Edward! Edward!" she screamed, getting into a frenzy, "Take me home! Take me out of this!"

It was almost an alien voice in the fierce male racket. Customers turned to see who was speaking. They saw the elderly gentleman succeed in snaring the hysterical woman back into the crib. Then the door closed. But the thin, querulous cry still sounded.

"Edward, I want to go home!"

Heads rose from neighboring cribs. There were guffaws of laughter. Derisive shouts sounded above the impacting voices around Shell and Lukey. The noise increased. Many customers swiftly drained their glasses and departed. Amongst them went the elderly gentleman and his friend. His head was erect but his glance was downcast. Several young men whistled loudly at him and laughed. Another bottle shot into the air and landed amongst a row of dummy whisky bottles, three of which crashed to the floor. Excited laughter greeted this minor event.

Suddenly there was a greater commotion from the end of the bar where Lukey was fighting. Shell had slipped from Lukey's grip and had fled into the heart of the mob thereabouts. Lukey flung off the barmen who held him and rushed after Shell. Customers stumbled all ways under the impact. More glasses were upset and broken. Shell dived deeper into the crowd and wiggled through it. Lukey saw him and struggled to reach him, but his left foot became entangled in the bird cage. He stooped down and wrenched off the crumbled wires and flung the thing away.

It struck an electric light and extinguished it and fell amidst a row of Guinnes bottles. The entire row toppled from the shelf and crashed on the floor, splitting open with a loud popping of corks and breaking glass and spilling the precious liquid in an oozing waste. Many hands seized hold of Lukey. In a moment he was limp and silent and abashed.

The barmen gathered round him and took hold of him with their big hands.

"Now . . . hold him boys! Hold him, the bloody wee nuisance!"

"Hold him! Hold him!"

It was Fencie, bursting his way through the throng and looming above Lukey with his bulk full of threat and his mouth brimming with words, and his arm raised to aim a blow.

Somebody pulled the arm down. Fencie grunted.

"Take him inside!" he said curtly. "Take him to the storeroom!"

The barmen rushed Lukey away. Others called for order. Others began to clear up the mess. One who had bolted for safety returned timidly. The customers looked at one another.

Everything had ended abruptly. Shell had disappeared. Lukey was removed. Suddenly there was no more excitement. The excited customers were disappointed. They began to exclaim.

"Bring him out! Bring him to us and let us see justice done!"

Fights began. Arguments rose and ended suddenly. Fencie ejected several rowdy customers and warned others.

"Any more of this and I will bring the police!"

The barmen exchanged glances.

"God help us all if he does!" they whispered.

"Did you hear number one let out the groan?" another whispered.

"It's desperate, desperate!"

Griffin came from the crib where he had remained during the uproar. His genial face smiled as he stood before Fencie.

"I hope, Larry . . . I hope you are going to take a lenient view . . ." he began.

Fencie frowned at him. He pointed to the broken mirror, to the wrecked shelves, the broken glasses and bottles and general ruin and disorder.

"A lenient view, is it? Take a look at the view yourself, mister! Just cast your eyes round! A nice picture it makes! A work of art!" he shouted.

"Very bad . . . a serious matter . . ." Griffin murmured, looking very grave.

"Just leave me to mind my own business and deal with that bit of artistic temperament, mister!" Fencie said, stamping away.

The clamor in the bar was beginning to subside. Griffin left. Fencie waddled through the slops and fragments of broken bottles and reached the end of the counter.

"Keep an eye on number one," he whispered to the senior

barman who was standing there.

He lifted his elbows and braced his shoulders as he strutted to the storeroom, which was a cold, dank little room full of empty casks, broken equipment, disused pails and measures, and a bad smell of sour beer. A waste pipe was splashing outside a tiny window high up on the damp wall. Lukey was sitting sullenly and in dejection on one of the casks with his hands between his knees. He looked up with a morose expression on his bruised face when Fencie entered.

"I suppose," Fencie said, slamming the door behind him, "I suppose you are feeling a wee bit tired after your exertions outside?"

Lukey was silent. He shrugged his shoulders and turned away.

"The damage is two hundred and twenty pounds!" Fencie said.

Lukey sniffed and remained with his head downcast.

"Well, come on!" Fencie said sharply. "What are you going to say? What suggestions have you to make as regards due restitution for the damage you have caused? I am waiting!"

"I have no money!" Lukey mumbled.

"Aye, no money and no sense!" Fencie retorted. He sat down and rubbed his hands together. "In that case, there is nothing more to be said."

Lukey glanced apprehensively at him.

"It's the police this time, Lukey," Fencie went on. "The last time you caused trouble and broke the fittings I took a lenient view. I forgave you. This time, it is worse. I am afraid it is the police for you this time."

Lukey made an angry gesture.

"What sense is there in that?" he snapped.

"Then pay up for the damage!"

"Two hundred and twenty pounds!" Lukey exclaimed. "Sure, I am an artist, not a publican!"

Fencie frowned. "Pay up, or go to prison!"

Lukey mumbled: "I am short of money at present."

"Then it will be six months in jug."

"Go ahead, then!"

"Six months this time . . . ."

"Go ahead! Have your revenge!" Lukey said.

Fencie cocked his head to one side. "I am not a man who relishes revenge," he remarked.

He put his hands in his pockets and looked at his shoes with their fine gloss which had been spoiled by the beer swills amidst which he had slipped. He appeared to be pondering a just settlement. Lukey saw only the head with its hair glistening under the naked electric globe. Something in the angle of the head on the shoulders suggested to him that Fencie was concocting a cunning scheme.

"Well," Fencie said, lifting his heavy gaze to Lukey. "I have a propositiin to make to you, Lukey!"

He looked at his prisoner and grinned so that his big stained teeth showed with the tongue moving over them. His lips as they closed made a sucking sound suggestive of the self-satisfaction which now possessed him.

"What is it?" Lukey mumbled.

"It is the only alternative besides the police," Fencie said. "One or the other. Which will you have?"

"What is it?" Lukey asked again.

"You will soon see," Fencie said. "Now, what is it to be? Make your choice!"

Lukey shrugged his shoulders. "I am not fond of kicking my heels in prison," he said.

"Then it is the proposition?"

Lukey nodded. At once Fencie went to the door and called to one of the barmen.

"Ring up old Fred and ask him to send Hughie or wee Billy with a cab. And make it sharp," he said.

He waited a few minutes while the barmen called "Time" and the bar emptied slowly. When he and Lukey returned to the counter the barmen where shouting lustily up and down the bar and in the passages and lounges upstairs, calling "Time." And already the premises were emptying and the pot-boys were bringing down trays loaded with empty glasses and bottles. In the big bar on the ground floor the barmen were washing the glasses under a tap from a small geyser. Others were wiping the counter and cleaning out the cribs. Lukey stood sullenly at the end, looking around at the disorder and emptiness. The voices and footsteps of the barmen echoed strangely in the place after the clamor which had at last subsided. The senior barman approached.

"Maybe your blood is cooled down, is it, you mad wee skitterer, you!"

Fencie appeared. "Sam, give us a hand with the fellow in number one," he said.

He glanced along the bar and into the cribs to make certain

that all customers had departed.

"Do you see the fine work you have done tonight?" the assistant said, addressing Lukey and pointing to the fractured mirrors and the empty shelves.

"He is going to make good for that mischief!" Fencie said.

He reached the door of the first crib. Pushing it open with a thrust of his thick shoulder, he went in, taking hold of Lukey by the arm and dragging him with him.

Johnny was lying across the little table amidst a pool of whisky. His left hand was raw and exposed and the wound showed black and ugly, with trickles of dried blood formed all across the skin. His cap had fallen to the floor, and his open overcoat revealed the great stain spreading from his sleeve across his breast. Fencie drew him upright against the wall of the crib. The eyes opened, and into the pallid face life gleamed thinly.

"It is Johnny!" Lukey said.

"Aye, it's Johnny, right enough," Fencie said, grinning at Lukey.

eleven

Fencie stood back from Johnny and tapped Lukey on the arm.

"I have ordered a cab for you," he said. "Hughie or wee Billy will be driving it, so there will be no questions asked and nothing said."

Lukey said: "But . . . it is Johnny!"

Fencie chuckled. "Sure, it's Johnny!" he said.

"What am I to do with him?" Lukey exclaimed.

"Take and get rid of him, that's all!" Fencie said. "You can take your choice. Drop him off somewhere in the dark. If you don't care for the idea, then I will have to hand you over to the police. What is it to be?"

Lukey looked at Johnny, who was sitting propped back against the wooden wall of the crib. The face was stained with blood, with dirt and mucus and splashes of whisky. Its expression had set in a stiff mask of agony over which momentary ripples of vitality passed like the strange, inexplicable movement of water in a stagnant pool. The eyes opened and in their depths Lukey saw the reflection of mysterious thoughts. The right hand rose as though to part from sight objects that interposed themselves between the eyes and the strange horizons which lay before them. The lips moved but no sound issued from them, although all over the face a straining impulse gathered the flesh and muscles, until once again the whole countenance was the mirror of the soul's agony.

"What am I to do with him?" Lukey whispered.

But he knew already what he would do. He had dreamed of this opportunity. He had committed all his imagination to the idea of it, deciding how he would pose Johnny, and in what harmony of color and line he would make the study of him, and telling himself what fear and despair, exultation and triumph would appear in the features. Now the idea increased in him, and he hardly listened to Fencie who was tapping his arm and instructing him:

"Take him out of this and lose him! Just drop him down somewhere in the dark, and forget about him. No questions. No talk. . . ."

Lukey sniffed. He looked at Fencie's hard, florid face.

"But the police . . ." he mumbled.

Fencie shrugged his shoulders. "That's your risk," he said.

Lukey shook his head and pretended to be perturbed.

"I am afraid," he muttered.

But he wanted this man, this soul, this precious thing in all its distress and agony and mystery and wonder.

"Here is ten bob," Fencie said, giving him a note. "That'll pay for the cab. Now, take him away!"

Lukey looked at him with a helpless expression.

"Suppose the police . . ."

Fencie frowned and made an angry gesture. He looked out along the empty bar. The assistants had got rid of the last customers from the lounges upstairs and had rapidly finished the cleaning of the glasses and the cribs. All of them were afraid of the advent of the police or some members of the Organization, and were anxious to depart. Their aprons and white jackets hung in a row near the far end of the counter; and already many of them were scrambling into their overcoats, which they had taken from a cupboard nearby.

"Hold on a bit!" Fencie shouted, beckoning to the nearest man. "Give a hand here!"

The man came forward grudgingly. The others hurried

away.

"Mr. Fencie!" the man said nervously. "It'll be ten years . . . ten years, if the police see us!"

"Ah, quit blethering, Tommy, and just go to the side door and see if the road is clear, and let us know when the cab is there!"

Fencie and the senior barman turned to Lukey and Johnny.

"You are for the road!" Fencie said, lightly touching Johnny's shoulder.

The eyes flickered slightly, but their dim orbs behind the intervening mists of the territory in which his soul hovered gave no sign that he had heard Fencie.

"Sure, there is only one road for him," the senior barman said. "Whatever way he goes, it is the same."

They lifted Johnny to his feet and carried him along the bar and into the passage, where the nervous barman was standing at the door.

"They are away," he whispered. "But there is no cab, and I'm telling you, Mr. Fencie, the police are up and down the road, I'm thinking!"

Fencie was panting. His breath trembled on his lips.

"Just put your head out and keep an eye on the road and let us know when the cab comes!" he said harshly.

"Mr. Fencie . . . if the police . . ."

The sound of hooves was audible above the whine and thrash of the wind outside.

"That's the cab!" Fencie said. "Now, just get out there and see if the police are about. Hurry!"

The man opened the door a little way and went out. Johnny groaned loudly.

"God help us!" muttered the senior barman. "He is going to pass out on us!"

Fencie sighed tremulously. The barman returned from the street.

"All clear!"

"Hold the door open for us," Fencie said.

They lifted Johnny and carried him into the dark street where the cab was standing at the curb. The senior barman opened the door. Lukey got in first. With a quick heave, Johnny was bundled in after him.

"Hold on now!" said the barman. He was still in his apron and jacket.

"Ah, God help him!" he murmured, getting in and

composing the lax body. "It's a pity of him!"

But Fencie had signed to the cabby and already the vehicle was moving.

"Hold on!" growled the barman, thrusting his head out of the window and then turning to Fencie, who had scuttled back to the door. "Blast you! You have no manners!"

The cab stopped. The barman settled Johnny comfortably and alighted, slamming the door and signing to the driver. Then again the cab started forward, rumbling softly over the cobbles, swerving slightly until the ancient horse increased its pace.

Lukey had not travelled in a cab since the time when he had attended his mother's funeral. Then he had worn a new black suit and had sat jammed between the fleshy flanks of his uncles. In the cab there had been a smell of whisky and hot cloth and upholstery, for it was summer and the sun was shining brilliantly from a cloudless sky. The hills around the city appeared near and very green, like friendly things gently flowing towards the city's heart. And since the early morning Lukey's sense of the solemnity of the day had been touched by a delicious feeling of newness and change filling his young life with dreams and promises, so that he enjoyed the sly air of sociability which broke across the quietude and tears which his aunts maintained. A life had ended. The familiar routine was concluded. Tomorrow and thereafter the days would be different. How, he did not know. But he anticipated them with secret wonder and joy. And he composed his dreams of them in fantastic delights.

He remembered the day vividly. Many years had passed since then, yet he felt as though they had been a mere incident leading to this moment when, again in a cab, his dreams at last reached their goal.

"This is my destiny," he thought. "I am to be a good artist. This thing has happened to me. I am to make a great study of this man Johnny."

He looked through the window and saw only the dark streets and the sombre shapes of big buildings. When he remembered that he had not given the driver an address, he leaned out and whistled softly to him. The cabby reined in the horse and leaned down.

Lukey peered cautiously about and then gave him a direction. The man grunted. The horse started to walk and finally to trot. Lukey got up from his seat and sat down beside

Johnny and spoke to him.

"Johnny," he said. "Johnny! How is it?"

Johnny turned his head to him, but in the darkness it was impossible to discern any expression on those pale, grimed features.

Suddenly, Lukey wondered what he would do with him after he had tended his wounds and made a portrait of him.

twelve

Shell's room in the big tenement was on the floor above Lukey's studio. It was a small place, crammed to overflowing with an assortment of junk which he had accumulated over the years: three big bird cages imprisoning several budgerigars; books which he had purchased for a penny or twopence each from the second-hand book-stalls in the Smithfield Market; bits of metal, wood, broken tools, broken pieces of furniture; pictures which Lukey had thrown away and which Shell had secretly retrieved; chipped and cracked crockery; a box full of rusty screws, nails, bent tacks and odd bolts; a big screen which he had never opened since the day when he had brought it to the room; a massive armchair piled high with books and junk and garments so that he was never able to sit on it. And his sunken little bed and an old chest of drawers against the wall from which many cobwebs hung. And a deep tide of newspapers and tattered magazines whose dates extended far back into the past. It all constituted his life's tale, the story of his aimless, impulsive moments of acquisition. The junk filled the place so that the door could never be opened more than the few inches necessary for the entrance or exit of his little body. Nor could the window be opened, or the fireplace given a fire, or the chimney opened, or the bed tidied and the room dusted. The place was a hole, a nest, into which Shell went furtively to sleep or to sit blinking like a tiny animal around whom life crashed and roared in its majestic passage through Time, while he huddled there amidst his wealth.

When he was not sleeping or sitting on his bed with his hands moving together and his prominent eyes blinking, the room was quite silent except for the chirping and singing of the birds. Yet it continued to reflect the character and nature of its occupant. Mice entered it and gathered the seed scattered from the cages or nibbled at the scraps of food which Shell sometimes dropped from his pockets or from the paper wrappings. From the newspapers, they tore fragments which they carried to their nests below the floors, the sound of their activity persisting for hours at a time and mingling with all the other sounds which softly disturbed the silence of the place when Shell was absent: the chatter of the birds; the creaking of floors and wainscot under a pressure which was surely that of accumulated Time; the tapping of beetles deep in the wainscot; the rustle of falling plaster from the ceiling; the cascades of mortar, brickwork and dust down the chimney; the springs snapping in the ancient armchair, or something else subsiding, expanding or contracting, as Shell's own life expanded, contracted, rustled, made sound and movement in the outer world which, on this tempestuous night, seemed to rise and thrust its immensity against the window on which its loud breath poured.

Shell had lowered a heavy black-out blind on the window and lit a naked gas jet. He was seated on his bed, with his hands touching the hurts which Lukey had given him. His jaws worked as though he were masticating something unpleasant. His eyes blinked, and he sighed repeatedly.

The chastisement was the worst he had ever received. There had been others, mere blows given in anger which he had accepted as the pressure of some discipline which Lukey exerted over him. But this recent one was heaviest of all. Yet he might have forgotten it had it not had so strange an effect on his spirit.

He wriggled his body, whereupon the bruises hurt him; yet when he extended his sensibilities deeper than those pains in order to find comfort from all the projects that supported his life, he discovered only a vast emptiness.

He was horrified. Something had been exorcised from him, expelled by Lukey's blows. For the first time in his life the sense of possession which extended over his plans which, in turn, were bred and developed by his nature, moved over a desolation which was denuded of hopes. A feeling of failure began in him. He became afraid. He could not recognize this new, terrible condition of his life now that so important a project had been quenched in all its springs in him. And remembering Father Tom's vague hints of a reward which would be better than money, he believed that he had lost all

211

hope of something of immeasurable worth which would have transformed his feckless, difficult life and given it ease and beauty. And as his thoughts dwelt on that loss, he felt within himself the sense of a new life, as though his spirit had already ventured towards horizons which, at a mere word or sign from the old priest, would have lifted their veils and admitted him. He heard its joyous clamour, the sounds of cool streams flowing through it, of breezes in its vivid foliage, of laughter across its meadows. Then his heart mourned his loss of it all. He had failed. Lukey had driven him from "The Four Winds," and by now Johnny was either delivered to the police or smuggled back to the Organization.

Shell sighed. Glancing around his untidy room, he felt revolted by what he saw. The mass of junk no longer delighted him or sustained his soul, which was mourning its loss of a better world and which could not be consoled by the things of a life which he had calculated to close for ever. Again, he sighed. He heard the big door of the house slam as somebody entered it, and he wondered if it were Lukey or Tober or someone occupying the other rooms who had returned. Waiting there in the cold and half light, he heard another door slam on the first floor. He knew then that it was one of his friends who had entered Lukey's studio which all three of them used as a common room. He rose slowly and rubbed his cold hands together as he crept down the stairs and ventured towards the big room.

He halted outside, putting his ear close to the jamb near the lock and listened. The door had long since shrunk, and consequently as he stood there he felt the cutting draught from the spiteful currents of wind which, on such a night as this, sped furiously to and fro about the old house whose structure was no longer able to exclude them. But above the whine of the wind he heard the rustle of paper in the room, and heard, too, a loud cough which he knew came from Tober.

At once his fears subsided. He opened the door slowly and went in, closing it softly behind him and standing there in the shadow before venturing forward. He saw a big man clad in a cap and a dirty overcoat and wearing a Queen's University scarf, sitting at the fire with his long legs outstretched and a large parcel of fried fish and chips steaming on his lap.

It was Tober. Tall, fleshy, taciturn and imperturbable, he turned slowly and saw Shell. Then he resumed his meal, lifting the succulent chip potatoes one after another and cramming them wolfishly into his mouth, where he masticated them with slow, ponderous movements of his jaws.

Shell edged round the room and timidly settled himself in the chair opposite him. Tober returned his stare, giving it back in a volume of heavy, impassive scrutiny which poured over Shell's tentative gaze and held it from penetrating to the secret, personal depths which were behind Tober's grey, unwavering eyes.

"It's a cold night," Shell said, with a deferential tone.

He watched the effect of this opening remark on the other, wriggling his little body into a comfortable position and darting little sharp glances which were intended to pierce the sombre curtain of Tober's stare.

Tober was silent. He continued to cram the food into his mouth. Using his fingers delicately, he lifted a crisp cutlet, and doubling it he stuffed it into his mouth where it collapsed in a couple of crunches from his jaws. Shell giggled nervously. His hungry stomach contracted spasmodically, and he leaned forward with an unconscious movement, like a dog ravenous at the sight of food.

He feared Lukey because of his wild tempers and the blows which often whirled from such moods. But he feared Tober in a different way. He knew that Tober would never strike him. Yet a glance from those cold, grey eyes in the unvarying expression of the face was more menacing than Lukey's strong, upraised arm; for in Tober's character and temperament there were forces which promised terrible conditions. Shell could not name them, but he knew that in the big body which, although only in middle age, was acquiring a stealthy obesity, there were hidden powerful things which seemed to be massed and so rigorously concealed from expression that the least anger would loosen them. They awed him. Nevertheless, in the same way in which he liked Lukey, so he liked Tober. The two of them bracketed his life and gave it stability. He admired Lukey for his strange talents and also because he was generous. And he admired Tober who was fearless and aloof and secret and in some mysterious degree free.

"The chips is nice," Shell murmured, indicating the big packet of them glistening and giving forth a tasty odor. "Good nourishin' food, Tober!"

Tober said nothing. He crammed his mouth with the food until the greasy paper was empty. Then, still chewing, he slowly rolled the paper into a ball between his slow, strong hands and threw it into the grate.

"Ah, dear help us!" Shell sighed. "Not a one left for wee Shell!" And he grimaced at the greasy little sphere of paper lying there and slowly expanding.

Tober leaned back in the chair and joined his hands over his stomach and belched heartily. He moved his feet slowly on the heels of his shoes.

"I'm desperate hungry," Shell murmured, sighing.

Tober grinned. He composed his body in a comfortable attitude, and slowly plunging his hand into the pocket of his overcoat, he drew out a big parcel similar to the one which had held his supper. Holding it as though he were about to toss it to Shell, he said slowly:

"Get up off your backside and make a taste of tea!"

Shell remained with his hands extended ready to catch the parcel.

"Tea!" Tober said, jerking his head towards the gas ring at the far end of the room. Leaning to one side, he dropped the parcel of fish and chips against the fender.

"When you have made the tea, Shell," he said.

Shell got up with alacrity and went to the cupboard where the food and crockery were kept.

"Aye, a taste of tea," he murmured. "And then a nice feed of fish and chips. Nothing better. No better food for prince or underling. Good, nourishing food . . ."

"Quit yammering, Shell," Tober said, murmuring in comfort, "and concentrate your bit of a mind on the preparation of some beverage for a thirsty underling."

"Tober!" Shell said sadly, "a bad thing has happened."

He came hurrying back to the hearth and stood beside Tober.

"A bit of misfortune. . . ."

Tober jerked his thumb towards the gas ring.

"There is no such condition as misfortune," he said blandly. "Go and make tea!"

Shell trotted back and lifted the kettle and placed it on the gas ring.

"Water in the kettle!" Tober said imperturbably.

"Ah, dear help us!" Shell said, lifting the empty kettle from the jets. "You're right, Tober! Fill the kettle first."

He sped out to the scullery. When he returned, he put the kettle on the ring and then moved again towards Tober.

214

"A bit of bad luck . . ." he began again.

"Light the gas under the kettle," Tober said.

Shell giggled. "Ah, sure! Light the gas . . ."

He ran across and struck a match and applied it to the jets.

"Now bring out the cups and the tea and the teapot," Tober said. "And the sugar."

When Shell had completed these small tasks he came back to Tober.

"I took the budgy round for a bit of advice," he said, rubbing his hands together.

Tober looked at his feet and continued to move them from side to side on the heels of his shoes.

"Well?"

Shell giggled. "You won't be cross like, will you, if I tell you, Tober? You won't, will you? Lukey was terribly cross."

"Go on," Tober said.

"I took and went to Father Tom," Shell murmured.

Tober heaved himself upright in the chair and stared at Shell with a look of disgust.

"You sneaking wee rat, you!" he said slowly and with vehemence.

"Tober! Man dear! Tober . . . now listen . . . wait until I tell you!" Shell whined.

He lifted his gaze timidly to Tober's awful stare.

"A wounded bird in a cage, and a wounded man hiding in a corner!" Tober said. "I know! I can guess! And away you trot to get your dirty bit of profit!"

"Sure, I have to live but!" Shell whimpered.

"What price did you ask for him?"

"Tober, I'm tellin' you the God's honest truth. . . ."

"What price?" Tober demanded.

"Sure, I never named the price! Father Tom knows I could go to the police and get me two thousand or whatever it is that's offered for information regarding Johnny. . . ."

Tober's big face was wrenched into an expression of extreme disgust.

"Shell, you are foul!"

"Father Tom never said so!" Shell protested. "He was decent like. He said I had to live but."

"How much did you ask?" Tober said.

"Tober, I never asked a lot. You know, I am not a hard man to deal with. I just said that I had to live, and he sort of agrees with me and says he has no fortune or anything, but he sort of hints he has something else he will give me. And when I ask him what it'll be, he says it is faith. A precious particle, he said. A bit of it to sort of work wonders. Something he has by him. And that's what I have lost."

Tober was frowning at him. "How did you know where you could find Johnny?" he said.

Shell grinned. "Sure, I heard tell . . . a friend of mine gave me word. I know rightly where Johnny was."

"You would," Tober said. "Like the rats know where the best food is."

"Sure, that's the way of things, Tober. I just went where I was told. . . ."

"Where to?"

Shell grinned as though he had been discovered in a despicable mischief. He sniggered.

"I saw 'Gin' Jimmy on the road, and he tells me that the fellow is away back a bit. I took my time. I went to Father Tom's first to see how it would be if I could bring the bird to him. Then back I come here to sort of think it out. And then away I go to find the bird . . ."

"Where?" Tober demanded.

"Sure, I took the way 'Gin' Jimmy tells me, and sure enough I see a strip of bandage blowing along the gutter, and by that I know. . . ."

"Where, I am asking you?" Tober shouted.

"Sure, it was in 'The Four Winds,' Tober, and but for Lukey I would have got him from Fencie!"

Tober turned away. "Smelling him out . . . like a blasted ferret or something! A damned little animal!"

Shell giggled. "Aye, I found him! I heard him, too! But Lukey comes out of a crib and sets on me. Hits out and near kills me!"

He lifted the corner of his lip and tilted back his head. A broken tooth showed, with the gum around the stump broken and bleeding.

"Serves you right!" Tober said.

"And that's the end of that," Shell said. "I come home."

Tober jerked his thumb at the boiling kettle and sat back in his chair.

"Make the tea," he said.

Shell crossed the big floor and dropped tea into the pot and poured boiling water into it.

"You know, Tober," he said, bringing the loaded tray to

216

the hearth, "Father Tom had a young lady with him, and I am thinking she was there to find Johnny."

Tober glared at him in silence. Shell giggled.

"And when I let on to Lukey what the plan is, Lukey says for me to bring Johnny here for to have his portrait painted."

"You are all mad," Tober mumbled.

"Sure, my intentions were honest," Shell declared.

"Pour the tea," Tober said. "You have lost your reward, and the woman has lost her man, and Lukey has lost his model, so that is that. Give me a cup of tea."

He leaned down and lifted the packet of fish and chips and tossed it to Shell, who caught it as deftly as a dog catching a bone. He greedily opened it.

"I could have done with the bit of faith the old fellow promised me," he muttered.

"It might have glorified your miserable bit of a soul," Tober remarked, accepting the cup of tea which Shell passed to him.

Shell related the whole of his interview with the priest and began to question Tober as to the nature of the reward which Father Tom had promised him.

"Eat your supper and stop yammering," Tober said, spreading his hands over his stomach and swinging his feet on their heels.

Shell was silent for a little while. At last he looked up with an innocent expression.

"Tober," he said, earnestly and almost eagerly, "what does it mean: faith? Faith?"

thirteen

The question struck Tober's mind like a tempest which stirred the ruin and chaos of his life and agitated the desolated hopes, lifting beautiful fragments for an instant before it hurled them into still greater confusion across the wastes of his vision. Then he was motionless in his being, silent, with his thoughts suspended for fear of committing himself to the regrets which were still concealed amidst that ruin.

He looked at Shell, who was eating voraciously, and he found some inexplicable comfort from his presence. Shell was small, poor, almost derelict, yet he was quick, vital. He lived. And that fact alone afforded Tober a degree of comfort, making it clear to him that there were strata below the one into which he had fallen, and that some essence of his former way of life was not quite lost to him. He clung to Shell, although that abject little being did not suspect it.

But in Shell's opinion, Tober's life was spacious and free. Actually, it was so because it lacked direction, hope and discipline. He was forty-three. For the past seventeen years he had worked as a casual laborer, digging roads, hauling loads, driving lorries, shovelling rubbish, pulling on ropes, filling hods, all of which brought him wages and tired his body so that he was able to sleep soundly. He found shelter and food with the money which he earned; and the weariness of his body enabled him to sleep deeply and forget his feckless life and awake to a vague hope that the day might offer him some miraculous chance.

Yet he knew that the miracle would never happen. Far back in time, behind years, across territories of experience, there was a life which had once afforded him a complete expression of his intellect and spirit. He had been confident and happy to such a degree that everything of his being was poised precariously on a high pinnacle from which a world of exciting vistas was visible. And everything of that being was concentrated on a purpose which his intellect had chosen for him. He was a medical student, and an idealist. But his idealism was his weakness which day by day had increased in him until it had drawn him towards disaster.

At this late day in his life, he sometimes remembered a face and a voice. Then in his soul there was an indescribable emotion, for the face and voice were the visible, audible things of a spirit which he had pursued and to which he had committed his whole life to the exclusion of all else. There was no return from that pursuit. For such a forthright, single-minded being as he was at that time, there was no hope of a return across those lonely regions. The ideal vanished from his life, passing into other societies, disentangling herself from the pursuit. He clung to her for a long time, unwilling to lose hope, distraught and lost. Only the necessity for living made him work. But it was work of the lowest kind.

In himself, something remained from the ruin. He possessed an intellect which permitted him to explore the world of the mind. He made strange journeys into those regions. He no longer grieved for his lost ideal, his lost ambitions. It was sufficient for him that he was alive and able to consider the mystery of existence.

But he had lost faith in many things, fundamental things to which others were attached. He had reached strange frontiers. He made odd friendships, with Shell, who was small and sharp and evil, but who was an expression of the life force; and with Lukey, whose vision pierced behavior and searched for the soul, the source, the impulse. And in this manner Tober had found a way of life which satisfied him, which was all that he desired or had faith in. The rest was futile and foolish.

Nevertheless, the question which Shell had asked disturbed him. He looked at the hungry little person munching the fish and chips.

"He has boundless faith in himself," he thought, "but he does not know it! He does not appreciate that faith is the secret of life, the seed of all things, the majestic, monstrous power. He does not know that it is the great weapon which destroys and creates, moves mountains and encompasses space and time. But only one man has completely possessed faith. And they feared Him so much that they crucified Him."

"I am wondering, you know," Shell said, "how old Father Tom would have given me a bit of it. What is it, Tober?"

Tober stopped swinging his feet on his heels. He looked down at Shell and spoke slowly and with conviction.

"It is life," he said.

The house door opened, whereupon the wild wind lifted its voices about the place, rushing swiftly into the hall and stairway, shaking the doors and windows and making a fierce lament through the chinks in the wainscot. The door slammed and footsteps sounded. Suddenly, the door of the room was flung wide open. Two figures stood on the threshold of the room.

Shell dropped the packet of fish and chips and scrambled to his feet and stood staring in horror at what he saw. Tober turned a bland, imperturbable gaze towards the doorway.

Lukey was standing there with his left arm supporting Johnny, whose right arm rested on Lukey's shoulder with the hand hanging over so that Lukey could hold it.

"Give us a hand, quick!" Lukey said.

Tober got up and strode over. Shell cleared away the remainder of the fish and chips and the tray. He drew out the armchair.

"Not that one," Lukey said, bringing Johnny into the room with Tober's assistance. "The one there!" and he jerked his head towards the big chair in which his models sat.

Shell hurried across and put cushions in it and helped the others to lower Johnny into it. Then all three of them stood back, staring at that pallid man whose eyes surveyed them with a filmed, vague gleam of life.

"Tober," Lukey panted, "do something for him! Wash his wounds and bind them up!"

fourteen

Tober took Johnny's right hand between the thumb and forefinger of his right hand.

"This fellow is in a bad way," he said.

Lukey brought out a large canvas nailed on its stretcher. He set it rapidly on an easel.

"Do something for him!" he repeated. "Bind up the wounds and . . ."

Tober looked sternly at him. "What are you going to do?"

Lukey was feverishly squeezing paint from tubes on a big palette and dropping oil and turpentine into a little aluminum container affixed to the palette. He did not answer Tober, who nudged Shell.

"Fill up the kettle and put it on the gas ring," he said. "And clean out a bowl and bring it in here with a lump of soap."

He removed his overcoat and scarf and tossed his cap on top of them. Removing his jacket also, he rolled his shirt-sleeves to the elbow; he waited for Shell, sitting meanwhile on the arm of a chair and watching Lukey, who had prepared his palette and was now arranging the powerful electric globe above Johnny's head.

"This fellow should be in a hospital, by the look of him," Tober said, jerking his head towards Johnny.

Lukey arranged the globe satisfactorily and took off his overcoat and scarf.

"Do you hear what I say, you madman?" Tober said.

"He is conscious!" Lukey said excitedly. "It'll be fine if he stays like this!"

220

Tober got up slowly and stood before him.

"Do you mean to stand there and tell me that you are going to paint a portrait of him?" he exclaimed.

Lukey's face was full of an expression of intense fervor and excitement. He selected brushes from a jar.

"Tober," he whispered, trembling, "I am not thinking of his body. Look at him! Do you see what is in his eyes? He is not thinking of life. When I have painted people they have all been concerned with their idea of life. This one is different. He looks at death. . . ."

"Yes, he is different," Tober said, emphatically. "He is dying. . . ."

"I know," Lukey said excitedly. "His soul is reflected in his eyes. There are great things in those eyes, Tober!"

"You damned madman!" Tober said.

Lukey lifted his palette and began to mix two colors.

"If I can have two hours of him, Tober . . ." he began.

Tober crossed to the cupboard and took out a big packet of bandages and lint.

"When I have finished with him he is going straight to a hospital," he said.

Lukey looked quickly at him.

"What?"

"I said to a hospital," Tober replied.

"Do you know who this fellow is?" Lukey exclaimed.

"There is no need to ask," Tober said.

"Well, then . . ."

"I am not bothering about who he is," Tober said. "I am going to patch him up and send him to a hospital. If he gets there soon there will be a chance of saving his life."

"But don't you know . . . don't you realize that he is doomed?" Lukey asked. "His life is . . . you could say it is lost already."

"That is another matter."

Lukey flushed angrily. "You are a cold-blooded devil!" he shouted. "Patching him up only so that they can try him and execute him!"

"I am not interested in what happens to him after his body is healed," Tober said.

"You are thinking of his life, I suppose?" Lukey said, contemptuously.

"It is all that matters to me: his body, which is wounded."

"There is more to be considered than the body, the flesh,"

Lukey said, and he began to make the first strokes on the canvas.

"He is not sound," he said to Tober. "His body is dying, but his soul is living, and it is greater than the body."

Shell entered with the kettle, which he set on the gas ring, and with the bowl which he had cleaned, and which he handed to Tober.

"Now bring me another bowl as well," Tober said.

"Och, Tober! Where will I find one?" Shell whined.

"Get out!" Tober said. "Do what I tell you!"

He sat down and watched Lukey.

"Why do you want to do this mad thing?" he said.

"Because there is something to be said about him before he dies," Lukey told him.

Tober smiled sardonically. "There is something to be said about all of us," he remarked. "You could take any one of us, man or woman, and say the same thing at last."

"He is nearer to death than he is to life," Lukey whispered, making swift strokes on the canvas, "and he is wise because of it. It is his soul lives now and is looking at us!"

His brush worked quickly on the canvas. A shape took color and depth thereon, confused, a mere foundation of a single hue upon which Lukey worked quickly and with conviction, as though amidst the paint was the expression which he sought to verify whenever his gaze went to the motionless figure in the chair.

Tober laughed uneasily. "You think you will find the reality of it in his body?"

"It is there, right enough!" Lukey asserted.

"Take care!" Tober said. "You will find something you might not understand!"

Lukey glanced angrily at him. "I understand what I see!" he declared.

"What is it?" Tober said.

"It is a soul which has suffered and which has no place amongst mankind," Lukey asserted.

"Is that all?" Tober asked cynically, pouring some boiling water in the bowl which Shell brought in. He began to wash his hands with carbolic soap.

"That is everything," Lukey said. "It knows that it is doomed."

Tober laughed. "So are we all, you poor fool!"

Lukey did not answer him. He continued to make quick,

confident strokes of the brush on the canvas until he saw Tober place a bowl of boiling water on a little table beside the chair on which Johnny sat. Then he stopped painting, for Tober at that instant had the demeanor of a surgeon; and something in the way in which he slit the packet of lint and the roll of bandages and opened a small case of instruments and dropped some of them into the bowl impressed Lukey.

"Do you want him on the settee?" Lukey said.

"I can manage with him as he is," Tober said. "Go ahead with your devil's work."

Lukey resumed his painting. "Is he really dying?" he whispered.

"We are all dying," Tober said, removing Johnny's jacket and disclosing the wounded arm.

"Can you do anything for him?" Lukey asked. "I mean, do you think you can save his life?"

"I shall try," Tober said, beckoning Shell over to help him.

"Keep your head out of the light," Lukey said to Shell, making a movement with a brush.

After that, there was silence while Lukey painted and Tober expertly cleaned and bound the wounds and Shell obeyed his murmured instructions.

Suddenly, Johnny moved. His head lifted slightly and his eyes opened wider; and as though he had heard and comprehended all that had been said since his arrival, he struggled to speak in reply. Only a loud groan issued from his dry lips, dragging its sound from his body at first in all the intense eloquence of agony and then with an exultation which expired swiftly. He seemed to sink into a coma then.

"Shell!" Tober whispered. "In the locker in my room there is a flask. Bring it."

fifteen

As soon as Johnny was settled in the chair in Lukey's studio, his body was eased in its agony. At first, he could not understand what had happened to him. He remembered being in a crib in a noisy bar . . . for a long time . . . for what seemed to him to be the whole of a lifetime, for his mind could recall nothing but the hours which he had spent in that place. He remembered how, when he had sat there, he had wondered how long he would remain, and why he was there, and how he had reached the place, and what all the noise and shouting and laughter was about. The noise frightened him, for it was a savage expression of life. It drove into his mind and obliterated the delicate fabric of memory and confused him. Then he tried to rise, whereupon pain clawed at him and his fears increased. He cried out in pain and terror. The sound of his own voice comforted him. It seemed to restore his spirit and lift it above pain and fear and the strange world in which he existed. Then he rejoiced; and his outburst that had started as a groan of pain and fear and despair assumed a quality of triumph over all the terrible conditions which beset him. For an instant, he experienced tranquillity. Then the noise in the bar began again on a different note, and he became afraid once more, for the sound had a questing tone which suggested something from which he had been in flight for almost the whole of his conscious life. He held his breath and remained quite still, remembering the beast of pain from which he had been hurrying, and wondering if the noise was a manifestation of that animal. The noise increased in volume and import, invading the ultimate regions of his consciousness, until its confusion and meaningless tangle of shouts, laughter, and crashing glass matched the chaos of the delirium into which he relapsed and from which he did not recover until faces loomed around him and arms lifted him.

In his spirit, he resisted the impact of those faces on his senses. And his body in which only a minute, precious particle of vitality remained, resented the efforts which the men demanded of him when their arms lifted him and half-carried him into the passage of the public house. He attempted to release himself, but his unavailing movements were scarcely perceptible. They merely consumed his strength, which he wished to conserve.

After that, he remembered only the sudden, drenching bitterness of the wind which flew out of the darkness and struck him. And he recollected vaguely the smell of the cab and its brief comfort. And, at last, there was this house, this big room with its firelight and shadows and the faces which hovered around him and spoke words, and other faces staring at him from pictures hanging low on the walls. And in the expressions of those portraits of men and women he recognized something of his own immeasurable dilemma and of all the questions which filled his fearful soul and drove themselves into his mind.

"What is it all for?" the men and women of the portraits seemed to be thinking. "Why are we alive? What is this great globe on which we exist? What are the millions of other globes out in space? Are they, too, a part of our existence? Are they inhabited, and if so, what is the purpose of our existence and that of other living creatures on other earths?"

And he realized that although the questions were ever in the minds of those people, the answers to them were there, too. But the men and women seemed uncertain as to whether the answers to all that lay in their minds were correct. They believed timidly in themselves, and were afraid to stand forth boldly in their belief, so that their characters were full of furtiveness and inconstancy. And only a few of them seemed resolute. But the purposeful expressions of these latter persons was an indication only of the evil things.

He turned to regard the faces of the living. And it was the same there as in the portraits, except that the questions were more urgent, more anxious for answers. It frightened him.

"What is it all about?" his own soul cried, and he tried to assemble his sensibilities to grapple with the huge problem of existence. But across his mind mists drifted making chaos, and a kind of soundless tempest overthrew the harmony of thought and admitted only meaningless visions that were actually the vistas of memory slowly offering themselves in disjointed fragments. He saw immense panoramas of his own life unfold. And his soul regarded them with indifference, rejecting them as trivial events that had no relation to the profound things of the soul itself. He saw himself as he had been in the days of boyhood and youth and early manhood, beyond an intervening gulf, preoccupied with foolish, material ideals that had no connection with the wonderful forces which had always existed in his soul.

"Oh!" he lamented in himself, "I have squandered years upon foolish fancies! I have wasted my life! I have never given my real strength to anything worth while!"

But he knew, too, that he had done only as the rest of mankind had done.

"We are all alike," he thought. "There are beautiful forces in us, truly glorious things, but we lack faith in ourselves to accomplish the full expression of those things. Instead, we squander our power in trivial affairs, trivial and bitter

225

pursuits."

Then his soul regretted its lost opportunities, and he tried to find the strength wherewith to tell the three men in the room of the miraculous, abundant powers that resided in their souls and bodies and which could be rendered to exquisite purposes if they would only have sufficient faith in themselves. But he had lost the power of speech. He had reached this ultimate region, this final belief in the wonder of life only when he no longer possessed the power of communicating it.

Somehow, he knew that it was not important that he sould communicate it. Sooner or later, it would bloom in the minds of all mankind. After endeavor, after ages of unrest and error and agony, the realization of it all would dawn . . . would fill the world with light . . . would release man from what was harsh and evil.

His thoughts relapsed into other visions of himself. He knew that he had slain a man and that this crime was of immense significance to his soul; but he lifted his terrified spirit from contemplation of it, for what mattered to him at that moment was his strange ability to command the actions of the three men in the room.

He looked at the big man whose sleeves were rolled to his elbows, whereupon that individual began to attack the pain in the wounds and abolish it. His hands were very deft and steady, and comfort flowed from them. And that was what he wished this man to do.

And when he looked at Lukey, he saw in that earnest countenance the reflection of a great question.

"Yes," he wanted to say to Lukey, "look at me and discover what is happening to me. Don't turn away from me. I am no longer afraid when you are standing there. Stay where you are, and discover what I am thinking, and consider how afraid I am, and write it all down, if that is what you are doing. Or painting. . . . But go on doing what you are doing! Don't fail! Presently, you will discover everything. . . ."

In the same way, when he saw Shell's prominent eyes watching him greedily, he knew that there was a hot purpose mounting in his mind.

"Do what you wish to do!" he wanted to say to him. "Have confidence in yourself! Don't be afraid or timid or resort to sly methods! What you think of doing is good. You know it is good, but you are still doubtful about something! You lack something. You know that, don't you? Don't be afraid. Take what you want. It won't overpower you. It is life! Is is faith! Take it!"

And as he continued to look at Shell, he knew that all that he wanted to tell him was audible to that timid, sly little spirit which hankered to enrich itself with faith, with the mysterious blessing which would transform its feckless existence. And because all three men seemed attentive to him, he felt at peace.

"There is only this peace," he thought. Then he was hushed at last in himself, and the anguish of pain and fear was like the edge of a tide receding in the distance.

He sat there for a long time, while the men washed and bound his wounds. He saw the lips of the men moving, but the sound which issued was no longer a harmony, but was the discord of argument. And as he watched them, he felt the peace disintegrating. Once again, fear began in him, and pain returned. He groaned and cried out. The man who had dressed his wounds gave him a little cup, putting it gently to his lips and raising it. He drank the brandy and felt revived.

Again the voices sounded, louder, quicker, full of contention which was of mortal existence. They shattered his calm and showed him terrible conditions. His fears increased.

"I am dying!" he told himself, and it seemed fantastic and horrible and unbelievable. He tried to rise from the chair, but the thought of death paralyzed his limbs. He fell back, groaning.

sixteen

"Lukey," Tober said emphatically, when Shell returned with the brandy flask, "this fellow must go to the hospital!"

Lukey frowned but continued to work feverishly at the portrait.

"What will they do with him there?" he demanded, angrily.

"Give him a blood transfusion," Tober said, folding his arms and leaning against the wall.

"Yes, but what good will that do?"

Tober said: "It will restore him. He has lost a good deal of blood."

"I am talking about the man himself, not his body," Lukey said.

Tober said blandly: "I am not interested in his fate as a human being! His arm and hand are badly wounded and his body is weak from loss of blood and from shock. He won't last much longer unless he gets a transfusion. That is all that I am interested in: the healing of his body. The rest is not my concern."

"It is the most important thing!" Lukey declared.

"Only the body is important when it is hurt or sick," Tober insisted, crossing to the hearth and seating himself. "It is life and must be preserved. Why should I bother myself with his stupid affairs that constitute his fate?"

"Because," Lukey said, "he has an immortal soul!"

Tober laughed in the heavy, slow fashion of a man who was seldom moved to mirth.

"That is a delusion!" he asserted.

Lukey continued to paint rapidly.

"I will prove to you that it isn't," he said.

Tober was silent for a little while. He watched Lukey, who appeared to be working feverishly. Whether this activity of Lukey's was because Johnny was dying and there was little time remaining, or because that tragic figure slumped in the model's chair inspired Lukey to a degree which he had never before reached, Tober did not know. He rose slowly and stood behind Lukey to examine the crude portrait. He saw something of extraordinary force and conviction shaping itself in the line and mass and color of the work. He shrugged his shoulders.

"But you are taking his life to do this," he said, pointing to the canvas.

"Well, then, give him something!" Lukey said. "Feed him a drop of brandy or whatever it is you have in the flask. Or give him an injection!"

"So that you can have him sitting there while the life dribbles out of him, is it?" Tober demanded.

He dragged Lukey from the easel and spun him about and confronted him. Suddenly Shell giggled and got between them and pushed them apart.

"The pot is calling the kettle black!" he said.

There was silence for several seconds. Lukey turned to the easel and resumed work. Tober leaned against the wall and frowned at him. Shell spoke.

"Youse ones are not givin' a damn for his life!" he exclaimed. "Talkin' about his body and his soul, and sayin' you will send him to a hospital or keep him here to paint a picture of him! It's cruel! It's a cruel way to be actin'! It's uncivilized. One of you says you will pack him off to a hospital, which is as good as handin' him over to the police! And the other one just lets him die in the chair!"

"He can go to a hospital when I have finished with him," Lukey said.

Tober walked towards the door. "He'll pass out before that," he said, standing with his hand on the door, "then you can bring the police and tell them what has happened. Maybe you will be able to explain everything to them."

"Sure," Lukey said, "I will tell them we found him on the street and brought him in to patch him up before we handed him over."

"They are not fools," Tober reminded him. "They would ask a few questions which would have to be answered truthfully."

He went out, closing the door loudly behind him. Shell sighed. Sidling up to Lukey, he whispered:

"What the hell are we to do now?"

"Go and get the flask from him," Lukey said.

Shell shook his head. "As like as not I'll get the toe of his shoe at my behind if I go to his room."

"Well, then, sit down and shut your trap," Lukey said.

Shell obeyed slowly, crossing to the hearth and seating himself there. He ate the last of the fish and chips which Tober had brought for him. Then he stretched out his legs as Tober had done.

"Lukey!" he called softly.

There was no answer from Lukey who continued to paint as rapidly as before.

"I'm thinking," Shell said.

"Take yourself off to bed!" Lukey said.

"Aye, I'm thinkin' I will," Shell said.

"Be quick about it!"

"I would, Lukey, only for not leavin' you in trouble down here."

Lukey ceased painting and turned to Shell.

"What's this you are saying?" he said.

"Lukey," Shell said, "how the hell are you going to get rid of him when you have done the picture?"

He waited for an answer. He saw Lukey frown and return to the easel. Then he knew that Lukey had not considered that question.

"You see?" Shell said, with an air of triumph. "It'll be trouble. For you. For Tober who has cleaned him up. And for me, too. Mostly for you but, for holdin' him here and not tellin' the police."

"Ah, quit blethering!" Lukey mumbled.

Shell yawned. He watched Lukey furtively. He rose and made a considerable noise with the tray and the crockery as he lifted it from the floor.

"Aye . . . I'm thinkin' I'll be gettin' off now to my wee bed, I'm thinkin'."

He crossed the room slowly and set down the tray near the gas ring.

"Well, good night now, Lukey!" he said, crossing to the door.

There was no answer from Lukey. Shell loitered at the door, opening it and standing there to cast swift, furtive glances at Lukey.

"Come in, or get out, but shut the door and keep out the draught!" Lukey bawled.

Next instant, Shell was gone. Then there was complete silence in the room, except for the sound of the wind outside the window. Presently Lukey spoke.

"Johnny!" he whispered, and he stopped painting and looked full at the pallid face.

"Johnny!" he repeated.

The figure in the chair stirred with an almost imperceptible shudder. His head lifted, and the ripple of vitality which had started from its source deep in his being travelled to the face and animated it. The lips moved slowly but without making sound, shaping words that issued silently as though they had sped instantly to the most remote distances. The eyes reflected the depth and profundity of thought. And the rest of the face—the haggard flesh about the cheeks and lips; and the muscles beneath that flesh, and the nerves which controlled the muscles—assembled into an expression of anger.

Lukey noticed it. He stood back from the easel and watched Johnny with curiosity. He became afraid. He hastily put down his palette and brushes. Two of the brushes fell to the floor. He stooped quickly and lifted them with trembling hands that had suddenly become clumsy. He kept his gaze on

Johnny, who rose painfully from the chair and appeared to be making an immense effort to speak.

"Take it easy, Johnny," he said nervously, making a gesture as though he were holding off Johnny, who, at that moment, swayed towards him.

"Sit down, Johnny, and I'll bring your jacket. Are you feeling the cold? Maybe . . ."

His voice dwindled in silence. Now he was very afraid, for that terrible figure seemed to have increased in stature. Johnny lurched forward, fastening his gaze on Lukey, who retreated rapidly and remained at a distance. Johnny followed him. Words broke loudly from his dry lips.

"Let me go!"

"Sure, sure," Lukey whispered.

He took up the jacket from the floor and offered it to Johnny.

"Shall I help you on with it?" he asked timidly.

He held up the garment in his hands and walked around Johnny in a wide semicircle.

"Open the door . . . and . . . and let me out of here!" Johnny shouted.

He stood facing Lukey and making wide gestures. A frenzied look appeared on his face, and his breath began to hiss in and out of his mouth through his clenched teeth. His right hand clawed above him, catching the flex which held the powerful electric globe which had been suspended above his head. With a single quick movement he tore the flex from its support. He grunted with satisfaction. The bulb swung towards him and struck his chest. Groping for it, he tore it from its socket and hurled it from him. Instantly the big room was in darkness except for the light from the fire, which threw sombre gleams on the walls and ceiling and along the floor. The bulb falling made a soft explosion. Johnny lurched towards the door.

His face showed red and devilish in its expression as the flames of the fire shone upon it. His shadow was huge, grotesque across the ceiling and walls, presenting him in a new and more terrible fashion as it jerked with all his movements. And he groped first in one direction, then in another, mumbling in an exasperated way, and trying to shout something whenever he saw Lukey.

Lukey remained in a frozen attitude of fear and bewilderment, edging in panic from the other, working his way towards the door, which he seized at last and flung open. He ran swiftly from the room, his heavy steps making an ominous thunder on the stairs which were covered only by a threadbare strip of dirty carpeting. He burst into Tober's room, panting, out of breath, at the climax of panic.

"Tober!" he exclaimed; then he swallowed his hard spittle and stood quite still, feeling foolish and yet still very much afraid of Johnny.

Tober was sitting up in bed clad in a stained blazer with the Queen's University colors. His hands were clasped behind his neck. The frayed sleeves of the blazer had slipped to his elbows, revealing his lean, strong arms. The neck of the garment was wide open over his chest. He yawned, and drawing down the sleeves to his wrist and folding the buttonless edges of the jacket across his chest, he settled himself deeper in the bed and winked at Shell, who had been talking to him before Lukey's arrival.

"Well, what is wrong now?" he asked Lukey, heaving his big body about on the bed, which squeaked like innumerable rats. He laughed tersely.

"Have you resurrected Johnny's soul or something?" he asked, before Lukey could speak. "Has it come alive on the canvas and proclaimed your cock-eyed genius?"

Shell nudged Lukey.

"What's goin' on, Lukey?" he said.

"I am scared," Lukey admitted, sitting down on the bed.

Tober yawned and drew the blankets to his chin.

"Well, you can go and be scared in your own room," he said. "I am wanting my sleep. I have a hard day before me, tomorrow, digging the road. . . ."

"Tober," Lukey said humbly, "come down and give me a hand with him! He is in a frenzy! He is tearing the place down!"

"Holy God!" Shell murmured.

"Take the flask," Tober said drowsily, "and give him a pull of it. And now clear out of here, both of you, and let me get my sleep!"

Shell had the flask in his hands.

"Leave it to me," he whispered to Lukey, drawing him off the bed. "Come on now, and we'll settle him."

He and Lukey closed the door behind them. Lukey hesitated and was reluctant to go back to the studio.

"Ah, come on!" Shell said. "Sure, he'll do us no harm! The

232

fellow is nigh dead, anyway. Sure, we'll just give him a taste of this stuff and that'll steady him and keep him quiet!"

He drew Lukey by the arm to the top of the stairs. There they halted. Lukey flung off his grip and moved back.

"He is fierce!" he said. "I am afraid of him.".

Shell peered down the stairs and saw a big shadow moving with menace to and fro in the light of the flames.

"Maybe we had better open the door and just let him sort of take himself off," he said.

"Get a cab or a taxi," Lukey said, following Shell down the stairs.

"Talk sense!" Shell exclaimed. "Sure, how would you pick up a cab or taxi at this hour of the night?"

"Take him to Father Tom," Lukey suggested.

Shell turned on him. "Aye, sure! Now you have had your way, eh? Sure! When you have finished with him like, I am left to do the hard work!"

They went down cautiously and approached the open door. Johnny confronted them at the instant when they stood on the threshold of the room. He was upright, with a look of rage wrenching the features of his pale face. Lukey drew back at once, running into the malodorous little scullery and bolting the door behind him. Shell put his head to one side and grinned. He nodded his head like a little doll as he moved slowly forward with his hands uncorking the flask.

"Mister!" he murmured, coaxing Johnny.

Johnny's face lost its look of rage and perplexity, and into the features an expression of curiosity flowed. Shell kept his gaze fastened upon him as he slowly approached and murmured in a soft, wheedling tone. He lifted the jacket and putting aside the flask he held out the garment.

"Come on, now, mister!" he said gently, "put this on you!"

He edged around Johnny and lifted the right arm and inserted the hand into the sleeve. He arranged the slit sleeve over the wounded arm. Next, he lifted the stained overcoat and folded it over Johnny's shoulders, all the time talking to him in a slow, cajoling tone, soft, even melodious, and yet sly and purposeful.

"Listen, mister," he went on, taking up the flask, "have you ever heard tell of Father Tom?"

Johnny was staring at the portrait on the easel. He took a step towards it and swayed. His right hand reached out to grasp it but his body overbalanced, colliding with the easel and sending the canvas toppling to the floor from which Shell quickly lifted it and set it in position once again.

"Ah, sure, never mind the thing!" Shell said scornfully. "It's just the way Lukey passes the time like. Listen, here, mister. . . ."

But Johnny's right arm had swung towards the canvas once more. His fingers swept over the wet surface and left a long smudge over the paint.

"Och, dear help us!" Shell whined. "Look at that! Now there will be trouble! Mister, mister! Come away out of that!"

Johnny struck the canvas again, whereupon another smudge appeared on its surface. Shell tugged at him, but a sudden fury possessed the other at the sight of his own features portrayed so vividly and impressively on the canvas; and breaking from Shell's grip, he tottered forward to the easel, pushing Shell away and sending him reeling backwards against a chair which overturned against a little table on which a vase stood. The vase crashed to the floor, taking with it a box of paint tubes and a small bottle of turpentine. Shell's body striking the floor made a dull thud. He groaned and rose slowly and saw Johnny grab the wet brushes and thrust them against the canvas and finally drop the brushes and strike the canvas, sending it sailing in a wide curve towards the wall, where it struck another portrait and brought it down. Both fell heavily to the floor, upsetting an assortment of jars on an upturned box. The jars spewed their contents across the floor and rolled against the split canvas. Johnny panted; then with a curious, deliberate air he shuffled across the room and entered the hall.

He hesitated there, swaying, looking about him as if he were trying to recognize the place. Shell followed him, moaning and whimpering at the threshold of the room. Slowly at first, and then with an increasing frenzy of activity, Johnny crossed the hall and gripped the handle. He muttered between his clenched teeth as he struggled with the lock. Suddenly, it turned, and at once the door burst open under the pressure of the wild wind outside. He was hurled back against the wall.

For a few seconds he remained there in the bitter blast and the confusion of sound which filled the hall, and which evoked shrill, shuddering draughts all over the old house. At last he moved forward, making a great effort, across the step, then down the short flight, until his form was lost to sight in the darkness.

Shell saw him disappear; and as Lukey came rushing from

the scullery to discover the ruin in the studio, he set off in pursuit of Johnny, clapping his bowler hat on his head and turning up the collar of his jacket as he brought the heavy house door fast behind him. The door slamming made thunder in the house. It reverberated for an instant and then subsided as the shrill, whimpering little currents of wind subsided. Then all was silent, except for the moan of the wind in the street and Lukey's lament as he surveyed the confusion in the studio and the torn, smudged canvas with its broken stretcher.

He lifted his work from the floor and examined it. The features with their wonderful expression were irretrievably erased, lost forever beneath the smudges and scratches. He let it fall from his hands as he sat down and let his thoughts move despondently. Presently, he became calmer. His despondency decreased. He thought of Johnny.

"His soul is his own," he thought. "He would not disclose it. He hated the things I put on the canvas when he saw them."

Then his thoughts moved slowly to contemplate his own life in all its efforts and purposes and ambitions.

"What am I to do? What am I alive for if it is not to believe in myself? What is my work in this world?"

And again he lamented the spoiled portrait, believing that he had touched a climax of expression, a pinnacle of perception, a moment of genius.

"It was all there," he told himself. "It was everything I have wanted to discover and paint."

He surrendered again to regrets; but later, when he undressed and got into bed at the far end of the room, his drowsy thoughts assembled of their own voliton about something precious and significant which had penetrated them and left its subtle seed therein. He felt it within him, transforming his life, and he wondered vaguely what it was. But in all the channels of his mind there remained a sense of loss which prevented him from appreciating what had happened to him. He believed only that he had suffered a profound disappointment.

Yet, in sleep, contentment welled in his soul and flooded his slumbering consciousness with the proud fire of a new experience which had fashioned anew his convictions, his sensibilities, and his belief in himself. Knowledge formed in his mind as he slept. Faith fashioned itself in his soul.

Tomorrow, and thereafter, a new life would develop for him, a new phase of his existence, and he would remember not what he had lost and what had been spoiled, but what he had found within himself.

seventeen

Snow was falling in small stinging flakes that whirled in eddies through the darkness. They came down on the long slant of the wind and turned in multitudes as the main current surrendered them to furious cross-currents that swept from side streets. In the darkness, they obliterated the familiar scene and created a new one in which the sound of the wind and the swift falling of the snow became the bitter features through whose confusion the edges of the pavements and the sharp outlines of buildings upon which the snow was already rimed showed faintly.

Shell pressed forward through it. He could not see Johnny. He hurried on, then he stopped and listened for the sounds of footsteps on the pavements. Only the roar of the wind and the hiss of the descending flakes were audible. Nothing else. It occurred to him that Johnny could not have come as far as this. Or perhaps he had gone in the opposite direction or gone straight across the road and fallen against the wall of the nearest house.

He turned back reluctantly. He had not walked more than twenty paces before he saw the outline of Johnny's form made distinct by the thin coating of snow upon him. He took him firmly by the arm.

"Lukey lost you, and so did Tober," he mumbled. "But Shell won't! I got ahold of you, and you're comin' with me, mister! You're comin' to old Father Tom's where there's a young woman waitin' for you!"

Johnny allowed himself to be led for several yards. Then he stopped and, jerking his body to a peculiar, stubborn attitude, he threw off Shell's grip with a violence which seemed to expend the last of his strength, for he fell towards Shell and leaned heavily against him in collapse.

"Och, for goodness sake!" Shell exclaimed, holding him off.

He deftly unfastened the flask and put its neck to Johnny's lips.

"Here! Get ahold of this! Take a good pull. There's a mile or more to go yet, with the police all around us!"

Johnny tipped back his head and swallowed until Shell snatched the flask from him.

"You've had enough! Now, come on!"

Shell took him by the arm. His grip was violently rejected as before.

"Go ahead, then!" Shell said, drawing aside and pointing along the street. "It's this way!"

Johnny braced himself and moved unsteadily forward, with Shell beside him. And in that fashion they continued. The snow changed to a freezing drizzle of sleet which fell like innumerable sharp needles driven by the wind and cutting the skin of face and hands. But the darkness was less impenetrable now that the outline of houses was clearer. Johnny stopped frequently to rest against walls and even to seat himself on the steps of houses, while Shell loitered nearby waiting for him and watching anxiously.

Often he heard police approaching. At once he returned to Johnny and dragged him off upon wide detours, or pushed him into deep doorways, where his tumbled form was invisible in the darkness, or impelled him into noisome places where he pushed him upon little mounds of rubbish and covered him with discarded sacking. Shell waited for several minutes until the patrols had passed. Then he returned to his man and set out again, through streets in which many people were returning homewards. Encountering them, Shell's will was poised in a fearful suspension of its powers. Nevertheless, always at the moment of encounter, some cunning expedient suggested itself to him, and as Johnny lurched and swayed about the pavement he linked his arm in his and swayed too, and sung in a loud voice and waved an arm in drunken fashion, until the two of them were safely past. But there were other late ones, and then more snow in a swift downfall which confused those two unsteady figures, and which left the surface of pavements and roadways covered with a treacherous, frozen slush. And then more police patrols.

Shell pushed Johnny into a ragged little front garden from which the railings had been removed for scrap metal, and in which the trampled, tattered shrubs were almost inadequate to conceal that dark, lumpish shape. Shell went on a short distance and waited in a doorway. From that vantage point, he saw more patrols converge on the district and assemble around

the street in which Johnny was lying. A Head Constabl
arrived and gave orders. A police car drove up and halted
Several officers alighted.

Shell groaned. "Now he'll up and show himself," h
thought. "In the middle of the party!"

He waited for ten minutes. The officers returned to the ca
and were driven away. The patrols set out in variou
directions. The Head Constable left with two sergeants. A hus
settled upon the street. Someone was staggering silentl
through the darkness. It was Johnny. As soon as he saw Shel
he mumbled and tried to hurry. Shell let him come on. H
walked ahead of Johnny, with his glance turned back to him
The road was clear. Shell became reckless. He passed severa
groups of night workers, and others coming off late shifts
Some of them turned to stare at Johnny, who swep
unsteadily past them towards the little guide who trotte
always a few feet ahead. Shell grew bolder. He crossed a roa
and waited on the far side for Johnny to follow him. Lookin;
back, he saw a tall, well-dressed man stop before Johnny
Shell's heart thudded and leaped in his breast.

"You're badly hurt!" the stranger exclaimed.

Shell drew nearer, hovering about the pair and seein;
Johnny put out his right arm to push aside the inquisitiv
stranger. He mumbled an incoherent sentence. Recognitio;
burst on the other man.

"Hold on!" he exclaimed in astonishment and excitement
Shell advanced slowly.

"What's wrong, mister?" he asked.

The man stared down at this odd being in bowler hat an
soaked jacket.

"This man is hurt," he said.

Shell sniggered. "I'm thinkin' he has drink taken, by th
smell of him!"

The stranger said quietly: "Do you know who this fellov
is?"

"Ah, he is some fellow has taken a good sup of drink,"
Shell said.

"He is the Chief of the Organization!" the other said. "H
is the man the police are looking for all over the city! Look a
him. He is Johnny, right enough!"

"Is that a fact?" Shell said.

"This man is a dangerous criminal!"

Shell sniggered. "Och, away out of that, mister! This fellov as drink taken . . ."

The stranger interrupted him. "He is the man who killed he cashier!"

Shell drew back slightly.

"God help us!" he muttered in awe, as he stared at Johnny. He nudged the stranger. "I'm gettin' out of this street efore the police comes and the shootin' starts!"

He fled rapidly, cutting swiftly across the narrow road and alting at a distance. He began to return slowly and oiselessly. From the shadow of a telegraph post, he watched he stranger look in all directions and suddenly hasten away owards a distant patrol. At once, Shell sped across the dark ad and seized Johnny.

"Come on! Quick!"

He dragged him swiftly forward, making speed with him. lore snow fell in angry showers which abated after several inutes, leaving the scene covered with frozen particles which he wind swept and held fast in little corners about doors and indows and gutters. The shrill current sweeping over the alf-frozen slush rose again with a keener edge which cut rough Shell's thin garments and laid a chilly touch on his ody. He gasped and shuddered as he trotted with Johnny and aited for him to advance, or sped on ahead while Johnny emained in hiding until corners were cautiously explored.

From somewhere close at hand, Shell heard the half-hour rike. The sound travelled clearly on the high wind, streaming bove the city, which was possessed now only by the night and he active patrols. Shell halted. He recognized the streets rough which he had come earlier in the evening. Then they ad been full of the echoes of the city's traffic and the patter f footsteps. Now they were deserted, except for the alert atrols. He became terrified, wondering how he would lead ohnny through these streets and past the police, who seemed him to be concentrated hereabouts in greater strength. He ghed. All his life his small, inquistive fingers had crept owards evil prizes which lay always beyond his reach under he noses of the police, behind the barriers of the laws. And nly now was he reaching for something good, for a blessing, or faith and hope. But, as ever, the police were around him. s always, they were ubiquitous.

"Ah, them fellows knows everything!" he told himself. Them ones hear whispers a mile off! There's no gettin' past he police! Clever! They beat all!"

Something collapsed in him. He believed that he would never be able to sneak through with Johnny to the old priest's home, which, as he slowly realized, was surrounded by a distant cordon.

"Somebody has told them . . ." he thought.

Beside him, Johnny seemed lost in a coma, with his body sagging in the embrasure of the wall. Faith, and a world of glittering marvels, lay at a distance in Shell's mind, tantalizing him and filling him with a mournful sense of failure which swelled in him and burst at last in his heart, leaving him exasperated.

"Ah, to hell . . ." he muttered.

He turned to Johnny.

"This way," he said, firmly, dragging him upright and leading him back along the way they had come. He took him to a distance where there were meagre front gardens before little villas.

"Listen, Johnny!" he said, putting his lips close to Johnny's ears. "Father Tom and the young lady is waitin' for you. I'm thinkin' we'll not be able to get through the police ring, so I'm leavin' you just here till I bring the old fellow and the young woman. See? Just get down behind these bushes and stay quiet like. Down you get, now!"

If he had heard at all, Johnny gave no sign of comprehension. There was only the high wind and the cold and the damp from the snow, and Shell's voice, whose words he could not muster into sense in the empty caverns of his mind, where all was a ponderous chaos of pain and dream. He flopped down, yielding at once to the weight of weakness and exhaustion which lapped his consciousness like a tide. Pain beat on him in a measure which he could not attune to his strength or overcome. But suddenly, at contact with the earth, there was a vague comfort, and silence, and no more effort demanded of him. Shell arranged his limbs and settled the overcoat over him.

"Don't stir out of here," he said emphatically. "Don't move!"

He scurried away on a wide detour.

eighteen

It was past midnight. A long time previously the housekeeper had brought Father Tom a glass of warm milk and some biscuits.

"Father Tom," she said quietly, touching his arm.

He moved slightly in his chair and looked up at her as though he had not been asleep after all. The barrier between wakefulness and slumber was so thin in him as to be almost negligible. He slept, but it was never so deep that he required time or an effort in which to assemble his senses from it.

"Yes?" he said. "Oh! Some milk!"

His hands reached slowly for the tray.

"You know, Father, it is late," the woman said. "It is after eleven."

Time was a factor which he had disregarded so frequently that he had gradually come to ignore it altogether, except when somebody from the world beyond his own compelled his acceptance of that condition. Otherwise, he lived only by the dawn and twilight, and by prayer which, in his life, was only a yielding of himself to the Will which had created all living matter.

"After eleven, is it?" he exclaimed. "Then . . ." and he was about to say that he would retire for the night. He remembered Agnes.

"Is the young woman in the little study?" he asked.

The housekeeper smiled. "Sure, she has gone," she said.

Father Tom sat upright and appeared distressed. His glossy hands made little gestures of anxiety.

"Oh, gone! And I have been dozing here! And I promised her . . . I told her . . ."

The housekeeper lifted the tray from his lap and set it upon a small table which she drew up to him.

"Well, there is no cause to worry, Father," she said. "She came down to me about half an hour after the Inspector had gone. . . ."

"Ah, you should have come to me and told me," he said.

"Sure, now, she was in the house quite a time, helping me with some ironing in the kitchen," the woman added.

She continued in a soft, melodious monotone, in the way in which one who lives amidst silence and almost alone will talk at length and recount details.

"She said she had had her sleep, and when she came from it and went back to you you were resting, and so she came to me to pass the time. Then when the work was finished, she took a bite of something with me . . ."

"Yes, yes, of course," he said, rising, "but where is she?"

"She said would I tell you that she would not wait, but would walk a little and come back later, if there was hope."

He shook his head and sat down again in the chair.

"I don't know," he mumbled, remembering hope and the terrible story.

"Go to bed, Father," she pleaded. "If there is a call I will hear it and knock on your door."

But he dallied with his supper before the dying fire, hearing the harsh wind rattling the windows and buffetting the house. His aged mind that had rejected time remembered the story which Agnes had related, and considered it as though it were an event which had happened far back in the years of his life. Yet the obligations which he had accepted with impressed on him, and he loitered at the fireside and was loth to retire, although in his heart there was a slight irritability as well as pity for Agnes and the man Johnny, and the police who were looking for Johnny, and the human race with its laws and its ambitions and ideals which conflicted with the laws.

"Oh," he exclaimed softly, half in anger, half in bewilderment, "I don't know why they concern themselves with so many trivial things!" And here he rose swiftly and struck his little weak hands together and frowned as he dwelt on the word.

"Silly, silly things! Their grandiose ideals! Their stupid dreams of grandeur! Their wretched Organization for shooting at the police and shouting nonsense across the bogs and wild mountains of this land! And . . . oh, all the rest of their hysterical gibberish!"

Then he smiled and was abashed as he passed a hand over his face, as though the idea of himself losing his temper and fulminating against mankind was a sin. Shrugging his shoulders as he walked slowly to the door, he mumbled to himself, asking how it was that if mankind were a creation of the Will and were a visible, sapient expression of the Creative Will which was eternal and omnipotent, it could be so petty, so evil, so . . . He hesitated. "But so splendid!" he added, aloud, remembering the woman who had come to ask for Johnny, not to restore him to the Organization, not to conceal him and heal him so that he might continue as before, but to go with him beyond life, rejecting the futile, incessant squabbles which were all that her proud nature, snatching him not only from the bitter things that had held him since boyhood, but from the laws, edicts, and the civic strife as well, and also from the terrible penalty which was demanded of him for his crime.

He paused to turn off the light, then slowly crossing the landing to his bedroom, he saw with pleasure that the electric fire was already glowing in the room. And because he was old and often tortured by cold weather, he was glad when he reminded himself that there would be a hot water bottle in his bed, with his night attire wrapped around it. He closed the door and began to remove his soutane. Above the little basin with its hot and cold taps and its neat array of toilet articles, he saw his reflection in the mirror as he approached to wash his hands and face and drop his dentures into the cup.

He was a long time going through this ritual. He could not hurry. Nothing of life compelled him to quicken his slow hands and make an effort. His limpid consciousness flowed without pressure, moving only because he was tired and wished to prepare for sleep. But he knew that after sleep there would be the dawn which always pleased him with its soft light before the clatter of traffic rode into it to crack wide open its subtle fabric and admit man's eager presence. But he enjoyed waking early to taste the quietude of the world in the first light. He anticipated it when he got into bed at nights, and he knew that because his appetite for sleep was slender and soon satisfied he would waken early. But tonight, something prevented him from anticipating the sleep and the dawn which would follow it. He wanted to know what had befallen Johnny. And wasn't Shell to return to him?

He remembered it all as he moved slowly about the room. Half an hour passed. By then he was washed and had changed his shoes and put on his bedroom slippers. He drew from his waistcoat the old silver watch which had been presented to him by the congregation in his first parish, long ago, so long ago that he had forgotten all of them. But he wound the watch every night and slipped it beneath his pillows and groped for it every morning to replace it in his waistcoat although he never glanced at it, and would not have known whether it was still working had he not heard it ticking.

After placing it beneath the pillows he went to the hearth and sat down. He still could not commit himself to sleep. He was wearing the thick, camel hair dressing-gown which was a present from somebody he had long since forgotten, but to whom he was unconsciously grateful whenever he donned the warm, comfortable garment. His hands slipped beneath the girdle and he sighed. He was praying.

He prayed in his own fashion, not upon his knees with hands joined, not making obeisance, for his body was old and long ago bowed in physical humility. It was his spirit and will that were bowed as they consigned themselves to the contemplation of the infinity of space which was God, of the volume of Time which was God, of humanity which was of God. He thought of himself, so small and so ancient and yet not forgotten by the Will which still granted him the boon of life. And he thought of Agnes and Johnny and Shell, and he waited for them.

How long he waited he did not calculate. Yet when the house door was lightly struck, he heard the sound without surprise and with satisfaction. He was ready. He rose slowly and went to the door of his room and opened it. Groping across the landing and switching on the light, he padded carefully downstairs, hearing the housekeeper open her door and whisper dryly to him.

"It is Shell, perhaps," he told her.

She followed swiftly in a dressing-gown, bidding him not to stand in a draught, not to catch a chill, not to wait in the hall in the cold. He stood aside obediently while she unbolted the big door and opened it.

It was Shell: a small, shuddering figure, pale and pinched by the cold, wet with snow and sleet.

"Is he . . . I'm sorry for troublin' you like . . . is he about? Is Father Tom . . ."

The old priest moved forward. "Yes," he said eagerly. "I am here, Shell! Come in!"

The housekeeper admitted Shell, who stood shuddering on the mat and rubbing his hands together.

"Oh, dear!" murmured Father Tom. "Why, you have no overcoat on you! And you are wet through, man! Take off your jacket now, and we'll hang it somewhere to dry!"

"Father Tom," Shell said, pushing up his fantastic little face at him, "I have him for you!"

"In here . . ." the housekeeper interrupted softly, opening the reception room and gently urging the old priest towards it. ". . . out of the draughts, Father."

244

"Eh? What? You have . . ." Father Tom said, blinking and following Shell into the room.

Shell nodded his head. "Johnny," he whispered.

"Oh! You have? Well, now, just a moment. Just wait a moment, please. . . ."

"I have him," Shell said, "but I don't rightly know for how long. I had to leave him tucked away while I come here to you."

Father Tom hesitated. He seemed uncertain what to do.

"I must find where Agnes is," he panted. "We must be sure that she comes with us."

But suddenly the thought of that terrible errand appalled him, and although he hurried out of the room and across the hall towards the kitchen, where a light was shining, he was still uncertain and hesitant and afraid. The door opened and the housekeeper appeared.

"Did she say in what direction. . . ?" he began.

A knocking sounded on the house door.

"I will go," the housekeeper said. "Maybe it is herself. Stand out of the draughts, Father, please."

Father Tom returned to Shell.

"She is here now," he said, hearing the housekeeper bring her into the hall.

Shell plucked his sleeve and nudged him with his elbow.

"You won't forget, will you, Father, will you?" he whispered. "The wee bit of reward you promised. The bit of faith. . . ."

"Faith?" Father Tom said, bewildered.

His complacent old face seemed full of an expression of anxiety and distress.

"Like you said, Father. Faith. That's what you said," Shell reminded him.

"Did I? Well . . . if I said that, then I will keep my promise," Father Tom said.

He turned to Agnes. She was standing in the doorway looking at Shell.

"Where is he?" she said.

"Sure, I have him for you," Shell said. "Along in the Square. We had better hurry but."

"Wait now," Father Tom said, "while I put on my boots and overcoat. . . ."

He hurried across the hall and up the stairs, calling after them to wait for him, to hold on a minute, to give him a couple of minutes.

"Ah, but, Father Tom!" the housekeeper called gently after him. "You will not be venturing out in this weather?"

He gave her no answer. She watched him, shaking her head and wondering would he wear the thin old overcoat, or would her leather coat fit him, and where was the big woollen scarf which, at one time, he had worn?

Agnes beckoned Shell, who nodded assent.

"Aye," he said, "I'm thinkin' so, too. I'm thinkin' we have no time to be waitin' while he dresses himself. Sure, there is no time to be dallyin' here like!"

The house door closed behind them. The housekeeper heard it in the kitchen, where she had found her heavy leather coat and the old woollen scarf.

"Maybe," she thought with relief, "he will not be going at all, now they have gone."

But he came plodding down a few minutes later, asking for his overcoat, and gently insisting that he must go, that he could not remain at home, and gratefully accepting the big leather coat which she draped like a voluminous cape about his shoulders and buttoned across his thin chest over which she drew the scarf.

"Sure, Father, they have been gone this five minutes . . . into the terrible darkness . . . and it will be hard for you to find them," she lamented.

He smiled confidently and braced his shoulders.

"It is only as far as the Square," he whispered. "Sure, I know the way to that and back!"

He let her open the door for him, and he drew in an icy breath and set himself to march out boldly down the little steps. He remembered at that instant the appalling, impenetrable darkness of mountain roads which he had travelled on foot and horseback at night, years ago, in the early years of his life as a priest in a scattered parish. The wind had swept like a cutting blade through the passes, down the naked screes, across the bogs. He recalled for an instant the roaring turmoil of it, and found within his old body some latent strength with which to meet it all again in the deserted streets leading to the Square.

He had promised the Inspector that he would bring Johnny to him at the Square. He knew that he would encounter the Inspector, and that he would be there waiting for him. And he believed that he would see Johnny, or that Agnes and Johnny would meet, and that if he failed to overtake Agnes and Shell it would not matter very much, for in the woman's heart there was sufficient faith to fulfil her. It was all that she required. There was nothing more he could give her. He was only an old spectator who had forgotten many things—ritual, dogma, the material world—and discovered at last a soul possessed of the supernatural gift.

nineteen

Shell set out on the wide detour by which he had made his way to the priest's home. He was silent. His speed was eloquent of everything in his mind. Presently, Agnes stopped.

He went on a few paces and then halted.

"Hurry," he said.

She waited for him to return to her.

"What is it?" he said.

"This is not the way to the Square!"

"Aye, I know! But the police are all around between the house and the Square. Thick as stars!"

"We will go the short way," she said.

"What's the sense in that?" he argued. "Sure, it'll only mean runnin' slap into a bunch of them!"

She did not answer him, except to walk on quickly. He let her continue, thinking that after half a dozen paces she would stop and wait for him. But she walked faster than before. He ran to overtake her.

"I'm tellin' you, miss: thick as stars!"

She continued as before, not speaking, her head held high and proudly.

"Hold on a wee bit!" he exclaimed.

His shoelace had broken. She glanced quickly at him but did not halt. For a few seconds he fumbled with the sodden ends of the lace, a tempest of anxiety rising in his mind as he heard Agnes's footsteps fade into the distance ahead of him. A shout sounded from somewhere in that direction. At once, he straightened himself and hurried after Agnes, running until his loose shoe suddenly flew off from his foot. He stopped then, feeling the bitter chill of the slush and ice on the pavement striking through his wet sock. He gasped, and his body shuddered. He prowled about that spot like a snuffling dog as he searched for the missing shoe.

Another shout sounded: a strange, inhuman cry lifting into the darkness and the wind. Hearing it, he stood quite still, no longer searching for the shoe.

"They'll lift him now!" he muttered in lament, realizing that Johnny had left his hiding place. "They'll be on top of him in a couple of minutes!"

A sudden thick flurry of snow began, coming down on the wind's ferocious slant and obliterating the dark outlines of houses, front steps, gutters. The big flakes stung his face and hands as he stood there peering about him. At last, he inclined his head against the cold drench of them on him and surrendered himself to disappointment and fear.

He had limped into the nearest doorway to shelter himself. Standing there and occasionally stooping to chafe his wet foot and restore its circulation, he heard footsteps.

"Father Tom!" he called, as the old man came near.

"Shell!" the priest said, from the whirling confusion of snow and wind.

He had stumbled over something on the pavement.

"Hold on!" Shell exclaimed, stooping and retrieving the shoe and holding it up for the old man to see.

"It came off me! Only for this breakin' its lace and flyin' off me, I might have saved him!" he said.

He drew it on quickly and contrived to tie it firmly while Father Tom waited patiently for him.

"It's this way," Shell said, taking the old man by the arm and trying to explain what had happened.

"I took her on a way that was safe, but she says she would take the straight road but, although I told her the police was there," he said.

An uproar of mingled voices broke from the darkness ahead of them.

"Hark at that now!" Father Tom murmured.

Orders were being shouted, and from all sides the sound of running feet lifted. Whistles blew. Excited voices called fresh orders across whose commotion a wild shout rose. Two shots sounded in quick succession. Their echo rose and was carried by the wind far away across the city in a curious, attenuated sound below which the shouts of command subsided abruptly.

The old priest heard them. He stood quite still for several seconds. At last he stumbled forward again, going towards the source of those sounds.

Shell hung back for a little while. He was afraid and uncertain of himself and of everything which composed his life.

"Shell!" Father Tom called.

Shell padded after him towards the Square.

twenty

A coma had descended on Johnny when Shell had left him. It passed after many minutes. Then he stirred and got painfully to his feet and tried to discover his whereabouts. He parted the shrubs and stumbled towards the pavement.

He was bewildered. Previously, for what seemed to him to be an eternity, there had been incomprehensible scenes through which he had been impelled. Now at last he was utterly alone in a bitter wilderness.

The snow abated slightly and finally ceased. The wind lulled for several seconds. In the ensuing silence, footsteps were audible. At once his soul filled with an access of joy and relief and hope. He knew that he was still alive, still attached to the things of mortal existence; and in himself he yearned for a release from all the conflicting confusion and chaos which had hurled him from place to place for so long a time. He kept trying to shout and attract the attention of the person who was advancing towards him.

His voice made only a rustling gasp. He wanted to express the sense of joy and hope that filled him, and also to see again a human face and hear words and taste contact with another human life and find peace, for he was becoming afraid of the weird pattern of experience through which he had travelled. He drew a deep breath and drove it from his lungs in a shout. He heard the sound which he made and he was pleased.

The effort deprived him of so much of his precious, final strength that he could no longer walk. He tried to lift his feet from the pavement. His limbs were cold, numbed, almost lifeless. He strained his ears to detect again the sound of advancing footsteps. Once more he shouted.

Now his fears were banished by something proud, defiant, fearless which welled in his soul and lifted the dying flame of his life into momentary brilliance. His shout was loud, clear, a cry of triumph over all the baseless fears that had ever beset him and influenced his life and rendered it small and vicious and stupid. It sundered the bonds that had constrained his emotional spirit, casting away the foulness of them and releasing him at last, so that he saw the sordid garments and felt a strange pity for his futile life. The pity was contrition; and his heart held it until it faded as the echo of his shout soon faded.

He was very weak. He stood against a wall and tried to discern his surroundings. He heard the oncoming footsteps and, lifting his head, he peered in their direction.

Now from all sides came the thud of running feet and a sudden clamour of voices shouting commands. From the last ripples of his life as a renegade in conflict with governments and the police, the old impulses of self-defence moved him. The cunning, the sly ruses, the bluffing and threats, all impelled him. But now, for the first time and the last time, he was without the strength to obey them.

He knew it. He knew that this was the end. Another hour at most would have sufficed for the little flame of his life to sink and expire in peace. He knew that, too. And with an immeasurable regret he realized that his death was to be characteristic of his violent life. And he feared it for an instant, and then—when the last shock of that terror had passed—he merely stood there, waiting, bewildered, hopeless, too weak to move, yielded in himself to the imminent wave.

He heard the oncoming police. They saw him and shouted words to him that were broken by the wild flurry of the wind, which streamed through the Square. He hardly heeded them. He was passive at last. His weakness increased rapidly, and mists of delirium rose from all the regions of consciousness and moved towards one another. He felt them closing steadily over the remnants of will and life, and he struggled to part them, for at that moment someone stood before him and spoke his name from all the familiar depths of mortal existence.

He made a terrible effort. He saw a face which his senses knew but which he could not name. It came nearer to him. It was a woman's: soft, fragrant, resting against his with an exquisite tenderness which he had never before experienced, and which was eloquent of many things of which his senses had been aware in the past when they had known this woman. In that instant, he heard her voice softly uttering his name and waylaying the terse shouts from the police. He felt her arms about him, encircling him warmly and supporting him. Her lips touched his, whereupon his senses came to life for that moment, tasting everything of her, at first on his lips and then in his soul, where the bloom came to effulgence with a soundless wonder and subtly possessed him. The ecstasy of that possession increased, lapsing at the instant when its wonder broke and spread like a tide over his soul and carried him forth into infinity.

She had fired twice, in quick succession, in the instant before the rush of the patrols towards her. Through the two hearts. The bodies were prone on the pavement when the police reached the spot.

And snow was already forming on them when the old priest and Shell arrived.

"It's finished," the Inspector said, addressing the priest. He removed his hat for a few seconds. His quick, tense breathing was audible as he leaned over the bodies beside which Father Tom had got to his knees.

"She got him," he said softly, "She took him, and herself. . . ."

The priest mumbled words and made the sign of the cross. He rose slowly to his feet.

". . . a few seconds before us, and shot him and herself," the Inspector said again. "Took him. . . ."

"She loved him," Father Tom murmured.

He moved unsteadily through the big groups of police. Then he halted and looked about for Shell and saw him, a pallid, horrified form who shuddered as he cried out in a thin voice:

"Killed him. . . ."

"Redeemed him!" the old priest said, resting a soothing hand on him.

THE END

THE LAW REVOLUTION by Melvin Belli *Non-Fiction*
Introduction by Erle Stanley Gardner

The "King of the Torts" has written a well of information about the law in America today, and the inevitable course it must take to stay with the times. ". . . exciting . . . tantalizing . . . always informative."
—Geddes MacGregor
Los Angeles Times

00008-125Z 240 pps. $1.25

Should you be unable to obtain any of these titles from your local bookseller, they may be ordered directly from the publisher.

LEISURE BOOKS, INC.
Department A
6340 Coldwater Canyon
North Hollywood, California 91606

Please send me____copies of each of the books I have checked. I am enclosing the payment plus 10¢ per copy for postage and handling.

Name_____

Address_____

City_____ State_____ Zip_____